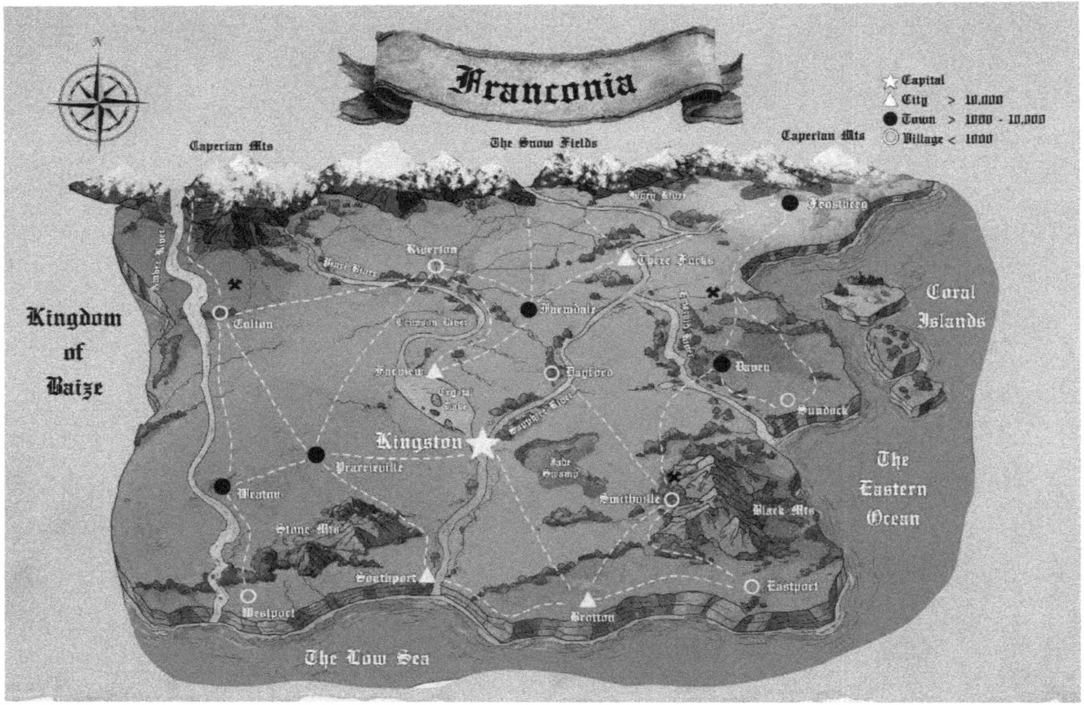

I0768341

Franconia
Capital
City > 10,000
Town > 1000 - 10,000
Village < 1000
Caperian Mts
The Snow Fields
Caperian Mts
Kingdom of Baize
Coral Islands
The Eastern Ocean
The Low Sea
Frostberg
Riverton
Three Forks
Colton
Farmdale
Raven
Sunduck
Bayview
Bayford
Kingston
Prairieville
Weston
Smithville
Black Mts
Stone Mts
Jade Swamp
Crystal Lake
Southport
Bratton
Eastport
Westport
Amber River
Pearl River
Ivory River
Crimson River
Emerald River
Sapphire River

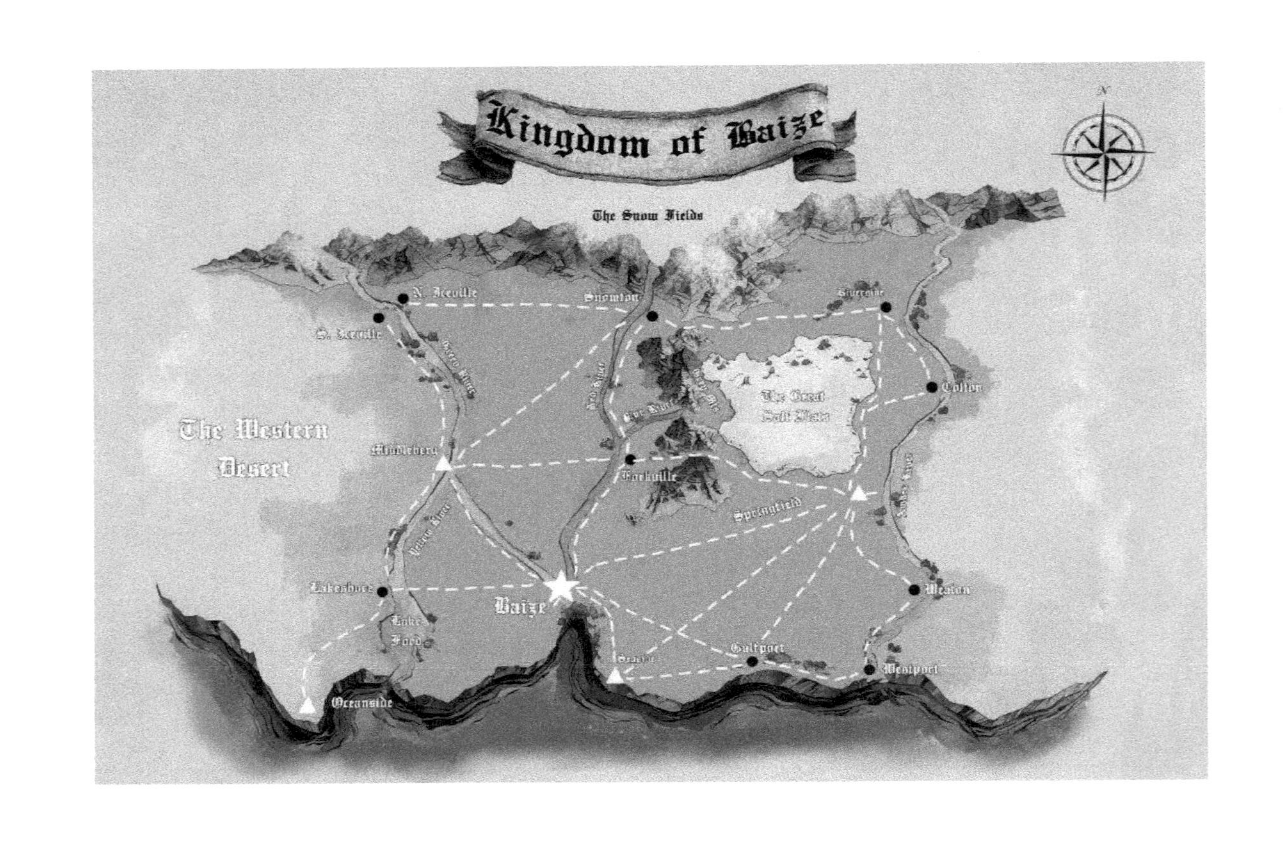

Kingdom of Baize
The Snow Fields
The Western Desert
The Great Salt Flats
N. Iceville
S. Iceville
Snowton
Riverside
Colton
Middleberg
Forkville
Springfield
Lakeshore
Baize
Weston
Lake Ford
Oceanside
Seaside
Gulfport
Westport
Snow River
Ice River
Eye River
Deep Arm
Yellow River
Salt River
N

THE CONFLICT OF INTERESTS

BY
ROBERT JONES

Copyright © 2025 by – Robert Jones – All Rights Reserved.

It is not legal to reproduce, duplicate, or transmit any part of this document in either electronic means or printed format. Recording of this publication is strictly prohibited.

Other Books by Robert Jones

The Honor of Dragons

The Valor of Sorcerers

The Compassion of Enemies

The Conflict of Interests

The Peace of Minds (Forthcoming)

"We [England] have no eternal allies, and we have no perpetual enemies. Our interests are eternal and perpetual, and those interests it is our duty to follow."

-Lord Palmerston, speech in the House of Commons, March 1, 1848

CHARACTERS

Wizards

Wizard Edward Francis, Royal Expeditionary Force (REF)
Wizard Noland, Headmaster, Franconian Wizards Academy
Wizard Faith, Gatekeeper, Franconian Wizards Academy
Wizard Toffin, Serums Instructor, Franconian Wizards Academy
Wizard Daniel, History and Enhancements Instructor, Franconian Wizards Academy
Wizard Mira, Seemings Instructor, Franconian Wizards Academy
Wizard Dylan, Forces Instructor, Franconian Wizards Academy
Wizard James, Chief of Army Wizardry, Baizian Army
Wizard Lake, Chief of Naval Wizardry, Franconian Navy
Wizard Cassandra, Court Wizard of Franconia
Mage Kathy, Assistant Court Wizard of Baize (on Special Assignment)
Mage Elianna, Headmistress, Middleberg School of Magic, Baize
Mage Andrew, Battle Mage, 1st Squadron, 1st Fleet, Franconian Royal Navy
Mage Curtis, Royal Expeditionary Force
Sorcerer Terry, Mentor, Franconian Wizards Academy
Sorcerer Donovan Francis, Royal Expeditionary Force
Sorceress Rachel Francis, Royal Expeditionary Force

Soldiers

Field Marshall Guzman, Commander, Franconian Army
General Diaz, Commander, Baizian Army
Admiral Cross, Admiral of the Fleets, Franconian Royal Navy
Admiral Vandall, Commander, Baizian Navy
Major Gerald, Commander, Royal Expeditionary Force
Commodore Matthews, Commander, 1st Squadron, 1st Fleet, Royal Franconian Navy
Senior Specialist Dirk, Assassin, 1st Company, REF
Senior Specialist Lance, Assassin, 2nd Company, REF
Captain Fletcher, Commander, 2nd Company, REF
Captain Smith, Commander, 1st Company, REF

Civilians

King Henry XI, King of Franconia
King Donald, King of Baize
Minister Leonard, Franconian Minister of Finance
Minister Williams, Baizian Minister of Public Works
James, Owner, Prestige Arms
Maria, James' daughter
Bruce, recluse who lives near Southport

Dragons

Ard, Great Dragon, Gek's grandfather
Gek, Great Dragon, Azure's mate
Cobalt, Sea Dragon, Gek's Father, Chief of the Sea Dragons
Azure, Sea Dragon, Gek's mate
Sky, Sea Dragon,
Bliz, Frost, Snow Dragons

Jasper, Amber, Stone Dragons
Rose, Fern, Fire Dragons

Table of Contents

Dedication

For Linda, with love

About the Author

Robert Jones served in the United States Army for 23 years before retiring. He currently works for the Department of Defense. This is his fourth novel. He lives in Northern Virginia with his wife, Linda, and he has two children, Donovan and Faith.

Foreword

Gek has a son! Unexpectedly, it's a human baby to go along with his Dragon daughter. Azure and Gek are going to have their hands full raising this blended family. Meanwhile, the conflict with the humans is still raging, although Gek has less of a stomach for it now, as he seeks to protect his children.

Wizard Edward has convinced King Donald of Baize that Franconia is *not* behind the recent attacks on his citizens and that it is really the dragons, trying to provoke a war between the two human kingdoms. Now Edward has volunteered to help dig a Great Salt Lake in eastern Baize to help keep the Salt Flats from spreading into the Amber River, creating an ecological disaster for both realms. Edward is aided in this endeavor by the attractive Mage Kathy, whom Edward has grown very fond of.

Donovan is engaged to his Mentor, Sorceress Rachel, and as soon as he passes his Sorcerer's Test, they'll both leave the Wizards Academy for assignments in the military or in one of the Regional Mage's Offices. After the wedding, of course.

Mage Andrew and the HMS VALOR have been reassigned to the Eastern Ocean and ordered to patrol around the Coral Islands, home of the Sea Dragons.

After a fierce battle, the Sea Dragons have offered a temporary truce with the humans. Will the truce last, or is it some ruse by the dragons?

Chapter One:

THE SORCERER'S TEST

Donovan grimaced as the fireball sped toward him. He had no idea whether it was a Seeming, a ball of flaming sawdust, or something else Wizard Noland, the hulking, dark-skinned Headmaster of the Franconian Wizards Academy, had conjured up to test him with. The Sorcerer's Test had really begun three days ago, on Twoday morning when Donovan had to cast a spell that would last for three days. Donovan had chosen the Tracer spell, the first spell that he'd learned when he arrived at the Wizards Academy a little over three years ago. On Endday morning, after Wizard Daniel had confirmed that Donovan's staff still had a Tracer spell on it, the test had begun in earnest.

The Sorcerer's Test had begun with a Military History exam, but it was unlike any test he had ever taken at the Academy. Wizard Daniel, a seasoned Battle Mage who had just recently passed the Wizards Test and been added to the Academy Faculty, was stocky, like a weight lifter, with dark hair. He walked with a limp from a battle injury that never quite healed right, but he had an easy smile and was a very good instructor. He arrived at the Lecture Hall precisely at the appointed time and posed the following situation: An enemy force, consisting of a Brigade of Cavalry, supported by six Fire Dragons, was advancing on Kingston. Using the forces known to be available in the city, plan the defense of the city. Include specific actions designed to protect the King and his five key Ministers. Donovan was given two hours to complete this task. Wizard Daniel turned the hourglass and limped out of the classroom.

Donovan started by making a list of the forces involved. On the enemy side, a Brigade of Cavalry was two Regiments; each regiment had four Squadrons, and each Squadron had three thirty-five-man companies, called Troops. So, a little over 900 horsemen, if he included the Brigade and Squadron staffs, plus six dragons. Donovan knew that Franconian Battalions normally acted independently. Deciding that, if he were the enemy commander, he would attack with six Battalions, each supported by a dragon, and keep two Battalions in reserve. Oddly, Wizard Daniel had not mentioned any enemy magicians. In Franconia, each Battalion was assigned a Sorcerer (who could only cast one spell at a time), and each Regiment had a Battle Mage (who could cast two spells simultaneously). Suspecting a trick, Donovan listed two Mages and eight Sorcerers in his Enemy Forces list.

Under Friendly Forces, Donovan knew that there were normally two Franconian Regiments, the 1st and

2nd, stationed in Kingston. Each Regiment had three Battalions of Infantry and one Squadron of Cavalry. Then he remembered that King Henry had recently ordered the Cavalry Squadron from the 2nd Regiment, along with their Sorcerer and the Regiment's Battle Mage, to move to Prarrieville to guard against an invasion from Baize. That left seven Battalions, one Mage and seven Sorcerers. Wait—he should also include the Kingston Regional Mage and his Sorcerer, plus the Court Wizard, to the list of Friendly Forces, as well as the King's Personal Guard, which had recently expanded to almost a hundred men (two companies). When he was finished, Donovan looked over his lists.

Enemy Forces	Friendly Forces
8 Sqdns Cavalry	5 Bns Infantry/1 Sqdn Cavalry
	King's Personal Guard
2 Mages	2 Mages
8 Sorcerers	8 Sorcerers
6 Dragons	1 Wizard

The balance of forces didn't look too bad. Donovan knew that defenders usually enjoyed the advantage of prepared positions and knowing the terrain better than the attacking forces. It would be an even fight if it wasn't for those damn dragons!

Well, the rivers would help the defense. First they would need to drop the bridges over the Sapphire and Crimson Rivers; that should force the attackers to approach from the north, most likely down the roads from Fairview and Hayford. Trenches should slow down the horses, or he supposed Fire could be used to spook the enemy horses. With the Franconian infantry on the walls around the city, armed with crossbows, defending against the soldiers should be relatively easy.

Now for the dragons and the magicians. The magicians were evenly matched; in fact, Franconia had a Wizard that the enemy lacked. Unfortunately, it was unlikely that one Wizard could defeat six dragons. Donovan decided to set that problem aside for the moment while he considered the challenge of where to place the King and his Ministers for maximum protection. *The palace dungeon? Probably not. He couldn't stay in the palace, that would be the first place the enemy magicians or dragons would look for him. What about a shop in the city? No good. He needed a secure place, big enough for the King and five Ministers.*

Then the answer came to him. Not only where to secure the King and his Ministers but how to solve the rest of the problem as well. Just then, Wizard Daniel entered to turn the glass to start the time for the remaining hour of the test. As he did so, he grinned and said, "Oh, by the way, I think I forgot to mention that the attacking forces have magical support with them. If they are supported as our troops are, there would be two Mages and eight Sorcerers in the attacking force. Please include them in your calculations."

"I anticipated that, Sir, and I'm done," said Donovan. "So soon?" asked Wizard Daniel. "Well then, tell me how you've decided to defend Kingston." "Sir, this is too easy. On the surface, the forces look pretty evenly matched," said Donovan, showing him the list of forces he'd compiled. "I see, so, how do we deal with the cavalry?" "Sir, trenches or fire could stop, scatter, or spook their horses. The enemy soldiers would not even reach the city walls."

"And the magicians and dragons?" asked Daniel. "At first glance, it looks like the magical forces are evenly matched," said Donovan. "But, when I considered where to put the King and his Ministers for maximum security against the dragons, the answer came to me." "And what did you decide?" "We secure them *here,* in the Wizards Academy, probably in the Mentor's quarters. We leave the Changed Ones, the Level Ones and Wizard Faith to guard the Academy and send the Level Twos, Level Threes and Mentors out to fight, along with the faculty. Even six dragons would have no chance against fifty of us."

Daniel smiled. "Exactly right, Donovan. Of all of the cities in Franconia, Kingston is the most secure. You forgot that there's one other element we might call upon; the rogue magicians in the city. I believe that there are actually several dozen that are too old to enter the Academy but have some practical use of their magical abilities, and we have a roster of all of those we have identified. Remember that if a similar situation ever arises."

"So I passed?" "You did, and it's because you used creative thinking. It might interest you to know that your classmate, Laura, spent both hours on this problem and never considered using any magical assistance from the Academy. She barely passed with a plan that would probably have seen most of our forces decimated and the King captured, injured, or fleeing for his life." "But she passed?" asked Donovan, concerned. "Barely. Which is why she was assigned to replace Sorceress Celeste in the Grotton Regional Mage's Office rather than being placed with a military unit."

Wizard Daniel rose from his chair and said, "Your next examination is Serums. Please go across the hall and begin. Wizard Toffin is expecting you, but you're quite a bit early." Daniel patted Donovan on the shoulder as he left and said, "I'll see you later for your Enhancements Test."

Donovan walked across the hall to the Serums laboratory, where he found Wizard Toffin, the portly Wizard with wild brown hair and a fluorescent orange waistcoat, dozing in his chair. Donovan cleared his throat as he approached, and Wizard Toffin sat up straighter and said, "Donovan! So soon? I didn't expect you for another glass yet! Well, everything about you happens sooner than we expect. Very well, your task this morning, as I'm sure you know, is to prepare a Love Serum, a Healing Serum for Mortal Wounds, and a Death Serum. You may prepare them in any order that you wish or simultaneously if you can. I'll explain how we'll test them once you're finished."

Donovan immediately set himself to the task of preparing the three Serums, knowing that they had to be perfect. Odorless, colorless, and, with the exception of the Healing Serum, tasteless. It took almost three glasses of time before all three were ready. "All right, Sir, these are ready to be tested," said Donovan skeptically. Wizard Toffin picked up the Love and Death Serums and put them into secure pockets in his waistcoat, leaving the Healing Serum on the stand on the table.

"So, my boy, I'm going to run off to court with your Serums. I happen to know that there is one domestic felon who needs another dose of Love Serum and another prisoner awaiting his last meal who will receive a dose of your Death Serum. Once both have been administered, I'll return and inform you of the results." "I guess it's fortunate that your brother is holding court today," said Donovan. "Please give him my regards." One of the judges in the Franconian Superior Court was Martin Toffin, Wizard Toffin's brother.

"You still think we schedule these tests randomly, don't you? My boy, you would have been tested last week if there were any court cases that would have required both Love and Death Serums." Donovan blushed in embarrassment. "How will you test the Healing Serum?" he asked.

Wizard Toffin smiled, "I watched you carefully as you prepared that one, and it is a Passing effort. You know, years ago, we made students test it on themselves. We enticed a sand viper to bite them, then had them swallow their Healing Serum immediately. Unfortunately, after we lost an otherwise promising Sorcerer during testing, we decided to eliminate that part of the test. Well, I must be off! I'll see you later this afternoon, hopefully with good news! Oh, your next test is Martial Arts; please saddle a mount and meet Wizard Faith in the Forces Training Area. I'll let her know you'll be early!" With that, Wizard Toffin hustled out of the Lecture Hall and jogged (slowly) towards the Gatehouse, waving for Wizard Faith.

Donovan moved quickly to the stable and saddled Stam, his rather short, white, Caspian horse, then headed over to the Forces Training Area. When he arrived, Wizard Faith was already there, mounted on an enormous Clydesdale. "You've got to be kidding me!" said Donovan. Wizard Faith smiled wickedly and said, "You never know who you'll be facing in combat or what they'll be riding. No spells, other than shields. First one knocked off their horse loses. Ready?"

Donovan wondered how in the world he was even going to be able to reach Wizard Faith with his staff when her mount was so much taller than his. He finally decided that he couldn't and that he would have to use his shield, but even that seemed like long odds. Then an idea came to him; previously, he'd always formed a round, pumpkin-sized invisible shield to deflect Faith's staff, *but whoever said the shield had to be round?* Instead, Donovan formed a long, thin, horizontal shield, about the width of his staff. As Wizard Faith charged in, he lowered his shield behind the Clydesdale's head and swept Faith off her horse while she was still ten feet away. Faith hit the ground hard, and Donovan reigned up quickly and dismounted to check on her.

"Are you all right?" "What was that?" asked Faith, groggily. Donovan smiled, "I formed my shield into a clothesline and dropped it behind your horse's head. Are you hurt?" "Only my pride," said Faith. "Who told you that you could make a shield in that shape?" "No one," replied Donovan. "Of course, no one ever told me that I couldn't either." Faith struggled to remount the towering horse, eventually giving up and walking him back to the stables. When she arrived, she said, "Sorry, Rachel. I tried to keep him here a few more weeks."

Donovan understood immediately, knowing that his Mentor and fiancé, Rachel Turner, was standing nearby, hidden under a Concealment shield. Mentors were not allowed to help their students in any way during testing and were only present in order to see what the students needed to improve on if they failed the test. "Donovan, Wizard Daniel should be waiting for you at the marina. Your Enhancements Test will be conducted on water."

Donovan nodded his understanding, and after returning Stam to the stable and handing him over to the stableboy, he walked briskly to the Academy boat dock, where Wizard Daniel was waiting. After Donovan climbed into the boat, Daniel cast off and said, "Now Donovan, we already know that your Seeking abilities are above and beyond what most magicians can accomplish." (Donovan had the rare ability to sense where someone was, just by thinking about them, without the need for an incantation or gesture.) "So, we'll begin with the Silence spell. Please cast the spell *on the boat*. The squeaking of the oarlocks annoys me."

Donovan said, *"SILENTIUM,"* while placing his left index finger to his lips, and the noise of the boat instantly muted. The power drain was more significant than Donovan anticipated, and he immediately reached for his water bottle. "You may release the spell," said Wizard Daniel. *"CODA,"* said Donovan, and the noise returned. "Next, I have cast a spell on something in this boat; please tell me what it is." Donovan looked around, then steepled his fingers and murmured, *"MAGNUS."* The boat's steel anchor began to glow with an eerie blue light. "Very good," said Daniel, "you may release the spell." Donovan released the spell and wondered what was next.

"Your last Level Three Enhancement spell is Healing of Mortal Wounds," said Daniel, "which is why we're on the river. I'm going to spear a fish and bring it aboard. Your task is to heal it and return it to the river. You must act quickly, or the fish will die. Do you understand?" Donovan nodded, and Daniel took a thin wooden rod from the pocket of his robes, enlarged it and sharpened the tip with magic. Then he scanned the river before thrusting the spear into the water, bringing up a large trout which he had speared cleanly through the body. The fish flopped around feebly as Donovan knelt down and placed his hands over the wound, palms down, and said, *"SALVARE."*

With the wound healed, the fish flopped around much more vigorously, and it took Donovan a minute to seize the slippery creature and return it to the water. "Nicely done," said Wizard Daniel. "Now, if you could please use a Wind spell and take us back to the dock, this part of your Sorcerer's Test is over."

Donovan easily executed the Wind spell and guided the small boat back to the dock. When they arrived, Wizard Daniel said, "Your next test is the Change spell. Wizard Mira is waiting for you in the Seemings and Changes Training Area. Good luck."

As Donovan entered the Seemings and Changes Training Area, he saw his former Mentor, Terry, a Fire Dragon Changed One, standing beside Wizard Mira and immediately knew what lay before him. He stumbled briefly, then felt a soothing hand on his back and heard Rachel whisper, "You can do this."

Wizard Mira looked at Donovan with concern in her eyes. "Donovan, we know this Change can be performed; Sorceress Celeste successfully made the change some weeks ago, but you will be the first student ever to attempt this Change. Do you know what I want you to Change?" Donovan nodded solemnly, "Yes. You want me to Change myself into a dragon." "Exactly right," said Mira. "Sorcerer Terry is here to help you. Terry?"

Terry said, "In order to make the Change, you must picture a dragon in your mind. I know that you have seen one before. That will be your model. Concentrate on that image and being able to retain the ability to speak. The transformation should happen immediately. To Change back, the spell is the same, think of returning to your true form, and rear up on your hind legs. Clapping your hands together is not a natural motion for a Dragon, but it can be done. Do you have any questions?"

"Will it hurt?" Terry smiled, "It should not. Just make sure you picture an *uninjured* Dragon in your mind. Do you understand what I am saying?" Donovan nodded. The only dragon he had seen before had eventually been riddled with crossbow bolts, and Donovan had cut off its head to take it to the King. It would not do to remember that image. Steeling himself, Donovan said, "I am ready." Terry and Mira stepped back to give Donovan some space.

Donovan closed his eyes and concentrated on the image of a large, golden dragon, glittering in the sun; he said, *"MORPHIOUS,"* and clapped his hands. Donovan's body *rippled* and transformed into a fifty-foot-long golden dragon. Donovan shook his head to clear it. Everything looked *smaller*. Before stepping away from Terry and Mira, he said, "Rachel, where are you? I don't want to step on you." Rachel dropped her Concealment shield and moved to stand by Wizard Mira, beaming. "I told you, you could do it," she said.

Donovan raised each foot, shook his tail from side to side, then spread his wings. He desperately wanted to try flying, but Wizard Mira read his mind and said, "Please don't take off, Donovan. You would panic the other students and staff. Return to your human form now, please."

Somewhat reluctantly, Donovan pictured himself as a human, reared up and clapped his short, dragon-arms together and recited the incantation. He dropped to the ground, human but without a scrap of clothing on. The remnants of his clothes were scattered on the ground in pieces. "Oh, my," gasped Wizard Mira, averting her eyes. Terry laughed, "Sorry, I guess I should have mentioned that. You have to take off your human clothes before you transform." "Now you tell me," groused Donovan. "At least I wasn't wearing my expensive new clothes."

To cover his nakedness, Donovan cast a Seeming of clothes on himself and walked back to the Mentor's quarters to get dressed. Walking in a Seeming of clothes was *weird,* but none of the students that they passed seemed to notice. Once they reached the dormitory, Wizard Mira said, "Donovan, you obviously passed the Changes Test. Once you're dressed, Wizards Dylan and Noland will be waiting in the Forces Training Area to administer the last part of your Sorcerer's Test. Good Luck."

After dressing and stealing a quick kiss from Rachel, Donovan headed to the Forces Training Area. Both Wizards looked relieved to see him. "How did the Change go?" asked Wizard Noland. "It went fine, but Terry should have warned me to take off my clothes before transforming. The Change tore them asunder and left me naked when I Changed back into human form." Both Wizards laughed. "We'll have to remember that for future tests," said Wizard Dylan. "Oh my," said Wizard Noland, "That can only mean that when Celeste landed on the HMS VALOR and transformed back into human form..." "She probably fainted from embarrassment," said Dylan, struggling to contain his mirth.

Eventually, the two Wizards regained their composure and said, "Donovan, please Blast that boulder over there." Donovan Blasted the boulder to rubble. Next, Wizard Noland asked Donovan to Paralyze Wizard Dylan. This spell was also executed perfectly. Wizard Noland then asked Donovan to cast a

Compulsion spell on Wizard Dylan and force him to do something that he would not normally do.

Donovan thought for a moment, then said, *"NECESSITAS,"* while crossing the index and middle fingers of his left hand. Once he felt the power drain, he said to Dylan, "Wizard Dylan, please sing me a song." Dylan began, *"My bonnie lies over the ocean, my Bonnie lies over the sea..."* "Enough!" said Wizard Noland, "Pass!" Donovan released the spell, and Wizard Dylan grimaced and shook his finger at him.

"I have already observed your Replication spells, and they are excellent. There is no need to repeat them. There are only two spells that remain to be tested. I need you to cast a Binding spell on one of us. It should be of short duration." Donovan thought, then said, "Wizard Noland, never tell anyone that you have heard Wizard Dylan sing." Donovan drew his right index finger along the ground, and the spell settled on Wizard Noland. Wizard Dylan smiled and said, "Pass."

"Donovan, your last spell is the most lethal in a magician's arsenal, and it is never to be used lightly or without cause. You know which spell I refer to?" Donovan nodded, "Yes, Sir. It is the Kill spell." Noland nodded somberly, and Donovan was shocked to see Wizard Mira leading Stam over to them from the stables. "Donovan, please kill your horse."

Donovan stood still, completely overwhelmed and shocked by Wizard Noland's order. He raised his hand but just couldn't do it. Stam had been with him too long and had been through too much with him. Even if it meant failing the Sorcerer's Test, Donovan resolved not to comply with the order.

"No, Sir. I'm sorry. I won't kill Stam just to prove that I can. There has to be another way." Surprisingly, Wizard Noland smiled, "Very good. I was hoping you would say that. If you had followed my orders blindly and killed without cause, you would have failed the test. Now, I assure you that this is just a Seeming of Stam, cast by Wizard Mira; if you look over there, you will see the real horse with Wizard Faith by the stables." Donovan looked over and saw Stam.

Wizard Noland then said, "Now, please demonstrate how you would use the Kill spell to dispatch this Seeming." Donovan raised his right hand and, with a quick slashing motion, said, *"TERMINA."* The Seeming vanished in a flash of light.

"The final element of the Sorcerers Test is to determine the strength of your shields. Are you prepared?" asked Wizard Dylan. Donovan took a quick sip from his water bottle, cast his shield and nodded. All hell broke loose.

It wasn't just Wizard Dylan throwing rocks, sand and nails at Donovan; Wizards Mira and Noland joined in as well. A maelstrom of debris struck his shield from all sides. Wizard Mira sent Seemings that looked like rocks at him. They passed right through his shield (because they weren't real). The Seemings didn't hurt, but they were certainly distracting. Finally, came the fireball. By now, Donovan was weary; his shield was battered, and his senses numb. Rather than wait for the fireball to reach him, he conjured a drenching gusher of water that fell from the sky and extinguished the fireball before it reached his shield.

The assembled Wizards all stopped their attacks in awe. "How in the world did he do that?" asked Wizard Mira. "He shouldn't be able to cast two spells at once!" "Donovan is just full of surprises," said Wizard Noland. "I think we've seen enough." Wizard Noland removed a scroll from his sleeve and read formally:

"Level Three Donovan Francis, pending verification of your Love and Death Serums by Wizard Toffin and the completion of your final task, you are hereby promoted to Sorcerer. You will receive your first assignment to the Armed Forces of Franconia in the coming weeks. Congratulations."

Rachel appeared by his side and wrapped him in an enthusiastic hug. "I guess we have a wedding to plan," she whispered.

Chapter Two:
WEDDING PLANS

"Gek, wake up!" Someone was slapping his face. Hard. *Why was he laying on the floor? Where was he, and why was he in human form?* Gek, the Great Dragon wondered. As he slowly came to his senses, he recognized the face above him. *Andrew.* That damn magic-user that he was compelled to protect because of his grandfather's Binding spell. *Why was the floor moving?* Then he remembered, he was on a ship, the HMS VALOR. He had come with Azure, his Sea Dragon mate, to negotiate a truce with the humans of Franconia.

Where was Azure? He remembered landing on the ship as a Dragon, then changing into human form; then Azure landed and transformed, but something had gone wrong. The transformation had taken way too long, and once complete, Azure was screaming in pain and bleeding profusely. The humans had taken her below deck to a cabin, and two Sorceresses, Anne and Celeste (who were identical twin sisters), had worked to heal Azure. Azure had screamed in pain for almost two hours before the cries had stopped. Then Celeste had come out of the cabin and said something to him. *What was it?*

"Gek!" said Celeste, coming into his field of view, "Azure is asking for you. Don't you want to see your son?" Gek shook his head to clear it. *What was this crazy Sorceress talking about? He did not have a son; he had a beautiful aqua and gold-colored daughter, Annalise. She had just hatched from her Dragon egg a few weeks ago! What was this nonsense about a son?*

Gek stood on shaky legs and staggered into the cabin to find Azure lying in the Captain's bunk, holding a baby boy wrapped in a gray towel. The baby was blonde with a single strand of blue hair on the right side. "Gek, we have a son," said Azure tiredly. "How is that possible?" asked Gek stupidly. "I guess I was pregnant with twins," said Azure. "I thought I felt a little bloated after laying my egg, but I had no idea that I was still carrying another baby."

"She was lucky to survive the birthing process," said Anne, coming back into the cabin. "Her energy level was very low when we got her down here. It was all Celeste, and I could do to keep her alive. Then she insisted that we save the baby. It was a near thing. The baby is weak but big for his age, if you know what I mean. Is it common for Changed One's births to be so difficult?"

"I have no idea," said Gek. "The other Changed Ones I spoke with about this only said that human childbirth was very painful and that once it began, Azure would not be able to change back into a Dragon without killing both herself and the baby." "Then she cut it awfully close," said Celeste. "As near as we can tell, her water broke during or immediately after her transformation into human form."

His head still swimming and having no idea how water could *break*, Gek knelt down beside Azure, "Are you OK?" he asked. "I am now. Thanks to these two," Azure said, pointing to Anne and Celeste. Gek stroked the baby's head gently too overcome for words.

"So, what are you going to name him?" asked Andrew from the doorway. "I have not given it any thought," said Gek. "When we thought the egg might be a son, we considered 'Ard,' after his grandfather, but that would be a strange name for a human."

"Hmm, yes, it would be. A human name with 'ard' in it—how about Richard?" said Anne. "Richard. Is that a common human name?" asked Azure. "I wouldn't call it common, but it's not too unusual." "I like it," said Gek. "Welcome to the world, Richard. I hope you know how complicated you have just made your parent's lives."

As expected, Donovan's Love and Death Serums worked perfectly, and as soon as Wizard Toffin reported such to Wizard Noland, Donovan was summoned to the Headmaster's cottage, where he was informed that he had passed his Sorcerer's Test and that he and Rachel would receive their first assignments in the coming days. "Sir," asked Donovan, "would it be possible to delay our departure for a couple of weeks? Rachel and I would like to be married here at the Academy, so her parents and all of our friends can attend. We don't know anyone in Fairview."

Wizard Noland thought it over for a few moments, then said, "Two weeks. That's all I can give you. Will that be enough time?" "I'm not sure that my father can make me a wedding dress that quickly," said Rachel, "but I'll go ask him right now. Thank you, Sir." Rachel gave Donovan a peck on the cheek and dashed out of the cottage, heading for the Academy gatehouse.

"Donovan," said Wizard Noland, "Now that you've passed all of your tests, I need to give you your final lesson about being a Sorcerer, which I believe you've heard before. It's just this—Never believe that an enemy is dead unless you have separated their head from their body. Your father has been 'killed' twice by enemies, only to regain consciousness later and strike them down. Remember that. It could save your life someday."

When Rachel entered her Father's tailor shop, he was surprised to see her, since it was earlier than when she normally visited. *Is anything wrong?* he signed. *No. Everything is wonderful! Donovan passed his Sorcerer's Test today, but that means that we have to get married in two weeks before we are sent to our new posts in Fairview! Can you make me a wedding dress that quickly?* Rachel's deaf father smiled and signed, *I began making your dress as soon as I met Donovan. I told you I thought he was a keeper.* Rachel was so happy that she burst into tears.

They arrived at the Great Salt Flats shortly before noon. The day was bright and clear, with only a slight breeze out of the north. Edward was relieved to see that the Baizian surveyors had been hard at work, laying out the boundaries of the reservoir they were going to dig. While the weather was near-perfect, the glare off the white sand and salt was blinding. It was going to take some getting used to. Once all of the eighty-four apprentice magicians were grouped into their fourteen teams of six magicians each, Edward said, "All right, as I said earlier, we will be working around the clock starting right now. Groups one through five will come with me and start digging. We will dig from noon until eight tonight; Groups six through ten will dig from eight this evening until four tomorrow morning, and Groups eleven through fourteen will dig from four until noon tomorrow. Each week, we'll rotate the schedule. Right now, while the first group is digging, I want the rest of you to go with Mage Kathy and set up our camp. There is one tent for each team and one field kitchen for each shift."

"We will also need latrines dug and shower stations erected. The first few days will be the hardest as we set up camp and adjust to our work shifts. The first group of diggers can follow me; the rest of you go with Mage Kathy. Move."

As the young magicians sorted themselves into their assigned groupings and prepared to head out, Edward had a quiet word with Kathy. "Once you get all fourteen tents set up, let the last shift try and get some sleep. I know it won't be easy. I want the adult engineers setting up the kitchens and tending the horses. Have the students use the Dig spell to construct the latrines; we'll need eight of them, four for men and four for women. Keep them separate and ensure as much privacy as you can. We'll fill in the trenches and move them every few weeks. Make sure the kitchens get cooking as soon as they're set up. We have a lot of mouths to feed."

Kathy nodded her understanding and led the young magicians to the campsite area, where they began unloading tents and other gear. Edward took the first group over to the corner post laid out by the survey crew. "Now, I want you all to watch closely so you get the idea of what we're going to be doing." Edward said, rather loudly, *"ENTRENCHO,"* while making a scooping gesture with his right hand and then turning his palm downward beside the trench he formed. The students approached the side of the trench and looked down. The hole was about ten feet wide, twenty feet long and thirty feet deep. The mound of dirt, salt and sand next to the trench was twenty feet long, ten feet high, and thirty feet wide. A second dig spell and Edward hit bedrock about ten feet deeper. The dirt beside the hole was now about fifteen feet high but not as wide as the lower tier.

Edward said, "Who knows the Wind spell?" Several students raised their hands, and Edward said, "Now, I am going to erect a vertical shield, going up the side of the trench, extending to the top of the mound. I want you to use the Wind spell to blow the dirt against the shield, ready—go." Edward erected his shield, and the students used Wind spells to blow dirt, rocks, sand and salt against Edward's shield until it was about twenty feet high. "Enough," said Edward. "Now watch as I use an Adhesive spell to stick the side of the trench and the wall above it together."

Edward said, *"FIRMENTO,"* while pinching the thumb and forefinger of his left hand towards the trench. The side of the trench and the wall above it were glued together solidly, and Edward informed the young magicians that he had also glued the trench wall to the bedrock below, creating a solid wall.

"Now, it's your turn," said Edward. "Group one, start where my hole ended and extend it north along the line the surveyors have laid out. I want two of you to dig, two of you who know how, to make the shield, and the last two to blow the sand against the shield. Once you have the hole dug down to bedrock and the wall at the same height as mine, take turns using the Adhesive spell to stick it all together. Groups three and five, come with me. Groups two and four, start digging the bottom edge of the trench at a ninety-degree angle to the first trench. I will return shortly."

Edward led the two groups of magicians north about a hundred yards and instructed group three to start digging a trench southward towards group one, which was proceeding north, towards them. Then he took group five another hundred yards north and told them to start digging their way south.

Once the odd-numbered teams were hard at work, Edward moved back to the corner and instructed Groups two and four how he wanted them to proceed. The students took to their tasks with enthusiasm, digging, shielding and blowing the spoils into walls. Edward was pleasantly surprised by the progress that was being made. After an hour, Edward called for a rest break, and the students sat and drank eagerly from their water bottles. A few minutes later, Mage Kathy arrived with some fresh fruit and cheese sandwiches for the teams.

The teams continued to dig throughout the day. After eight hours, the next shift of five teams of apprentice magicians arrived to take over. This time, Edward set three teams to work on the southern boundary, and two groups began digging south-to-north. It was more difficult digging in the dark. Fortunately, the moon was nearly full, and the sky was cloudless. Still, Edward made a mental note to order torches that could be placed along the trenches to improve visibility.

Kathy returned at about mid-shift with hot soup and tea for the young magicians. "How's it going?" she asked. "Actually, much better than I expected," replied Edward. "It's only about thirty feet down to bedrock here, and the students are working hard. Once we start moving further into the Flats, I expect it to become more difficult, even though we'll be vanishing the spoils instead of making walls out of them."

"Why do you think it's easier here?" asked Kathy. "It's because we're at the edge of the Salt Flats. There isn't as much sand and salt here as there will be as we progress towards the center. I'm also not really sure what's going to happen if we get a heavy, sustained rain." Kathy looked thoughtful, "How big a problem is rain going to be?" "It depends. How many of these magicians will be able to cast a weather shield while digging? A weather shield takes almost no energy, but it only *deflects* the rain. I need to give it some thought while we have time. Ideally, we'll be able to capture some of the rainwater for drinking, cooking and showering. I'd hate to have to bring all of our water all the way from Springfield."

"How long do you plan to work tonight?" asked Kathy. "I'll supervise all three shifts and get the first shift started tomorrow before I head back to camp for some rest. My water bottle is full of Stamina Serum, so I'll be OK for a while," said Edward quietly. Kathy squeezed his hand, "Just don't overdo it. It would look *terrible* if you passed out and had to be revived by a twelve-year-old." Edward laughed, "I suppose it would at that. I'll see you in the morning; you get some rest too." Kathy nodded, gave Edward a quick kiss on the cheek and headed back to the base camp. Several of the apprentice magicians snickered at the public display of affection. "Shut up and dig," said Edward good-naturedly.

The 2nd Company of the Royal Expeditionary Force arrived in Kingston two weeks after departing Springfield. It had been a hot, dusty, but otherwise uneventful trip. Captain Fletcher dismissed the company to stable and feed their mounts while he went to report their arrival to Major Gerald, the Force commander. The newly-promoted Mage Curtis bid his farewells and headed over to the Wizards Academy to report his return to Wizard Noland, the Headmaster of the Academy, and deliver Edward's messages to Noland and Donovan.

As he approached the non-descript gatehouse, the door opened, and Wizard Faith greeted him enthusiastically. "Curtis! Welcome back! How was your trip?" Wizard Faith, the Gatekeeper for the Wizards Academy, was a petite, attractive woman with dark hair. "The trip was exciting, what with the dragons and all. There was also the exploding flour barrels and the conquest of Springfield. How are you liking your new job?" asked Curtis. Wizard Faith had recently been recalled from the city of Southport, where she had been the Regional Mage. Upon her arrival in Kingston, she had been given and passed the Wizard's Test, and assigned as the Gatekeeper for the Academy. The previous Gatekeeper, Wizard Stuart, had been a dragon 'Changed One' (a dragon in human form) who, in coordination with Wizard Loren, the Academy History and Enhancements Instructor, was plotting to kill the other Changed Ones at the Academy who would not join them in their conflict against the humans.

The scheme had been unmasked by Wizard Noland and Mage Edward, and Loren and Stuart had both had their hands removed so they could not transform back into dragons or perform any lethal spells. Stuart and Loren had been held for questioning, but Wizard Noland had not accounted for Stuart's advanced age and all of the Healing spells and Serums he was taking to maintain himself, and Stuart had died before he could be questioned thoroughly. Loren, on the other hand, had been a wealth of knowledge, divulging the dragon's plans, the location where the Dragon Council normally met, and how to transform from a human into a dragon. Unfortunately, Loren had managed to kill herself before divulging any further information.

"You must have dinner with me tonight and tell me all about this exploding flour. We already knew about the dragon ambush," said Faith smugly. "I forgot, Major

Gerald has been back for several weeks now, and he undoubtedly reported what happened," said Curtis as they walked into the Academy courtyard together.

"Well, that and the fact that Edward's son, Donovan, can also perform the Seeing spell. You see, Minister Jasmine reported to the King that the Royal Expeditionary Force had been ambushed and nearly wiped out. Wizard Noland didn't believe it, so he asked Donovan to try the Seeing spell. Donovan found one company of the Royal Expeditionary Force outside Prarrieville, one company in Springfield, Wizard Edward halfway to Baize, and the echoes of seven dead Fire Dragons on the hills near Springfield. By the way, it looked like Edward was being followed by an enemy Wizard," said Faith.

"No. That's Wizard Timothy from Springfield. He's going with Edward to talk to King Donald about these dragon attacks," explained Curtis. "Edward was going to talk to the King of Baize? Alone? Is he out of his mind?" "No, but he certainly is fearless. He acted like he was going for a walk in the park. He spent a little over a week in Baize, then came back to Springfield in the company of a very attractive Baizian Mage." "How attractive?" asked Faith, teasingly. "Nowhere near as pretty as you," said Curtis, blushing. "Good answer," said Faith. "Let's get you to Wizard Noland."

They walked across the courtyard to the cottage of the Headmaster, and as usual, the door opened before they stepped onto the front porch. Wizard Noland, the Headmaster, greeted them warmly, "Mage Curtis! Welcome back! Please come in, I've heard great things about you!" Curtis grinned as he and Wizard Faith entered Noland's cottage.

Noland waved them to seats in the parlor and said to Curtis without preamble, "Before we begin, I want you to know that I've heard about your exploits against the dragons, and I heartily endorse Wizard Edward's promotion of you to Mage with no further testing required." Curtis looked relieved, and Wizard Faith clapped him on the back enthusiastically. Curtis had been somewhat skeptical of the legality of a battlefield promotion to Mage, even though Edward had assured him that it was legitimate.

"So, have you given any thought as to what you'd like to do next?" asked Noland. Curtis gave Faith a sidelong glance, then said, "Well, Sir, I'd really like to stay here in Kingston if I could. Wizard Edward said that he didn't think that the Kingston Regional Mage's position had been filled yet and that I might be a good fit." "Edward has a keen mind for these things. That's exactly what I was thinking. Besides, the King knows that you can perform the Seeing spell. He was most upset when he learned that Edward had chosen you to be the Sorcerer to accompany the Royal Expeditionary Force to Springfield. Apparently, aside from you two, only Mage Roark in Three Forks can conjure that spell. The King is very insistent that someone with that ability remain in Kingston at his beck and call."

"I heard that Edward's son, Donovan, can also cast that spell," said Curtis. "Who told you—oh, I suppose you did, Faith. Yes, but Sorcerer Donovan is needed elsewhere, and I think I need to remove him from Kingston. He's made some enemies here." "*Sorcerer* Donovan?" asked Curtis, "but he's only been here for-" "Three years, six months and two weeks. Yes. I know. He's passed every test required in record time. There's never been a student who advanced so far, so fast. He can even cast two spells at once for a limited time, and he can probably cast *three* spells at once for a few moments. He's extraordinary."

"That reminds me, I have a message from Edward for you and also one for Donovan," said Curtis. Wizard Noland twirled his finger around his head, and Jerry, his door warden, appeared instantly. "Jerry, go find Sorcerer Donovan and bring him back here. He's probably with Rachel." "At once, Sir," said Jerry, bolting for the door. "Rachel?" asked Curtis.

Noland and Faith smiled, "Yes, Donovan is engaged to Sorceress Rachel, who was his Mentor. Now that he's passed the Sorcerer's Test, they're planning their wedding here at the Academy before they depart on their first assignments," said Wizard Noland. Curtis looked stunned, "Things certainly happen fast around here." "Only when it applies to Donovan. When do you expect Edward to return? I know that Donovan is anxious to tell him about his passing the Sorcerer's Test and the wedding, not necessarily in that order."

Curtis looked down, "I doubt that Edward will be able to make it. He's elected to remain in Baize for several months, helping them with a civil engineering project." Before he could explain further, Jerry entered with Donovan in tow.

"You asked to see me, Sir?" asked Donovan. "Yes, please sit down. Donovan, this is Mage Curtis. He has just returned from Springfield with the 2nd Company of the Royal Expeditionary Force. He has a message for you from your father," said Noland. "Where is he? Did he come back with you?" asked Donovan excitedly. "No," said Curtis, handing over the messages to Noland and Donovan. "His message should explain everything." Noland took the message from Curtis and, oddly, smelled it, then smiled. "Why did you do that?" asked Curtis.

Wizard Noland said, "It's something that Edward and I worked out many years ago when we suspected that some of our messages to each other were being intercepted and altered with magic. Not that I doubt you, Curtis; it's just something I do automatically with messages from Edward. You see, if the message is altered in any way, even by adding so much as a comma, the parchment will smell like oranges. That was how I unmasked that traitor, Jasmine."

"Jasmine, you mean *Minister of Internal Security, Jasmine?"* asked Curtis. "Yes. King Donald of Baize sent King Henry a message, promising to remove his troops from the border and asking to restore normal relations with Franconia. Jasmine intercepted the message and altered it in a way designed to infuriate King Henry. After the King read the message, I asked to see it. The message *reeked* of oranges, so I asked Jasmine why she had altered the message, then I changed her into a marble statue when she tried to attack me."

"So Jasmine was a dragon Changed One, as Edward suspected," said Curtis. "Yes. It's very fortunate that Edward and I worked out the message spell all those years ago," said Noland. "Why oranges?" asked Curtis. Noland smiled, "My parents were orange growers," he explained, "growing up, I had to eat oranges three meals a day. Now, I find the smell distasteful. Edward thought it was funny." Donovan experimentally smelled his message. It smelled like parchment. He opened it and read:

Donovan,

It appears that I will be remaining in Baize for much longer than I anticipated. I have agreed to help King Donald of Baize construct a giant reservoir to contain the spread of the Great Salt Flats that have been expanding for decades and now threaten to reach the Amber River. If the salt gets into the river, it will poison the fish and all the wildlife downstream. We must not let that happen.

I have asked the King to allow me to remain here for some months as we dig this enormous hole that I hope will fill with water and contain the threat.

I hope you are doing well and studying hard. Mage Curtis can perform the Seeing spell if you ever need to locate me. I will send you additional messages as soon as I am able.

Dad

P.S. I have met someone that I am very fond of. Her name is Mage Kathy. I hope she will agree to return to Franconia with me once this project is over.

E.F.

Donovan re-read the message and then passed it over to Wizard Noland. Noland scanned it quickly and smiled widely. "It's about time," said Noland. "What do you mean by that?" asked Donovan. "I mean that your mother has been dead for over five years. If your father can find happiness again with this Mage Kathy, I wish him well. *And so should you.*"

Wizard Faith started at the mention of Mage Kathy. "*Mage* Kathy?" she asked. "That's what Edward's message says," said Noland, looking to Donovan for permission for Faith to read his father's message. Donovan nodded his consent. "I met a magician named Kathy a few months ago. She was traveling to Fairview on the ship that brought me here from Southport. I detected her spark from the dock and, since she was too old for enrolment at the Academy, I suggested the standard Binding spell— you know, never to harm another with magic or counterfeit coins, but she refused." "What?" said Noland. "Yes," said Faith, "she explained that, as an attractive woman, I should understand that she sometimes has to use magic to dissuade aggressive men and that our standard Binding spell would leave her defenseless. So, I modified the spell, requiring that she would not *unjustly* use magic to harm another. She agreed, and we parted ways at the dock in Kingston. I wonder if it could be the same woman."

Noland looked over at Mage Curtis. "Have you met Mage Kathy?" Curtis nodded. "Describe her." "Mage Kathy is about five foot six, with long blonde hair and blue eyes. I would estimate that she is in her early thirties. She is very shapely—Ouch!" said Curtis as Faith kicked him in the shin. "That sounds like the magician I met on the HMS UNSINKABLE," said Faith. "What would a Baizian Mage be doing in Franconia? Spying? She told me that she was returning to Fairview after visiting her sick sister in Westport."

"Did she ask you about anything else?" asked Noland. "She seemed very interested about the dragon that the Royal Expeditionary Force killed near Farmdale. She also asked how they managed to kill it after Edward was killed," recalled Faith. "It sounds like she was sent to find out what she could about the dragon. I suppose I can understand King Donald's curiosity. I think we should give Mage Kathy the benefit of the doubt for now," said Noland.

"Should I cancel the Binding spell?" asked Faith. "I think that would be a good idea. If she's with Edward they might get into all sorts of situations that would require magical solutions. Edward has a knack for finding trouble. If Kathy doesn't know the spell has been lifted, she should still be cautious using magic *'unjustly,'*" said Noland. "*CODA PROMISA*," said Faith, drawing her left finger along the floor; sparkling bits of magic rose from the floor and settled on Wizard Faith.

"So, how do we let Edward know about your promotion and wedding?" Noland asked Donovan.

"Well," said Donovan, "I know one way to get a message to him quickly."

Mage Andrew

Chapter Three:

NEWS

Commodore Matthews knocked on the door to his cabin gently. "Come in," said Azure softly. The Commodore entered, finding Azure sitting in his captain's chair, nursing a small baby boy. "I don't mean to be rude, but I do need my cabin back soon, and I suspect that the two of you came here for a reason, not just for you to give birth." Azure laughed gently, "Yes, Commodore, Gek and I flew here to arrange a more permanent truce between the Sea Dragon Clan and the humans of Franconia. We have been given authority to negotiate such a Treaty by the Sea Dragon Clan."

Commodore Matthews stroked his beard and said, "I thought that any Treaty would have to be agreed to by the Sea Dragon Clan Chief. Forgive me, but I do not think you are that dragon, and I am certain that your companion is not, since he is a Great Dragon." Azure smiled, "You are correct, Commodore, but Cobalt, the new Sea Dragon Clan Chief, was delayed by other matters and was unable to make the trip here. We do have his permission to formalize the Treaty, however. You see, Cobalt is Gek's father."

"When you're finished with what you're doing," said the Commodore, looking at the suckling baby, "we should sit and talk. I'll ask Mage Andrew to assist me with our discussion. I must tell you, though, that any Treaty that I agree to will have to be approved by the Chief of Naval Operations and King Henry of Franconia. It may take some weeks to inform them of our discussions and receive their instructions regarding any Peace Treaty."

"I understand completely, Captain. It will also take us some time to inform all of the members of our Clan of any agreement that we reach. Not all Sea Dragons live on the islands, you see. There are many who have moved to the mainland over the decades since our last disastrous Treaty with you humans." Commodore Matthews nodded, not quite understanding what Azure meant by the *last Treaty*. He would need to talk to Andrew.

"I will await you on deck," said the Commodore. Once up on deck, Commodore Matthews sent for Andrew to order a table and four chairs to be brought out, along with a pitcher of water, several rolls of parchment, ink and quills. Andrew arrived shortly, "You asked for me, Sir?" "Yes. It seems these dragons have come to negotiate a more permanent Peace Treaty between the Sea Dragons and the 'humans of Franconia,' as Azure put it. Azure mentioned the last 'disastrous Treaty' between dragons and humans. Do you know anything about that?"

Andrew briefly explained that, two centuries ago, the people of Franconia agreed to provide the dragons with a tribute of 20,000 head of cattle every two years, in exchange for the dragons agreeing not to eat humans." "So, what happened?" asked Commodore Matthews. "We gave the cattle slow-acting poison before we delivered them to the dragons. Most of the dragons of that era died from the poison or were killed by the army as they writhed on the ground, overcome by the poison. It was not our finest moment." The Commodore grunted his agreement.

"That's going to make it difficult to negotiate a Treaty that is fair to both sides. Why do you think they're asking for a truce now?" "It could be that we hurt them more than we knew in the last battle, or it could be something else entirely. I'm just not sure, Sir."

Just then, Gek and Azure arrived on deck, with Azure carrying the sleeping child. The two humans and two dragon Changed Ones took their seats across the table from one another. "So," began the Commodore, "what kind of terms did you have in mind?" Gek looked at Azure and she nodded for him to take the lead in the negotiations. "Our proposal is just this: the Sea Dragon Clan will agree not to sink any Franconian ships and not to attack your ports on land, provided that you agree not to attack us. Additionally, what you call the Coral Islands are to be ceded to the Sea Dragon Clan in perpetuity. There are to be no human structures built on our islands."

The Commodore sat back in his chair, considering the proposal. Andrew whispered something in his ear, and he said, "No. You must agree not to *attack* our ships. Under your proposal, you could attack them as long as you did not *sink* them. However, I will agree not to construct any *permanent* facilities on the Coral Islands, but our ships must be able to anchor in the cove on the northernmost island in the event of a storm."

Gek and Azure conferred quietly, and then Gek said, "Define *permanent*." Commodore Matthews smiled and said, "Any structure that is not made of cloth, like a tent." "Why would you want to erect a tent on one of our islands?" asked Azure. "I concede the point," said the Commodore, "We will agree not to construct *any* structures on the islands. Do we have an agreement?"

"One last point," said Gek, "a maximum of three ships may anchor in the cove at the same time." "Five ships," said the Commodore, "Our Navy usually operates in groups of five ships. In the event of a storm, the entire Squadron must be able to take shelter. I could not protect three ships and leave the other two at the mercy of a storm." "Four ships," countered Azure. "No, again, I cannot leave one ship out in a storm." "Very well, five ships, but no one is to come ashore," said Gek.

"Agreed," said the Commodore. "Will all of the dragons agree to this?" Azure looked at Gek and shook her head. "No," said Gek. "We cannot speak for the other Dragon Clans. This agreement is with the Sea Dragon Clan only." "So, what you're saying," said Andrew, "is that our ships might still be attacked by Stone, Fire, Great or Snow Dragons."

Gek hesitated, then said, "Snow Dragons seldom venture far from the Snow Fields, and the Fire and Stone Dragons should only be living on the west side of the Amber River, outside the boundaries of Franconia." "What about the Great Dragons, like you?" persisted Andrew. "I do not speak for the Great Dragon Clan," admitted Gek, "but I will ask them to cease their attacks on your ships."

"What about the Kingdom of Baize?" asked the Commodore. "This agreement would only apply to Franconia," said Gek. "You do not have the authority to speak for the other humans that live on the west side of the river. If a Treaty is to be made with them, it will be a separate negotiation."

The four of them sat for a while, considering the agreement they were about to make. Finally, the Commodore said, "I will present these terms to the Admiral and the King: Sea Dragons will not attack Franconian ships or port facilities, and we will not attack them. We will cede ownership of the Coral Islands to the Sea Dragon clan but retain the right to shelter up to five ships at a time in the cove on the northernmost island in the event of a storm. There will be no structures built on the islands, and no one will come ashore. Gek will ask the Great Dragon Clan to cease their attacks on Franconian ships."

"How long will it take to receive an answer from your king?" asked Azure. The Commodore thought, "With favorable winds, I can be in Grotton in two weeks, then another two weeks to get the draft Treaty to the King. I have no idea how long it may take for him to reach a decision. Let's call it three months." "How long is a human month?" asked Gek. "One cycle of the moon," replied Andrew. "Will that be long enough for you to inform the rest of your clan?"

"It should be. We can move faster than humans. Once your king approves the Treaty, what then?" "*If* the King approves, he will draft a formal document, with lots of flowery words, then send it back to me. Once you sign the document, I will ask Mage Andrew to cast a Binding spell on all signatories to ensure we keep our word this time." Gek nodded. "That should suffice. I guess it is time for us to be on our way now. Please say goodbye to Anne and Celeste and thank them for their help. We will not forget them."

With those parting words, Gek disrobed and transformed into dragon form and Andrew helped Azure climb aboard his back and secured the baby in a cross-body pouch. Gek lifted off, flying north towards the Coral Islands and home.

Donovan, Rachel, Wizard Noland, and the rest of the Wizards Academy faculty headed down to the Academy boat dock. It was almost sunset. After opening the portal and walking out onto the dock, Wizard Noland addressed the four Academy instructors, "Donovan is going to transform into a Great Dragon in order to deliver a wedding invitation to his father, who is currently somewhere in Baize, near the Great Salt Flats. Once he has delivered his message, he will return. You are all here in order to see what a Great Dragon looks like in the event that you ever need to transform into one yourselves."

"You will note that Donovan has a backpack with a set of clothes in it. As we discovered during the course of his Sorcerer's Test, transforming into a dragon will destroy your human clothes, and when changing back into human form, you are left naked." The five Wizards laughed loudly at this news, and Donovan blushed.

"Donovan, we will turn our backs while you disrobe and complete the Change spell."

The Wizards turned their backs while Rachel grinned and held out her hands to receive Donovan's garments. Once naked, Donovan winked at Rachel, then said, *"MORPHIUS,"* while clapping his hands together. In a flash, a large golden dragon was standing on the riverbank. "You can turn around now," said Donovan. The teachers gasped in awe of Donovan in dragon form. They walked around him, examining him from every angle in order to remember what a dragon looked like in case they ever had to transform themselves. "How do you feel?" asked Wizard Faith. "Hungry. Even though I just ate. I guess Terry was right about that." The Wizards laughed.

"You have to remember to transform into a dragon that can talk," said Donovan. Otherwise, you will not be able to Change back into a human." The Wizards all nodded their understanding. "Very well," said Wizard Noland, "Donovan, you'd best be off. I believe that it will take you almost two full nights to reach your father. Remember to transform back into a human before entering their camp. I know that you used the Seeing spell earlier today to determine his location. *Do not* alarm any people on your way there. Find a good hiding place before sunrise, and Change back into a human. Only travel at night when in dragon form. Oh, here is your new Sorcerer's Concealment cloak. It might come in handy." The Wizards moved off, back towards the Academy, leaving Rachel alone with Donovan.

"You'd better hurry back here as fast as you can. I can't believe that you're leaving me alone to make all the arrangements for our wedding," said Rachel. "What arrangements?" asked Donovan. *"What arrangements? Why, the caterer, the flowers, delivering the invitations, the decorations! There's a ton of work to do and less than two weeks to do it!" "At least Wizard Noland has relieved you of your Mentor duties. That should free up some time."

"Have you thought of anyone specific we should invite?" asked Rachel. "Your parents, probably the King, Marshall Guzman and his wife, Major Gerald and the Royal Expeditionary Force, plus all the students here and the instructors and Mentors. Maybe even the staff." Rachel frowned, thinking about how many people that was going to be. "I wish my cousin Andrew could make it, but he's probably still at sea on the HMS VALOR."

"Who do you think should perform the ceremony?" asked Rachel. "How about Judge Toffin? I am sure he would be happy to." "That's a good choice," said Rachel, putting Donovan's new cloak into his backpack and handing it to him. "Well, you'd better get going.

Don't talk to any strange dragons on your way!" Donovan wrapped Rachel up with his tail for a 'goodbye' hug, then released her and told her to stand back, since he'd never tried flying before.

Rachel backed up as Donovan spread his wings and took off, clipping one of the elm trees along the river as he passed. Rachel stood on the dock and watched as he slowly faded from view; then she headed back to her quarters to begin the task of putting on a magician's wedding with only two weeks' notice.

Donovan flew on through the night. The feeling was exhilarating. He flew as fast as he could, hoping to make it to the banks of the Amber River before dawn. He made it (barely), settling down in a cornfield. He transformed back into human form, put on his clothes, and settled in for an uncomfortable day. It was hot. While the corn was fairly tall, it didn't really provide any shade. If he hadn't been so tired from flying all night, Donovan doubted he would have gotten any sleep at all.

He was awake as night fell, but he waited until it was fully dark before disrobing and transforming back into a dragon. He didn't want the farmer to see him. When he felt it was safe, he took off, flying west. From the air, he saw the Amber River, then the city of Springfield, so he knew that he was getting close. A few minutes further west, he saw a sprawling encampment of tents and campfires, with a lot of activity going on for so late at night. Donovan landed about half a mile from the southern edge of the campsite and transformed back into human form. He put on his silver-grey trousers with the burgundy shirt and his concealment cloak and headed toward the camp.

He was surprised not to find any sentries around the camp and that most of the inhabitants were children. There were a few adults sitting around the campfires, but they almost seemed to be ignoring the children. Then Donovan realized that all of the children had the spark. This was a camp of teenage magicians! *What was his father thinking?*

Near the center of the camp, Donovan spotted a large tent that seemed to have a guard in front of it. *That's probably where my father is,* he thought. Throwing back his hood and allowing his cape to slip open, Donovan walked up to the man, who was dozing in his chair and cleared his throat. The man came awake immediately.

"What do you want?" he asked. "I need a word with Wizard Edward, please," said Donovan. "The Wizard asked not to be disturbed until dawn. Go away and come back tomorrow." Donovan stood there stunned, "Wizard Edward is my father, and I need to see him immediately. Either you can wake him up, or I will."

The man looked like he was about to argue the matter, then seemed to notice the Concealment cloak and decided that maybe he should make an exception in this case. "One moment." The man opened the tent flap without looking in, "Excuse me, Wizard Edward, but there's someone out here claiming to be your son. He says he needs to see you immediately."

Donovan heard the shuffling of not one but two people on the other side of the tent flap. A moment later, Edward emerged, wiping his eyes. "Donovan! What are you doing here? Why aren't you in school? How did you get here?" Donovan smiled, "It's good to see you too, dad." Edward reached out and put his hand on Donovan's shoulder, "Well, you're not a Seeming. Where did you get that cloak? What's going on?" A moment later, an attractive woman with long blonde hair emerged from the tent, pulling her robe closed and tying the sash. "Edward, what's wrong?"

"Kathy, this is my son, Donovan—Donovan, this is Mage Kathy. I'll ask again, why aren't you in school, and how did you get here?" Donovan asked, "Is there someplace private we can talk?" Edward looked at Kathy, who grinned like a cat that had just swallowed a canary. "Come on in, Donovan. It's nice to meet you, but this is certainly a bit of a surprise," said Kathy. Kathy led Donovan and an embarrassed Edward into the tent. Donovan took note of the table with several camp stools around it and the lone double bed that had recently been made.

As they settled onto the camp stools, Donovan asked, "Is there anything to eat around here? I know it's late, but I'm starved." Kathy smiled and went back to the tent flap, where she asked the bemused guard to bring them some tea and soup from the kitchen. While they waited, Edward walked over to the wash basin and splashed some cold water on his face. The guard returned shortly with three bowls of hot soup and a kettle of tea. Once the guard left, Donovan cast a Silence spell around the tent.

"OK, now talk," said Edward, overcome with curiosity. "Well, I needed to bring you this invitation," said Donovan, handing over an embossed, cream-colored envelope. Edward opened it suspiciously.

Sorcerer Donovan Francis

Sorceress Rachel Turner

Invite You to Share in Our Happiness

7 May

10:00 am

Franconia Wizards Academy

"You're getting married? Wait, *Sorcerer?* That's impossible! You've only been at the Wizards Academy for—" "Three years, six months, and two weeks, according to Wizard Noland," finished Donovan. "Apparently, I set some kind of record." Edward rose and hugged his son enthusiastically. "That's wonderful! I'm proud of you! Tell me about Rachel."

"Rachel was my Mentor after I moved up to Level Three. We've been dating for the last six months or so. Her father is Brian Turner, the tailor in town who makes the Concealment cloaks for the Royal Guard." "The tailor who's deaf?" asked Edward. "You know him?" *I have known him for years,* Edward signed. *I had no idea you knew sign language,* responded Donovan in sign. *Sign language is a useful skill for a Battle Mage,* responded Edward. "Ahem," said Kathy, "What are you two saying?" "I was just telling Donovan that knowing sign language is a useful skill for a Battle Mage."

"Wait, when did you graduate? How on earth did you find me? You must not have gotten the message I sent with Mage Curtis! May 7th? That's in less than two weeks! You'll never make it back in time!" said Edward, his mind racing with questions.

Donovan smiled, "So many questions. First, I passed my Sorcerer's Test four days ago. I found you with a Seeing spell. I met Mage Curtis three days ago, and I have plenty of time to get back to the Academy." Edward sat down and shook his head. "How is any of that possible? It took us two weeks to get to Springfield from Kingston!" "I flew," said Donovan.

"What do you mean, you flew? When did you learn how to fly?" asked Edward. "During my Sorcerer's Test, Wizard Mira asked me to Change into a dragon. Terry told me how. It's something we'd been discussing at the Academy for a while. If dragons can Change into humans and back again, why can't we?" Edward put his head on the table and groaned. "You used the Change spell to transform yourself into a dragon? Do you know how dangerous that was?"

"Well, Sorceress Celeste did it first. I figured that if she could manage it, so could I." Edward looked at Kathy and said, "Did I tell you that my son was impulsive?" Kathy smiled and took his hand. "So, tell me, how did Sorceress Celeste know what a dragon looked like? You can't Change into something you've never seen before!"

Donovan sighed, "It's a long story. Celeste was transporting a young man from Grotton to the Academy. Mage Charles had apprehended him on the docks and knew he had the spark. Neither of them knew that he was a dragon Changed One. His mate, a Sea Dragon, attacked the coach just outside the Jade Swamp; the Changed One, who said his name was Gek, was injured when the Sea Dragon used the Dig spell to stop the coach. The Sea Dragon was distraught because she didn't know how to heal her injured mate. Celeste offered to heal him if they spared her. She did, and they did. So, Celeste saw a Sea Dragon and was able to change into one to deliver a message to Mage Andrew on board the HMS VALOR."

Edward put his head in his hands, "How can Andrew be a Mage already? It hasn't been a year since he left the Academy!" "After the Sea Dragons attacked Sundock, Admiral Cross sent Commodore Matthews to take command of 1st Squadron. The Squadron's Battle Mage was killed on the HMS COMFORT when the dragons attacked it. Since the VALOR had been having so much success against the dragons in the Low Sea, Wizard Lake promoted Andrew to Mage."

"You certainly miss a lot when you're gone for six months," said Edward. "You mean while you're off killing seven Fire Dragons, straightening out a foreign city, confronting a neighboring King and killing his Court Wizard?" asked Donovan. Kathy laughed out loud.

"He's got you there, Edward!" "I suppose that Mage Curtis told you about the Fire Dragons?" "No. While you were gone, Minister Jasmine reported that the Royal Expeditionary Force had been ambushed by dragons, magicians, and the Baizian Army and nearly wiped out. She said that the remnants of the force were fleeing back to Franconia and being pursued by dragons." Edward glared, "Remind me to kill her when I get home." Donovan smiled, "No need. Wizard Noland turned her into a marble statue after she altered the message from King Donald to King Henry. That trick with the orange scent is pretty slick."

"That doesn't explain how you knew about the Fire Dragons," said Edward tiredly. "When Wizard Cassandra told Wizard Noland what Jasmine had reported to the King, Noland asked me to try the Seeing spell to see if I could locate you and the Expeditionary

Force. I found you, halfway to Baize, one company of the Expeditionary Force in Springfield, and the other almost to Prarrieville. I also detected the echoes of seven Fire Dragons in the hills just east of Springfield."

"You detected me from that far away? Impressive!" "I guess so, but I wound up passing out and ending up in the Infirmary for three days before I woke up. Rachel was pretty mad at Wizard Noland over that."

"OK, let me get this straight— You're a Sorcerer, Andrew is a Mage, you're getting married in less than two weeks, you can Change into a dragon, and Michael killed Jasmine. Anything else interesting happen?" "Well," said Donovan mischievously, "I saved a Kingston Superior Court Judge from a deranged criminal and received a Special Commendation for it; I had the idea to give one of these Concealment cloaks to all Academy graduates; one of the replacement soldiers in the Royal Expeditionary Force was a Changed One who tried to assassinate Marshall Guzman at the Royal Ball, but I stopped him, and Wizard Faith tried to make me fail my Sorcerer's Test by riding the Academy Clydesdale when we fought on horseback."

"Why would someone try to assassinate the Marshall?" "He was considering issuing Concealment cloaks to the entire Royal Guard. I guess Minister Jasmine didn't like that idea." "So, only the Royal

Expeditionary Force has the cloaks?" asked Edward. "Yes. And the magicians, but we had to make Concealment horse blankets for Major Gerald." "Why?" "When the troops were riding in their cloaks, you could still see the horses. It looked damned funny, too," said Donovan. "I should have thought of that. When we attacked the dragons, we rode around behind them at night, then dismounted. I never thought of the horses," said Edward.

"Anyway, now Rachel's father is the official tailor for the Wizards Academy. He makes all the cloaks. We add the Concealment and Stamina spells, so they cost a lot less than they used to, but he should have a steady income from all the new Sorcerers." "It seems like you've had a busy winter and spring. One more question: Why would Celeste need to change into a dragon and go find Andrew?" "Oh, I'm sorry. Wizard Noland needed to tell him that his mother passed away. I guess she was your sister-in-law." Edward sighed, "Yes. She was your mother's older sister. She was very kind, although her husband never believed that Andrew had the spark. That's why Andrew ran away to go to the Wizards Academy."

Edward rubbed his bleary eyes, "So, is that it? No more big news?" Donovan shrugged, "Just one more thing, apparently Andrew and I are both descendants of Wizard Amanda, you know, the one who helped the dragons two hundred years ago? Well, according to Loren, the Dragon Council is under a Binding spell that any progeny of Wizard Amanda must be spared by the dragons, so I'm feeling pretty good right now."

Chapter Four:
CHANGES

They landed on Acropo before they realized their mistake. Gek and Azure looked at each other stupidly, realizing that there was no way to get baby Richard through the underwater cave that led to the Sea Dragon colony's system of caverns. "Now what?" asked Azure. Gek thought for a minute, then said, "I suppose we should go back to Perfo and use Cobalt's cave until the children are grown." "Are you serious? It is going to be almost a year before Annalise can fly and probably ten years or more before Richard can cast a spell to change into a Dragon!"

"Hey, I am just making suggestions," said Gek defensively. "We cannot stay here, in the hot sun, with no water, and we cannot get Richard into the cave. At least on Perfo, we will have a cool cave with fresh water while we try to figure things out." "Fine. But I need to go tell Aqua that we are back first," said Azure. "I do not think that is a good idea," said Gek. "Annalise will see you for sure and want to come with you. I think we need to postpone that introduction until we are settled. You can come back and get her later today." *"Fine,"* said Azure, in a tone that meant it was definitely not "fine."

The two dragons flew back to Perfo, the southernmost of the Coral Islands, where they found Cobalt's mountaintop cave empty. They entered and sat in the cool shade of the cave for a short while before Richard woke up and began crying. Azure handed the baby to Gek. "Here, I think he needs his diaper changed." Gek looked at her quizzically, "his what?" Azure sighed, "His diaper. Change into human form, and I will show you what to do."

Gek grumbled but complied with Azure's demands. Once in human form, they placed the baby on a flat rock, and Azure took a new diaper out of the bag that Anne had given her. She removed the wet diaper and showed Gek how to put on a clean, dry diaper. "What do we do with this thing?" asked Gek, holding the wet diaper at arm's length. "You go and wash it and then hang it outside to dry. We only have a few of them, so we will have to re-use them."

Gek grumbled some more but found a shallow hole with some water in it and he rinsed out the diaper, then took it outside to dry. When he returned, Azure was breast-feeding Richard. Gek stared, fascinated by the process. "Stop leering and get me a blanket," said Azure. "Once he falls asleep, I am leaving for Acropo. You will have to stay here and watch him." Gek started to protest, then thought better of it. This was going to be a difficult year.

The baby nodded off to sleep, and Azure handed him gently to Gek. "Keep him warm. I will return soon." "What do I do if he wakes up?" "Play with him, rock him back to sleep, give him some water. I do not know. I will be back soon."

Azure left the cave, transformed back into dragon form, and headed for Acropo as fast as her wings could carry her. When she arrived at the island, she immediately dove under the water and entered the cave of the Sea Dragon Clan. When she broke the surface of the grotto that was the entrance to the cavern system, Annalise was there with her grandmother, Aqua. "Look, there is mommy!" said Aqua tiredly.

The baby dragon squealed with delight and ran to Azure. "Hello, Anna! Have you been a good girl while I was away?" Aqua humphed, "Hardly. She has cried for you every night and been a terror to the other children of the Clan. I think there must be too much Great Dragon in her. Where is Gek, by the way?"

Azure sighed, "We have a complication, I did not realize it, but I was pregnant with twins. After I landed on the ship to begin the negotiations with the humans, I went into labor. It was a near thing. It took two human Sorceresses, Anne and her sister Celeste, to save me and the baby." "BABY? YOU HAVE A HUMAN CHILD?" said Aqua, aghast. "Yes," said Azure, "a boy.

We named him Richard, after Gek's grandfather." Aqua sputtered. "How flattering," said Ard, entering the grotto with Cobalt close behind him. "Where are they now?"

"Gek and the baby are in Cobalt's cave on Perfo, since we could not figure out a way to get Richard in here safely," said Azure. "Ard, you look wonderful, by the way." Ard grinned, "Thank you, I feel much better. I am not sure how long the Healing spell will last, but at least I will have a chance to see my great-grandchildren."

"Cobalt, are you OK?" asked Azure. "Fine, I just put too much power into the healing spell. I guess you two can use my cave for a while. As Clan Chief, my place is here with the others. So, were you able to conduct the negotiations with the humans?" asked Cobalt.

"Yes. We had to agree not to attack their ships or port facilities. The humans agreed to our ownership of these islands, and they agreed not to attack us and not to build any structures on our islands. We did have to agree to allow up to five of their ships to anchor in the cove on Acropo in the event of a storm, but no human is allowed to come ashore." Ard and Cobalt considered her words for a few minutes, and then Ard said, "I suppose that is as much as we could hope for. Will all of the humans abide by this Treaty?"

"The ship Captain said that he would have to send the agreement to the Admiral in charge of the Navy and the human King. He said that it might take as long as three cycles of the moon to get an answer. Once the Treaty is agreed to, Sorcerer Andrew said that he would cast a Binding spell on everyone who signs the Treaty to make sure they do not break their word."

"You saw Andrew? What does he look like?" asked Ard. "He is about average height for a human, with light brown hair. He is younger than I expected for a Mage," replied Azure. "Any other impressions of him?" "Gek said that he was a very impressive magician and calm under pressure. When I went into labor, Andrew grabbed a pot of boiling water to bring to my room." "So? That does not seem so impressive," snorted Cobalt. "Gek said that the pot scalded deep burns on both of Andrew's hands, but he did not drop it or even comment on the pain until after he delivered it to the Sorceresses treating me." "Hmmm, an individual with a very strong will then," observed Ard.

"Well, we need to head back to Perfo. I am sure that Richard is awake by now. Can Anna swim to the surface yet?" Azure asked Aqua. "Yes. That is why we are here. She has gone off in search of you twice now; once, we had to comb the island before we found her sleeping in the shade of a palm tree. The second time, she was swimming in the water around the island! It is a wonder that she was not eaten by a shark," said Aqua. "You know there are no sharks in these waters," said Azure. "No, but there are certainly other dangers to a young baby Dragon. We were most fortunate," said Cobalt.

"I guess I will have to carry her to Perfo," said Azure. "It will be many months before she learns to fly." "Or swim strongly enough to reach the other islands or the mainland. Do you and Gek have a plan for what you will do?" asked Cobalt. "Not yet," said Azure. "We could really use some advice." "Let us get to Perfo first, then we can discuss matters and maybe come up with a solution," said Ard.

Aqua yawned and said, "If it is all the same to you three, I will stay here. I am exhausted from chasing Annalise all around the caverns. I am not as young as I used to be." The four Dragons dove into the grotto and surfaced a short distance from the island. They swam to the beach, where Azure grabbed Annalise in her talons, and the three adult Dragons took flight for Perfo, Annalise shrieking in fear and delight, on her first flight.

Edward shook his head to clear it and said, "I need some air." Donovan and Kathy followed him out of the tent to the nearby fire ring, where they took seats on one of the crude wooden benches around the fire. The man who had been guarding Edward's tent followed them over, "Do you need anything else, Sir?" "No, Frank. We're fine," said Edward kindly. "So, I guess this really is your son, then," said Frank. "Yes. Donovan, this is Frank, one of the two men who are kind enough to protect my rest and privacy during the few short hours I allow myself to sleep. Frank, this is my son, Donovan. Actually, it's Sorcerer Donovan now."

"I'm pleased to meet you, Sir, sorry about the misunderstanding earlier. It's just that everyone in the camp seems to want to disturb your father's rest lately." "I understand, Frank. Thank you for your diligence and reasonableness." Frank grinned, "He doesn't look much like you, Sir Wizard, but he kind of *acts* like you, if you know what I mean." Frank laughed and moved back to his post outside Edward's tent.

"So, dad, *what are you doing here?*" asked Donovan. Edward sighed as he uncorked his water bottle and took a sip. He shuddered slightly and said, "Too much Stamina Serum, too often. I need to slow down." Kathy placed a comforting hand on his back, massaging Edward's aching muscles. Finally, Edward said, "Well, son, you said that Mage Curtis delivered my message, so you know that we're trying to contain the Great Salt Flats." Donovan nodded and said, "Yes. I read the words, but without knowing what the Great Salt Flats are, that didn't tell me very much or why you thought it was going to take so long."

Edward used a Wind spell to clear off a patch of ground in front of the bench, then he used a Sand spell to place a small pile of sand in the center of the cleared area. "The Great Salt Flats is a large area covered by sand, mixed with salt, like this," said Edward, pointing to the pile of sand. "When it rains," Edward used a Water spell to drop a cup-full of water on the pile of sand, "the sand and salt spread out, carried outward by the rainwater. When the sun evaporates the water, the area of sand and salt is bigger."

"I understand," said Donovan, "and the sand and salt is moving downhill, towards the Amber River." "Exactly!" said Edward. "So, we started at the eastern and southern edges of the Salt Flat and began digging an enormous, U-shaped trench, fifty miles long and twenty-five miles high on each side. We are using the spoils from the trench to make twenty-foot-high walls on the outer edges of the trench. Once we get the trenches finished, we'll excavate the sand and dirt in the middle. When it rains, the water will create a large reservoir and keep the Salt Flats from expanding."

"So, what are all the children doing here?" asked Donovan. "They are the ones doing the digging and wall-making. King Donald would not release his adult magicians for this task because of the looming conflict with the dragons and maybe even the Franconians. So, I convinced him to send me his apprentice magicians to build the reservoir. The Dig spell is easy to learn, so are the Shield and Wind spells. The Adhesive spell is the most complicated one they're using."

"I don't understand," said Donovan, "what does a Shield spell have to do with building a reservoir?" Edward explained, "I have them divided into groups of six. Two of them dig the trench and deposit the spoils on the outside edge of the trench. Two others make a flat shield along the edge of the trench, twenty-feet high, the last two use Wind spells to blow the sand and dirt against the shield. Then the two diggers use an Adhesive spell to glue it all together, right down to the bedrock, so the water can't get under the trench walls."

"Is it working?" Edward smiled, "Using five teams per eight-hour shift, we've been able to dig a mile of trench and wall each day. That means in ten weeks, we'll have the U-shaped borders of the reservoir done and be ready to start excavating the middle." Donovan whistled, "That's quite an accomplishment, but there's still an awful lot of sand and dirt to excavate."

"Tell me about it. I'm also worried about what will happen when it rains," said Edward. Donovan thought about it and said, "Yes, a lot of rain will probably fill in the trenches, and you'll have to dig them out again. Still, with walls twenty-feet high, I don't think the water will get over them, and it's still the same amount of sand to be excavated, right? It'll just be along the edge instead of in the middle." Edward grinned, "You're right. I hadn't thought of it that way. Thanks."

"Is there anything you'd like me to do while I'm here? Rachel wants me back at the Academy *yesterday* to help with the wedding plans, but if there's anything you need…"

"Come to think of it, there is something you can do. Besides the rain, the melting snow keeps flowing down from the Grey Mountains to our west and the Caperian Mountains to the north and expanding the Salt Flats. If you could fly around and tell us where the channels are that bring the water down, that would be helpful. We'll need to create reinforced channels to bring the water into the reservoir. They tend to dry up and fill with sand after the rain ends," said Edward. "Happy to. So, do you think you'll be able to break away for a couple days to come to the wedding? You and your plus-one, that is," said Donovan, looking at Kathy.

Edward thought for a minute, then said, "I guess we could ask Wizard Timothy from Springfield to come take over for a week. It would be a nice break. So, how do you change into a dragon?" Donovan was incredibly happy to be able to teach his father something. "You have to picture a dragon in your mind and think of being able to speak, then perform the Change spell. I know you've seen a Great Dragon before, but what about Mage Kathy?"

"Kathy knows what a Stone Dragon looks like," said Edward. "Really? How did that happen?" asked Donovan. "We were scouring the palace of King Donald for Changed Ones, when one of the servants transformed into a Stone Dragon and attacked." "How did you kill it?" asked Donovan. "Well, I started with an incredibly strong Wind spell that kept him pinned to the ground. I guess Stone Dragons are not very strong fliers, but our blast spells had almost no effect on him. I doubt that even a crossbow fired at close range would hurt a Stone Dragon." "But Sorcerer Justin killed one in Weaton!" said Donovan. "Yes," said Edward, "but at the cost of his own life."

"Then how did you kill it?" "Your father enclosed it in a shield," said Kathy proudly. Donovan thought for a moment, "So, you suffocated it?" "Exactly right! You need to tell Wizard Noland this, so he can spread the word among the magical community." Donovan nodded, then said, "There really shouldn't be any Stone Dragons in Franconia. The Stone and Fire Dragons should all be living on the west side of the Amber River." "And just how do you know that?" asked Edward. "Loren told Celeste. She also let slip that the Dragon Council usually meets in that abandoned rock quarry just north of Colton," replied Donovan.

"I knew that Loren would be a wealth of information. I'm glad we didn't kill her," said Edward. "Not anymore. She was so distraught about telling Celeste how to change into a dragon that she killed herself the next day." "How did that happen?" asked Edward. "She went into the stable and goaded a horse into kicking her in the head. It wasn't pretty." Edward shuddered.

"I don't know how to breathe fire, though," said Donovan. "There must be a trick to it that I haven't figured out yet." "Why would you need to breathe fire?" asked Edward. "In case I get into a fight with another dragon while I'm in dragon form," said Donovan reasonably. Edward yawned. "I'm sorry, son, I should have thought of that. I'm just tired." "So, what's the schedule around here?" asked Donovan.

"Well, the third shift of five groups of young magicians came on duty at four hours after midnight, and they'll work until midday. I usually check on them around dawn to see how much progress they've made and take them their breakfast. The kitchen should be preparing it right now. Then the next shift starts at midday and works for eight hours, then the last shift relieves them," explained Edward. "And when do you rest?" asked Donovan. "Not often enough. That's when," said Mage Kathy, firmly. "I'll take breakfast to third shift. You stay here and talk, then get some sleep. I'll wake you at midday." Kathy gave Edward a kiss on the lips, then moved off toward the kitchen. Donovan raised his eyebrows inquiringly.

"Yes. Kathy and I are involved. I don't know if it will last or if we'll be able to make it work, being from two different kingdoms and all, but I really like her." "You mentioned that in your message. Wizard Noland said that he was happy for you and that it was about time." "And what do you think?" "I just met her about half a glass ago, but she seems to care about you. Oh, by the way, Wizard Faith said to tell you that she removed the Binding spell she'd placed on Kathy," said Donovan. Edward smiled, "That's a relief. I was worried that Kathy would correct some upstart teenage magician and end up dead from the Binding spell. Please thank Wizard Faith for me." Donovan nodded.

Edward opened his water bottle again, and Donovan said, "Don't. Go get some sleep. I'll put on my Concealment cloak and walk around the camp for a while, just to check things out. Then I'll find a place to take a nap. I've been flying all night. Tomorrow, I'll check the water channels for you before I head home." Edward nodded wearily and headed back inside his tent.

Donovan pulled up his hood and closed the Concealment cloak, disappearing from sight. He strolled around the camp, looking for any signs of trouble, but all he found were sleeping children and a few roaming adults, mostly tending the campfires or talking with the cooks. He noticed Mage Kathy loading boxes of food and drinks into a wagon, presumably to take to the third shift. On an impulse, Donovan quietly climbed onto the wagon as Kathy guided the horse down the well-trodden path to the dig site.

After they'd left the camp, Kathy said, "So, Donovan, I'm sure you have a million questions." Donovan smiled as he lowered his hood. "Very good," he said. "What gave me away? I thought I was pretty quiet." "You were, but I expected you to tag along, and you might notice that I sprinkled a little flour on the wagon running board. I saw your footprint in the flour."

"You're clever. I like that," said Donovan. Kathy laughed softly. "That's the same way I detected Specialist Dirk in Baize. By his footprints on the dusty floor." "I didn't know that Dirk went with my father to see the King," said Donovan. "You're very observant.

Dirk is probably the best Specialist in all of Franconia." "I'll take your word for it," said Kathy, "but I doubt that's what you wanted to talk about."

Donovan sat in silence for a while, then said, "As far as I know, my father hasn't even *looked* at another woman since my mother was murdered. Yet, he seems quite taken with you, and in a very short time." Kathy grinned, "And you're wondering if I slipped him some sort of Love Serum?" Donovan blushed and said, "The thought had occurred to me."

"No, Donovan, I have not given Edward any type of Love Serum. He saved my life by killing King Donald's Court Wizard, Louis, then again when he shielded me from an exploding barrel of flour in the courtyard, so I was naturally grateful, but your father is *honest, humble and very capable.* Do you know how rare that is in a magician? Almost all of the male magicians I have met in Baize are deceitful, egotistical, and narcissistic. I admit that I pursued him, almost from the moment we met, and I am not sorry that I did." Donovan smiled, "That's all I wanted to hear. You two have my blessing, although you really don't need it. By the way, Wizard Faith asked me to tell you that she removed the Binding spell, so you can use magic any way you please now." Kathy smiled with relief. "So, Mage Kathy, do you really think this crazy idea of digging a lake is going to work?"

"Are they gone? asked Commodore Matthews. "Yes," said Andrew, "they just flew out of sight." "So, Andrew, what do you think? These Sea Dragons were pretty quick to want to make our truce more permanent." "I agree. I suspect that we hurt them more than we realized during the last battle, still…" "'Still' what?" asked the Commodore. "The wording of the proposed treaty is interesting. They agreed not to attack our *ships*," mused Andrew. "So?" "So, they did not agree not to attack our *sailors*. We'll need to close that loophole in the final Treaty."

"You think they'd exploit that technicality?" "In the last Treaty with the dragons, they agreed not to *eat* people. They didn't agree not to *kill* people, just not to eat them. They're not stupid. Actually, they're quite cunning. We better not underestimate them." "You're right, of course. I'll add a note about that with the message I send to the Admiral and the King," said the Commodore.

Just then, Sorceress Celeste came up on deck, "Well, this has been exciting, but I guess I should be heading back to the Wizards Academy." "On your way, could you deliver the draft copy of the Treaty with the dragons to Admiral Cross at Navy Headquarters in Grotton?" asked Andrew. "It would save two weeks of travel for us, and get this process moving along faster. You could also tell the Admiral about the possibility of using Sorcerer 'Changed Ones' to deliver messages and orders to ships at sea."

"Go back to Grotton? What if I run into Mage Charles?" asked Celeste, clearly uncomfortable with the idea. "You apologize to him for deceiving him, explain what really happened, and tell him that you're on a mission from Wizard Noland and Commodore Matthews. I doubt he'll give you any trouble. In fact, you should probably make a point of going to see him, even if you don't run into him on your way to see the Admiral," suggested Andrew.

"You're right, of course. OK, I'll do it. Do you have the draft treaty ready for me to take?" "Give me a few minutes to add some thoughts to it," said Commodore Matthews. "Why don't you go spend a few minutes with your sister? Andrew will bring you the message pouch once I'm done." Celeste went below deck to find her sister, Anne, who was resting in Andrew's cabin. "Why aren't you up on deck, enjoying the fresh air and sunshine?" asked Celeste. "Because the sailors stare. I'm the only woman in the Franconian Navy, and while I can defend myself and handle any crude comments by the crew, I can't stop their staring, and it makes me uncomfortable," explained Anne.

"That's terrible! Have you spoken to Andrew about it?" "No. What could he do anyway? Most of the time, Mage Andrew is on this ship while I'm on a different one. The only reason we're both on the VALOR now is because my ship, the COMFORT, was sunk by the dragons. As soon as another ship arrives, I'll be transferred to it. Besides, I don't want Andrew fighting my battles for me."

Celeste thought for a moment, then said, "Now that you're a dragon-friend, I would expect the other dragons to avoid attacking whatever ship you're on, just like they avoid the HMS VALOR. That should be a great benefit to your new shipmates. It might help them accept you easier." Anne brightened at the thought. "I hope you're right, both about the dragons and my new shipmates. Thanks. So, when are you leaving?" "Commodore Matthews is adding some notes to the draft treaty and has asked me to take it to the Navy Headquarters in Grotton on my way back to the Academy. Mage Andrew suggested I stop by the Grotton Regional Mage's Office and see Mage Charles, to apologize and explain what really happened on my way to Kingston with Gek."

Anne nodded. "That's probably a good idea." "I know, but it's not a conversation I'm looking forward to." Anne patted her sister's arm and said, "You'll be fine, and I'm sure you'll feel better once you clear the air with Mage Charles." Celeste nodded. Just then, Andrew opened the door and said, "The message pouch is ready. Are you two about done?" Anne rose from her chair and gave her sister a hug, "We are now," she said.

The three magicians headed up on deck where Commodore Matthews was waiting. "Here is the message pouch, I'd wait for a reply before leaving the Headquarters building. The Admiral might want to add a note to the King. He might also ask you to return to the VALOR with a message. This could be a new calling for you—'Official Messenger of the Royal Navy'"

"That's an interesting thought, Sir. I will certainly consider it," said Celeste. "If you leave now, you should be able to make it to Grotton by tomorrow morning," said Andrew. "I'd recommend landing and transforming at night. Oh, here are some clothes for you to wear after you transform. Sorry that they're men's clothes, but other than your sister, there are no women in the Navy, and Anne only has the clothes on her back right now." Celeste smiled her thanks and packed everything into a sturdy canvas bag, then she walked to the rear deck as sailors cleared a space for her.

To the sailor's great disappointment, Andrew cast a Seeming of a curtain across the ship to give Celeste some privacy as she dropped her blanket and transformed into a Sea Dragon. She seized the bag in her talons, extended her wings, and leaped into the air, climbing quickly until she was lost in the clouds. "That was very kind of you, Andrew," said Anne softly. "Celeste would have been mortified to have all these sailors staring at her again." "Well, I actually did it for both of you. You're identical twins, right?"

Cobalt, The Sea Dragon

Chapter Five:

ARRANGEMENTS

Rachel was frazzled. There were just *so* many things to coordinate for the wedding. First, she had to replicate dozens of wedding invitations and get them out (done). There was so little time. Fortunately, Wizard Noland had suggested sending just *one* invitation to Major Gerald, inviting the entire Royal Expeditionary Force, rather than getting a roster of the force (a restricted item) and filling out fifty-one individual invitations. Once she had all of the invitations delivered, she started looking for caterers. She expected about a hundred people from the Wizards Academy, including all the students, instructors, Mentors and the staff. Since she was inviting all the Academy cooks, she couldn't very well expect them to prepare food for the reception. Then, there was the Expeditionary Force and selected Ministers at the Palace. All told, she was expecting just over two hundred people.

There was no single caterer in Kingston that could accommodate such a large order in under two weeks, so Rachel had to contact several, and some of the caterers said they would have to outsource various bakers and serving personnel if they got the contract. The florists proved impossible. No one could possibly provide enough flowers for such a large event on such short notice. Rachel eventually enlisted Wizard Mira's help. The flowers, other than her bouquet and Donovan's boutonniere, would be Seemings. At least that would make clean-up easier.

She had no idea what to use for decorations. Between herself and Wizard Noland, they had determined that the Academy courtyard was too small for such a large event, and they would have to use the Forces Training Area, since the Enhancements and Seemings Training Areas were overgrown with knee-high grass and had boulders scattered about, while the Forces Training Area was mostly sand. Rachel needed about two hundred chairs, a white carpet runner for the aisle, musicians, and a podium for Judge Toffin (who had enthusiastically agreed to perform the ceremony).

She also had to stop by her father's tailor shop in town for fittings to make sure her wedding dress fit perfectly. She decided that she would wear the same shoes she wore for the Royal Ball (which would make Donovan smile). For bridesmaids, Rachel selected her three Level Three students, Joyce, Hope and Mary. She chose Wizard Cassandra, the Franconia Court Wizard and her former Mentor, as her Maid of Honor. Rachel knew that Donovan wanted Andrew, his cousin and first Mentor, to be his Best Man, but Andrew was at sea and it was uncertain if they could get a message to him and he could get to the Academy in time. Well, *that was Donovan's problem*, and it served him right for leaving her to arrange everything.

Donovan had been gone for two days, so he should be back in two more (assuming there were no complications). That would leave them a week until the ceremony. Rachel really thought she'd have more time to plan something this important. "Everything going OK?" asked Wizard Cassandra from the doorway. "Hi, Cassi, everything's fine. I'm just a bit overwhelmed, trying to put this together by myself in only two weeks." "Well, there's your problem," said Cassandra, "you're *not* alone. There are lots of people willing to help you. You just need to ask. What are you struggling with?"

"Chairs." "Chairs?" "Chairs," repeated Rachel. "Do you know where I can get two hundred chairs in a week?" "Well, you could probably borrow all of the chairs in the Lecture Hall to start with." "That's only about fifty. Where do I get the rest?" "You ask Wizard Noland to have the Level Three students replicate them this week. How many Level Threes are there at the Academy?" asked Cassandra. "About twenty-five, I guess." "That's only six chairs each, a very manageable number. You weren't thinking of renting that many chairs, were you?" Rachel blushed with embarrassment. "Girl! Donovan and his father may have coin, but they won't if you spend it all on chairs! The only thing you should have to pay for is the food and the musicians."

"The food is also a problem. Because of the short notice, I may have to engage several different caterers to have enough food," said Rachel. "What are you serving?" "Roast beef, fish, maybe a chicken dish, sides, and dessert," said Rachel. "No. This isn't a dinner; it's a *reception.* All you need are finger foods, some punch and the wedding cake." "THE CAKE! I FORGOT THE CAKE!" screamed Rachel. "Relax," said Cassandra, "I've already instructed the Academy bakers to start planning for the wedding cake. That's something they can make in advance, once you approve the flavors and the design. I'll also take care of the caterer."

"I just want everything to be perfect," said Rachel. "Don't worry, *it won't be,*" replied Cassandra. "What?" "Relax, no wedding is ever perfect. No matter how long you have to plan it, or how much coin you have, or how much help you enlist, something will go wrong. The musicians are going to play the wrong song, or the Best Man is going to misplace the ring, or the caterer will make the wrong onion dip, or the cake will have the wrong topper. But that's not important. All that's important is that you and Donovan are there, and there is an officiant and enough witnesses to make it legal in the eyes of the crown. Everything else is *window dressing.*"

"Judge Toffin is going to perform the ceremony, Donovan will surely be here, and there will be more than enough witnesses," said Rachel, smiling. "Good. Now, let's go talk to Wizard Noland about those chairs."

They heard Richard's screams even before they landed on Perfo. Annalise had fallen asleep during the flight, so Azure set her down gently on the sand, took her human clothes out of the diaper bag, and changed back into human form. She entered the cave to find Gek rocking and shushing Richard without success. He looked up as she entered. "Finally! What took you so long? He has been screaming for you for hours!" said Gek. "Give him to me," said Azure. She took the baby, who instantly quieted. "How did you do that?" asked Gek. "He is just hungry and wet. You should have changed his diaper!" "*You* took the diaper bag! The diaper from earlier is not dry yet! If I had been in dragon form, I could have used some fire breath to dry it, but in human form, all I could do was wait!"

From outside the cave Gek heard Cobalt and Ard laughing loudly at the exchange. Gek rose and headed outside, "You think this is funny?" he demanded. "Hysterical," replied Cobalt. "You see, I remember having a similar conversation with Liza several years ago—except for the part about the diapers." All the noise woke Annalise, who padded over to Gek and sniffed him. She looked at him curiously, not really sure what to make of this strange creature who smelled like her father.

"Great. What should I do now?" Ard thought for a while, then said, "I suggest that you take off those rags you call clothes and transform back into a dragon. She might think of it as some kind of a game." Cobalt shrugged, not really having a better suggestion. Gek stripped off his still bloody shirt and tattered trousers and changed back into a Great Dragon. Annalise ran and hid behind Ard's legs, then peeked around to look at Gek. Suddenly recognizing him, she bounded to his side.

"Hello, Anna," said Gek, "I know this must seem strange to you." Annalise walked around Gek, poking him with her nose, as if trying to make him change back into the other figure, "No. That is not how it works, Anna. I will change back later." Anna seemed to understand, and she stopped poking Gek and peered inside the cave. "Azure, we are coming in," called Gek.

"Are you sure that is wise?" asked Azure. "No, but I am sure that it is necessary," said Gek.

Gek, Anna, Ard and Cobalt entered the cave and found Azure in human form, nursing the baby, who now had on a clean, dry diaper. Anna approached cautiously, sniffing the air. She walked over to Azure and poked her with her nose. "Hello, Anna. Yes, it is mommy." Annalise continued to poke Azure's arm. "What is she doing?" "I think she is trying to get you to change back into a Dragon," said Ard. "Not yet, Annalise, your brother is still hungry," Anna looked at the baby in Azure's arms and sniffed him; a low growl started in her throat.

"No!" said Azure, "this is your brother. You will not growl at him." Anna accepted the rebuke stoically. "Gek, go wash out his wet diaper and put it out to dry. I had no idea that he was going to wet himself so often. We will need to get more diapers." Gek said, "Ard, could you take Annalise outside and play with her? I do not want her thinking she can force me to change forms whenever she wants."

Ard laughed and said, "Annalise, come outside and play with grandpa." The baby dragon reluctantly headed out of the cave, where Ard scooped her up, placed her on his back, and went bounding off through the sand dunes, Anna squealing with delight. Gek quickly transformed back into human form, put on his tattered clothing, and proceeded to wash the diaper and place it outside to dry. "So, it seems like Anna has accepted our ability to transform back and forth into human form, but she seems less than pleased with her brother," said Gek.

"She will come around in time," replied Azure tiredly. "I am just not sure how we are going to get any sleep if we cannot get them both on the same sleep cycle." "I am sure it will get better in a few days," said Cobalt from the entrance. "Liza often despaired of getting any rest while you were growing, Gek. Even once you could eat solid food, she complained that she had to spend hours a day hunting prey, and it was so much easier when you just wanted Dragon milk." "That is not much comfort," said Azure. "It should be. There are many more fish in the sea than there was prey in the Snow Fields," said Cobalt. "You will have a much easier time finding food than Liza did."

Kathy stopped the wagon at the first group of young magicians who were diligently digging the trench. She and Donovan dismounted and unloaded the boxes of food and a small keg of cider that made up the worker's breakfast. The students quickly descended on the wagon, eager for a break and some food after a tiring night of digging. As the group of apprentice magicians consumed their meal, Donovan walked around the top of the trench, inspecting their work.

The trench was about thirty feet deep and ten feet wide, with a wall on the outside edge. Donovan could sense the Adhesive spell, which bound the trench walls to the bedrock at the bottom and the wall at the top. Looking west, he saw the vast expanse of the Great Salt Flats and understood what his father was talking about. There were some places in the trench where the wind had already blown some sand and salt back into the trench. Not much, but rain would fill the trench with even more sand. Donovan thought for a moment, then said, "Mage Kathy, a moment?"

Kathy walked over to where Donovan was standing, "Yes, what is it, Donovan?" "My dad said that he was concerned about what would happen when it rains. He said that the sand over there," said Donovan, pointing, "would flow back into the trench and have to be excavated again." "That's true," said Kathy. "We haven't had more than a sprinkling of rain so far, but I'm sure it won't be long before we get a thunderstorm with lots of rain. There are two concerns, first that the young magicians won't be able to hold Weather shields and Dig at the same time, which could delay the work;

and second, that the inner walls of the trench may collapse."

"I can't help with the Weather shields, but I do have an idea that might keep the sand and salt from pouring into the trench," said Donovan. "Really? What do you have in mind?" Donovan walked to the top of the trench, on the inside, and said, "Watch." He concentrated, then said, *"THERMO INTENSIF,"* while holding his left hand, fingers closed, against his chest. The sand along the inner edge of the trench began to smoke, then *melted* into a large sheet of glass, as Donovan released the spell.

Mage Kathy walked over to the now smooth and shimmering sheet of glass. She reached down to touch it, and Donovan said, "DON'T! It's still hot!" Kathy pulled her hand back just in time and nodded her thanks to Donovan. She walked back to him and said, "So, you used the Heating spell to melt the sand into glass. How does that help us?" "Well," said Donovan, "when it rains, the water will flow into the trench, but the sand, salt and underlying soil should stay firm. When you excavate the center, you will just be disappearing some glass along with the other material. It will slow the trench digging, but it might prove faster in the long run."

"How much power does it take to heat the sand that much?" asked Kathy. "Why don't we move down a bit and you can try it yourself," said Donovan. They walked down to the next area of exposed sand, and Kathy conjured the spell, turning the sand into glass. When she was done, she said, "Well, it's not too bad. Some of the older apprentices would certainly be up to it, at least in short sections. You think we should do this along the entire trench?" "At least the Southern and Eastern trenches. Based on what my father told me, I doubt that much water will flow into the trench on the west side," answered Donovan.

"I just wonder how well it will work," mused Kathy. "Let's find out," said Donovan. He walked back to the now cool, glassy area and said, *"AQUARITOUS,"* while making a cupping gesture with his right hand and turning it upside down. A hundred gallons of water rained down on the glass, pooled briefly, then poured over the edge and into the trench. The underlying soil held firm. Kathy smiled and said, "You must have inherited your father's creative thinking! We never considered doing this. What about the water in the trench?"

Donovan thought for a moment, "Well, you could evaporate it with the Heat spell, or just leave it and see how long it takes to evaporate naturally." "Let's leave it for now," said Kathy, "we still have four more groups of magicians to feed." Donovan took one last look at the trench and said, "It might be a good idea to pour some water into the entire trench. If you look closely, there is a spot down there where the wall of the trench is not completely adhered to the bedrock. I'm sure there are other spots as well. This is a good way to test the seal. It would be unfortunate if there are too many gaps and the water gets under the walls." "You're right about that. We'll check the rest of the trench before we dig any further," said Kathy.

Mage Kathy and Donovan proceeded up the trench line, feeding and checking on the other two groups of magicians, then headed south and fed the groups working on the southern edge of the trench. Once all of the diggers had been fed, they returned to the camp. Kathy parked the wagon next to shift two's kitchen. "I'll take a snack to the second shift about four hours past midday," explained Kathy. Donovan nodded and yawned. "You must be tired," said Kathy. "I forgot that you flew all night to get here. Why don't you go lie down in my tent? It's right next to your father's. Bill should be on guard duty now. I'll tell him not to let anyone disturb you."

"Thank you," said Donovan. As he entered Mage Kathy's tent, he hesitated before climbing onto her cot, then realized that there was a thin layer of dust on it, indicating that it had not been used in a while. He used a Wind spell to clear the dust, then laid down and pulled his Concealment cloak around him as a blanket. He was asleep in minutes.

He awoke a few hours later to the sound of a knife, gently slicing open the tent's canvas on the side opposite the door flap. Donovan pulled his cloak closed and waited. After completing the vertical cut, the assailant hesitated for a few minutes, probably waiting to see if anyone heard the noise; then, he slipped inside the tent and moved quickly to the water pitcher sitting on the table. He dropped something into the water, then made his escape. Or almost. Donovan seized him with a Tether spell and called out for the guard. Bill rushed in to see what the noise was about.

The assassin was a tall, middle-aged man, about forty years old, with red hair. Within seconds, Edward and Kathy entered the tent, and Kathy asked, "What happened?" "This fellow cut a hole in the back of your tent and slipped something into your water pitcher. I doubt it was vitamins," said Donovan, still holding the man's arms at his sides. "Hmm," said Edward, "tall, red hair, he's probably a Fire Dragon Changed One. Do you recognize him, Kathy?"

"Yes," said Kathy, "he's the one who brings us firewood from Springfield each day. Although, I recall his hair being brown, not red." Edward moved to confront the man, "Who sent you?" he asked. "No one *sends* Dragons anywhere," snarled the Changed One. "Why did you attempt to kill Mage Kathy?" "Because she murdered my daughter, Char," replied the bound man. "Char? You mean Charolette?" asked Kathy. "The same," sneered the man. "The right of vengeance is mine."

"So, what should we do with you?" asked Edward. "We could set you free under a Binding spell to never harm a human, remove your spark and leave you as a dim-witted human, or kill you right now." "I will never submit to one of your Binding spells," said the man." So be it," said Edward. *"TERMINA,"* said Donovan, unexpectedly. The man fell dead at Edward's feet. Kathy and Edward recoiled in shock. "Why did you do that?" demanded Edward. "So you didn't have to," said Donovan. He looked down at the corpse and said, *"DELERE,"* while flicking his right wrist towards the body, removing the assailant's neck.

"We could have questioned him further, then removed his spark," said Edward. "I doubt he knew much, and I'm tired of murderous dragons," said Donovan wearily, "and how would you explain him to the children here? If they learn that there was a dragon Changed One in camp, it wouldn't be good for their morale." "I guess that's true," said Edward. While they were talking, Mage Kathy used the Remove spell to vanish the body of the Changed One.

"Kathy told me about your idea of melting the sand into glass along the edge of the trench and testing the trench for leaks. Both ideas are excellent. I wish you could stay and help us with this project, but I know you need to get back to the Academy for your wedding. Has Michael told you where your first assignments will be?" asked Edward.

Donovan smiled at the compliment and said, "Yes. I'm going to be assigned to the 3rd Regiment in Fairview, and Rachel will be assigned to the Fairview Regional Mage's Office. What can you tell me about those positions?" "The 3rd Regiment is commanded by Major Stone, a good man, if a bit cautious. The Fairview Regional Mage is Mage Ryan, and his office is usually very busy. There are apparently a lot of rogue magicians that live in, or move to Fairview because of the wealth of the city. The good news is that Rachel will get to visit her family in Kingston fairly regularly as she transports drag-ins to the Academy."

"I hadn't thought of that. I'll be sure to mention it to her. I know that she's never lived anywhere but Kingston, and I think she's a little apprehensive about moving," said Donovan. Edward smiled, "I understand that feeling. Your experience will help ease the transition. However, I do foresee one awkward conversation you need to have with Rachel *before* you move to Fairview." "What conversation is that?" asked Donovan, confused. "Maria," said Edward. "You need to let Rachel know that you two dated when Maria lived in Kingston. It would not be good for your wife to run into an old girlfriend unprepared." Donovan winced.

Changing the subject, Kathy said, "I understand that we're getting our last influx of apprentice magicians today. Wizard Timothy sent a Messenger Hawk saying that he was bringing about twenty new students down. They're from Middleberg and Lakeshore, the two cities that are the farthest away from Springfield. In fact, I think I know one of the magicians that should be arriving from Middleberg." "Really?" asked Edward.

"Yes," said Kathy, "Mage Elianna sent a young man named Stephen to deliver a message to me, informing me that Wizard Louis had tried to poison her and all of her students at the Middleberg School of Magic during his *inspection* visit. Stephen was very resourceful in making his way to Baize undetected by Wizard Louis, who put some effort into finding him and preventing the message from being delivered." "How did he manage that?" asked Edward.

"He travelled the last leg of the journey by boat, while Louis was diligently searching the road. It was quite an impressive achievement. While he was in Baize, he stayed in my room for his protection." "Indeed," said Edward, raising an eyebrow. Kathy laughed, "I will tell you what I told Stephen: that he could stay in my room but not in my *bed.* I think he was somewhat disappointed." Now, it was Edward's turn to laugh, "You see, son, these conversations are not always as difficult as you imagine. Nevertheless, I may have a private word with Stephen when he arrives later today."

Azure and Gek got almost no rest their first night on Perfo. It seemed that in true Dragon form, Richard was constantly hungry, waking up every couple of hours, and Annalise awoke wanting food as soon as Richard fell back to sleep. Azure grew so tired of transforming back and forth from human to Dragon, she eventually decided to not even put her human clothes back on between feedings, which pleased Gek immeasurably. "Do *not* get any ideas," warned Azure, "and hand me that blanket."

The next morning, they discussed the problem. "I do not think Richard is comfortable in this cave. Annalise is used to sleeping on the floor, but I believe that human babies sleep in small, soft beds. Maybe that is why Richard keeps waking up," said Azure. "It could be," said Ard, "but what other choice do we have?" Gek and Azure looked at each other and said in unison, "Bruce!" "Bruce?" asked Ard and Cobalt.

"Yes, Bruce," replied Gek. "He is a human that we stayed with for a while outside the city of Southport while we were shadowing the VALOR. He has a driftwood hut, just off the beach. He was married to a Sea Dragon Changed One for many years. He identified me as a Changed One almost as soon as we met. He was very kind for a human, and I am sure he would let us stay with him for a while. He would know more about caring for a human baby than any of us do, even though he and his wife never had any children."

Cobalt asked, "Are you sure that Annalise would be safe there?" "Yes," said Azure. "I just hope that Bruce will be safe from Anna. She can be a handful. I guess it is a good thing that she cannot breathe fire." Ard laughed, "Gek was almost two years old before he learned how to breathe fire; how long does it usually take for a Sea Dragon baby to learn to spit a harmful stream of water?" "Not long," said Cobalt, "maybe a year at most."

"Is there any training required," asked Ard, "or do they just come by it naturally?" "Training?" asked Azure, "what kind of training are you talking about?" "Dragons that breathe fire have to learn how to ignite their inferno and hit what they are aiming at. Great Dragon babies do not know how to breathe fire from birth. Why, if they did, they might injure their parents or set their homes on fire if they could just breathe fire without any training."

"Is Annalise more Great Dragon or Sea Dragon?" asked Azure, alarmed. "Will she spit water or breathe fire? How can we tell?" Ard considered the question, "Well, she certainly swims like a Sea Dragon. To tell if she will be able to breathe fire, I would need to look at the inside of her mouth." Just then, Annalise came sneaking back into the cave, looking to see which form her mother was in at the moment, and disappointed to find her in human form.

"Anna, come here," said Azure. The baby Dragon ran and jumped into her mother's arms, jostling Richard in the process. "Open your mouth, dear; grandpa wants to count your teeth." Anna looked at Azure without understanding. Azure demonstrated by opening her mouth wide and saying, "AHHHH." Anna mimicked her mother, and Ard peered inside her mouth. "This Dragon has inferno sacs. Not as many as a normal Great Dragon, but some. She will eventually be able to breathe fire. Maybe she will be able to do both; spit water *and* breathe fire! That would be extraordinary!"

In Ard's excitement, he had been too loud, and he woke Richard, who began to cry. Azure sighed, "Here we go again. I am beginning to think that some Dragon parents eat their children, not because the parents are hungry, but because the babies will *not shut up and leave them alone!*" Both Cobalt and Ard laughed, and Annalise looked at her brother and bared her teeth.

"Anna, stop that!" said Gek, "come outside with me while your brother has breakfast. Mommy will feed you soon." Anna climbed down off Azure, slapping Richard with her tail as she did. "I saw that, Anna," said Gek, "and it was not very nice." Anna stuck out her tongue and ran over to Ard for protection.

Cobalt watched the exchange and said, "This is common behavior between Dragon siblings, but you will need to protect Richard. His skin is very soft, and what would be a playful nip to another baby Dragon could cause him serious injury." Gek looked worried. "If they cannot get along, eventually, you may need to consider a foster family for Richard, at least until he is old enough to defend himself," said Ard.

"I hate that idea," said Gek. "As do I," said Ard, "but until Annalise is old enough to understand what a Binding spell means and does, which she will not for almost a year, one of you will have to stay with baby Richard at all times to protect him from her. Do not let her deceive you by pretending to accept him. She is likely to attack him the first chance she gets in order to resume receiving all of your attention." Gek looked over at Annalise, who stared back at him and smiled, the very picture of innocence.

Wizard Timothy and a contingent of twenty-one apprentices and one Mage arrived late in the afternoon. Edward and Kathy greeted the arriving students warmly, quickly dividing them into three groups of six, with the three oldest apprentices forming a smaller team. Edward explained what they were doing, and that the three new groups would be split among the three shifts, starting with the third shift at eight glasses past noon (in about two hours).

Tents for the new students were quickly erected, and cots, tables, and chairs were put in the tents. Apprentices were shown where the kitchens, shower facilities and latrines were located. Edward gave them the standard "no fighting" lecture, and told them that the work was proceeding faster than he anticipated, so they might all be done in less than a year. The three oldest new arrivals were taken aside by Mage Kathy and informed that they would constitute the Magical Inspection Team, responsible for testing the seals of the trenches, and melting the sand along the edge of the trenches into glass.

Mage Elianna, who had accompanied her students to the project, stayed in the background until Edward and Kathy had finished giving the new arrivals their instructions. "Kathy, it's good to see you again! This is quite a project you two have undertaken," said Elianna. "Edward, this is Mage Elianna, Headmistress of the Middleberg School of Magic. Elianna, this is Wizard Edward of Franconia. This project was all his idea and I really think it will work." Edward shook hands with Elianna, "Pleased to meet you, Elianna. Are you planning to stay with us, or were you just escorting your students here?"

"With no beginning magicians to teach, there was really no point in my remaining in Middleberg, so I thought I'd join you. I'm sure you need all the help you can get," answered Elianna. "You're right about that," said Edward. "I'll have a private tent set up for you near ours. That way, you won't be disturbed by inquisitive young magicians at all hours of the day and night." "She can just have my tent," said Kathy. "You know I'm not using it." Elianna raised her eyebrows, asking the unspoken question.

"Why don't you two go have a chat and catch up? I'll go and let the cooks know that they'll need to start making food for twenty-two more magicians," said Edward. "I'm sure they'll be thrilled with *that* news," said Kathy. "They should be. I told them earlier that we were expecting fifty," said Edward with a wink. Kathy and Elianna laughed as Edward headed off in the direction of the kitchens.

As soon as Edward was out of earshot (hopefully), Elianna said, "So, dish. What's this about you not using your tent?" Kathy blushed slightly and said, "Edward and I are sharing his tent. He's the most exciting man I've ever met and one of the kindest. When the Franconian Royal Expeditionary Force marched on Springfield, by order of King Henry, seven Fire Dragons tried to ambush them in the hills outside the city. Edward detected the ambush, moved the force around behind the dragons, and killed them all. Then he spared the citizens of Springfield, established a Healing Clinic and restored law and order, before he traveled to Baize with Wizard Timothy to meet with King Donald."

"Was King Donald expecting him?" asked Elianna, shocked. "No. During the meeting, Edward agreed to be questioned under Truth Serum, but that snake, Wizard Louis, presented him with Death Serum instead. Edward Compelled Louis to drink his own poison. Louis died instantly." Elianna smiled, "Just what that murderer deserved." "I agree. Later, Edward saved me from an exploding barrel of flour."

"Do tell. Why would a barrel of flour explode?" asked Elianna. "Wizard Timothy told the King that

Edward used barrels of flour to kill two of the Fire Dragons. Apparently, flour is very flammable. A Sorcerer with the force loaded ten barrels of flour into an open wagon, removed the tops of the barrels and used a Wind spell to waft the flour into the air. When the flour was ignited, it consumed the attacking dragons. King Donald was skeptical of the story and demanded a demonstration in the palace courtyard. I was chosen to blow the flour into the air and ignite it. The resulting fireball filled the entire courtyard. If Edward had not shielded me from the explosion, I might not have survived."

"So, for saving your life, Edward expected..." Elianna left the rest of the thought hanging in the air for Kathy to finish. "No. As I told Edward's son, Sorcerer Donovan, who is here, by the way, *I* pursued Edward. Not the other way around," said Kathy. Elianna smiled, "I don't suppose Edward has a brother?" Kathy laughed, "No, and his son is getting married at the Franconian Wizards Academy next week. That reminds me, now that you and Timothy are here, Edward and I were discussing slipping away to attend the wedding." "That's no problem. Just tell me how things work around here, and I'll be happy to take over for a while."

Edward returned and said, "The cooks are overjoyed! So, how about we give Timothy and Elianna a tour of the works and get the new Inspection Team working. I figure that they'll only be able to work during the day, since they would have trouble inspecting the trench in the dark."

The three-person inspection team consisted of Stephen, Toby and Olivia, the three oldest and most advanced of the arriving apprentice magicians. They decided that Mage Elianna would supervise and help the Inspection Team. They each mounted a horse and proceeded to the southeast corner of the trench. When they got there, Edward explained how he wanted the sand and salt along the inner edge of the trench to be melted into glass and how they should test it with water, then inspect the trench wall's seal to the bedrock below.

The team each took turns melting the sand. It took a bit of energy from each magician, but they were able to take turns and rest between spells. "I want you to alternate between the southern trench and the eastern trench each day. Once you get caught up to the current digging effort, it should be much less work each day. We need to hurry, as I have no idea how long we have before the summer rains come," explained Edward. "You mean, you want us to start *now*?" asked Toby. "*Right now*," said Edward. "Kathy and I will stay and help you get started, but you three and Mage Elianna will be working independently for the most part. Mage Kathy or I will check on your progress periodically. Any questions?"

"How long are we expected to work?" asked Olivia. "Today— until just before sunset. You start tomorrow at one glass after sunrise and work until an hour before sunset. Someone will bring you food and water at regular intervals throughout the day. As I said, once you catch up to the current digging, your work hours will be the shortest in the camp, and we may even be able to start getting you three prepared for your Sorcerer's Tests." The last bit of news added an enticing incentive to the three magicians, and they hurried over to the edge of the trench and began melting sand in earnest.

Chapter Six:

SAND AND SNOW

Donovan stayed in the camp until just after sunset. He decided that he should fly out to the mountains in the dark, then look for the water channels in the morning since he would have little chance of finding and tracing them in the dark. "There are most likely ravines and gorges in the mountains that the water and snow melt flow down through onto the plains, from there, the channels may be wide and shallow, or narrow and deep. I haven't explored the north end of the Salt Flats, so I have no way of knowing. Just do your best and hurry back. I don't want you to be late for your own wedding," said Edward. "Me either," said Donovan. "See you tomorrow."

Donovan went outside the camp and demonstrated to his father, Wizard Timothy, and Mages Kathy and Elianna how to transform into a dragon, warning them about the issue with *clothes*. Then he took off, flying low until he had cleared the camp and the completed section of the trench, then rising up and heading towards the mountains in the west. A few short hours later, he found a secluded glen at the foot of the mountains and settled down for a brief nap before sunrise. Everything was going according to plan.

The ten Snow Dragons attacked the town of Snowton just after dawn, catching the sleeping townsfolk completely unaware. Breathing ice, the Snow Dragons began freezing entire families inside their homes and turning the roads to black ice. When the lone company of Baizian soldiers emerged to fight the Dragons, they were quickly routed, their swords and arrows completely useless against even the smaller Snow Dragons. The Snow Dragons became overconfident, chasing the fleeing humans for sport, taking their time and dragging out the hunt. They really didn't care about the town's alarm bell ringing constantly, pleading for help. *Let them come. We will freeze them all,* thought Bliz, the Snow Dragon Clan Chief.

When Donovan arose at dawn, something didn't feel right. His ears were ringing. No, it was the sound of a bell tolling constantly. Deciding to investigate, he soared into the air and looked around. In the cold morning light, he saw a small village in the distance, just on the other side of a pass through the mountains. Then he saw movement. While a dragon's eyesight was better than a human's, a quick Sight enhancement spell showed Donovan that the town was under attack by Snow Dragons.

Without a second thought, Donovan raced towards the fray. He stayed low, out of sight behind the mountains, until he crested the mountaintops and saw the smaller Snow Dragons around the town beneath him. Donovan wished that he had worked harder to learn how to breathe fire, *still I have the element of surprise*, he thought. He dove towards a group of three Snow Dragons, slashing one with his talons, biting off the head of another with his teeth, and striking the third with a powerful blow from his tail.

After that, it was a melee! Snow Dragons swirled around him, screaming, asking what he was doing, and blowing sheets of ice at him. The ice was cold but did not slow his attack. He killed or wounded six of the Snow Dragons before one of them got above him and slashed his face with their talons. Donovan screamed in pain, and fire erupted from his mouth, incinerating the attacking dragon. Seeing the fire breath, the remaining Snow Dragons fled back to the Snow Fields, cursing all Great Dragons and vowing vengeance.

Donovan descended to the town and transformed back into human form. He began using Heat spells to thaw the ice-encased dwellings and melt the ice covering the road. Slowly, the townsfolk emerged from their hiding places and came forward to thank Donovan for his timely aid. Sorcerer Fredrick from Snowton healed Donovan's wounded face but informed him that he would always bear the scars. "Great, Rachel is just going to love this!" said Donovan.

After the town was settled (at least as much as can be expected after a Snow Dragon attack), Donovan departed, telling the people that he had another task to complete that morning. He transformed back into a dragon and flew off, back over the mountains, looking for water channels. He found several deep gorges that led to shallower, now dry wadis, that meandered downhill towards the Great Salt Flats. Deciding that he had done enough for one day, Donovan flew back to the camp, arriving a little after midday.

The appearance of a golden dragon caused panic among the young magicians, and Donovan cursed himself for forgetting to transform back into human form out of sight of the camp, but he was *tired*, and his face hurt. As soon as he landed, he transformed back into human form and cast a Seeming of a cape around himself. Some (but not all) of the panic subsided.

"DONOVAN! Why did you do that? You nearly caused a stampede among the students! Fortunately, almost half of them are sleeping and many others are in their tents. What happened to your face?" Donovan sat down on the sandy soil and took a long drink from his water bottle. As he was gathering his composure, Wizard Timothy and Mage Kathy arrived.

"Snow Dragons attacked a small village on the other side of the mountains. I heard the town's alarm bell—dragons can hear exceptionally well, by the way, and I went to investigate. It looked like about ten Snow Dragons were in the process of turning the town into a block of ice, so I swooped in and started killing them. Snow Dragons are much smaller than Great Dragons, but one of them got above me and slashed my face. I screamed, and fire came out, killing the Snow Dragon that scratched me, and the few remaining Snow Dragons fled back to the Snow Fields."

"I changed back into human form and did what I could to help the village. The local Sorcerer, I think he said his name was Fredrick, healed my face but said I would always have the scars. How bad is it?" asked Donovan. Edward cleared his throat and said, "Well, it's *noticeable.* It seems like Sorcerer Fredrick did a passable job. Maybe one of the Wizards at the Academy can clean it up a bit. I'd try, but cosmetic wizardry is not my area of expertise. I'm more of a 'mortal wounds' kind of healer." Donovan nodded his understanding.

Edward helped Donovan to his feet and led him to his tent, telling everyone they passed that everything was alright and that the dragon they saw was a friend and not a threat. Once inside the tent, Edward asked, "I hate to ask after all you've been through, but did you have a chance to check on the water channels?" Donovan smiled, his mouth twisting in an unfamiliar way, "Yes. There are several deep gorges in the mountains that lead to dry ditches that head towards the Salt Flats. I'm sorry, I didn't have enough time to trace them all the way to the Salt Flats. It's been a busy day." Edward laughed. "Why don't you get a couple hours of sleep. You still have to head back to Kingston tonight." Donovan groaned. "I know, and Rachel will kill me if I delay any longer."

Donovan rose unsteadily and walked back to Mage Kathy's tent, forgetting that it was now occupied by Mage Elianna. He collapsed on the cot and was asleep in seconds. "When Elianna gets back, make sure she knows that Donovan is sleeping in her tent. I would hate for there to be a misunderstanding," said Edward. "I'll tell Bill and be on the lookout myself. It won't be a problem. How do you want to explain the dragon to the children?" asked Kathy.

Edward thought for a moment, then said, "I've always found the truth to be the best explanation. We tell them that some magicians have learned how to transform into dragons and that what they saw was my son, returning from a scouting expedition around the Salt Flats. That should ease their minds." "You know what I really like about you? It's your unwavering commitment to honesty, in both the big things and the small ones," Kathy said before giving him a kiss.

Celeste landed in Grotton just after nightfall. She set down in a fallow soybean field just outside of town. Quickly changing into her ill-fitting sailor's garb, she began walking towards the city. It was nearly midnight when she reached the city center and proceeded immediately to the nearest reputable inn. Having been briefly stationed in Grotton, she knew the good inns, from those to avoid. She rang the bell on the reception desk, and a bleary-eyed night manager emerged from the back room. "Yes, can I help you, Miss?"

"I need a room for this evening, please," said Celeste. The clerk looked at the board behind him and saw the key for room six was hanging on the hook. "Yes, ma'am, Room six is available. That'll be three silvers, payable in advance, please." Celeste rummaged through her handbag and came up with three silver coins that she handed to the desk clerk. He examined the coins closely before handing over the key to the room. "Room six is just along the hallway on the left," he said, "Good night, Miss." "Good night," said Celeste.

Upon entering her room, the first thing Celeste did was apply an Adhesive spell to her door and window. While the door had a key, Celeste did not trust such things and preferred to see to her own security. The precautions turned out to be unnecessary, as no one disturbed her sleep, and Celeste rose refreshed but still somewhat pensive about what the day might bring. She waited in her room until just after eight in the morning, when she was sure that the Navy Headquarters building would be open and manned. She returned her key to the front desk and strode off quickly towards the Admiralty, hoping not to run into Mage Charles along the way.

Celeste entered the Navy Headquarters building and told the receptionist that she had an urgent message for Admiral Cross from Commodore Matthews on the HMS VALOR. "Please wait right here, and I will see if the Admiral is available," said the receptionist, looking disapprovingly at Celeste's attire. She returned a few minutes later and said, "Follow me, please." She led Celeste downstairs and opened a heavy door. Once Celeste entered, the door was slammed shut and bolted.

Celeste found herself in a detention cell, not understanding why. She decided that she had two options: she could wait patiently for someone to come and question her, or she could blast the door off its hinges and go find the Admiral herself. Ultimately, she decided that discretion and patience would serve her better than any aggressive action, so she settled into one of the two wooden chairs in the room to wait.

About an hour later, the door opened, and Mage Charles entered. "Celeste! What are *you* doing here? And what's this nonsense about having a message from Commodore Matthews? The HMS VALOR is currently patrolling around the Coral Islands! There's no way you brought a message from him!"

Celeste steeled herself, then said, "It's good to see you again, Sir. I had planned to come by your office after I delivered my message to the Admiral so I could explain what happened to me on my trip to Kingston with Jed," "You told me a fanciful tale about being attacked by brigands! Are you saying that's not what happened?" asked Mage Charles.

Celeste took a deep breath and said, "Jed was a Great Dragon Changed One. The coach was attacked by his Sea Dragon mate just outside the Jade Swamp. Azure, the Sea Dragon, blew the driver off of the coach with a blast of water. The poor horses went mad, both from the loss of the driver and the appearance of a dragon. They galloped down the trail out of control until Azure used a Dig spell to make a ditch in front of the coach. The horses fell into the ditch, and the coach was catapulted end-over-end until we came to rest upside-down. Jed was still paralyzed from my spell, and he was tossed about the inside of the coach like a ragdoll."

"Then Azure ripped the door off the coach and dragged Jed outside. She was distraught, not knowing any Healing spells to help her mate. Jed was in a bad way. He had a head injury, a shattered shoulder, broken ribs and internal injuries. He was probably going to die. Feeling compassion for them, I offered to heal Jed, whose real name is Gek, and they agreed to let me try in exchange for not killing me. I gave him some Healing Serum I had in my bag and tried the Healing spell for Mortal Wounds. I think it worked because he recovered somewhat. In any event, he climbed onto the Sea Dragon's back, and they flew off toward the coast."

"Why didn't you tell me the truth?" asked Mage Charles. Celeste gulped, "Because I didn't think you'd believe me. You were so angry." Mage Charles considered her answer for a while, then said, "You may be right, but I might have given you the benefit of the doubt."

"I'm sorry," said Celeste. "Anyway, when I returned to the Academy, Wizard Noland asked me to interrogate Wizard Loren, the former History teacher who turned out to be a Snow Dragon Changed One. She always liked me, and one time, she forgot that her water was laced with Truth Serum, and she told me how dragons can change into humans and back again." "WHAT? Are you saying that you can change into a dragon?" asked Mage Charles. "Two kinds, actually. Now that I have seen both Sea Dragons and Great Dragons, I suppose I could transform into either one."

Mage Charles sat down in the other wooden chair. "So, what were you doing on the HMS VALOR?" "Wizard Noland sent me with a message for Mage Andrew. His mother passed away. While I was there, Gek and Azure landed on the ship to negotiate a Peace Treaty with us. That's the message I have for the Admiral. Can you tell me why I was thrown into a detention cell?"

Mage Charles smiled, "Because the Admiral said it was impossible for anyone to bring a message from Commodore Matthews while he's at sea. He thought you were a spy or an assassin. He would have sent Wizard Lake down here to question you, but the Wizard is in Southport, visiting family. So, he sent for me."

Celeste just sat there, waiting for Mage Charles to make a decision. Finally, he said, "OK, let's go see the Admiral. I just hope you can prove what you say." When they entered the Admiral's office, the Admiral said, "Mage Charles, since you escorted this young woman into my office, I assume you've questioned her and determined that she's not a threat." "I have, Sir. Admiral, this is Sorceress Celeste, formerly of the Grotton Regional Mage's Office, currently on detached duty to the Wizards Academy. She has an incredible story and potentially an ability that will enable you to communicate with our ships at sea."

"Indeed? I would be very interested to learn about such. Now Miss, you told my receptionist that you had a message for me from Commodore Matthews. How is that possible?" Celeste said, "Because I have learned how to change into a dragon and deliver messages to ships at sea. Provided they don't shoot at me." The Admiral sat up straighter in his chair, "Really? If that's possible, it would be a boon to the Navy. We wouldn't have to rely on Messenger Hawks that can't find ships at sea. Incredible! Now, what's this message?"

Celeste handed over the oilskin message pouch that Commodore Matthews had given her to deliver. The Admiral opened the pouch and read:

Admiral Cross,

This message should be delivered to you by Sorceress Celeste, a petite young woman with auburn hair. Her identical twin sister's name is Anne. Sorceress Anne is currently the only woman serving aboard a Franconian Navy ship. Celeste has the ability to change into a dragon, which is how she is getting this message to you while I am miles away at sea.

We have sailed around the Coral Islands several times without incident, so I believe the truce with the Sea Dragons is holding. Two days ago, two dragons landed on my ship under a flag of truce and requested that we agree to a more permanent Peace Treaty. The draft Treaty is enclosed. I informed the dragons that any such Treaty would have to be endorsed by you and approved by the King.

We have agreed to meet again in three months, by which time I hope to have the King's approval of the Treaty. The Sea Dragons are informing the rest of their Clan about our agreement. While the Coral Islands are their home base, many Sea Dragons have relocated to the shores of the mainland.

These dragons are cunning, and I recommend that we examine the wording of any Treaty carefully. Mage Andrew pointed out to me that this draft Treaty states that dragons will not attack our ships or port facilities, but it does not say they will not attack our sailors. We need to be very precise with our words.

Horatio Matthews
Commodore, 1st Squadron
1st Franconian Fleet

The Admiral looked up from reading the message, "So, how is your sister, Anna?" he asked. Celeste smiled, "My sister *Anne,* was fine when I left her two days ago, Sir." The Admiral smiled. "Very good. Now, not that I doubt you or Mage Charles here, but would you mind changing into a dragon for me?"

Edward woke Donovan at sunset. "Son, it's time to get up. You need to be on your way back to the Academy." Donovan shook his head to clear it as he sat up, trying to remember where he was. *I'm in a camp near the Great Salt Flats in Baize,* he thought groggily. *Why did the right side of his face hurt?* Then he remembered the Snow Dragon attack. He stumbled over to the water pitcher and splashed some warm water on his face. Shaking like a wet dog, Donovan emerged from the tent to find his father and Mage Kathy waiting for him.

"Your trip home should be faster than the one that brought you here," said Edward. "Why do you say that?" asked Donovan. "The prevailing wind in Franconia blows from west to east. You were fighting a headwind all the way here, so it should be easier going back with a tailwind behind you." "I hope so," said Donovan. "I'm still pretty beat." "Just don't push it," cautioned Edward. "You have plenty of time. Where did you take off from? You can't just leave from the Academy; the shield won't permit it."

Donovan grinned, "You have to leave by the portal at the boat dock. There's just enough room for a dragon along the riverbank." "Of course," said Edward. "Well, if you fly high enough and hide above the clouds, you might be able to make it without stopping. Here, have some Stamina Serum," said Edward, offering his water bottle. Donovan took a healthy swig and said, "Thanks. Well, I guess I'll be on my way. I hope to see you two in a week."

"Goodbye, son. Take care of yourself. We'll be along directly." Kathy turned away as Donovan removed his clothes and placed them in his pack before transforming into a golden dragon. Without another word, Donovan soared into the sky, flying east. "That must be an incredible feeling, to fly like a bird," mused Edward. "We'll find out in a week," said Kathy, taking his arm, "Right now, it's time to Dig like a mole."

Chapter Seven:

FINAL ARRANGEMENTS

Donovan landed at the Academy boat dock around midday the following day. He had flown through the night with only a brief stop to rest and drink some Stamina Serum from his water bottle before resuming his journey from the Great Salt Flats back to the Wizards Academy. He was tired but not completely spent; flying was not as easy as it appeared to be. For one thing, dragons were much too heavy to glide or 'float' on the wind like birds. As soon as you stopped flapping your wings, you began to fall, *rapidly*. You had to stop flapping and angle your wings in order to turn, but you lost altitude as you did so.

Donovan was disappointed that he had not been able to reproduce the fire breath he had employed against the last Snow Dragon. There must be something that he did in the heat of the moment that he didn't realize. He would need to talk to Terry, his former Mentor, who was a Fire Dragon Changed One.

Donovan quickly changed back into his human form and put on his clothes. He was in a hurry to see Rachel, but it wouldn't do to go running around the Academy naked. Once clothed, he opened the portal and headed for his and Rachel's room. He needed a shower, *badly*.

He got as far as the Academy courtyard before Rachel came running to him.

"Finally! What took you so long? And what happened to your face?" she asked. Donovan grimaced, awkwardly. "My father asked me to scout around the north end of the Great Salt Flats to determine where the rainwater and snowmelt were coming from out of the mountains," began Donovan, "then I ran into a pack of Snow Dragons that were attacking a small town. Snow Dragons are much smaller than Great Dragons, but there were about ten of them. I killed or injured six or seven, but one of them got above me and clawed my face. The local Sorcerer healed the cuts but said I would have scars. Is it bad?"

Rachel examined the three scars that went from the corner of Donovan's mouth, diagonally up to just below his right eye. "Well, we'll always know which is your 'good side' now. Didn't I tell you not to talk to any strange dragons? Maybe one of the wizards will be able to do something about the scars," said Rachel tactfully. "I hope so. I asked my father, but he said that cosmetic wizardry wasn't his area of expertise, that he was more of a 'mortal wounds-type' healer," replied Donovan. "Can we get to our room? I need a shower." Rachel smiled, "You certainly do. So, what is your father working on, and will he be able to make it to our wedding?"

"My father and Mage Kathy are digging an enormous hole to try and contain the expanding Salt Flats in eastern Baize. They have about a hundred young apprentice magicians, most of them about Level Two, I would guess, who are using the Dig spell to create a U-shaped trench along the bottom and the sides of the Salt Flats. Once they get the trench dug, they'll start removing the dirt and sand in the middle, so when the rains come, it will create a giant reservoir," explained Donovan.

"They're using some of the excavated spoils to build a wall on the outside of the trench, then using the Adhesive spell to stick the wall to the trench and the trench to the underlying bedrock. I think it might work, but it's going to take *months* to finish. My dad did say that he and Kathy will try to make it to the wedding. I showed them how to change into dragons, so it should only take them a couple of days to get here." Rachel smiled at the news.

"So, how are the wedding preparations going?" asked Donovan. "All of the invitations are out, and we've started getting replies; the King sends his regrets, but he'll be in Southport, inspecting the renovations and upgrades to his Winter Palace; the Royal Expeditionary Force will be here, and all of the Academy and staff will be there, of course. I'm just waiting on replies from a few of the Ministers." "It's probably a good thing that the King can't come. If he came, *every* Minister would feel obliged to attend, plus his personal guard and all the extra security," opined Donovan.

They arrived at the Mentor's dormitory and entered their room. Donovan stripped off his dirty clothes and headed for the shower. Rachel considered joining him but decided that doing so would delay them for at least a glass, and they still had lots of things yet to do. She stood outside the shower and said, "Judge Toffin agreed to perform the ceremony. We have to use the Forces Training Area because Wizard Noland says the courtyard is too small for that large a gathering. I've arranged for chairs for two hundred people. The flowers will have to be Seemings, since no florist in town would take on such a large order on such short notice." Donovan grunted, understanding.

"All we really have left to finalize is the catering, and Wizard Cassandra is helping me with that. She'll be my Maid of Honor, and my three Level Three students will be my Bridesmaids. Have you considered who you want to be, your Best Man and your groomsmen?" Donovan hesitated, then said, "I had hoped that Andrew could be my Best Man, I haven't really thought about any others. Maybe Jacob, Leo and Evan?" Rachel smiled, "That's an inspired choice. I'm sure they would all be overjoyed." Donovan grinned as he emerged from the shower, "OK, that takes care of the wedding party, assuming that Andrew can make it. What else do we need to do?"

"We need to decide on the wedding cake. The Academy bakers have agreed to make it for us. *You* need a tuxedo. We need to hire some musicians and finalize the catering order," said Rachel. "Then I guess I'd better get over to see your father as soon as I'm done talking to Wizard Noland." Rachel said, "My father doesn't make tuxedos, and you certainly don't *buy* them. You rent one from the shop in town. I'll take you there once we're done with the Headmaster. We can talk to the caterer and see about musicians after that." Donovan yawned loudly. "Oh no, you don't!" said Rachel, "I don't want to hear about how tired you are. You just take some Stamina Serum or something! We have work to do!" "Yes, Dear," said Donovan.

Wizard Noland greeted Donovan warmly as he approached, "Donovan! Welcome back! How was the trip? What on earth happened to your face?" Donovan was *really* getting tired of being asked 'What happened to your face?' by everyone he met. He explained what had happened and how he was injured, and that his father had said that he would be here for the wedding. Then he asked about the possibility of Andrew being his Best Man.

"I anticipated this request, so I sent Wizard Faith, in dragon form, of course, to locate the VALOR and deliver your invitation and request to Andrew. Hopefully, his commander will release him for a couple of days to attend. We should know when Faith returns tomorrow." Donovan smiled and thanked Wizard Noland for his foresight. "We need to go into town and make the final arrangements," said Donovan. "Sir, do you have any idea where we might find some musicians to hire?"

Wizard Noland told Donovan and Rachel to visit the Kingston Opera House and make inquiries. He said that there were always musicians looking for outside work between performances, and their prices were usually very reasonable. "Don't offer more than four silvers per person," he advised., "and you don't need the whole orchestra! A six-piece combo should do. Talk to Miss Karla, the Orchestra Director, she'll know what you need. More experienced musicians charge more, but they're more skilled, so choose your players wisely."

Donovan and Rachel expressed their appreciation for the recommendation and headed into town. The first stop was the tailor shop owned by Rachel's father. When they entered, Brian, Rachel's father, who was deaf, signed, *Donovan! It's good to see you again! What happened to your face?* Donovan sighed and signed, *I was attacked by a pack of Snow Dragons. Is it really that bad? Do they make veils for grooms?* Brian and Rachel both laughed, then Mr. Turner signed, *No, but you might consider using some makeup. At least for the wedding.* Donovan said he would consider it, then Rachel shooed him out of the shop so he wouldn't see her wedding dress, "Go across the street to the tuxedo rental shop. Tell the owner you are marrying Mr. Turner's daughter, and he'll give you a discount on the rental. *Do not select that hideous orange tuxedo he's been trying to offload for years!* Select something conservative, please. My bridesmaids are wearing yellow dresses if that helps."

"Maybe he has a neon yellow tuxedo," mused Donovan. "If you do that, I'll use a Remove spell, and you'll be standing at the altar in your underwear!" said Rachel. Donovan grinned as he left the shop; his parting words were, "And what if I'm not wearing any underwear?"

Closing the tailor shop door quickly behind him to avoid being hit by a thrown shoe, Donovan walked across the street and found Max's Tuxedo Rental shop. He entered and was greeted immediately by Max, the proprietor. "How can I help you, Sir?" asked Max. "I'm getting married next Endday to Rachel Turner, Brian's daughter. I know it's short notice, but I need a tuxedo."

"Of course! Of course! Come right in. I've actually heard news about the wedding and was expecting you. Let's see what we can do." Max led Donovan to the racks, where there were several tuxedos in many different styles and colors. "Rachel said that her bridesmaids were wearing yellow, if that matters," said Donovan. "Yellow! An excellent choice for a May wedding! Why, I have the most gorgeous orange—" "No. Not the orange one. Rachel was very specific about that." Max looked crestfallen. "I just can't get anyone to try that one. It's a shame, really, because, other than the color, which I admit was a bold choice, it's the finest in the shop." Inspiration struck Donovan, and he said, "Let's take a look at it, I might be able to make it work."

Max smiled and said, "Here it is," The tuxedo was made of what appeared to be brilliant orange satin, with gold sparkles and a silver-grey silk interior. It certainly was *colorful.* In a way, it reminded Donovan of the brilliant orange shirt that Rachel was wearing the day they met. "I have an idea," said Donovan.

A glass later, Donovan left Max's, and both he and the owner were very happy. He walked back across the street to Mr. Turner's shop and knocked discretely, "Is it safe for me to come in yet?" he called. "Yes, come on in. Did you get a tuxedo?" asked Rachel. "I did indeed, and you were right, Max gave me a significant discount.

Are you ready to head over to the caterers, or should we book the musicians first?"

"Let's go to the Opera House first," said Rachel, "the caterer should already be working on our order; we just need to pay the deposit and make our final selections." The two of them left arm-in-arm and walked over to the Kingston Opera House. "Have you ever been here before?" asked Rachel. "No, my father went a few times, but I always begged off," said Donovan, "You?"

"I went once with my mother when I was little. I haven't had a chance since I entered the Academy." Donovan nodded his understanding as they entered through the wide, intricately carved double doors. They were met almost immediately by a man in a bright red vest, wearing a top hat. "May I help you?" he asked. "Yes," said Rachel, taking the lead, "We are getting married at the Wizards Academy next Endday, and we need to hire some musicians. Wizard Noland suggested we speak to Miss Karla. Is she available?"

The man bowed and said, "May I have your names, please?" "I'm Rachel Turner, and this is Donovan Francis," replied Rachel. "Please follow me." He led them down the hall to an office with windows facing the street. He knocked gently and cracked open the door, "Excuse me, Miss Karla, but there are a couple of magicians from the Wizards Academy who would like to engage some of our musicians for a wedding next week." "Please, Harold, show them in," said an elderly woman with grey streaks in her hair.

Donovan let Rachel proceed him into the office. "So, a wedding next week, is it? You two certainly waited until the last minute, too—You're the one who captured that assassin at the Royal Ball, aren't you?" Karla asked Donovan. "Yes, ma'am, and I'm sorry for the short notice. You see, I've just passed my Sorcerer's Test, and Rachel and I will be leaving for our first assignments in Fairview in just over a week," explained Donovan.

Karla smiled and said, "We can certainly accommodate you. You're quite the celebrity, you know." Donovan shrugged humbly. "Now, what were you thinking, six or eight musicians? Strings or brass? Will the King be in attendance?" asked Karla. "King Henry will be in Southport next week," said Donovan, "so he sent his regrets." "Better for you," replied Karla. "Otherwise, you would need the Royal Trumpet Squad, in addition to the other musicians. Is the venue inside or outside? It makes a difference, you know."

"The ceremony will be at the Wizards Academy, outside in the Forces Training Area, if you know what that is," said Rachel. "Hmm, outside, I'd recommend eight musicians so the sound carries better." "So, would you like brass or strings?" "Strings. Definitely, your eight best, including a harpist," said Donovan. "First chairs?" asked Karla, "Those are more expensive, you know." "I'm aware," said Donovan. "Very well," said Karla. "Are there any particular songs you would like played, other than the Bridal March, of course?" Rachel rattled off a few of her favorite songs, and Donovan deferred to her choices.

"I understand; eight of our best string musicians, at six silvers each, comes to four golds and eight silvers…" Donovan handed over five golds and said, "Keep the change." "Thank you very much," said Karla. "I'll coordinate our arrival and set up with the Academy Gatekeeper, Wizard Stuart, isn't it?" "No, Wizard Stuart retired. The current Gatekeeper is Wizard Faith. I'll tell her to expect your visit," said Donovan.

As they left the Opera House, heading for the caterer, Rachel said, "You said that you'd never been to the opera." "And I haven't," replied Donovan, "but I've been to plenty of concerts, my love." "We didn't have to have the best musicians," said Rachel, "we could have bargained for less experienced—" "No," said Donovan, cutting her off. "You deserve the best, and I have the coin. Besides, I didn't want to spend half a glass negotiating. I have other plans for this afternoon," Donovan said with a leer. Rachel blushed.

The visit to the caterers was uneventful. Wizard Cassandra had done a masterful job of selecting an assortment of snacks and finger foods that would be well-received by their guests and wouldn't break the bank. The caterer did inform them that she had to subcontract out for several additional servers because of the short notice, but neither Donovan nor Rachel thought much about it.

With everything decided on except the cake, Donovan and Rachel headed over to Edward's house. Donovan said that he needed to pick up some more money, since paying the numerous wedding expenses had depleted his ready cash. A glass later, they left the house, both looking a little winded but happy. They returned to the Academy, where Noland greeted them at the door.

"How did everything go?" he asked. "Very well," replied Rachel, "all we have left to do is decide on the cake." Wizard Noland nodded his understanding and watched them as they headed towards the Mentor's dormitory and the kitchen.

The cake proved to be much more complicated than either Donovan or Rachel expected. Donovan wanted *chocolate* cake, but Rachel was horrified at the thought. She wanted a white cake with peach icing between the layers, with white frosting and yellow icing flowers.

Donovan eventually conceded the chocolate cake for some orange frosting along with the yellow flowers. Rachel looked at him suspiciously and said, "This better not be because you rented that outrageous orange tuxedo!"

Donovan assured her that his tuxedo was not orange and said he wanted the orange trim on the cake to remind him of the orange shirt she wore the first time they met. Rachel was flattered and agreed to the frosting, but she still had a sneaky suspicion that Donovan was not telling her the whole truth about his tuxedo.

With all of the wedding preparations completed, Donovan headed over to the Infirmary in the hopes that there was a Healer there who could do something about his scars. He was becoming very self-conscious at the stares he was getting. "Tsk, tsk, tsk," said Margret, the Chief Healer at the Academy. "I cannot make them completely vanish, but I should be able to make them less obvious," she said. "Virginia, come here, please," she said to her assistant. "Please fetch me some fish oil, a lemon, and some Epsom salts from the medicine cabinet." The young assistant rushed off and returned quickly.

"Now Donovan, this will likely sting a bit, but I need you to hold *absolutely* still until I'm finished. If you flinch or move in any way while I'm working, it will likely make the scars worse. Do you understand?" Donovan nodded and steeled himself for the procedure.

It felt like Margret was applying a hot branding iron to his face, Donovan could only speculate, but he suspected that she opened the wounds, poured in lemon juice and fish oil, then topped the concoction off with salt. Nevertheless, he held as still as he could, but his eyes began to water, and a tear dripped down his left cheek. After what seemed like an hour, Margret placed a gauze patch over the scars and said, "Leave this on for two glasses, and whatever you do, don't talk or open your mouth! You'll tear open the wound, and I'll have to start over again, with less promising results the next time." Donovan nodded his understanding.

"Come back and see me tomorrow, and I'll check on your progress. Here is a pad and charcoal for you to write any messages while you are letting your face heal." Donovan wrote THANK YOU on the pad, then tore off a new sheet and wrote: I CAN'T TALK. MOUTH HEALING. DON'T MAKE ME LAUGH!

The next few nights did not go any better for Gek or Azure. It was difficult to get Richard to sleep in the cave unless Azure was holding him (in human form). They tried padding a shallow hole with seaweed, sea sponges, and even sand, but nothing seemed comfortable enough for the baby. They were also very tired of having to protect Richard from Annalise. The baby dragon's attitude towards her brother had not softened, and Gek and Azure were at a loss for how to punish a two-month-old baby dragon.

They finally decided that they needed to visit Bruce and at least see if he had any suggestions. So, on the evening of the fourth day on the island, Gek, Azure, Anna, and Richard flew towards Southport. It was a two-day flight, and they had to stop just east of the Jade Swamp. They dared not camp inside the swamp for fear of alligators and vindictive baby dragons. Of course, as soon as they landed, both babies were hungry and wanted food *now*. Azure decided that Richard could wait, since humans needed less food than dragons; besides, she was already in dragon form.

Once Annalise was fed and was resting under the watchful eye of Gek, Azure transformed back into a human and fed Richard. Since both children had been awake all day during the flight, both Gek and Azure were hopeful that they would sleep through at least part of the night. No. While Richard was content to sleep for a while, Annalise wanted to go explore the swamp, which kept either Gek or Azure awake and alert, ensuring that Anna did not wander off into danger. By the time Anna grew tired of the game and settled down to sleep, Richard was awake, demanding food.

Neither Azure nor Gek got much rest that day. The following night, they flew on to Bruce's house, arriving just before dawn. Gek transformed into a human and knocked softly on the driftwood door. "Who's there?" came Bruce's gruff voice from inside the hut. "It is Gek and Azure," said Gek.

"Well, come in, come in!" yelled Bruce. Gek opened the door to find Bruce sitting in one of the old wooden chairs, his leg propped up on the crate that served as the dining room table. There were wooden slats along the sides of his left leg, held in place by strips of cloth. "What happened to you?" asked Gek. "Well, I was fishin' this big piece of driftwood outta the surf, and a wave smashed it into my leg. I managed to drag myself back home and put on this splint, but I haven't been able to do much else for a while."

"When did this happen?" asked Gek. "Oh, not more than a week ago, I reckon.'" "Let me get you some food and water," said Gek. "I appreciate that. Where's Azure?" "She is outside with our children," said Gek. "Children? What kind?" "A human baby boy and a baby girl dragon," answered Gek. "WOOOHOO! You two are in for it now!" said Bruce with a smile. "Tell me about it," grumbled Gek. "We have not gotten much sleep lately, and Annalise, our daughter, seems to hate her brother."

"Nothin' unusual about that," said Bruce. "Even among human children. Of course, a baby dragon is a whole other matter, I suppose." "Yes," admitted Gek, "with her sharp teeth, she could really injure Richard if she tried." "How old are they?" asked Bruce. "Annalise is almost two months old, and Richard was born about a month ago."

"Any other problems besides the sibling rivalry?" asked Bruce. "Well, we cannot get any sleep. It seems that one or the other of them is always hungry and crying for us. We decided that Richard was not comfortable in our cave on the Coral Islands. Anna does not mind sleeping on the ground, but I think human babies need something softer to sleep on," said Gek.

"You have that right. I may be able to help you both. Have Azure come in; you know where the back room is. It's going to get a bit warm later today, but it's better than being out in the hot sun," said Bruce. Gek went out and told Azure it was all right to come in. She handed Richard to Gek, then coaxed/pushed Annalise inside the hut. Annalise walked into the hut cautiously, saw Bruce in his chair and went over to sniff him. She pushed her nose against his good leg.

"What's that about?" asked Bruce. Gek smiled, "She is trying to get you to change into a dragon." "Fat chance of that," grumbled Bruce. Anna eventually gave up the attempt, sat back on her hind legs and growled at Bruce. "NO!" shouted Gek, "Bruce is our friend!" Anna ceased her growling and began exploring the rest of the structure. Azure said, "We really appreciate your help, Bruce. How is your leg?" "Well, I don't think it's broken. At least it hasn't swelled up. It's just sore. I think I did more damage to my knee than my leg. Why don't you take Anna into the back room and make her comfortable?"

Azure and Anna headed back to the "dragon room' at the back of the hut, which Bruce's Sea Dragon wife used when she felt the need to revert to her true form. Mother and daughter laid down on the dirt floor, and Azure was asleep in minutes. Annalise explored the room, sniffing the corners and generally getting acquainted with this new place, which was much different from both the cave on Acropo and the one on Perfo. Eventually, Anna curled up next to Azure and fell asleep.

Gek held Richard and rocked him for a while, while Bruce tried to get comfortable with his splinted leg. Finally, Gek said, "You know, I might be able to heal your leg." "Really?" asked Bruce. "Yes," said Gek, "I am not an expert, but I did watch Cobalt, my father, heal another dragon once. I would be happy to try." Bruce thought for a moment, then said, "Sure, go ahead. Just don't turn my leg into wings or a dragon tail."

Gek put Richard down on the floor briefly, then moved to Bruce's side. Remembering the spell, he placed both hands over Bruce's knee and said, "*SALVARE.*" Instantly, Gek collapsed to the floor, while Bruce grinned happily and proceeded to remove the splint. "It worked! Why, I feel ten years younger! Thank you, Gek! Oh no! Too much power. Well, after the month you've had, I guess you need your sleep anyway. I'll take care of Richard for now; you just rest," Bruce told the sleeping Changed One.

Leaving the sleeping baby on the floor for a moment, Bruce went out to the crude lean-to storage hut outside his house and retrieved a worn and faded cradle. He quickly dusted it off as best he could and brought it back inside. Then he retrieved some old blankets from a chest in the corner and placed them in the cradle. He gently picked up Richard and laid him in the cradle without waking him (an incredible accomplishment).

Bruce sat in his chair and wondered what was in store for him next. He was very glad to be healed, and it wasn't just his leg that felt better, but he had a feeling that his life just got a lot more complicated.

Wizard Faith, in the form of a Great Dragon, circled the HMS VALOR, holding a white dress. The sailors below seemed to understand her intent and cleared the aft deck, creating space for her to land. She landed gently on the deck, then said, "Would you gentlemen please turn around and give a lady some privacy?" The crew reluctantly turned their backs, realizing that they would *not* be feasting their eyes on a naked woman this morning.

Faith quickly transformed into her human form and put on the dress. "Thank you, gentlemen. Does anybody know where I can find Sorcerer Andrew?" The Bos'n approached and said, "Mage Andrew is below, meeting with the Commodore. If you wait here, Miss?" "Wizard Faith," said Faith. "Wizard Faith," continued the Bos'n, "I will fetch them immediately."

The Bos'n ran to the steep staircase leading to the lower decks and moved quickly to the Commodore's cabin. He knocked urgently. "Yes? What is it now?" asked the Commodore gruffly. "Sir, there's a Wizard Faith who just arrived. She wants to speak to the Mage." Andrew opened the door, "Wizard Faith? But she's the Gatekeeper at the Wizards Academy! How did she get here?" "She arrived as a big golden dragon, just like Sorceress Celeste did, only she knew that she was going to be naked when she changed back into a human, and asked the crew on deck to turn their backs." Andrew laughed. "I guess the ability to change into dragons is spreading to the rest of the magical community. Shall we go see what she wants, Sir?"

The Commodore rose from his chair and said, "Yes, I don't suppose it would be a good idea to keep a Wizard waiting." The three men headed up on deck and found Faith examining the Seabow. "Wizard Faith! It's good to see you," said Andrew. "What do you think of my invention?" Faith turned and said, "It looks very efficient. Does it work?" "Incredibly well," said the Commodore. "Commodore Horatio Matthews, at your service. What can we do for you this fine day at sea?"

"I'm Wizard Faith, Commodore, and I have a message for *Mage*? Mage Andrew. I hope I didn't alarm your crew," said Faith. "Dragons landing on my deck and changing into humans is becoming a normal occurrence," said the Commodore. "Although a single Great Dragon is new. The last one came in the company of a Sea Dragon." "Gek and Azure?" asked Faith. "You know them?" asked Andrew. "I know *of* them from Sorceress Celeste. We have never met," replied Faith.

"Yes, they were here a few days ago to negotiate a Peace Treaty between the Sea Dragons and the Franconian Navy. Then Azure suddenly went into labor and delivered a baby boy right here on the ship. It was an extraordinary day." "She had a baby *boy*? How was that possible?" "Apparently, if they are in human form when they give birth, the child is human. When in dragon form, they lay a dragon egg. It seems that Azure laid an egg a month ago but didn't realize she was carrying twins."

Faith shook her head and said, "I don't envy those two; having two children of different species is going to be a challenge. Anyway, the reason I'm here is to deliver this to Andrew," said Faith, taking a cream-colored envelope out of her satchel and handing it to Andrew.

Sorcerer Donovan Francis

Sorceress Rachel Turner

Invite You to Share in Our Happiness

7 May

10:00 am

Franconia Wizards Academy

"Donovan is getting *married*?" exclaimed Andrew. "Wait, 'Sorcerer' Donovan Francis? You're telling me that Donovan passed his Sorcerer's Test already? But he hasn't been at the Academy for four years yet!" "Nevertheless, he passed all the tests," said Faith. "The reason I'm here is that Donovan would like you to be the Best Man at his wedding. That is, if the Commodore can spare you for a few days."

Andrew looked to the Commodore. "Well, since Sorceress Anne is aboard, and the dragons have ceased hostilities for the time being, I see no problem in your taking a week's leave to attend your friend's wedding," said the Commodore. Andrew smiled. "Let's go tell Anne."

After informing Anne of his imminent departure for a week, Andrew and Faith returned to the aft deck. "You'll need a bag of some sort to put your clothes in," said Faith. "When you transform back into a human, you'll be naked, and if you don't take off your clothes before changing into a dragon, you'll destroy the clothes you're wearing." Andrew grinned, "I know. Celeste was mortified when she transformed on a ship full of men without a stitch of clothing on." Faith laughed, "I guess we should have prepared her better for the mission!"

Andrew retrieved his sailor's duffle bag and disrobed, stuffing his clothes in the bag quickly. Faith addressed the assembled sailors, "Gentlemen?" The sailors reluctantly turned their backs, and Faith quickly disrobed and made the transformation. Now, in dragon-form, she said to Andrew, "Look at me. Picture a dragon in your mind as you invoke the Change spell. Make sure you think of a dragon that can speak, or you may never be able to change back." Andrew gulped.

Steeling himself, Andrew looked at the gold dragon before him and created a mental image of the dragon in his mind—one that could speak and said, *"MORPHIOUS"* while clapping his hands. He instantly transformed into a Great Dragon. The sailors on deck clapped their hands at the accomplishment. "All right, get back to work," Dragon-Andrew told the crew.

"Ready?" asked Faith. "Ready," replied Andrew, spreading his wings. The two golden dragons lifted off the ship, heading west towards Kingston and the Wizards Academy.

Chapter Eight:

THE MOST IMPERFECT WEDDING

They landed at the Academy boat dock after a long day and a half flight from the HMS VALOR. Faith landed first, and Andrew flew in circles until she had transformed and gotten dressed. Andrew landed and resumed his human form, dressing quickly. They entered the Academy through the portal that could only be opened by a Sorcerer and proceeded to the Headmaster's cottage. Wizard Noland greeted them warmly, "Mage Andrew! Faith! Welcome back! So, how was the flight?" "Tiring," admitted Andrew, "It's not as easy as it looks, especially when you're trying to stay out of sight above the clouds. It's very cold up there, and the air seems thinner, so you have to flap your wings harder."

Wizard Noland nodded his understanding. "So, how's life at sea?" "It was pretty exciting there for a while, with all the Sea Dragon attacks, and I guess the HMS VALOR didn't see the worst of it. How do you suppose that the dragons knew which ship I was on?" asked Andrew. "Probably from either Stuart or Loren. It really wasn't a secret around here," said Noland.

"Well, since the Sea Dragons have proposed a Peace Treaty, things should be pretty calm now," said Andrew.

"A Peace Treaty? Why would they do that?" asked Noland. "We were under orders from Admiral Cross to patrol the Coral Islands. We sailed around them a couple of times but didn't find any Sea Dragons around. Then I went ashore on the big northern island, and we found hundreds of dragon tracks." "Really? Hundreds?" "Sure, but it was pointed out to me later that dragons have *four feet*, so it might only have been a few dragons." "Hmm, I suppose that's true," said Wizard Faith.

"The frightening thing was that I noticed one set of footprints was following us," said Andrew. "A Concealment shield?" asked Noland. "I suspect so. So, I loudly proclaimed that there was nothing on the island and we should return to the ship. I guess I fooled the dragon because we made it back without incident." "Then what happened?" "Well, we were ordered to patrol the islands and engage the dragons. We couldn't just sail home. I had the idea to set the small, southern island on fire and see what happened."

"I take it that the dragons were not happy with your plan," opined Faith. "No, they were not. About a hundred of them attacked us. They sank the HMS

COMFORT, and we thought we'd lost Sorceress Anne. They dropped a mast on her from above. The mast punched right through the keel, and the ship went down fast." "How did Anne survive?" asked Faith. "Her shield was strong enough to withstand the shock from the mast and crashing through the two decks and the keel below, but she was pushed deep underwater and had to hold on for quite some time before she was able to make it to the surface," "Anne always did have good shields," confirmed Noland.

"Anyway, with the new Seabows, we killed and injured a lot of dragons. Then, two of them rose together at the stern of the VALOR; one was trying to penetrate my shield with a fine stream of water when the other saw the name of the ship and yelled, 'It is the VALOR!' and moved between us. I killed him with a Blast spell to the throat. Then, all the other dragons retreated. I guess they didn't expect the HMS VALOR."

"Undoubtedly not, and the Binding spell on the members of the Dragon Council is what has been protecting you. Most likely, the dragon that intervened, was one of the dragons that was bound by the spell. Now tell me, what is a Seabow?" asked Noland. Andrew smiled, "I took the crossbow you sent me and enlarged it to four times its normal size. We mounted them on pedestals that can traverse and elevate. Then I devised a crank mechanism to draw back the bow, it takes two men or a magician using a Strength Enhancement. We put one Seabow on each side of all four ships. They fire long harpoon-sized bolts. We learned later that we killed or injured fifty-two Sea Dragons."

"How did you determine that?" asked Wizard Noland. "Once Anne surfaced, she had to swim to the shore of the island we'd set fire to. She passed out once she got on shore and was found by a Great Dragon, who mistook her for Celeste." "Let me guess, Gek?" asked Noland. Andrew smiled, "The very same. Anyway, Gek and Azure decided to spare Anne's life because of her relationship to Celeste. It seems that Azure went to the northern island, which the dragons call Acropo, to check on her Clan. She found a great many injured and dying Sea Dragons. Azure returned to Perfo, the southern island, and convinced Anne to help heal the injured dragons, but Anne insisted on a Binding spell that any dragon she healed would never attack a human again. The injured dragons agreed. Anne says she healed and Bound thirty-three Sea Dragons, and another two died of their wounds. Anne said that she overheard that another seventeen dragons had perished in the battle, including the Clan Chief."

"Anyway, after Anne healed the dragons, the new Sea Dragon Clan Chief, Cobalt, proposed a truce. The Sea Dragons will not attack our ships as long as we do not attack them. Cobalt says that he does not speak for the other dragon Clans, and that the truce does not apply to Baizian ships because we do not speak for them. A few days ago, Gek and Azure landed on the HMS VALOR under a flag of truce and proposed a longer, more formal Peace Treaty. The Commodore and I negotiated a draft of the Treaty and sent Celeste with a copy for Admiral Cross and one for the King. She should be here in a few days. We agreed to meet with the Sea Dragons again in three months to finalize the terms."

"Well, the King isn't here right now. He's in Southport, inspecting his Winter Palace. I don't expect him back for a month. I guess we'll have to send the Treaty to him by dragon. Faith, can you send a Messenger Hawk to Southport, telling them to expect a 'friendly dragon' to arrive soon with an urgent message for the King?" Faith left at once, headed for the Academy Message Center.

"One other thing, after Azure changed into human form on the VALOR, she went into labor. I guess she didn't even know she was pregnant. It took both Anne and Celeste to keep her alive and deliver the baby. It was a boy, and they named him Richard," said Andrew. Noland whistled, "Well, that should certainly complicate their lives, having a human son. It might make them more amenable to humans. We'll just have to see."

"So, Donovan actually passed the Sorcerer's Test?" asked Andrew. "Indeed, despite Wizard Faith cheating and riding the Academy Clydesdale against him during the Martial Arts Test," said Noland. "The Clydesdale? How did Donovan even reach her with his staff?" "He didn't, according to Faith; instead of conjuring a round shield to deflect her staff, he made it linear, like a clothesline, and scooped her right out of the saddle." "HAH! I would have loved to see that! But why was Wizard Faith trying to make Donovan fail?" "I suspect that Rachel asked her to defeat him so that they could remain at the Academy for a few more weeks. They're going to have to leave shortly after the wedding," said Noland.

"Where are you assigning them?" asked Andrew. "Donovan will go to the 3rd Regiment in Fairview, and Rachel will be assigned to the Fairview Regional Mage's Office," said Wizard Noland. "So, the wedding is the day after tomorrow?" "Yes. Now that you're here, I think all the arrangements are complete. You should go find Donovan and let him know you've arrived. You'll probably find him in the Infirmary."

"The Infirmary? What happened to him?" "He went to deliver a wedding invitation to his father, who is still in Baize. While he was there, he interrupted a Snow Dragon attack on a small Baizian town. He killed six or seven Snow Dragons, but one clawed him across the face. Margret is trying to reduce the scarring." "That boy has a knack for finding trouble," grinned Andrew. "It's a good thing that he's usually able to get himself out of it."

Andrew walked across the courtyard to the Academy Lecture Hall and proceeded up the stairs to the second floor, where the Infirmary was located. As he entered, he heard Margaret scolding, "Stop squirming and hold still! I'm almost done. There! That's the best I can do. Now get out of here, and try not to come back again." Donovan nodded, stood up and turned to find Andrew standing in the doorway. "Andrew! You made it!" he went forward and embraced his cousin and former Mentor.

"Let's see the damage," said Andrew, looking at Donovan's face. "Not bad, considering. You really should be more careful." Donovan laughed as they headed down the stairs, "I would have been fine if I knew how to breathe fire," he whispered. "After I got clawed, I screamed, and fire came out, killing the Snow Dragon, but I was never able to repeat the process. I still need to ask Terry how it's done. So, how's Navy life? I heard you made Mage already! Congratulations!"

Andrew related all of his adventures aboard ship, about the Treaty and the new Seabows. "Hmm, I wonder if something like that would work for the Royal

Guard," mused Donovan. "They're pretty big," said Andrew, "It's not something you can carry around with you; even a wagon would have a hard time." "I was thinking about mounting some on the parapets of our castles and garrisons," said Donovan. "A mobile version would be nice, but you're right; something that big would be cumbersome."

"So, where's Rachel? I hardly remember her from my time here. Mentors for Level Ones didn't interact much with those for Level Three students." "She's in town at her father's shop for yet *another* fitting. Honestly, you'd think her father could get her measurements right!" "Her father is a tailor?" asked Andrew. "Yes, he's Brian Turner, the tailor who makes all the Concealment cloaks for the Academy," replied Donovan. "Whoa! Slow down. Since when do magicians get Concealment cloaks?"

Donovan smiled and told Andrew about his idea to issue Concealment cloaks to all new Sorcerers, so they could save their spell for another purpose. "That's brilliant! Where do I get mine?" asked Andrew. Donovan grinned and said, "Right this way." Donovan escorted Andrew to the Academy supply office and rang the bell on the reception desk. A wizened elderly man appeared. "Yes?" "This is Mage Andrew, newly returned to the Academy. He needs his new Concealment cloak," said Donovan.

"Just a minute, let me get my list," said the Supply Master, "Last name?" "Perrucci," said Andrew. "I got a Sorcerer Andrew Perrucci here…" "I've been recently promoted," said Andrew. "Then I need a different cloak," said the man, "Mages get one with a crest on the pocket. One minute." The Supply Master went into the back room and returned with a Concealment cloak, folded inside out. "Try it on," he said. Andrew put the cloak on, and it was a bit big for him but fit reasonably well. "They're sized big," said the Supply Master, "in case you're carrying something. That looks about right. Sign here, please." He pushed over a ledger with a list of all of the magicians in Franconia on it. Andrew noted that less than half of them had received their cloaks yet.

"We recommend that when you take it off, you fold it inside out so you can find it again," explained the man, "There's a one-gold replacement cost for any lost cloaks. Just so you know, all the cloaks have Secrecy spells on them, so they can't be replicated." "Thank you very much," said Andrew. The Supply Master just waved as he returned to the back room.

"A one-gold replacement cost?" asked Andrew. "It actually only costs us about five silvers, since our Level Three magicians put the Concealment, Stamina, and Secrecy spells on the cloth," said Donovan. "I think the extra is just a deterrent,"

"So, what next?" asked Andrew. "Is everything ready for the wedding?" "I hope so," said Donovan. "The ceremony will be in the Forces Training Area, and the students and staff will set up the chairs tomorrow, so no Forces training for the next two days unless it's on boats. The food will arrive just after dawn on the day of the wedding. The Academy bakers are making the wedding cake. We couldn't get any florists to provide what we needed on such short notice, so all the flowers will be Seemings conjured by Wizard Mira and the Level Twos. The musicians will arrive at about eight to set up. We went with all strings, so not much infrastructure required. I'll pick up my tuxedo tomorrow. Am I forgetting anything?"

"Do you have the ring?" Donovan slapped his forehead, "The ring! How could I be so stupid! We need to get to the jeweler's right now!" Andrew smiled at Donovan's discomfort. "Relax, the longest wait for rings is the sizing. As magicians, we can do that ourselves. Let's go."

Donovan and Andrew headed over to the Kingston Jewelers, where Donovan had purchased the engagement ring for Rachel. The sales clerk recognized him immediately, "Have you come for the wedding band?" she asked. "Yes," replied Donovan. "I'm glad you're here, since you know exactly which engagement ring I picked out." The girl smiled and said, "Of course.

We set the matching wedding bands aside when we sell an engagement ring; if you don't come back in a year, we figure that it didn't work out and put the band back in the case. Here is the ring you need." Donovan happily paid for the ring and as he and Andrew were turning to leave, they ran into Rachel and her father, entering the store.

"Fancy meeting you here," signed Donovan. Rachel blushed and her father made the sign for laughing. *"Rachel, you remember Andrew. He just flew in today to be my Best Man."* Rachel's father signed, *"What do you mean, 'flew in'?"* Rachel signed, *"I'll explain later."* "It's nice to see you again, Mage Andrew. I'm glad you could make it. *It's my honor,"* signed Andrew. Donovan stared, *"When did you learn to sign?"*

Andrew signed, *"There once was a girl in Southport..."* Rachel and Donovan laughed, and her father signed his amusement. Before they left, Donovan took Rachel aside and whispered, "Do you need any money? This place is pretty expensive." Rachel kissed him on his 'good' cheek and whispered, "We have it covered, but thank you for asking. I'll see you later."

Donovan and Andrew left the jewelers and headed back to the Academy by way of the Happy Maid Tavern, where Donovan paid for lunch. "I figured that this might be better than Navy food," said Donovan.

Andrew smiled, "They don't call it 'mess' for no reason. Thanks." After lunch, Andrew asked who Donovan had selected for his groomsmen, "Evan, Jacob and Leo," said Donovan. "Just a final 'Thank You' before I leave the Academy." "Do they have appropriate outfits?" asked Andrew. Donovan's face fell. "Oh, no! I completely forgot about them! What are we going to do?"

"We are going to run back to the Academy and get them to the tuxedo rental shop right now," said Andrew. "I just hope Max has something in their size." Donovan and Andrew raced back to the Academy and ran to the respective kitchens, gathering Evan from the Level One dormitory, Jacob from the Level Two kitchen, and Leo from the Level Three bakery. They all rushed out to the tuxedo rental shop with apologies to the supervisors of the three groomsmen. As they entered the shop, Max came out from the back room and said, "Welcome back! Are you here to pick up your tux?" "Yes, and I need tuxedos for my three groomsmen here. I can't believe that I forgot about them."

Max looked confused, "But Wizard Noland brought these three gentlemen over almost a week ago for fittings. Their rentals are right here, ready to go." Andrew laughed hysterically. Donovan paid Max and smiled, shaking his head.

Azure woke at the sound of Richard crying. Checking to ensure that Annalise was still asleep, she quickly transformed and put on her human clothes. She slipped out to what passed for the living room of Bruce's hut and found Gek sleeping on the floor, with Richard in some sort of wooden bed next to him. Bruce was walking around the kitchen, preparing some fish for them.

"Gek! Wake up! What are you doing sleeping?" asked Azure. Bruce came over and said, "Leave him be. He passed out after healing my leg. I'm sure he'll come around soon. How are you doing, Azure?" "I'm sleep-deprived and tired of changing back and forth between human and Dragon. How long have I been asleep?" she asked. "A few hours," said Bruce. "I know it's got to be tough, having one of each."

"You have no idea; it seems that as soon as we get one of them to sleep, the other starts crying," complained Azure. "And you rush right over to comfort them, right? Well, there's your problem," said Bruce. "What?" asked Azure. "Look, babies cry because they're hungry, wet, messy, or bored. If you've recently fed them, they're probably not hungry. If Richard's diaper is dry, that's not the issue either; he's just bored. You just need to let him cry himself back to sleep."

"Are you kidding me?" asked Azure. "Not at all," said Bruce, "while Celeste and I never had any children of our own, we spent a lot of time around Changed Ones who did. Just because one of them is crying doesn't mean you have to rush to their side. If you do, they'll learn that all they have to do to get your attention is cry. It's like Annalise bumping you with her nose; if you change every time she asks, then *she* is in charge, not you." Azure considered his words, then smiled.

"It won't be easy at first," cautioned Bruce, "your natural instincts as a parent will be to go and comfort your baby, but you have to let them learn how to put themselves back to sleep. Otherwise, you'll be a basket case in a month." Azure smiled and said, "I am really glad we came to you. Where did you get that bed for Richard?" "The cradle? Believe it or not, it washed up on the beach a few years ago. I have no idea why I kept it, but it comes in handy now."

"Do you have any suggestions for how to handle Annalise and her dislike of Richard?" asked Azure. "Well, Once upon a time, I heard about something called negative reinforcement, which means that when Anna acts aggressively towards Richard, you punish her by giving Richard more attention. Eventually, Anna will figure out that the less mean she is to Richard, the more attention she gets from you. I don't know if it will work with a baby dragon, but you could try," said Bruce. Azure nodded.

"I have another question; you said Richard might be 'messy.' What did you mean by that?" "Well, right now, both of your children are getting an all-liquid diet, right?" Azure nodded. "Well, once Richard starts eating solid food, what he doesn't digest will come out the other end. Changing *those* diapers is a whole other experience." Azure grimaced, "How long does that last?" "Why, until he learns to go to the bathroom by himself and doesn't need diapers anymore. Maybe two years." "TWO YEARS!" exclaimed Azure. "Maybe less. Changed One's children tend to mature much faster than normal human babies."

"What about Annalise?" "Once she starts eating solid food, the same thing will happen, but she doesn't wear a diaper," said Bruce with a wink.

Endday morning dawned bright and clear without a cloud in the sky. The caterer arrived right on time, and she and her workers began setting up the canopy and refreshment tables. The musicians arrived next and found their place and began tuning up. The guests began arriving about an hour before the ceremony, with the Royal Expeditionary Force leading the way, their scarlet and gold dress uniforms looking magnificent. As they mingled about, Major Gerald took the opportunity to confer with Wizard Noland.

"Sir, I have a request. Given the dragon threat, do you think it would be possible to assign some organic magical support to the Royal Expeditionary Force? When we went to Springfield, we had Wizard Edward and Sorcerer Curtis. When I returned with Second Company, we had no magical support, and I realized how much I've come to rely on it lately," said the Major. Wizard Noland thought for a moment, then asked, "You're thinking a Sorcerer for each company?" "If possible, Sir. We've done a lot of split operations in the past; even during the attack against the dragons outside of Springfield, each company took one hill and fought three dragons each. It's just a thought; I know our magical assets are stretched a little thin right now."

"I'll give it some thought. When do you think you'll be sent out again?" asked Wizard Noland. "Not before the King returns from Southport, certainly. After that? It could be anytime." Noland nodded and said, "Well, I guess we better take our places; it looks like they're about to begin."

Donovan moved through the crowd, shaking hands with those he knew, Senior Specialists Lance and Dirk, the company commanders of the Royal Expeditionary Force, and Marshall Guzman. He searched for his father and Mage Kathy, but they were nowhere to be found. Then he moved to the front of the crowd and stood by the altar, chatting with Judge Toffin and Andrew. He wore a shimmering silver-grey tuxedo with what appeared to be flecks of mirror embedded that sparkled in the sunlight. Under the jacket, he wore a brilliant orange waistcoat and an orange bow tie. As Rachel's mother was escorted to her seat in the front row, the musicians struck up the Bridal March and Rachel, escorted by her father, began walking down the white carpet towards the altar.

Rachel looked stunning. Her dress was studded with tiny pearls that shimmered in the sun. Her hair was down, just reaching her shoulders, and Donovan noticed that she was wearing the shoes he bought her for the Royal Ball. Her father stopped and kissed her on the cheek before she completed the walk to the altar.

"Nice shoes," said Donovan. "Nice tie," replied Rachel with a wicked smile. Donovan's head was buzzing. So much so that he didn't really hear anything that Judge Toffin said. He had eyes only for Rachel. At one point, Andrew nudged him and handed him the ring. Donovan refocused his attention enough to say, "I do," as he slipped the ring on Rachel's finger, expertly resizing it as he did. Rachel did the same, and Judge Toffin said, "I now pronounce you man and wife. You may kiss the bride." Donovan and Rachel exchanged a passionate kiss, then turned and walked quickly back down the aisle.

The wedding cake was cut, and the music was excellent. Rachel said, "I like your choice of tuxedo." Donovan replied, "Well, to be perfectly honest, this is the orange tuxedo. When I talked to Max, he said that this tuxedo was the finest one in his shop and that he just made a mistake with the color. I examined the outfit and it really is outstanding. So, using magic, I turned it inside out. See?" Donovan opened the jacket, exposing a brilliant orange satin lining. "Why did you pick this one?" asked Rachel. "I wanted to remember the fantastic orange shirt you wore the first time we met. Besides, Max was so happy, that he sold me this tuxedo for the cost of a rental." Rachel laughed.

Everything was going perfectly until Donovan smelled a familiar and very unwanted scent. "DRAGON!" He shouted, turning and scanning the crowd for the Changed One that had infiltrated the festivities. One of the caterers *rippled* into a Stone Dragon, and the mayhem began.

The dragon tail-whipped the pavilion, scattering the tables and wedding guests. He turned towards the red-clad Royal Expeditionary Force and spewed fire. "Oh no, you don't," shouted Rachel, casting a protective shield in front of the soldiers. The dragon fire sheeted off Rachel's shield, striking some of the Academy students, some of whom erected their own shields in time and some who didn't. Blast spells began striking the dragon, but they seemed ineffective. The dragon ran through the crowd, slashing with his talons and whipping his tail from side to side.

Donovan suddenly remembered his father's advice about how to kill a Stone Dragon. He stepped to the front and cast a shield completely around the dragon. It wasn't going to work. The dragon was incredibly strong, and Donovan's shield was being struck by Blast spells, hurled rocks and anything else the frightened Academy students could throw at the dragon. "STOP FIRING!" shouted Donovan. "What are you doing?" screamed Wizard Noland. "I'm suffocating him!" yelled Donovan. "HELP ME! My shield is buckling!" Instantly, Donovan felt Rachel's shield surround his, reinforcing the containment, then Wizard Noland's, Daniel's, and Faith's, then a dozen more.

"STOP firing at the Dragon!" said Wizard Noland's booming voice, and the assault stopped. The dragon suddenly realized what was happening and rammed the shield with all his might; he slashed it with his talons, then breathed fire at it, not realizing that the fire rapidly consumed the remaining air inside the shield. He rammed the shield again, desperately, and Donovan felt his shield shatter, and he fell to his knees.

Fortunately, the other shields held, and the dragon quickly collapsed to the ground. The magicians held the shield for long minutes, just to make sure the beast was dead. Finally, Wizard Noland commanded them to release their shields and begin tending to the wounded. Wizards treated the most badly injured first, sending some Level Ones to the Infirmary to retrieve the Academy's supply of Healing Serum.

The triage and healing went on through the afternoon. Most of the injuries were shock or burns, but there was also an assortment of broken bones and lacerations. Rachel went and checked on her parents, who were both unharmed but in shock. When the casualty count came in, there were ten dead and fifty wounded. Among the dead were three soldiers from the Royal Expeditionary Force, the caterer, two Level Ones, two Level Twos, Leonard, and Sorcerer Terry.

Donovan sat with Rachel and cried. *How could he have been so stupid? He should have checked everyone who entered. This was all his fault.* Wizard Noland came by and sat with them. "I hope you realize that this wasn't your fault. The faculty should have checked everyone entering. We all just got caught up in the joy of the moment. I'm sorry." "I should have listened more carefully," said Donovan. "The caterer told me that she was going to have to hire sub-contractors. I just never considered…"

"Donovan, you detected the dragon before anyone else. It was your shield idea that helped us kill it. What made you think of that?" "My father killed a Stone Dragon in the palace in Baize. He told me that he had to suffocate it with a shield. I meant to tell you, but I forgot because I was distracted by all the wedding plans. Then I couldn't hold him. I tried…"

"Donovan, as accomplished as you are, you are not as strong as a Wizard! Also, I doubt that Edward had to contend with dozens of magicians hitting the outside of his shield with Blast spells while he tried to suffocate a Stone Dragon! You did well." "But Terry and Leo are still dead," said Donovan, sadly. "Yes. Terry fought hard, and he protected his wards, all of whom survived. Leo was just in the wrong place at the wrong time," said Wizard Noland.

In the midst of the carnage, Edward and Kathy came rushing up. "What happened?" asked Edward. "There was a Stone Dragon Changed One among the caterers; he transformed and attacked. Donovan enclosed him in a shield and yelled for help. We eventually killed the dragon, but we have ten dead and fifty wounded." "What can we do?" asked Mage Kathy.

"Go and see if there are any more wounded that need help, maybe cast some Stamina spells on the magicians that have been tending the wounded. I will meet you later in my cottage," said Wizard Noland. "We are going to have to cast Secrecy spells on everyone," said Edward. "We can't have news of dragon Changed Ones circulating around Kingston. There would be panic." Noland nodded and called Wizard Faith over. "Gather the uninjured Level Threes and man the gatehouse. Cast Secrecy spells on everyone before they leave the Academy. We can't have news of this catastrophe spreading." Faith nodded her understanding and headed off, calling to the Level Threes she saw." "It's a good thing that no one can leave except through the Gatehouse," said Edward. "How will you explain the civilian deaths and injuries?" "The only civilian death was the caterer, Doris. I guess I'll have to claim that one of her heating elements exploded, killing her and injuring the others. That will explain the burns." Edward said that that was a believable explanation, and then he turned to Donovan.

"Are you all right, son?" asked Edward. Donovan nodded wearily. "What kept you? You missed my wedding." "I know. It turns out that Stone Dragons fly much slower than Great Dragons. We left two days ago and came as fast as we could. I'm sorry we weren't here. We could have helped." "I couldn't hold him," said Donovan sadly, "the Stone Dragon. He eventually broke my shield. If it hadn't been for the others, he would have escaped." "NO!" said Rachel. "You held him long enough for the rest of us to wrap our shields around yours. He was *never* going to escape."

"When you killed the Stone Dragon in Baize, was anyone shooting Blast spells at your shield while you held him?" Edward smiled, "Is that what happened? No, son. There were only three magicians present when I shielded that dragon, and neither James nor Kathy fired a Blast spell at the dragon after I shielded him." "Well, that's some comfort," said Donovan. "Dad, Mage Kathy, this is my wife, Rachel."

Edward smiled and said, "It's a pleasure to meet you, Rachel. Donovan has told us a lot about you. *How are your parents?* Edward asked in sign. "They are uninjured," replied Rachel. "But they are confused and in shock. I told them to go home and that we would explain what happened to them later."

"Why don't you two go get cleaned up? We can take over from here," said Edward. Donovan and Rachel rose unsteadily. Leaning on each other, they limped to the Mentor's dormitory. As they entered, Donovan observed, "You lost your shoe again." Improbably, Rachel laughed.

Chapter Nine:

THE MORNING AFTER

Donovan groaned as he woke the next morning. Every muscle in his body was sore. Rachel rolled over and winced, clearly not in much better shape. "I guess we should get up and see what's happening today," said Donovan. "There's probably still some cleaning up left to do, and we have to find your wayward shoe." They both got up gingerly and headed to the shower. The warm water helped, as did mild Healing spells they conjured for each other.

They left the Mentor's dormitory to a dark and gloomy day. Dark clouds covered the sky and rain fell in buckets. "I guess it's a good thing we got married yesterday," said Rachel. Donovan could only nod. They both erected weather shields and proceeded to the Forces Training Area. Shockingly, the area was clear and there was no evidence that anything at all had happened there just twelve short hours ago. The broken pavilion was gone, as were the chairs, tables, and the altar.

Rachel watched curiously as Donovan roamed around the area, staring at the ground. "What are you doing?" she asked. "I'm looking for your missing shoe," replied Donovan. "You'll never find it now," said

Rachel, "it looks like someone used a Wind spell and swept the entire area. There aren't even any scorch marks left." Suddenly, Donovan stooped and dug in the loose sand with his hands. "Found it!" he said triumphantly.

"How in blazes did you do that?" asked Rachel. "Easy. I put a tracer spell on them as you were walking down the aisle yesterday. Just in case." Rachel frowned, "My beautiful wedding dress, and you were looking at my shoes?" "It only took a second, and I can tell you exactly how many pearls are on that dress, even though that was *not* what I was concentrating on," said Donovan with a smile.

Donovan shook the sand and mud off the shoe and used Wind and Water spells to clean it off. Shoe recovered, Rachel and Donovan headed back to the courtyard, where they found Edward and Kathy sitting on the bench under the Magnolia tree. "Ah! There's the happy couple," said Edward. "How are you two this morning?" "Sore," admitted Donovan, "even more so than after my Sorcerer's Test." "I imagine," replied Edward. "The rigors of combat are much more taxing than even the most arduous test. All testing has a safety element built in to ensure that the subject will survive; in combat, there are no such safeguards."

"So, when are you two leaving?" asked Donovan. "Tonight. I'm sorry it's so soon, but we have to get back to the project. Kathy isn't even supposed to *be* here, in Franconia, I mean," said Edward. Donovan and Rachel sat on the bench next to Edward and Kathy. "Don't forget to pick up your Concealment cloak from the Supply Master before you leave. In fact, if you ask Wizard Noland, he might even authorize one for Mage Kathy," said Donovan.

"An excellent thought! I'm glad you reminded me," said Edward. "So, have there been any *repercussions* from yesterday yet?" asked Rachel. Edward shook his head, "No. Michael notified the student's parents last night, and Major Gerald is taking care of notifying the next of kin of the three soldiers in the Royal Expeditionary Force who were killed. All that's left to do is talk to the caterer's family." "Was she married?" asked Donovan. "No, but her mother still lives in Kingston. It's going to be a difficult conversation for Wizard Noland," said Edward.

"When do you think we'll have to leave for our first assignment?" asked Rachel. "New Sorcerers who are not appointed as Mentors, usually only have a few days to put their affairs in Kingston in order before leaving the Academy. That's entirely up to Wizard Noland." "I guess we should go have a talk with him," said Donovan. "He's talking with Major Gerald right now.

You should probably wait until he's done." "I wonder where Andrew is this morning?" said Donovan.

As if on cue, Andrew came stomping across the courtyard, clearly agitated. "That Supply Master is a moron!" he said. "I went by to see if I could pick up the Concealment cloaks for the other Sorcerers in my squadron, and he refused, saying that they had to be signed for." "If that's the case, it's going to take a long, long time to get them issued to all of the magicians who are spread across Franconia," said Edward. "That's exactly what I told him," said Andrew, "but he still refused!"

"He's probably just following orders. I'll speak to Michael about it this morning. I guess there's no point in trying to get a cloak for Kathy yet; she's undoubtedly not on his list."

They sat quietly for a minute, then Donovan asked, "So, what are your thoughts about what happened yesterday?" Edward said, "Clearly, there are more Changed Ones in Kingston. I admit, I'm surprised that there was a Stone Dragon here, since they're all supposed to be on the other side of the Amber River, but there must be more Changed Ones in the city. I expect Michael to beef up the Kingston Regional Mage's Office, under Mage Curtis and instruct them to increase their efforts to find those in the city with the spark, and any Changed Ones, of course."

"How big is the Regional Mage's Office?" asked Kathy. "It's just a Mage and three Sorcerers, well two now, since I don't think a replacement for Sorcerer Zak has been named yet," replied Edward. "Actually, there's only one Sorcerer, since Sorcerer Chad had his spark removed and is currently serving on a Road Crew," said Donovan. "How did that happen?" asked Edward, shocked. "He tried to kill Judge Toffin after a convicted felon pulled a shiv out of his sock and tried to murder the judge. Sorcerer Chad was busy flirting with the court scribe and was inattentive. Judge Toffin dismissed him from any further court duties. Chad didn't take it well," said Rachel.

"Is that what you got the Special Commendation for?" Edward asked Donovan. "I stopped the convict; Wizard Toffin paralyzed Sorcerer Chad," explained Donovan. "So, now the Kingston Regional Mage's Office only has one Mage and one Sorcerer. I'll need to speak to Michael about that. That is, if he hasn't thought of it already," said Edward.

"We should go check on my parents," said Rachel. "I'm sure they're confused about what happened yesterday, especially my father." "Yes," said Edward, "and you need to impress upon him the need for secrecy.

He was the only person here yesterday that we couldn't put under a Secrecy spell." "Because he's deaf?" asked Rachel. "Correct. I had a brief talk with him before they left, but it would be better coming from the two of you." Rachel nodded, and she and Donovan headed towards the Gatehouse.

After they left, Edward said, "I need to go find a cook in the Royal Expeditionary Force. I promised to try healing a friend of his. Would you like to join me?" Edward asked Kathy. "Well, I'm certainly not going to sit around here alone!" said Kathy. "Let's go." As they left the Gatehouse, Wizard Faith said, "Hello, *Mage* Kathy. It's good to see you again." Kathy blushed. "Sorry for the deception, *Wizard* Faith, but I was unsure how a Baizian Mage would be received in Franconia."

"I understand. If you haven't heard, I removed the Binding spell," said Faith. "I heard, thank you. I did have a close call once. When I got back to Baize, I was accosted by three thugs on the waterfront, and I had to blow them into the sea when they wouldn't leave me alone. I guess the spell decided that it was *justified.*" Faith laughed. "So, where are you two off to?"

"I need to find Corporal Fry of the Royal Expeditionary Force," said Edward. "He has a friend that I promised to heal while we were on our way to Springfield." "Corporal Fry, the cook?" asked Faith.

"The same," said Edward. "He's here," said Faith. "Here, where?" asked Edward. "He's in the Infirmary. He was burned by the dragon after the wedding," said Faith. Edward immediately reversed course and headed for the Academy Infirmary, Kathy following close behind.

When he entered, Edward called out for Margret, the Chief Healer. "Yes, Wizard Edward?" "Where is Corporal Fry from the Royal Expeditionary Force? I understand that he was injured yesterday." "Yes," said Margret, "he's in bed three." "How bad?" asked Edward, fearing the worst. "He was burned on both arms, but not badly," said Margret, "We just kept him overnight for observation to make sure there was no infection." Edward breathed a sigh of relief, "Can I see him?"

"Of course," replied Margret, "right this way." They walked down the row of beds and stopped at a bed on the right side, Corporal Fry was sitting up, insisting that he was fine and that he needed to get back to his command. "Hello, Corporal," said Edward. "Wizard Edward! Am I ever glad to see you! Would you please tell this nurse that I'm fine and I can leave?"

Edward said, "Let me check your injuries first, then we'll see about getting you out of here." Edward examined the cook's arms, which had second-degree burns. They were blistered but had been expertly tended to. Edward reached inside his robe and extracted a vial of Healing Serum. "Here, drink this. It doesn't taste very good, but it should heal your burns immediately."

Corporal Fry looked at the vial suspiciously, then drank it down, grimacing as he did. "Ugh, it tastes like burnt eucalyptus leaves!" said the Corporal. "As it should," replied Edward with a smile. As they watched, the cook's red and blistered arms returned to a normal color, the blisters vanishing as if they had never been there.

"Sir Edward," said Margret disapprovingly, "there was no need to spend a Healing Serum on those burns! They would have healed by themselves in a couple of days!" "I know," said Edward, "but the Corporal is a friend and former comrade, and I have plenty of Healing Serum stored up, some of which is about to expire soon. Are there any other members of the Royal Expeditionary Force in here?" "Only two," said Margret. "Take me to them, please," said Edward, "Corporal, please wait here for a moment. I'll return shortly."

Edward was taken to the two other injured soldiers and he gave them each half a vial of Healing Serum, completely healing their relatively minor wounds and instructing Margret to discharge them so they could return to duty. "Sir Wizard, you know we can't give Healing Serum to every patient who arrives with only minor injuries..." began Margret. Edward forestalled her, "Yes, I know, but I have an affinity for the soldiers of the Royal Expeditionary Force. It was my Serum, so your stocks are still intact. I will inform Wizard Noland of my actions prior to my departure later today. Thank you for your expert care of Donovan. I don't know anyone who could have done a better job." Margret blushed, completely calmed by Edward's kind words.

As they left the Infirmary, Edward asked Corporal Fry to take him to his friend with the burns that Edward had promised to attempt to heal. The Corporal led them to a small shack near the garrison compound. He knocked, and a weak voice told them to enter. The Corporal's friend was seated (uncomfortably) in a wooden rocking chair, a glass of ale on the table beside him.

"Burt, this here's the Wizard I told you about. He's going to try to heal you." Burt started to rise, but Edward waved him back down. "No need to get up, Burt, I know it's painful. How long ago were you burned?" "It's been almost a year since that fool put the flour barrel next to the fire," said Burt. The Palace Healer did what he could, but..." "But he wasn't a magician," finished Edward. "So, first, we're going to try a Healing Serum. This is the strongest I can make, and it's specific to burns. It may not heal everything after so much time, but it will surely help."

Edward handed over the vial of Healing Serum, "Corporal Fry here can tell you that the Serum does not taste good, but it's usually effective." Burt took the vial, smelled it briefly, then drank it down. Burt closed his eyes as the Serum did its work. It took several minutes, and Edward was becoming concerned that it wasn't enough. Then Burt opened his eyes and smiled. "Sir Wizard, I feel good as new! Thank You!" "Just take it easy for a few days, Burt, and stay indoors. It'll be a few days before the healing is complete, so stay out of the sunlight, a sunburn will feel like your skin is on fire. In three days, you should be well enough to go back to work."

"How can I ever repay you?" asked Burt. "Just keep the flour away from the fireplace," replied Edward.

"Have you given any thought to my request for magical support for the Royal Expeditionary Force?" Major Gerald asked Wizard Noland. "I have, and while you're correct that our magical resources are stretched thin at the moment, I had an idea last night that might suit you, but it's a bit unorthodox," said Wizard Noland. "What did 'ya have in mind?" asked Gerald.

"How would you feel if I assigned Sorcerers Donovan and Rachel to your command?" Major Gerald sat back and considered the idea. Donovan was well respected by the soldiers of the Royal Expeditionary Force, even before he became a Sorcerer, but the idea of a woman as a member of his command was new. Wizard Noland continued, "I only offer this because Donovan is an exceptional magician and is a known quantity among the men of the Expeditionary Force. As his *wife*, I dare say that Sorceress Rachel wouldn't have to deal with any unwanted attention from your men, despite being the only woman in the organization."

"And, she did save several of them with her shield yesterday. I can tell you that that act did not go unnoticed by my soldiers. OK! As you said, it's a little unorthodox, but I believe that Donovan and Rachel will make excellent additions to the Royal Expeditionary Force," said Major Gerald. "Then I shall inform them today and have them report to you this coming Endday. I assume it will be alright if they find a house in town?"

"Perfectly OK. All officers, Squad Leaders, Healers and Specialists are permitted to live in their own quarters. It's only the Privates and Corporals that have to stay in the barracks. I'll expect them on Endday.

Thank You." Major Gerald left the Headmaster's cottage and headed back to the garrison, considerably happier than he was when he entered the Academy.

Gek woke to the sound of Richard crying. He shook his head and looked around. "Where is Richard?" he asked out loud. "He's in the back room in an old cradle I fished outta the surf a while back," said Bruce from the kitchen, "and Azure fed him just before she went out to play in the surf with Annalise. His diaper is dry, so just sit here and let him cry." "What?" said Gek, "but he is crying!" "Yes, and all babies cry," said Bruce. "That doesn't mean that you have to rush right over and tend to 'em. I told you, he's not hungry or wet. He's just awake and bored. You need to let him cry himself back to sleep so he learns how. Otherwise, the two of you will never get any rest."

Gek sat back down and asked, "How long have I been asleep?" "About six hours. I told Azure that you had to wake up on your own. You put too much power into healing me. Not that I'm not grateful, but you overdid it." "So, it worked?" "It did indeed," said Bruce, "and I'm very grateful. Now, how about some food?" "Now that you mention it, I am starving!" said Gek.

Bruce laughed, "That's one thing all you dragons have in common; you're always hungry. How about some lamb stew?" "What is a lamb?" asked Gek. "It's a baby sheep," said Bruce. "I figured you might be tired of fish by now."

Gek picked through the stew, eating the meat and skipping the potatoes and other vegetables. The gravy was excellent. After finishing three bowls of stew, Gek sat back and sighed contentedly. "Thank you, Bruce. It has been a while since I had anything but fish, and Azure has been craving some strange fish lately." "That just comes with being pregnant," said Bruce. "Her appetite should return to normal now."

"I sure hope so," said Gek. "I really do not like squid, octopus, or eel." Bruce laughed. Just then, Azura and Anna returned. Anna ran over and started poking Gek with her nose. "Not now, Anna," said Gek. "I will play with you later. Anna seemed to understand, and she walked over to the corner of the room, where she curled up and went to sleep. "Is Richard still asleep?" asked Azure. "He woke up a few minutes ago and started crying. Bruce told me to just let him cry for a while, and he would eventually stop and go back to sleep on his own, which I guess he has," said Gek, just noticing that the baby was no longer crying.

"Do you think I can go in the back without waking him? I need some sleep, too," said Azure, tiredly. "Maybe," said Gek. "If he wakes up, just ignore him, and he should fall back to sleep, right Bruce?" "Right." Azure quietly entered the back room and laid down. She was asleep in minutes.

"So, did you two ever find any more Sea Dragons along the coast?" asked Bruce. "Very few," said Gek quickly. "Although we did not get very far in our search because of Azure being pregnant." "I reckon' I can understand that. How far did you get?" "About halfway between Grotton and Eastport," said Gek. "We found a few Changed Ones, but not many Dragons." "I'm not surprised," said Bruce. "Well, since you two seem to have this under control for the time being, I got to go look for some more driftwood. I'll be back by nightfall." Bruce left the shack and headed back down the beach, looking for driftwood, which seemed to be his only hobby.

Gek sat and wondered; *What were they going to do now? He could not just leave Azure and the twins with Bruce and go off to fight the humans, but he needed to do something! Well, the next Dragon Council was in a couple of weeks; he could decide what to do then.*

Rachel and Donovan entered her father's shop and found him working on Concealment cloaks for the Academy. *Are you all right?* Rachel signed. *I am uninjured,* he replied. *How are you two? We are well,* signed Rachel. *Do you want to talk about yesterday?* Brian put down his work and said, *I do not understand. How could a dragon get into the Wizards Academy?*

Rachel looked at Donovan, and he shrugged. "We should probably just tell him," he said. Rachel said, "We should probably tell them both." Donovan nodded his agreement, and Rachel went upstairs to find her mother. *That was a beautiful dress you made,* Donovan signed. *Thank you. It is something I've been working on for several years,* signed Mr. Turner.

When Rachel returned with her mother, she signed, *We need to explain what happened yesterday. We have discovered that dragons can change themselves into humans. One of the caterer's assistants was a dragon, masquerading as a human, what we call a 'Changed One.' When Donovan detected him and yelled, "Dragon!" the dragon transformed from a human, back into a dragon and attacked.* Rachel paused her explanation to ensure her parents understood.

You mean that some of the people in Kingston are actually dragons in disguise? asked Mr. Turner. *Yes, but we do not know how many there may be. It's probably a very small number,* signed Rachel. "Why have we not been told about this by the crown?" asked Rachel's mother. Mr. Turner pointed his finger emphatically in agreement. "Because it would cause a panic," said Donovan. "Imagine what would happen if everyone suspected their neighbor of being a dragon in disguise."

"How did you detect the dragon?" asked Rachel's mother. "I smelled him," said Donovan. "Dragons have a sort of *reptilian* smell." *Yes. I have smelled it before,* signed Mr. Turner. *You have? Where?* Asked Donovan. *Oh, here and there about town. There were several students I met yesterday that had that smell too,* signed Mr. Turner. *Yes,* signed Rachel, *there were ten students at the Academy who are Changed Ones. You allow them in the Academy?* asked Mr. Turner. *Yes, but they are under a Binding spell, never to transform back into a dragon and never to injure a human. One of the Changed Ones died yesterday, defending his students.*

How long have you known about this? he asked. *Several months,* signed Rachel. *I'm sorry that I couldn't tell you.* Mr. Turner nodded his understanding. *I'm sorry he ruined your wedding.*

He did not ruin our wedding, signed Donovan. **He ruined the reception**.

When they returned to the Academy, Andrew was waiting for them, and he was in a much better mood. "Wizard Noland ordered the Supply Master to let me sign for the cloaks for the rest of the magicians in my squadron. He also issued one to Mage Kathy. That means that I have to leave now. I need to get back to the ship in case the Sea Dragons change their minds," said Andrew.

"Take care of yourself," said Donovan. "Look us up the next time you're in Fairview." Andrew smiled, "You're not going to Fairview. Wizard Noland has something else in mind for you two." "What?" asked Donovan and Rachel together. "I guess you'll just have to ask him. It's not my news to tell. Anyway, I'm headed to the boat dock to make the Change and be on my way. I'm sure I'll see you soon." Donovan and Andrew embraced briefly, and Rachel gave him a kiss on the cheek. "Goodbye, take care," she said. Andrew nodded, slung his seabag over his shoulder and headed toward the Academy boat dock.

"I guess we should go find Wizard Noland and find out where we're going and when we have to be there," said Donovan. They headed over to the Headmaster's cottage, and as usual, the door opened before they got there. "Come in, you two. Did you see Andrew before he left?" "Yes, Sir, he just left, heading for the boat dock," said Rachel. "Well, sit down. We have much to discuss." Donovan and Rachel sat side-by-side on the sofa, and Wizard Noland said, "I've decided to change your assignments. Instead of going to Fairview, I'm assigning you both to the Royal Expeditionary Force."

As evening fell, Edward and Kathy made their way to the boat dock. When Edward opened the portal, they found Donovan and Rachel sitting on the bench near the boats. "Ah, there you are! We wondered where you two had gotten off to. We looked for you but were afraid you were still in town, and we wouldn't get to say 'goodbye.'" "Have you heard about our new assignments?" asked Donovan.

"Yes, and I think they're inspired," said Edward. "The Royal Expeditionary Force has been lacking organic magical support for years. Before the dragon, Major Gerald never believed that he needed any; now he can't envision going out without a magician." "But I'll be the only woman in the Force!" said Rachel. "Just as Sorceress Anne is the only woman in the Royal Navy, and Wizard Cassandra is the first woman to be appointed Court Wizard. Times are changing," said Edward.

"I'm just not sure this is a good idea," said Rachel. "Let me ask you a couple of questions," said Edward. "First, are you worried about the men in the Force treating you badly because you're a woman? Or are you worried that your husband will do something foolish to protect you if your life is threatened?" "Probably a little bit of both," confessed Rachel. "I thought so," said Edward. "First, if someone treats you badly, *you are a Sorceress!* You deal with it! You don't go running to Donovan or Major Gerald! The soldiers will understand and respect that. Second, if the situations are reversed, and Donovan's life is threatened, what would you do to protect him?" "Anything," said Rachel. "Exactly! Being married gives you both extra incentive to protect each other and the soldiers of the Royal Expeditionary Force."

"Another thing, Donovan, you have treated Major Gerald as a confidant and a friend in the past. That relationship is about to change. He is about to become your commanding officer. You do not question his orders in front of his men. You may make suggestions, but only in private, and whatever he decides, goes. Do you understand?" Donovan nodded. "Now, I understand that you will report for duty on Endday. You'll be permitted to stay in your own house when the Royal Expeditionary Force is in garrison in Kingston. You may live in my house if you wish, or find someplace of your own. I know that newlyweds often want to find a house of their own. As a wedding present, you may take twenty golds from my savings under the laundry tub."

"Please magically lock my door when you leave. We may not be back for a while," finished Edward. Without another word, Edward and Kathy began to disrobe. Donovan and Rachel turned their backs. Once both of them were in Great Dragon form, Donovan said, "Hurry back and keep us posted. We'll try not to be late for *your* wedding."

Senior Specialist Dirk

Chapter Ten:

TRANSITIONS

“If you want me to change into a dragon, we’d better go outside. Otherwise, I’ll destroy your office, Admiral,” said Sorceress Celeste. “A wise precaution,” said Admiral Cross. Celeste followed the Admiral and Mage Charles into the courtyard of the Navy Headquarters complex. It was fairly deserted at this early hour, but there were still a few officers and other civilian employees occupying the benches that were scattered around the open grassy area. “Admiral, I’d recommend clearing the courtyard. You may not want everyone to witness this,” said Celeste.

“Quite right,” said the Admiral, “Mage Charles, would you handle that, please?” Mage Charles murmured a spell to enhance his voice and then shouted, “CLEAR THE COURTYARD!” Charles’ booming voice rattled the windows and sent everyone scurrying inside. “All yours, Celeste.” Celeste moved to the center of the courtyard and asked, “Could I trouble you two to turn your backs for a moment? You see, if I change into a dragon now, I’ll destroy these human clothes. Frankly, that’s why I’m wearing this sailor’s outfit because I destroyed my dress when I transformed at the Wizards Academy. Also, when I change back, I’ll be naked, which amused the crew of the HMS VALOR, despite their amazement at a dragon changing into a woman." Both the Admiral and Mage Charles smiled at this information, but they both obliged Celeste and turned their backs while she disrobed.

A moment later, Celeste said, "OK, you can turn around now." The Admiral and the Mage turned around, and their mouths fell open. Before them stood a 40-foot-long blue-green Sea Dragon. "Celeste?" asked Mage Charles, tentatively. "Yes, Mage Charles, it is still me." The Admiral circled the dragon, examining the wings, the claws and the scales. "So, this is what a Sea Dragon looks like," said the Admiral. "Yes, Admiral. I can also change into a Great Dragon if you like." The admiral nodded, and Celeste reared up on her hind legs and clapped her forelegs together; the Sea Dragon *shimmered*, then, with a flash of light, transformed into a much bigger, golden-scaled Great Dragon.

"Are all Great Dragons bigger than Sea Dragons?" asked Mage Charles. "I think so," replied Celeste, "but I can only transform into ones that I have seen. May I change back into human form now? I think I am attracting attention." "Of course," said Admiral Cross. Celeste waited. "Oh, right," said Mage Charles, turning his back. Celeste transformed back into human form and dressed quickly. When she was done, she said, "I understand that there are also red Fire Dragons, grey or black Stone Dragons, and white or light-grey Snow Dragons. I've never seen one of them, so I can't transform into one yet."

"Incredible," said the Admiral. "Let's go back to my office. We need to talk." "Of course, Sir. Might I suggest that Mage Charles remain in the courtyard and cast a few Seemings of dragons for a few minutes? That might provide a plausible explanation for anyone who witnessed my Change spells." "An excellent thought! Mage Charles, if you would?" "Of course, Sir. I'll be in in a few minutes."

Mage Charles proceeded to produce Seemings of Dragons in the courtyard, then dissolve them by touching them. They vanished in flashes of light. He hoped that the deception worked; the last thing they needed was the dragons finding out that human magicians had learned how to change into dragons.

When he arrived back at the Admiral's office, Celeste and the Admiral were having tea. "I hope you understand why I had you placed in a holding cell when I heard what I thought was an outlandish story about your having a message from Commodore Matthews," said the Admiral. "I understand completely, Admiral, and it was a wise precaution. These dragons are cunning, but I have found that some of them can be reasoned with," said Celeste.

"So, how is it that you were able to change into a Sea Dragon in the first place?" asked the Admiral. Celeste hesitated, then told the Admiral the whole story about escorting Gek to the Academy, the crash, and the meeting with Azure. The Admiral listened closely, then nodded. He thought for a moment, then said, "Sorceress, I would like to offer you the newly created position of Official Dragon Messenger to the Royal Navy. It will take some time to get the word to all of the Royal Navy, but I can send out Messenger Hawks today, to inform the other squadrons."

"I would be happy to serve in such a capacity, Sir, but I would have to clear it with Wizard Noland. He's in charge of all magical appointments in Franconia. And I still have to deliver a copy of the draft Peace Treaty to the King, but I will certainly ask him when I return to Kingston," said Celeste.

"Excellent!" exclaimed the Admiral, "And, since we have two Fleets, it might be best if we had two Dragon Messengers, one for each Fleet. Please ask Wizard Noland if there are any other magicians who can make the change and would be willing to serve in this capacity." "I will certainly pass on your request, Sir. Now, if it's not too much trouble, is there somewhere I can get a few hours of sleep today? I only travel at night in dragon-form so as not to alarm the people."

"Your Majesty, Snow Dragons have attacked the town of Snowton!" said James, the newly-appointed Court Wizard of Baize. "Snow Dragons?" asked King Donald. "That's the report, Sire. Apparently, they attacked just after dawn a week ago, scattering the townsfolk and routing the Third Infantry Company, whose weapons were useless against these ice-breathing creatures," said James.

"What were the casualties?" asked the King, dreading the answer. "Five dead and a dozen wounded, Sire, most with frostbite." "So few? How did so many of the townsfolk survive the attack?" asked the King. "It seems that a golden Great Dragon entered the fray shortly after it began and attacked the Snow Dragons, driving them off before they could do significant damage to the town." "Why would a Great Dragon attack his Snow Dragon cousins?" asked King Donald, confused.

"Sorcerer Fredrick with the 3rd Infantry reported that the Great Dragon was actually a Franconian Sorcerer, named Donovan, who had changed into a Great Dragon to help his father, Wizard Edward, conduct a survey of the northern edge of the Great Salt Flats. While he was flying along the north edge of the Salt Flats, Donovan heard Snowton's alarm bell and went to investigate. He allegedly killed six of the Snow Dragons and wounded one or two others before they withdrew back into the Snow Fields," said James.

"How did Sorcerer Fredrick determine this?" asked the amazed King. "Donovan was wounded in the battle, Sire. One of the Snow Dragons clawed his face. After the Snow Dragons fled, Donovan landed in the town square, transformed back into a human and began using Heat spells to remove the ice from the buildings in town, freeing the inhabitants. Sorcerer Fredrick healed Donovan's wounds as best he could."

"Incredible! Please draft me a letter, thanking King Henry for his Sorcerer's assistance. Edward never told us that Franconian magicians knew how to change into dragons. I wonder why he failed to mention it," mused the King. "Sire, if you recall, Wizard Edward was very reluctant to divulge the existence of crossbows until we told him we had one. It may be that he didn't tell us everything he knew, or maybe this is a recently discovered talent," said Wizard James.

"We could always ask Mage Kathy. If Edward's son knows how to transform into a dragon, and he was present at the dig site, then Kathy may know something useful." "You're right, of course," said the King.

"Please send a Messenger Hawk to Springfield and ask Mage Kathy what she knows about this incident. That should be enlightening." James composed the message and sent it immediately. It read:

Mage Kathy,

I have received reports of a Snow Dragon attack on Snowton. Sorcerer Fredrick reported that the Snow Dragons were driven off by a Great Dragon, which turned out to be Wizard Edward's son, Donovan. I was under the impression that Donovan was still a student at the Franconian Wizards Academy, and I had no idea that Franconian magicians knew how to change into dragons. I would like to know what you know about this attack and this remarkable ability that allows magicians to transform into dragons.

Donald, King of Baize

"What about this one?" asked Donovan. "It's too close to the marketplace and too noisy," replied Rachel. Donovan sighed. This was the fifth house they had looked at, and all of them had been "too something" for

Rachel. "Too small," "too close to the neighbors," the kitchen was "too small," or the house was "too close to her parent's house." Rachel was looking for the "perfect" place, and Donovan was afraid that they wouldn't be able to find it in three days (which was all the time they had).

It was fortunate that Donovan had been able to cast a Seeing spell to find all of the houses for sale or for rent in Kingston. Otherwise, they would have had no chance, but after crossing out the houses in the "wrong" neighborhoods, they were rapidly running out of options, and his map was a mess of red ink that would have to be cleaned up later. "How about this one?" Donovan asked, pointing at a cottage on the outskirts of town, near the river.

"Hmm," said Rachel. "The area looks OK. I don't know if the sound of the river will be soothing or annoying, but I guess we could go take a look." They rode out and found a small, cozy cottage with two bedrooms, a dining/living room with a fireplace, an ample kitchen, plenty of storage space, and a small stable for their horses. It wasn't as nice as their room at the Academy, but it was the best they had seen. "How much?" Donovan asked the seller. "Well, for a nice young couple like you, thirty golds, and it's all yours." Donovan started to agree, but Rachel cut in, "We'll give you Twenty golds, and the furniture stays." "Twenty-five golds, and you keep the furniture," said the man.

"For twenty-five, we get the furniture and a load of fresh-cut firewood," countered Rachel. "Done. When do you want to move in?" "How about tomorrow?" asked Donovan. The man smiled, "Meet me here at noon tomorrow and we'll get everything signed and legal," said the man, extending his hand. "You have a deal," said Donovan. "I'll bring the gold tomorrow."

The seller waved and mounted his mule, heading back into town. "We may have overpaid," said Rachel, "and *you* are a terrible negotiator." "I know," sighed Donovan, "it comes from having easy access to coins. I never really had to consider the cost of things growing up. I had everything provided for me." "Well, *those* days are over, Mister Moneybags. We no longer have your father's coins to rely on, and I'm not even sure how much we get paid each month as Sorcerers in the Royal Expeditionary Force," said Rachel.

"Nobody knows because we've never had a Sorcerer assigned to us before," said Dirk, lowering the hood of his Concealment cloak. Rachel jumped and started to raise a shield, but Donovan grabbed her hand before she could complete the gesture. "Hello, Dirk. You ever scare my wife like that again, and I'll turn you into a toad," said Donovan jovially.

"Sorry, I thought you knew I was here," said Senior Specialist Dirk, the Assassin/Scout for the 1st Company of the Royal Expeditionary Force. "I did," said Donovan, "but I think Rachel was focused on the size of the closets. Rachel, this impetuous fellow is Senior Specialist Dirk, he's the 1st Company's Specialist. You've already met Specialist Lance from 2nd Company." *It's nice to meet you, Sorceress. I apologize for startling you,* said Dirk in sign language. *No matter. I'm sure I'll be able to return the favor soon enough,* replied Rachel in sign. *Does everyone in the Expeditionary Force know sign language?* signed Donovan. "No. As far as I know, only Lance, Major Gerald and I are proficient, but we're teaching Corporal Knox," said Dirk.

"So, what were you doing following us?" asked Donovan. "Well, I knew that you two would be looking for a house today, so I decided to tag along and see what you came up with. Then I could look very smart later by telling you that I knew where you lived. By the way, I think you made an excellent choice. That last place was a dump!" Rachel laughed. "I think I'm going to like you, Senior Specialist Dirk."

The following day at noon, Donovan and Rachel signed the Deed and became first-time homeowners. After handing over the twenty-five golds, Donovan asked for the key. "Key? There ain't no key! What do you think this is, some wealthy merchant's manor? There's a latch on the door. That's all most folks need. If you want a lock installed, you'll have to talk to the locksmith in town. Well, good luck to you!"

Donovan seethed, but Rachel said, "Let's get our things unloaded from the cart and we'll just use an Adhesive spell until we can get a real lock installed. They spent the rest of Foursday unloading their belongings and arranging the house to their satisfaction. When they were done, Donovan asked, "Do you want to eat one last meal in the Mentor's dining room? Starting tomorrow we have to start cooking our own food, and I can tell you, I cook about as well as I negotiate."

"We might as well," said Rachel. "Besides, we still have to remove our names from our doors and check out with Wizard Noland. In fact, why don't we just Adhere up this place and spend one last night at the Academy? The shower in my room is certainly much nicer than the one in this cottage, and *that,* my dear, is your first home improvement project." They returned to the Academy, and Donovan made a final check of his Level Three room to make sure he wasn't leaving anything behind. Then he removed his name from the door plate using a Remove spell and headed over to the room he'd been sharing with Rachel in the Mentor's dormitory.

Dinner was uninspiring, but at least they didn't have to cook it themselves. They turned in early and awoke refreshed. After a quick shower, they headed down to the dining room for breakfast. All of the Mentors were there to wish them well, and the food was excellent. After breakfast, Rachel returned to her room and removed her name from the door plate. "I guess that's it then," said Donovan. All we need to do is say our farewells to the faculty, and we can be on our way.

As they exited the Mentor's dormitory, all of the Wizard faculty was assembled to bid them farewell. They came forward one at a time, gave them words of encouragement and told them to come back anytime if they had a question or needed help with something. Wizard Toffin presented each of them with two vials of Healing Serum, Truth Serum, and Stamina Serum, in a carved, decorative chest. "I hope you will not need any of this anytime soon. Remember, it will only last for–" "Six months, if stored in a cool, dark place," Donovan and Rachel finished.

Finally, Wizard Noland walked them to the Gatehouse. Outside, Donovan's horse Stam, and the Chestnut, Ginger, favored by Rachel, were saddled and waiting. "A final gift from the Academy," said Wizard Noland. He then presented Donovan with an elaborately carved truncheon. "You are not a Mage yet, but in order to conjure the Seeing spell on a map, you will need this." After they had mounted, Noland stepped back, raised his right hand, and said formally, "Go forth in strength, Sorcerer Donovan Francis and Sorceress Rachel Francis, serve the Kingdom above all personal desires, and return to us when you are prepared to test for the rank of Mage." With that, Noland turned abruptly, entered the Gatehouse, and closed the door firmly.

They rode quickly to the Kingston garrison, where the Royal Expeditionary Force was billeted when they were in the city. They dismounted and tied their mounts to the hitching post, then proceeded inside to find Major Gerald in his office. "Sorcerer Donovan Francis and Sorceress Rachel Francis reporting for duty, Sir," said Donovan. "Come in and shut the door, please," said Gerald. "First of all, welcome! The Royal Expeditionary Force has never had organic magical support before, and that was a serious oversight on my part, that I'm only too happy to correct."

"Donovan, I know that you're familiar with how the Royal Expeditionary Force is organized, but I'll refresh your memory and explain it to Sorceress Rachel. The Force has two identical companies, a Captain commands each company, which consists of three eight-man squads, each led by a Senior Sergeant. The entire force is mounted. The first squad in each company are all bowmen, with short swords for close-in work; second squads are all swordsmen with long swords, shields an' daggers. The third squad in each company has two axmen, two spearmen, one of whom is the cook, a Healer, the best archer in the company, and a Senior Specialist. Each company carries extra spears, arrows, crossbows an' other gear in their wagon with the food and other supplies. You two will ride in your own wagon or on your mounts, depending on the situation, as you see fit."

"While the Force is officially stationed here in Kingston, we're seldom here. The King sends us out to wherever there's trouble. In fact, as soon as he returns from Southport, I expect to receive orders to deploy somewhere, probably somewhere close to Baize, if I had to guess. Donovan, I'm assigning you to 2nd Company, and Rachel, you will provide magical support to 1st Company. Most of the troops are off today, but we'll resume field exercises on Firstday. I assume you both have Concealment cloaks?" Both Rachel and Donovan nodded.

"Very good. Tomorrow, you'll be issued the Concealment blankets for your mounts. As far as your pay goes, you'll each be paid the same as the two company commanders, which is five silvers a week, payable twice monthly. I'd appreciate it if you didn't let anyone know your pay. The only people who are paid more are myself and the two Senior Specialists. Rachel, have you met them yet?"

Rachel said, "Yes, I met Senior Specialist Lance some months ago, after you returned from Springfield, and I met Dirk when we purchased our house on Midweek. He startled me, and Donovan threatened to change him into a toad if he did it again." Gerald smiled, "Ha! That'll teach him!" "Not really," said Rachel, looking at the corner of the room, "right Dirk?" Dirk lowered his hood, looked at Donovan and smiled, "She wasn't startled, so no need for any frog spells." "Dirk! What are you doing here?" asked Major Gerald.

"I thought I'd take the Sorceress around and introduce her to the rest of 1st Company, Sir," said Dirk diplomatically. Major Gerald grunted his disbelief but said, "Good idea. Why don't you two head out? I need a word with Sorcerer Donovan." Rachel and Dirk left the office and headed over to the area where Second Company was billeted. Once they left, Major Gerald said, "I take it that your father and Mage Kathy have returned to Baize?"

"Yes, Sir. They left the day after the wedding," replied Donovan. "Anyway, the reason I wanted to speak to you alone, is that Sorceress Rachel, *your wife,* is the only woman in the Royal Expeditionary Force. I'm sure that she's a competent magician, but this may be a difficult assignment for her. Being your wife will help because everyone in the Force likes and respects you, and no one would do anything to cross you. No hazing, or initiations or any of that nonsense. However, if problems arise, Rachel has to solve them herself, you understand?"

"Yes, Sir. My father told us something like that before he left. Good. Now, there is a *perception* among some of the Royal Guard that magicians are aloof and think they're better than everyone else because they can do magic. Your father overcame that stereotype by being kind and helpful to everyone. I expect you and Rachel to follow his example."

"We'll do our best, Sir. One question, how do we address everyone?" "A very good start. You call the Company commanders "captain" or "sir," the Sergeants "Sergeant," and the Healers "Healer." You call me Sir or Major." You can call Dirk and Lance by their first names. Everyone will call you Sorcerer Donovan or Sir, and your wife Sorceress Rachel or Ma'am, unless you give them permission to just use your first names, which I wouldn't advise for the first month or so. We need to get the men to think of you as 'Sorcerer Donovan,' not just 'Donovan, Sir Edward's son.'"

"Anything else we should know, Sir?" "Yes, while in garrison, you can dine in the Officer's Mess. It's a lot better than our field rations, and you'll run out of coin pretty fast if you decide to cook your own food every meal." Dinner is at six, breakfast is at six, and lunch is generally at midday. I would recommend eating in the mess as often as you can. Once Rachel returns, you are released for Endday activities. Be in the courtyard ready to ride at seven tomorrow morning."

Edward and Kathy landed half a mile outside of the campsite an hour before sunset. With Kathy transforming into a Great Dragon, they made much better time returning than they did going to the Wizards Academy, despite the headwind. As they walked into the camp, they heard the cooks preparing dinner for the second shift amid the threatening rumble of thunder.

"Well, we knew it wouldn't last forever. I guess we'll find out today what happens when we get heavy rain. I hope the Inspection Team made good progress on melting the sand into glass on the inside of the trench while we were away," said Edward. Kathy yawned and said, "I say we let Elianna or Timothy take the food to third shift while we get some rest. It's been a long night and a long couple of days. We can check on the trench after the storm passes."

"Good idea," agreed Edward. Why don't you head for our tent, and I'll just inform Elianna or Timothy. This looks to be a real gully-washer, I think I'll just have them bring second shift in, and we'll wait this storm out. We're *way* ahead of schedule anyway. I just hope this storm doesn't set us back too much." Kathy headed off to their tent, and Edward walked over to the kitchen where the cooks were just finishing up the dinner meal. The cooks were looking at the sky with concern.

"Once you finish getting dinner prepared, button down the kitchen and head for your tents," said Edward. "I'm going to bring second shift in until this storm passes." The kitchen staff looked relieved and very appreciative. "We'll be done in just a few minutes, Sir. Thank you," said the senior cook. Edward walked over to the wagon where Wizard Timothy was waiting, "Hello, Tim. I see you held off the rain until we returned." "Welcome back, Edward! How was the trip and the wedding?" asked Wizard Timothy.

"Stone Dragons fly so slowly that it would almost have been faster to ride a horse," replied Edward. "We missed the wedding and got to the Wizards Academy just in time to help clean up the aftermath of a dragon attack." "How could a dragon get into the Wizards Academy? I thought that place was shielded." "It is, but one of the caterer's assistants was a Stone Dragon Changed One. Donovan detected him during the reception, just before he transformed and attacked. There were ten killed and about fifty wounded before Donovan could get a shield around the beast and suffocate him," explained Edward. "HAH! Like father, like son, I guess," said Timothy. "Well, Donovan was the only one who knew the best way to kill a Stone Dragon. What he didn't count on was all of the other magicians firing blast spells and hurling rocks at the dragon, striking the outside of Donovan's shield. Fortunately, some of the Academy faculty realized what Donovan was trying to do and reinforced his shield. It was apparently a close call."

"I'm sorry to hear that, Edward. Was anyone close to you killed or injured?" "No, just one of Donovan's former Mentors, Sorcerer Terry. Terry was actually a Fire Dragon Changed One. He defended his students and was killed in the process. If he'd been able to transform back into a Fire Dragon, he might have survived, but we placed a Binding spell on him that prevented that." Just then, a clap of thunder boomed.

"Tim, why don't you just head out and bring second shift back in until this storm passes. We're way ahead of schedule, and this looks like a big storm. I told the cooks to just set dinner aside. You'll need the room in the wagon," said Edward. "An excellent idea! I'll leave right now." Timothy climbed up onto the driver's seat and got the skittish horses moving. Neither of them looked very happy to be pulling a wagon into the approaching storm.

As Wizard Timothy was leaving the camp, Mage Elianna came in with a wagon full of very grateful young magicians. "I heard the storm approaching and thought I'd bring in the teams to wait it out," she said. "Excellent thinking!" said Edward. "Dinner is ready. They can pick it up from the kitchens and eat in their tents. We'll just hunker down and wait out the storm. I need one or both of you to stay awake and watch for any damage from the storm. I'm going to my tent to try and get some sleep."

As Edward approached his tent, he found Frank at his post, looking worried. "Frank, head back to your tent. No one is going to bother us during this storm." Frank nodded his thanks and sprinted away, just as the first raindrops began to fall.

The storm lasted for two full days. The wind howled, tents flooded, tent poles snapped, Canvas was ripped from latrines, and campfires were impossible to light. It was fortunate that the camp was inhabited almost entirely by magicians. Flooded tents were immediately dried, tent poles and canvas repaired, Seemings (which were unaffected by weather) were erected around the latrines to provide privacy, and Edward, Timothy, Kathy and Elianna erected Weather shields around the kitchens so the cooks could prepare hot meals, even in the driving rain.

On the third day, the clouds broke, and the sun rose above the Great Salt Flats like a giant orange ball. The temperature soared, and the humidity made it feel like a sauna. "I guess we should go check on the trench," said Edward. "Timothy, keep everyone here. Have the students make any necessary repairs to the camp; we'll resume digging at noon with first shift. Elianna, Kathy and I will be back as soon as we check on the walls and the trench."

They rode quickly to the eastern edge of the trench. From a distance, they could see that the walls were still standing. When they arrived at the northern-most section of the trench, they could see that the thirty-foot deep trench had about fifteen feet of water in it but that the walls had held and, while some of the melted sand had slid a little ways towards the trench, it had not fallen in, and there was very little sand in the trench. The greatest damage was to the surveyed outline of the reservoir. The rain had wiped the survey line off the ground, and sand and salt had spread beyond where the line had been.

"Now I see first-hand how the Salt Flats keep expanding," said Edward. "No matter, we'll keep driving north along the line we had. We need to get the surveyors back out here. I'm sure they'll be disappointed. They were almost finished. Hopefully, the lines on the west side are undisturbed, since all the water flowed in this direction. Let's go check the south trench."

The southern trench had more water in it. About five feet more, but the walls were holding. It seemed that the Inspection Team had not been able to melt all of the sand along the southern trench, and where they left off, the inner walls of the trench had collapsed, sending sand and salt down into the trench. "We'll need to Remove this sand," said Edward, "and re-establish the inner wall. From now on, we melt sand as we Dig." Like the eastern section, sand and salt had advanced beyond the surveyed lines for the trench.

"This wasn't really unexpected," said Edward. "But I was surprised by how intense and how long the rain lasted. It's all right. Once we get this trench and wall system built, we won't have to worry about this again." "What about the water in the trenches?" asked Kathy. "In this heat, it will evaporate in a few days," replied Edward. "I don't want to spend any time evaporating it with magic. We need to keep digging and erecting these walls. At the rate we're going, it should only take us another five weeks or so to finish the three sides of the trench. Then we can start excavating the middle."

"Gek, the baby wants you." "Which one?" asked Gek, groggily. "It is Annalise this time," said Azure wearily. "It is the middle of the night," said Gek. "What could she possibly want now?" "She should not be hungry. Maybe she just needs to go outside and relieve herself. Just take her outside and try not to wake Bruce. I think he is getting tired of the constant walks and feedings." "Him and me both," grumbled Gek. Gek was in Dragon form, so he had to transform and put on his ragged clothes. They had already discovered that trying to creep through the house quietly in Dragon form just did not work. They invariably knocked over a lamp or a chair or a table, waking everyone in the hut in the process.

Gek scooped up Anna in his arms (a task that was becoming increasingly difficult as the baby Dragon grew) and headed for the door. They managed to get outside without waking Bruce or Richard (a rare feat) and proceeded down to the shore. Annalise rushed ahead, splashing happily in the surf. Gek sat on the sand, watching his daughter play. The gibbous moon shone brightly, illuminating the area and reminding Gek that the next Dragon Council was only a few days away. He would need to be leaving soon.

Gek was roused from his thoughts by Annalise's growling. She had found a sand crab that had emerged from the sand to change position on the beach as the tide ebbed. Anna pounced, grabbing the unfortunate sand crab in her jaws and crunching it like a cracker. "Anna, NO," whispered Gek softly as he rushed to her side. Too late. The baby Dragon swallowed the crab, shell and all and romped down the beach looking for more. Five crabs later, Anna returned to Gek's side, looking very pleased with herself. "Well, mommy will be pleased that you are eating solid food. I just hope you can digest crab shells," said Gek. "Are you ready to go back inside?"

While Anna could not speak yet, she was gaining an understanding of what was asked of her at an alarming rate. Gek could only hope that Richard would mature as fast. The diaper-changing routine was getting old quickly, and Bruce had warned them that once he started eating solid foods, it would get more unpleasant.

Gek scooped her up and carried her to the back room where they slept and plopped her down on the dirt floor next to Azure. "Any problems?" asked Azure sleepily. "No. She just ran around in the surf and then started eating sand crabs," said Gek softly. "Really? Maybe she is ready for solid foods!" "Maybe, we will see how she does. I expect an unusual day today."

Gek rolled back up in the sand-covered blanket and tried to get comfortable. He was sure that Richard was going to be awake soon, which would undoubtedly wake Anna. *It sure would be nice for them both to sleep through the night once,* thought Gek as he drifted off to sleep.

Chapter Eleven:

AND ALL THE SHIPS AT SEA

ndrew landed back on the deck of the HMS VALOR with a "Thump." He still wasn't used to flying (and landing) as a Sea Dragon. At least no one had fired at him. A crossbow bolt, fired at close range, could kill a Sea Dragon, and Andrew didn't even want to think about the damage a Seabow bolt would cause. After quickly changing back into human form and putting on his clothes, he carried his parcel down to his cabin and unwrapped the four new Concealment cloaks. Separating his from the rest, he hung his inside-out in his small closet and headed out to find the Commodore.

He ran into him almost immediately. "Andrew! Welcome back! How was the wedding?" asked Commodore Matthews. "It was the most exciting one ever," replied Andrew. "But we really could have done without the party crasher." "Party crasher?" "Yes. A Stone Dragon Changed One infiltrated the Wizards Academy posing as a caterer, in all the excitement of the wedding, no one noticed until my cousin, Sorcerer Donovan, the groom, smelled him and yelled, 'Dragon!'

The dragon transformed and started wreaking havoc. You'd think that a hundred magicians could have handled one Stone Dragon quickly, but we had ten killed and about fifty wounded before we were able to take it down."

"Why was it so hard to kill?" asked the Commodore. "The Stone Dragon's scales were incredibly hard," said Andrew, "I doubt that a normal crossbow would penetrate deep enough to cause serious injury. The Seabow might be more effective, but there wasn't one handy; besides, none of the wedding guests were armed. We all tried using Blast spells or blowing rocks at it, but nothing was working." "So, how did you finally manage to kill the beast?" "Donovan put a shield around it," replied Andrew, still amazed at the idea. "A shield? How would that kill a dragon?" asked the Commodore. "Donovan put the shield *all the way around* the dragon. Eventually, the dragon used up all the breathable air inside the shield, and the dragon suffocated." "That actually worked?" "Surprisingly well, actually. You see, with the shield around it, the dragon's fire couldn't reach us, and the fire burned up the air inside the shield very quickly. The dragon also couldn't bite anything or slash us with its talons or tail," explained Andrew. "It's a good thing that Donovan thought of using a shield then," said Commodore Matthews.

"He got the idea from his father, Wizard Edward, who killed a Stone Dragon using a shield in the King's palace in Baize." The Commodore looked at Andrew suspiciously. "Now, what would a Franconian Wizard be doing in the palace in Baize?" "It's a long story," said Andrew. "My uncle went to Baize to convince King Donald not to attack Franconia. He believes that the dragon's plan is to get Baize and Franconia to go to war, then they'll attack us both after we've bloodied each other."

The Commodore considered this idea for several minutes, then said, "He might be right. Still, that's taking a heck of a risk. Did it work?" "I think so. At least, Baize is withdrawing some of their troops from the border. I think Wizard Edward may be on to something, I mean, all of the attacks on our ships have been by dragons. I don't believe that we've ever been attacked by Baizian warships." "That's true," mused the Commodore. "Well, as you said, you've certainly had an exciting couple of days. While you were gone, we completed repairs on the three remaining ships in the Squadron and have started making some more Seabows. Sorceress Anne is very good at repairing ships, by the way. I think the crew is really beginning to like and respect her."

"I'm glad to hear that sir. As soon as we can, we need to spread the word to the rest of the fleet magicians about the best way to kill a Stone Dragon. I know we haven't been attacked by any yet, but that could change at any time." "You're right about that. This truce only applies to the Sea Dragons. The dragons we negotiated with made that clear enough. I wonder why we haven't had to deal with the Fire, Stone or Snow Dragons yet."

"According to Wizard Noland, the Fire and Stone Dragons should only be living on the west side of the Amber River. Of course, the fact that one got into the Wizards Academy means that that may not be the case anymore," said Andrew. "And I understand that the Snow Dragons seldom venture far from the Snow Fields, so unless we sail much farther north, we shouldn't see any of them."

The Commodore grunted, "And a good thing, too. Sea Dragons are bad enough. A fire-breathing dragon could flame our sails, and we'd be dead in the water. So, Andrew, do you feel like taking another flight to Grotton this evening?" Andrew grimaced, "Sir, I'm pretty tired right now. Flying is not as easy as it looks. You have to flap your wings *every damn second,* or you start to fall, and being so big, dragons fall really *fast*. It might be better to send Sorceress Anne—give her some practice at using the Change spell."

"You think she can do it?" "Absolutely. It took me two nights to get here from Kingston, so she should be able to get to Grotton in about a night and a half. Besides, the Admiral already knows about Dragon Messengers, since Celeste took him the Treaty." Andrew smiled, "Plus, it'll be a small joke on the Admiral, since Anne and Celeste are identical twins." The Commodore laughed, "OK, let's do it. Did you learn anything else while you were in Kingston?"

"Yes. Jasmine, the Minister of Internal Security, was a dragon Changed One; Wizard Noland turned her into a marble statue; Wizard Noland would like a Seabow to replicate and mount on some of the castle walls, and each magician in Franconia is being issued a Concealment cloak. I have three for the magicians assigned to first squadron," said Andrew. "Wow! That's a lot of news for only being gone a week! What are these Concealment cloaks?"

"Come down to my cabin, and I'll show you," said Andrew. "They're really quite remarkable." The Commodore and the Mage headed down the passageway to Andrew's cabin. Andrew took the cloak from his closet and put it on, vanishing from sight. "Fantastic!" exclaimed the Commodore, "But what good is it on a ship?" "Well, if we wear them during the next dragon attack, the dragons won't be able to see and attack the magicians, so we might be able to do more damage. Otherwise, I guess they're only good for sneaking around on board if there was ever a chance of a mutiny."

"HUH. That's unlikely. Could you put the spell on our sails?" "I suppose I could," said Andrew, "but then you wouldn't be able to see if they were taut against the wind. I can't cloak the whole ship. It wouldn't do any good anyway because we'd be seen by our wake," said Andrew. "Well, let's give it some thought. These cloaks ought to be good for something. In the meantime, let's go find Sorceress Anne." Andrew grabbed the cloaks from his bed and followed the Commodore up on deck, where they found Anne replicating Seabow bolts.

Anne rose as they approached, "Mage Andrew! Welcome back! How was the wedding?" Andrew quickly related the story, including the best way to kill a Stone Dragon. "Incredible! I would never have thought of that!" said Anne. "That's why I need you to fly over to Fleet Headquarters in Grotton and inform Admiral Cross and Wizard Lake. After the last time, I don't want the Admiral thinking we're withholding information. He might bust me right back down to Captain and Andrew to Sorcerer," said the Commodore.

Anne laughed and asked for directions to the Navy Headquarters building in Grotton. Andrew gave her the new Concealment cloak with the warning to always turn it inside out when she put it down, or there was a chance she would never find it again. He also asked her to deliver the cloaks to the Sorcerers on the VICTORY and the VICEROY on her way that evening. "Remember to take off your clothes before Changing and take them with you. We're going to have to work something out about that if we keep Changing into dragons and back again, maybe a curtain of some kind on the aft deck…" The Commodore handed Anne the message pouch with the warning to the Admiral about Stone Dragons. "Try not to be seen, Sorceress. I don't want you scarin' the folks between here and Grotton. It's probably best if you land outside of town, change, then walk in. I'm sure we'll eventually figure out a dragon landing pad near the Headquarters, so messengers won't have to walk so far. Give the Admiral my regards."

"I am going to have to leave tomorrow in order to get to the Dragon Council on time," said Gek. "I know," said Azure, "and I wish I could go with you, but I cannot leave the babies alone with Bruce." "If we had more time, we could take Annalise to Acropo and leave her with your mother, and Bruce could watch Richard. It would only be for a couple of days…" "And we may do that *next time*," said Azure, "but I think they are still too young right now. Richard is growing rapidly, much faster than a human child, according to Bruce, and Anna knows how to swim and is starting to catch her own food, but she is a long way from her first flying lesson."

"Whatever the Council decides, it had better not be another truce! I, for one, want revenge for my father's murder!" said Azure angrily. "You cannot," said Gek reasonably. "WHAT? WHY NOT?" "Because you are bound by the truce. Cobalt promised that the Sea Dragon Clan would not attack the ships if they did not attack the Clan. *I* can fight, but you cannot without breaking the truce." "Then perhaps we should break it before it is finalized with some Binding spell!" said Azure. "We are already bound by one spell I wish we could break; I want to avenge my father!"

"Have you forgotten all of the wounded and dying Dragons after the last battle?" asked Gek softly. "I have not. I keep imagining you, lying on the floor with one of those iron spears through you. I miss my mother, but I do not want to risk your life or the children if I can avoid it."

"Then the Dragon Council had better come up with a way to take the fight to the humans on land!" said Azure. "We need space and access to prey! Gek, how many children do you think we are going to have? Dozens? We have hundreds of years together ahead of us! We cannot continue to hide and hope to avoid detection." "You make excellent points," conceded Gek, "and I will certainly raise them with the Council." From the back room, they heard Richard crying.

Celeste landed at the Academy boat dock and changed into her human form. She quickly donned her sailor's outfit, determined to procure some women's clothes while she was in Kingston. She opened the portal and sat down on one of the benches. Wizard Faith arrived moments later, curious as to who had opened the portal without informing her. "Sorceress Celeste! Welcome back. How was your trip?"

"Hello, Wizard Faith. My trip was very interesting. Flying is not as easy as it looks, and almost immediately after I arrived on the HMS VALOR, Gek and Azure, a Great Dragon and his Sea Dragon mate, landed on the ship under a flag of truce." Celeste explained about her acting as a messenger and flying a copy of the Peace Treaty to Admiral Cross in Grotton. "What did the Admiral say when a dragon landed in Grotton?" "Nothing. I landed outside of town during the night and walked in. I stayed in an inn and went to the Navy Headquarters building the next morning," explained Celeste.

"That was probably for the best," said Faith. "The next morning, when I told the receptionist that I had a message for the Admiral from Commodore Matthews, they put me in a detention cell until Mage Charles came to question me," said Celeste. "That was undoubtedly awkward," said Faith. "Yes, but it gave me a chance to explain what happened on the way here with Gek and apologize to Mage Charles. I don't think he really believed me until the Admiral insisted I change into a dragon to prove my story."

"I'm sure they're convinced now." "Yes. In fact, the Admiral wants to make me the official "Dragon Messenger" for the Royal Navy. I told him that I would have to clear it with Wizard Noland. By the way, when you change back into a human from a dragon, you end up naked." "I know," said Wizard Faith. "We found out during Donovan's Sorcerer's Test. Wizard Mira made him change into a dragon to pass his Changes Test. When he transformed back, he was naked." "I still had it worse, standing there naked in front of a ship full of randy sailors." Faith smiled, "I know. I had to deliver a message to the VALOR myself, only I was better prepared. Still, it's an inconvenience."

"You went to the VALOR! Why?" asked Celeste. "After Donovan passed his Sorcerer's Test, he and Rachel wanted to get married here at the Academy before they left for their first assignments in Fairview.

Donovan wanted Mage Andrew to be his Best Man, so Wizard Noland sent me to deliver the invitation." "Wow, things sure happen fast around here. I've only been gone a couple of weeks."

"You don't know the half of it! During the wedding reception, one of the caterers was a Stone Dragon Changed One; Donovan smelled him and shouted a warning. The dragon transformed and started wrecking the place. We had ten killed and about fifty wounded before we were able to kill the beast." "No! Who was killed?" asked Celeste. "Mentor Terry, two Level Ones— Mark and Rex, two Level Twos— Kyle and Matt, Leonard from the Level Three kitchen staff, the caterer, and three soldiers from the Royal Expeditionary Force." "My gosh! I would have thought that with so many magicians around, it would have been relatively easy to kill one dragon."

"Stone Dragons are hard to kill. Their scales are much thicker than Great Dragons. Donovan finally had to put a shield around it and suffocate it." "A shield? That's certainly a new approach to killing a dragon!" "Yes. It seems that using a shield may be the only way. Blast spells certainly had no effect on it. If you become a Dragon Messenger, you need to spread the word." "I'll definitely do that. On that note, I better go see Wizard Noland," said Celeste.

As she entered Wizard Noland's cottage, she passed Minister Leonard, the Franconian Minister of Finance, who was just leaving. "Celeste! It's good to see you. Come in," said Wizard Noland. Celeste sat down on the sofa and asked, "If you don't mind my asking, sir, what was Minister Leonard doing here?" Noland frowned, then said, "It seems that Jasmine, the former Minister of Internal Security, drained the Royal Treasury, replacing the chests full of gold with Seemings. Minister Leonard was conducting an audit of the funds when he discovered the theft. The Kingdom is missing over ten thousand golds, and the Minister is worried that the King will blame him."

"Ten thousand golds? What are we going to do?" asked Celeste. "I told Minister Leonard that Jasmine probably just hid the golds somewhere and that I, and a few magicians will come over and search her old quarters and the store rooms to see if we can find where she hid them. I suspect that she actually just Removed them with a spell, and we'll have to replicate the golds without anyone knowing. We certainly can't let the Finance Minister or the King know that magicians can replicate golds. We'd spend all of our time making coins, which would ruin the economy of the Kingdom!"

"Jasmine certainly tried to ruin us," said Celeste. "Anyway, sir, the reason I'm here is that I brought a proposed Peace Treaty with the Sea Dragons for the

King's approval." "The King is inspecting his Winter Palace in Southport," said Noland. "I don't expect him back for at least two more weeks. What did the Sea Dragons propose?" "That if we cede the Coral Islands to them and agree never to build a structure or go ashore on the islands, they will not attack our ships or port facilities as long as we do not attack them. We are permitted to anchor up to five ships in the sheltered cove on the northernmost island in case of a storm, though."

"Hmm. What does the Admiral think?" "He and Mage Andrew think we need to get the dragons not to attack our *sailors,* not just our ships. They want to be very specific if we are to agree to a Binding spell," said Celeste. "Yes. We must be very careful with our wording. The last time, both sides used vague wording to try and trick the other. What about the other dragon clans?" "Azure said that the Sea Dragons can't speak for the other Clans and that the Treaty does not apply to the Kingdom of Baize because we do not speak for them."

"That's very true. I worry that if we agree to a truce with the Sea Dragons, the Fire and Stone Dragons will start attacking our ships, and fire on a ship is a very bad thing." "Andrew is replicating more Seabows, placing six on each ship in the first squadron. He can do that because there are only three ships left in the squadron, and they saved some of the crew of the HMS

COMFORT. The other ships will need more sailors assigned if we install additional Seabows," said Celeste.

"Which means that only our battleships will be able to carry six Seabows. Our frigates won't have the space for the additional crew," mused Wizard Noland. Celeste looked surprised at Wizard Noland's knowledge about Franconian warships. "I spent several years as a Sorcerer in the Royal Navy," explained Noland. "And I know all about how bad a fire on a ship can be and how hard it is to extinguish one."

"That reminds me, sir, Admiral Cross offered me the newly created position of Official Dragon Messenger of the Royal Navy. He immediately saw the benefits of being able to send messages to ships at sea and between ships in different squadrons. He asked if we had enough Sorcerers to deploy two to the Navy, one for each fleet."

Wizard Noland considered the request for a few moments, then said, "Anne is still aboard the HMS VALOR, isn't she? With the loss of the HMS COMFORT, first squadron has an extra magician that could be used for such an assignment. I imagine it will take at least a year to replace the HMS COMFORT. What are your thoughts, Celeste? Would you like to be a Dragon Messenger? The idea of identical twin sisters as dragon messengers has a certain appeal, and I know that Anne cannot be entirely happy as the only woman in the Navy." "She says the sailors stare," replied Celeste. "She spends most of her off-duty time in her cabin. The sailors aren't disrespectful, exactly, but she can't keep them from staring without sounding insecure." Noland nodded understandingly.

"And what about you?" asked Noland. Celeste smiled and said, "Sir, I would really like this to be my 'second chance.'" "Very well. Once you have delivered the draft treaty to the King, you may return to Grotton and inform the Admiral that you and your sister are now assigned as the Dragon Messengers of the Royal Navy."

King Henry

Chapter Twelve:
COUNCILS

"WHERE ARE THEY? Those traitorous, back-stabbing Great Dragons!" shouted Bliz as soon as he arrived at the abandoned rock quarry for the Dragon Council meeting. Ard and Gek walked forward, and Ard said, "'Traitorous?' What are you babbling about, Bliz?" "ONE OF YOUR CLAN ATTACKED US WITHOUT WARNING! WE LOST SIX SNOW DRAGONS IN AN ATTACK ON THE HUMAN TOWN OF SNOWTON! DO YOU DENY BEING INVOLVED?" shouted an enraged Bliz. "I absolutely deny it," said Ard calmly. "Why would a Great Dragon attack you?"

"SHOW ME YOUR FACE! BOTH OF YOU!" yelled Bliz. Both Ard and Gek walked towards the much smaller but very angry Snow Dragon Clan Chief. Bliz examined them closely. "It was not either of you," he said finally. "But I will find the Great Dragon traitor and have my revenge!" "Calm down, and tell us what has happened," said Cobalt.

"As requested, ten of my Clan attacked the human town of Snowton. We were destroying the town; the humans fled in fear or cowered in their dwellings, which we covered in ice. Then, a Great Dragon swooped down from above, slashing, tearing, killing my kin without warning and without mercy. My mate got above him and slashed his face, but he turned and murdered her with a blast of fire! The three survivors retreated to the safety of the Snow Fields. So, what do you have to say for your Clan, old one?" Bliz asked Ard.

"Why would one of my Clan attack you?" asked Ard reasonably. "Besides Gek, the only other member of the Great Dragon Clan that I know of is Ig and his family. Ig is looking for Changed Ones in the towns of Oceanside and Lakeshore, far, far, from Snowton and the Snow Fields." "Then who could it be?" raged Bliz.

"It is as I feared," said Ard, "it must be a Great Dragon Changed One, who had friends or loved ones among the humans of Snowton. That is the only explanation I can think of." Bliz hesitated, considering, "You really think a Dragon Changed One would turn on one of his kin and attack?" "I do not know," said Ard. "Maybe if it were Great Dragons that were attacking the town, the Changed One would have tried to talk them out of their attack, but he did not give his Snow Dragon cousins the same consideration. You are sure it was a male Dragon?"

"Yes, he was a male. I saw that much before he struck me from behind with his tail and sent me crashing into a strand of pine trees." "This is unexpected," said

Jasper, the Stone Dragon Clan Chief. "This could happen again, to any of us." "I feared that there were some of our Changed Ones who would refuse to fight alongside us," said Cobalt. "Many of the Sea Dragon Changed Ones have taken human mates; some even have children. I did not expect them to help us, but I never considered that they might fight against us!"

Gek, speaking for the first time, said, "Azure and I found many Sea and even a few Snow Dragons who we would not even ask for help from because of their ties to the humans." "Where is Azure?" asked Rose, the Fire Dragon Clan Chief, "I expected to see her here." "She is with our daughter, Annalise," said Gek, not wanting to mention Richard. "Azure gave birth a short time ago, and Annalise is not able to fly yet, so she stayed home and allowed me to attend."

Cobalt and Ard looked at Gek sternly but decided to let the omission pass. "So, what should we do?" asked Jasper. "Which human kingdom is likely to have more Changed Ones?" asked Ard. The Dragons all looked down, considering. Finally, Gek said, "I have never been on the west side of the river, but I know from experience, that in Franconia, there are magic-users in every city and town who hunt for those with the spark of magic. When they find them, they are unwillingly sent to the wizards academy for training. Is it the same in …" "Baize," said Rose, "and no, on our side of the river, those with the spark of magic are exalted. A Dragon Changed One who did not wish to be found could live in Baize for a hundred years and never be discovered."

"So, it is likely that if this became common knowledge among our kin, many Dragon Changed Ones would move to the west side of the river in order to live in a place where they were less likely to be discovered," said Ard. "Which means we are less likely to be attacked by a Changed One if we attack in Franconia," deduced Gek.

"*Less* likely, but it could still happen. We need to adjust our strategy to account for this new development," said Cobalt. "What do you suggest?" asked Jasper. "First, we must abandon our plan to keep the humans in Franconia neutral. Our future attacks should focus on the humans on the east side of the river. Also, we must fight as one."

"What do you mean by that?" asked Rose. "So far, we have fought as individual Clans, Fire Dragons attack Riverside, Snow Dragons attack Snowton, and Stone Dragons against Weaton. We must combine our individual skills, Fire *and* Great Dragons, Stone *and* Sea. If the Snow Dragon attack on Snowton had had a couple of Fire Dragons with them, the Great Dragon

Changed One might have been driven off or killed," said Ard.

The Dragon Clan Chiefs were silent for a long time. This was *not* how Dragons fought. Ever! Still, a Sea Dragon spraying water that could be frozen by a Snow Dragon or a Stone Dragon assisting an attack by Fire Dragons could be very effective if coordinated properly. "This is an interesting idea," said Rose, "and one that will require the consent of all our Clans. I recommend that we return to our Clans and discuss this cooperation. It could be effective, but it is not the Dragon way."

"So, how do we proceed?" asked Bliz. "Return to your Clans and discuss this idea. Can we work together for the benefit of Dragonkind? If so, we plan new combined-Clan attacks; if not, we accept the risk of being attacked by Changed Ones of different Clans. In any event, I suggest that our ancient agreement for the Stone and Fire Dragons to remain on the west side of the river be annulled. If Fire and Stone wish to settle in Franconia, so be it," said Ard.

"I have other news," said Ard, "the woman that I was guarding, Beverly Perrucci, has passed away of old age. The only remaining descendants of Wizard Amanda are Beverly's son, the magic-user Andrew, who is serving aboard the HMS VALOR, and Donovan Francis, who, I believe, is still in the Wizards Academy."

"I have another idea for the Dragon Council's consideration," said Gek tentatively. The other Dragons looked at him questioningly. "Only the human magic-users are aware that Dragons can Change into human form. If our ability became known..." Now, the Dragons looked very skeptical. "Our ability to speak and understand humans has been a secret for two hundred years! Dragons have died rather than divulge that secret!" said Ard. "I know, but if it *did* become known by the humans, they might turn on each other, each suspicious that the other was a Changed One. It is just a thought."

"A dangerous one," said Ard, "but one we may have to consider in the future. Times change, perhaps Dragon Clans can cooperate, and maybe it is time to show the humans all of our capabilities. We will consider this and discuss it again at our next Council meeting. In the meantime, I suggest we confine our attacks to the humans on this side of the river as we consider our next moves. Cobalt, what is the status of your truce with the humans?"

"We have proposed a Peace Treaty that states that we will not attack Franconian ships or port facilities in exchange for ownership of the Coral Islands and a pledge that Franconian ships will not attack us," replied Cobalt. "But this Treaty does not speak to attacks on land?" asked Ard. "It does not, so even a Binding spell would not prevent us from attacking humans on land," said Cobalt. Ard smiled wickedly.

"Mage Kathy, a Messenger Hawk just arrived for you from King Donald," said Kimberly, the Chairwoman of the Springfield City Council. "From the King? I wonder what he could want. We've only been here a little over a month." Kathy and her staff were in Springfield, operating the Procurement Office for the dig site. She had been meeting with vendors and merchants for the past few days, trying to keep up with the constant need for provisions, water, firewood, and a host of other commodities that kept the construction site going.

"I have no idea, but this poor Messenger Hawk looks like he's been through the wringer. He must have gotten caught in that big storm we had a few days ago. It's lucky he got here at all," said Kimberly. "So, how's the work going?" "We're way ahead of schedule, despite the storm. It seems that it's only about thirty feet down to bedrock, instead of the hundred feet we were expecting. If we don't get any more big storms, we should have the outer trench and walls finished in about a month. Then the hard part starts."

"I would have thought that excavating the middle would be easier," said Kimberly. "Well, it's true that we'll be Removing the spoils, instead of making walls out of them, but how do we get the children in there? We'll probably have to move our campsite to somewhere inside the U-shaped trench, so we don't have to go all the way around each day. I'm just not sure what Wizard Edward has in mind. I don't want to have to move the camp several times as we excavate."

"I see your problem. Wherever you move the campsite to, it's going to take longer to get supplies to you." "You're right. I hope Edward has a solution. Well, that's a problem for another day. I guess I should see what King Donald wants," said Kathy, opening the message scroll. Kathy read the message from the King quickly, then told Kimberly and her accounting staff that she needed to head back out to the campsite at once and confer with Edward. "Is everything alright?" asked Kimberly. "Yes, but I have to explain something to the King. I might be gone for a few days, she told her staff. Remember to check every invoice carefully; we are almost halfway through our funding for the quarter already."

Kathy rushed out of the office that she had secured for her and her staff and headed for the stables. "Mage Kathy! Where are you going in such a hurry?" asked Captain Douglas, the commander of the Baizian infantry battalion that had recently returned to Springfield. "I need to go out to the construction site and confer with Wizard Edward about a request I just received from the King." "Would you mind if I tagged along? I haven't met Wizard Edward yet, and I've been curious about this enormous project you two are up to in the Great Salt Flats."

Kathy considered the request for a moment, then said, "Of course, commander. It's high time you met Edward and got a look at the project." Kathy and Captain Douglas saddled their mounts, and the commander told the stable boy to inform his second-in-command, Lieutenant Hill, that he was going out to the construction site and would be gone for a few hours.

As they rode out of Springfield, the Captain asked, "So, as I understand it, you're digging a giant hole in the ground where the Salt Flats are, in the hope that it will keep the salt from expanding towards the Amber River. Is that right?" "Correct, Captain. We're currently digging a U-shaped trench, about ten feet wide, that goes all the way down to bedrock. We have the apprentice magicians digging the trench and piling the spoils along the outside edge; then, using an Adhesive spell, we're cementing the sides of the trench to the bedrock and the dirt walls above the trench."

The Captain tried to picture what Kathy was describing in his mind but was having difficulty understanding. "Let me get this straight, you dig a trench, all the way down to bedrock and pile up the excavated dirt on the outside. Then glue it all together?" Kathy smiled, "Something like that, Captain. But the Adhesive spell we use makes the dirt as hard as rock and will hold up to the water that will later fill the reservoir." "And you're using *children* to dig this hole?" "Also correct. The Dig and Adhesive spells are some of the first ones we teach apprentice magicians. The students have gotten very adept at using these spells, and we're ahead of schedule with the project."

They rode for another hour, making small talk, before the edge of the campsite came into view. "That's quite a large operation," observed the Captain. "Yes, we have a little over a hundred apprentices and fifty or so adults in the camp." "What are the adults doing?" "They are the surveyors, engineers, cooks and wagon drivers. They also stand watch over the camp during the night. We can't ask the children to dig all day then stand watch during the night."

"I'm not sure how effective a child would be on guard duty," Captain Douglas scoffed. "Captain, these *children* are all magicians and would probably be more than capable of defending the camp if we asked it of them. Please remember that." "I apologize, Mage

Kathy. I meant no insult." "I'm sorry, Captain, I'm just a little protective of these apprentices. They are working so hard and at such a young age. I've already had to pull two wagon drivers and one cook out of holes that a young female apprentice dropped them into after they made an inappropriate remark to her." The Captain laughed. "I shall certainly keep that in mind."

They rode up just as Edward was leaving his tent. "Kathy! I thought you were staying in town for a couple of days to finish setting up the Procurement Office," said Edward. "I was, but I received a Messenger Hawk from the King that I need to talk to you about. The poor bird must have been on the way here during that big storm. It's lucky he made it to Springfield at all." "Hmm, you're right about that. In Franconia, Messenger Hawks are trained to fly directly between cities. Most Messenger Hawks try to fly through or over storms, and we've lost some over the years when they weren't able to make it through safely. So, what does the King want?"

"I'll tell you in a minute. Edward, this is Captain Douglas, the commander of the 1st Infantry Battalion that returned to Springfield a few weeks ago." Edward came forward and offered his hand. "Wizard Edward Francis, Captain. It's a pleasure to make your acquaintance." The Captain shook Edward's offered hand tentatively. "I don't bite, Captain. So, how was your trip from Westport?"

"It was hot and dusty, Sir Wizard. At least I was mounted. The poor foot soldiers had a long march. It was fortunate that we got to Springfield before that big storm rolled in a few days ago." Edward smiled and said, "I understand perfectly, Captain. Did you bring any magical support with you? I imagine there are quite a few of your troops with blistered feet." The Captain hesitated, and Edward said, "Captain, I'm just asking a simple question, not trying to spy out your strengths and weaknesses. If I wanted to, I could conjure a Seeing spell and determine if there was a Sorcerer or a Mage with your force."

The Captain gulped, then said, "Yes, Wizard Edward, Mage John, our Battalion Battle Mage came with us." "When we have a chance, we should meet him," Edward said to Kathy. "Captain, is there anything that your troops need that we might be able to provide? I know that the barracks were pretty bare when the last Company of the Franconian Royal Expeditionary Force pulled out. I hope they didn't leave a mess." "No, sir. The barracks were probably cleaner than we left them. We left in quite a hurry," said the Captain, not quite sure what to make of the foreign Wizard.

Edward looked over the Captain's shoulder and saw Mage Elianna loading the wagon to take the afternoon snack to the digging teams. "Mage Elianna!" Edward yelled, "Come and meet the commander of the 1st Baizian Infantry Battalion, Captain Douglas." Mage Elianna stopped what she was doing and came over to greet the Captain. After introductions were made, Edward said, "Elianna, why don't you take the Captain with you and show him the project? I'm sure that's one reason he came all the way out here." Elianna eagerly agreed and she and the Captain went back over to the now loaded wagon and headed out to feed the first shift.

After they left the camp, Edward asked, "So, what does the King want now?" Kathy handed over the message, and Edward read it quickly. "Well, I knew he was going to find out eventually. What do you think we should do?" "Send a Messenger Hawk?" asked Kathy hopefully. Edward laughed. "That explanation would take about ten Messenger Hawks! No, I think a more *demonstrative* explanation is in order." You don't mean…" "Yes, I do. One or both of us is going to have to Change into a dragon and go see the King."

Wizard Noland sat at his desk pondering. The Stone Dragon scale on the desk before him was perplexing. It was harder than steel, fire-proof (as far as he could tell) and generally inflexible. It could, however, be replicated using magic. Wizard Noland had gathered a little over a hundred of the Stone Dragon scales off the carcass of the dragon that Donovan had killed during his wedding reception. The question was, *what use could he make of them?*

They were too heavy for armor, even if he could find a way to punch holes in them (which he hadn't yet) to string them together in overlapping bands. Just then, Wizard Daniel knocked on the door. "Come on in, Daniel, I'm in the study," said Noland. "You asked to see me, sir?" asked Wizard Daniel. "Yes. I need your help. I'm trying to find a use for these Stone Dragon scales I took off the carcass. They're harder than steel, but I'm not sure what use we can make of them."

Daniel picked up one of the scales from the desk. It was about the size of a wooden roof shingle, flat on the top and rounded on the bottom. "They're heavy," he observed. "Yes," replied Noland, "they're about twice as heavy as the Great Dragon scales that the Royal Expeditionary Force brought back from the dragon they killed outside of Farmdale. It's no wonder that Stone Dragons can't swim; the weight of these scales would make it impossible."

"I guess we could use the Adhesive spell and stick them on wooden shields for the knights…" mused Daniel. "They would still be much heavier than their current shields," said Noland. "I guess we could just Adhere them to the castle walls," said Daniel, "it would make for good fire protection…" "No," said Wizard Noland with a grin, "not the *walls,* the roofs!" "The roofs?" "Yes, we might have to reinforce the rafters to compensate for the extra weight, but with enough of these, we could make all of the roofs in Kingston fireproof in case of a dragon attack."

"But, how do we make them stick?" asked Daniel. "We can't send out magicians as roofers for every building in the city! We'd never get any training done." Noland stopped to consider the problem. "We replicate the scales and give them to the carpenters in town. I'm sure they can figure out a way to attach them to the roofs. We should probably send some to the other major cities and have the Regional Mages and their staffs start replicating Stone Dragon scales too." Daniel nodded.

"In the meanwhile, on Endday afternoon, I need you, Mira, Jeffery and Wizard Dylan to come with me to the palace. We have to replicate some gold." "Gold? I thought replicating coinage was illegal!" "It is, but Jasmine apparently emptied about ten thousand golds out of the treasury in an attempt to undermine the kingdom. The Finance Minister discovered the theft and is somewhat frantic, worried that the king will blame him if the missing gold isn't recovered. I told him that Jasmine probably just hid the gold and we would come over and search for it. I suspect that she actually just Removed it. Jasmine didn't need the gold." Daniel whistled, *"Ten thousand golds! Even with four of us, that's going to take quite a while to replicate."*

"I know," said Noland, "and we can't let anyone know what we're doing. If the King ever learns that magicians can replicate coins, we'll never be doing anything else, and the resulting inflation would wreck the economy of the kingdom!" "How long before the King returns from Southport?" asked Daniel. "He'll undoubtedly return by ship, so we probably only have a couple of weeks," said Noland. "Then I guess we better get started."

Celeste approached the King's palace in Southport carrying the draft Peace Treaty in a standard messenger pouch. When she asked the soldier guarding the door to the audience chamber where she might find the King, the guard was less than cooperative. "How is that your business?" asked the burly armsman. "Messengers report to the Message Center on the third level."

Somewhat taken aback, Celeste said, "I have an urgent message for the King from Admiral Cross, the Franconian Chief of Naval Operations." "I don't care. All messages go to the Message Center. They will decide if it's important enough to show to the King."

"You don't understand—" began Celeste, before the guard reached out to grab her by the shoulders. "*LIGARE,*" she murmured while making a fist with her left hand. The soldier immediately froze, paralyzed by the spell. "A little more courtesy on your part would have been advisable," said Celeste as she opened the door and entered the chamber.

Alerted by the sound, King Henry looked up from the swatches of cloth he was inspecting on the conference table and said, "What's the meaning of this? Who gave you permission to enter? I asked not to be disturbed!" "Your Highness," said Celeste, crossing the floor, "I am Sorceress Celeste, and I have an urgent message for you from Admiral Cross." The King seized the proffered message pouch and said, "What could the Admiral be sending me, all the way from Grotton?"

"Sire, I believe it is a proposed Peace Treaty from the Sea Dragon clan," said Celeste. The King blinked hard, then said, "Say that again." "I said, that I believe that the Admiral sent you a copy of a draft Peace Treaty between the Franconian Royal Navy and the Sea

Dragons, Your Majesty." The King sat down. "A Peace Treaty?" he asked. "Why would the Sea Dragons want a Peace Treaty with us?"

Celeste explained, "Sire, as I understand it, the 1st Squadron, under Commodore Matthews, fought a fierce battle with the Sea Dragons, during which, many of them were killed or injured, including their Clan Chief. After the battle, the dragons proposed a temporary truce, stating that if we did not attack them, they would not attack us. A few weeks later, Two dragon Changed Ones landed on the HMS VALOR and proposed a more permanent Peace Treaty. Commodore Matthews sent the draft Treaty to Admiral Cross, who asked me to deliver it to you."

"And just how could you have gotten the Treaty to me so quickly?" asked the bewildered King. "Sire, some of your magicians have learned how to Change into dragons, much like many of the dragons have learned how to change into human form. Once the two dragons departed the HMS VALOR, I transformed into a Sea Dragon and flew to Grotton with the draft Treaty, then from Grotton to Kingston, where I thought to find you, then to Southport when I learned you were here. I only left Grotton three days ago."

"That's incredible!" said the King. "This could make Messenger Hawks obsolete!" Celeste smiled,

"I'm glad you approve, Sire. Commodore Matthews has arranged another meeting with the dragons in three months to finalize the Treaty, if it meets your approval." "Well, let's see what it says," said the King, scanning the document. "Hummph, I cede ownership of the Coral Islands to the Sea Dragons and agree not to build any structures there. We agree not to attack them, and they agree not to attack our ships or port facilities. We are allowed to anchor up to five ships in the cove on the northern island during storms, but no one is to come ashore. Hmm."

"Sorceress, do you know anything about the Coral Islands?" "I believe that's where the Sea Dragons make their home, Sire. There is no fresh water on the islands, and the fishing around the islands is said to be very poor, probably because the Sea Dragons have eaten all of the fish in the area. Other than the sheltered cove mentioned in the Treaty, I don't believe that those islands have anything of value on them."

"Well," the King mused, "this Treaty would certainly get the Merchant Council off my back, if it would stop the raids on our shipping. What is your opinion, Sorceress?" "Sire, I'm much too young to offer an opinion about such heady matters of state," said Celeste demurely. "Come now, you can't be much younger than I am. I would like your opinion." "Sire, if I remember correctly, Mage Andrew expressed a concern about the precise wording of the Treaty." "How so?" asked the King. "Well, the Treaty states that the dragons will not attack our *ships or port facilities;* it doesn't say they can't attack our *sailors.*" "How could you attack a sailor without attacking his ship?" asked the King. "I suppose a dragon could swoop down and grab a sailor off the deck and carry him off," speculated Celeste.

"Hmm. Quite right," said the King. "I will discuss this with my Ministers and have a reply ready for you within the week. In the meanwhile, I will have a room prepared for you, Sorceress. Thank you *very* much for bringing this to my attention." "It was my pleasure, Sire. I will cancel the Paralyze spell I cast on your guard on my way out. You see, he didn't want to let me in." The King smiled. "Bruno is a competent guard but a poor judge of character. Once you release him, tell him I want him to show you to the guest quarters."

Celeste smiled, bowed to the King and left the room. The King watched her leave, admiringly.

Senior Specialist Lance

Chapter Thirteen:

STICKS AND STONES

Breakfast in the Royal Expeditionary Force Officer's mess was better than expected. Donovan and Rachel both managed to wake in time to shower and get over to the dining facility a little after six in the morning. Donovan expressed remorse that they no longer had a wake-up service (Leo) and worried that one day, they would oversleep and be late for duty. "*I* was getting up at five on my own, long before you came into my life," said Rachel. "I'm sure we'll adjust to the new place and manage just fine."

The first night in their new home by the Sapphire River had been much different than their time at the Wizards Academy. There were strange sounds outside, the creaking of the trees as they swayed in the wind, and the sound of raindrops on the roof as a light rain storm swept through the area just after midnight. The shower in the cabin was also smaller and less efficient than the one they had in the Mentor's quarters; it didn't automatically refill, so they had to magically Replicate and heat the water in the tank several times before they were clean.

After breakfast, they rode to the barracks occupied by the Royal Expeditionary Force when they were in

Kingston (which wasn't often). They arrived a little before seven and were on time for morning muster. As the soldiers stood in formation, Major Gerald addressed the men. "For those of you who don't know it yet, we've recently received two new members. Most of you know Donovan from our little excursion to Farmdale a few years ago. He has just graduated from the Wizards Academy and been assigned as magical support to the Expeditionary Force." There was a round of applause from the assembled soldiers. Donovan waved, somewhat embarrassed.

"*Sorcerer* Donovan will be assigned to 2nd Company, and his wife, Sorceress Rachel, will support 1st Company." Rachel also waved. Some of the soldiers smiled, remembering how Rachel had protected them against dragon fire during the reception after her and Donovan's wedding, while other soldiers looked skeptical or confused. "I know that Sorceress Rachel is the first woman ever assigned to the Royal Expeditionary Force, and there will likely be some procedures that we'll need to adjust. We'll work those situations out as we encounter them."

"The King is still in Southport and is unlikely to return for at least two weeks," Major Gerald continued, "this morning, I want to work on individual skills. Swordsmen, draw wooden wands from the rack and pair off. Archers, I want you to work on rapid fire this morning. Fire all ten of your arrows as fast as you can, and try to keep them on target. Axmen, Wizard Noland from the Wizards Academy has constructed a target for you. It's a wooden dragon with actual dragon scales on it. I want you to practice running at the target, striking a blow that can penetrate the scales, then rolling away. Remember what happened to Corporal Wade? A dragon isn't going to give you a chance at a second blow if you just stand there. Healers, you practice staff work with the magicians. This afternoon, we'll work with the crossbows. Dismissed to your squads."

The soldiers moved off to their respective training areas, the swordsmen picking up wooden practice swords from racks along the wall, while the archers moved off to the nearby archery range. Healers Bone and Wells walked over to Donovan and Rachel, carrying their staffs. "I imagine your staff work has improved since we last sparred," Healer Bone said to Donovan. "Sorceress, I'm Healer Bone, and this is Healer Wells from 2nd Company," said Bone to Rachel.

"It's nice to meet you, Healer Bone, Healer Wells. Healer Bone, Donovan has told me how you beat him black and blue when you sparred. I hope he's improved, since *I* was one of his instructors." "Well, let's stretch and then find out," said Healer Wells. The four of them did some standard stretching exercises to warm up their muscles, then paired off, Donovan against Healer Bone, and Rachel with Healer Wells. As they began sparring, Donovan quickly realized that he was not the only one who had improved. If possible, it seemed as if Healer Bone was even faster than before, and Donovan speculated that the Healer had probably been going easy on him when they sparred almost four years ago as they traveled from Farmdale to Hayford. While the Healer was fast, Donovan was able to anticipate most of his strikes and was holding his own until Healer Bone stuck one end of his staff in the sandy soil of the training area and, using the staff, threw sand in Donovan's eyes.

The sand struck home because Donovan had neglected to cast a Weather shield in front of his face, not expecting sand from the Healer. Reacting quickly, before the Healer's staff could strike him, Donovan said *"NERVO"* and made a grabbing motion with his right hand, seizing the Healer in a strong Tether spell. Donovan rubbed the sand out of his eyes and deliberately placed his staff on Healer Bone's shoulder. "My point," said Donovan with a grin as he released the spell.

From across the training area, Healer Wells laughed, just before Rachel swung her staff low and swept his feet out from under him. He landed hard. Donovan and Rachel approached and gave each other a "high five" as they switched sparring partners. The swordsmen who had been watching the bouts stood with their mouths open. They had rarely seen anyone score a touch on one of their Healers, and seeing them both go down within seconds of each other was shocking.

Healer Bone grimaced, "No more magic spells," he said, smiling, "No more sand," replied Donovan. "Agreed," Donovan began sparring with Healer Wells. Having never sparred with him before, Donovan chose to begin on the defensive, sticking to blocks and counter-strikes. It soon became apparent that, while Healer Wells was very good with a staff, he was not as good as Healer Bone. Donovan began attacking, spinning, ducking, and lunging. He struck the Healer three times before Healer Bone called a rest break.

As they walked over to the water barrel, Healer Wells said to Healer Bone, "They're both very, very good." "So I saw. I want another crack at Donovan, though, this time with no magic spells." Donovan nodded his agreement. As they sparred again, Donovan asked, "Were you going easy on me before?" Healer Bone replied, "No. I just underestimated you. You were much more skilled than I anticipated." After sparring for another half a glass, Healer Bone asked, "What other spells have you learned to use while sparring with a staff?" Donovan immediately conjured a Seeming of four rocks and sent them speeding toward the Healer's face. When he ducked, Donovan's staff was there.

"Impressive, anything else?" "Swing at me with one hand," said Donovan, grinning, "and I'll show you." Wasting no time, Healer Bone switched his staff to his left hand, thinking to throw Donovan off, and swung his staff in a lightning-fast attack. *"REDUCTO,"* murmured Donovan, reducing the Healer's staff to the size of a twig. The Healer, without the counterweight of the staff, spun around and fell to the ground. "DAMN! That was good," said Healer Bone. "From now on, no magic spells when we spar. That was embarrassing." "Agreed," said Donovan.

A glass later, Major Gerald called a halt to the morning training sessions and dismissed the soldiers to lunch. Donovan, Rachel and the two Healers headed to the Officer's Mess with the other Officers. The two Healers took seats together and began discussing strategies for future sparring sessions with Donovan and Rachel. Major Gerald came over and sat with the two magicians. "So, you two certainly didn't disappoint me this morning," he said. "I had hoped that you were both proficient with staffs, at least enough to hold off the Healers. I admit, I didn't expect ya to beat 'em. So now all of the soldiers know you can fight. If ya didn't realize it, everyone except the archers was watching.

Donovan smiled, "They're both very good." "No," said Major Gerald, "they are both *the best* in the Royal

Guard. You two made a very good first impression today," said Major Gerald.

After lunch, the soldiers moved to the newly constructed crossbow range. Targets were set up on bales of hay, with a stout wooden fence behind the targets to keep the soldiers from losing the crossbow bolts if they missed. The soldiers began loading and firing the crossbows. Some were capable marksmen, but most were still slow to load the cumbersome weapons. Donovan noticed that one soldier's crossbow kept firing before the soldier was ready. "Can I see your crossbow?" he asked. "It seems to be firing before you're ready." "You're right about that, sir. It's got a hair trigger, for sure." "Let me see what I can do," said Donovan. Taking the crossbow, Donovan used an Enlarge spell to tighten the trigger lever, so that more force was required to activate it. "Try it now."

The soldier loaded the crossbow, took aim, and fired, striking the bullseye. "That's much better, sir. Thank you." Donovan nodded and proceeded down the line of soldiers, looking for any more weapons that needed adjustments. Rachel noticed that one soldier was having a difficult time drawing his crossbow. "Is everything OK?" she asked. "Yes, ma'am, I just tweaked my back sparring this morning, and drawing this thing is hard under normal circumstances; with a bad back, it's very painful. Rachel moved behind the soldier, placed her right hand over his lower back, palm down, fingers closed and said, *"ALIEVIO."* The soldier flexed his back and smiled, "Thank you, Sorceress! That feels so much better." "I'm glad I could help," said Rachel.

When the training ended for the day, Donovan and Rachel mounted their horses to return home (deciding to forgo the evening meal in the Officer's Mess and try cooking their own dinner in their new place), one of the soldiers in 1st Company said to his neighbor, "Did you see how she healed Pinkerton's back? She could be a real help to us." The other soldier leered at Rachel as she started to ride away and said, "I sure hope she helps me with *my* problem," he said, making a crude gesture. Suddenly, a palm-sized rock struck the back of the speaker's head, and he went down, seeing stars. As he got up and looked around to see who threw the rock, Rachel turned in her saddle, pointed at her eyes with two fingers, and then at the soldier.

"Nicely done," whispered Donovan. "Thanks, I just hope I don't have to do it too often."

Sorceress Anne landed as close to Grotton as she could without being seen. It was almost dawn, so she quickly changed into human form, dressed, and headed into the city to find the Navy Headquarters Building. Commodore Matthews had given her a crude map of the city and some general directions, but she was still going to have to search around a bit to find the right place.

She eventually found the four-building complex a short distance from the piers where the Royal Navy ships docked. Before entering the complex, Anne looked around for a suitable dragon landing area for future visits. She noted what appeared to be an abandoned warehouse a short distance from the Headquarters buildings. Anne walked around the warehouse until she found a faded sign that said "Navy Surplus - RESTRICTED AREA. KEEP OUT." Realizing that if a magician magically removed the roof of the building, a dragon could easily fly in and land (depending on what the inside of the warehouse looked like). Anne decided that she would speak to the Admiral about it.

As she walked into the Navy Headquarters building, the receptionist said, "Sorceress Celeste! Welcome back! Are you here to see the Admiral?" Anne reddened and said, "I *am* here to see the Admiral, but my name is Sorceress Anne. Celeste is my identical twin sister." The receptionist didn't miss a beat, "No matter. Follow me, please. I'm sure the Admiral will see you immediately." Anne followed the receptionist down a short corridor that led to Admiral Cross's office. The receptionist knocked and said, "Admiral, there's a Sorceress here to see you." "Please show her in, Betty," said the Admiral.

Anne entered the office, and the Admiral made the same mistake that most people did, "Celeste! What brings you back so soon? Did Wizard Noland agree to my request?" Anne said, "I'm sorry, Admiral, but I'm not Celeste. I'm her identical twin sister, Anne. I've been serving aboard the HMS COMFORT in 1st Squadron under Commodore Matthews." "Sorceress Anne! Forgive me. I've heard good things about you! What brings you to Navy Headquarters this fine day?"

"Sir, I brought you a message from Commodore Matthews. With two magicians on board, both of whom know how to Change into dragons, he felt that he could send me without compromising his command." Anne handed over the message pouch, which the Admiral opened quickly. After reading the message, he asked, "Do you know what this says?" "Yes, sir," replied Anne, "it says that the only way to kill a Stone Dragon is to enclose it in a shield and suffocate it. The Commodore thought you should have this information as soon as possible."

The Admiral nodded, "That's one thing I like about Horatio; he keeps me informed. What say you and I go over to Wizard Lake and tell him the news? He just got back from Southport." The Admiral led the way to the Chief of Naval Wizardry's office, which was just two doors down the hall. They entered, and Admiral Cross introduced Anne to Wizard Lake.

"So, you're the famous Sorceress Anne, the only woman in the Royal Navy!" said Wizard Lake. "Yes, sir," replied Anne. "Remember how I told you that Sorceress Celeste was able to change into a dragon and deliver a message to me from the HMS VALOR? Well, her twin sister, Anne, has just done the same." "Really?" asked Wizard Lake. "That's remarkable! What information was so urgent that it needed to be delivered by a dragon?" The Admiral looked to Anne for an explanation. "Sir, it seems that a Stone Dragon attacked the Wizards Academy a short time ago, and to kill it, they had to enclose it in a shield. Wizard Noland says that a shield may be the only way to slay a Stone Dragon. The Blast spells conjured by the magicians at the Academy were ineffective."

"A shield? What good would that— I see, they suffocated it!" "Yes, sir. And while inside the shield, the dragon was unable to attack with fire, teeth or talons," said Anne. "Ingenious!" said Wizard Lake, "Wizard Noland is a very clever magician." "He is indeed, sir, but it was Sorcerer Donovan who thought of using the shield against the Stone Dragon." "Well, I would like to buy that Sorcerer an Ale!" said Wizard Lake. "So, you flew all the way here to tell us that?"

"Yes, sir. Commodore Matthews thought that we should spread the news, even though no Navy ships have been attacked by Stone Dragons." "That's true," said Wizard Lake, "and from the reports I've seen, Stone Dragons can't swim, and they don't fly very well, so I doubt that they'd ever try attacking a ship at sea. I suppose they could do a lot of damage to one of our port facilities, though."

"Sir, on that note, I saw what looked like an abandoned Navy Surplus warehouse near here. Is it being used for anything?" Anne asked the Admiral. "That old shack? I would've had it torn down years ago if I had the funding. Why do you ask?" "Well, sir, it occurred to me that if we removed the roof, it would make an ideal landing spot for Dragon Messengers." The Admiral considered the idea and said, "It's awfully close to the port. Wouldn't somebody see a dragon landing inside? We don't want to give away our secret."

Anne considered the problem for a moment, then said, "The Dragon Messenger could cast a Concealment spell before taking off or landing, Sir. And with our Concealment cloaks, we could travel to and from the warehouse in human form without being seen." "Excuse me? Concealment cloaks?" asked Wizard Lake. "Yes, sir. Wizard Noland has had Concealment cloaks made for all of the magicians in Franconia. If I had known that I would be coming to Grotton so soon, I would have brought yours with me."

Wizard Lake smiled and asked, "Why would a Wizard need a Concealment cloak?" "Well, sir, if you had a Concealment cloak, then you'd be able to use all three of your spells without using one to cast a Concealment *shield*. The same goes for Mages and Sorcerers." "That's brilliant! I've seldom had to cast three spells at once, but with this trouble with the dragons…, this is a significant accomplishment. But, I suppose I'll have to go to Kingston to get my cloak."

"Let's walk over to that old warehouse and see if it will do," said Admiral Cross. It was a short walk to the warehouse, and when they arrived, the door was locked. "Allow me, sir," said Anne. A quick Remove spell on the lock and the door swung open on rusty hinges that creaked loudly. The three of them entered and found rows of empty, decaying racks and shelves that once held Navy supplies and equipment.

"We'd need to get rid of all these racks," said the Admiral, "then shore up the walls before we remove the roof, or the whole structure could collapse." The two magicians looked at each other and nodded in unspoken agreement. Anne moved to one side of the structure, while Wizard Lake took the other. Using Remove spells, the old and empty racks and shelves were disposed of quickly, leaving a large, empty warehouse that had plenty of room for a dragon to land in.

"Will this work?" asked the impressed Admiral. "I think so, sir," said Anne. "But when I remove the roof, I'll have to construct some sort of drainage system to channel the water out of the building when it rains." Wizard Lake nodded in approval. "Should we spruce up the exterior?" asked the Admiral. The two magicians gave it some thought, and then Wizard Lake said, "It might be better to leave it looking like it is, at least on the outside. That way, no one would suspect we're using it for anything important." "I like it," said Admiral Cross. "Can you two handle the rest of the modifications? I have a mountain of paperwork to get through this morning."

"Of course, sir. Thank you for taking the time to inspect the building with us," said Wizard Lake. After the Admiral departed, Wizard Lake looked at Anne and said, "Well, I guess we better get started."

By the end of the day, the roof was gone, the interior of the walls reinforced, and the cement floor of the warehouse was sloped so any rainwater would flow to the corner of the building farthest away from the door and out into a drainage culvert that led to the sea.

Wizard Lake said, "I think this might work." Anne said, "If you step back, sir, I'll make one last test."

The confused Wizard moved to the front door, and Anne walked to the center of the building, cast a Seeming of a curtain for privacy, disrobed, then clapped her hands and Changed into a Sea Dragon. She spread her wings and still had plenty of room to turn around in the large, empty structure. She then reared up and clapped her dragon forelegs together, changing back into her human form, quickly casting a Seeming of clothes.

"Amazing," was all the Chief of Naval Wizardry could say. After Anne got dressed, they replaced the lock on the front door with a much sturdier one than had been there when they arrived and headed back to the Navy Headquarters building, feeling very pleased with themselves.

As Gek landed outside Bruce's hut, Annalise came bounding towards him. "Hello, Anna. Have you been a good girl for mommy?" From inside the hut, Gek heard Azure (in human form) screaming, "Annalise! Get back in here!" The baby dragon cringed at her mother's tone and hid behind Gek's legs. "I guess that answers that question," said Gek, "come on, in we go." As they entered the hut, Gek saw the problem immediately; Richard's wooden cradle was lying in pieces, with baby dragon teeth marks all over it.

"What happened?" asked Gek. "What do you think happened?" asked Azure crossly. "I was playing with Richard, and Anna got jealous and came in here and destroyed his bed!" Gek sighed. "I guess we are going to have to find another bed for Richard. He was almost too big for that one anyway." "That is not the point!" exclaimed Azure. "I know, but what do you suggest we do about it?"

Disciplining the baby Dragon had been almost impossible for Gek and Azure. Bruce had suggested that, when Annalise acted aggressively towards her brother, they should respond by paying more attention to Richard and ignoring the baby Dragon, but it did not seem to be having the desired effect. If anything, being punished this way increased Anna's resentment towards her sibling.

Bruce returned from his morning 'driftwood search' and saw the broken cradle on the floor. "Well, I didn't think it would last much longer," he said wearily. "What do you mean?" asked Azure. "Well, Anna has been chewing on that cradle for about a week now. I think she's teething. It was only a matter of time before that old cradle gave way." "Teething?" asked Gek. "Sure, most infants need to chew on things as their teeth grow in. It helps ease the pain. Richard will eventually need something to chew on, too, but I don't recommend wood," said Bruce.

"What can we use for a bed for Richard?" asked Azure. "I've had my eye on an old shipping crate in the lean-to. If we pad it with enough blankets, it should work." "Gek, change into human form and help Bruce get this crate. I will look for some blankets," said Azure. "There should be some blankets and towels in that chest over there," said Bruce, pointing. "We'll be right back with the crate."

Gek went into the back room, transformed, and put on his tattered human clothes. When he emerged, Azure said, "We really should get you some new clothes. Those look like rags." "I know," grumbled Gek. "Especially since someone blew a hole clean through my shirt. It just has not been a priority lately."

After Bruce and Gek brought the medium-sized shipping crate inside, Azure lined it with towels and blankets and placed Richard inside. He immediately curled up and fell asleep. "A'fore long, you two are going to need a proper crib for him," said Bruce. "What is a crib?" asked Gek. "It's a bed for infants. At the rate that boy is growing, he'll be crawling and walking soon. Do all Changed One babies grow so fast?"

"I have no idea," said Azure. "Why do you say he is growing 'fast'?" "Well," replied Bruce, "just from looking at him, I'd say he was about six months old. If he was a human baby, that is. I estimate that he's growing about three times as fast as is normal for a human. At that rate, he'll be moving about on his own in no time. Once he learns how to climb out of this crate, you two will be chasing him all over the hut! Anyway, a *crib* is a bed with high rails, like a fence. It's designed to keep infants in their beds, so parents don't have to watch them every minute. Once the child learns how to climb out of their crib, that respite is over."

Gek yawned, "This is all very interesting, but I need some sleep. I have been flying all night. Bruce, can you watch Anna for a while? I need to talk to Azure in private for a minute." Bruce nodded and said, "Anna, how about we go down to the beach?" Anna looked at Azure questioningly, then bounded out the door when her mother nodded. "Be back in a few," said Bruce with a wink.

Gek and Azure moved into the back room, and Azure asked, "So, what did the Dragon Council decide this time?" "It was a very argumentative meeting," began Gek, "apparently, a Great Dragon Changed One attacked a pack of Snow Dragons that were assaulting a human village on the other side of the river. He killed six or seven of them before the others retreated back into the Snow Fields. Bliz, the Snow Dragon Clan Chief, was very angry." "I can imagine," said Azure. "Did he accuse you?" "Yes, but one of the Snow Dragons scratched the face of the Great Dragon before they fled, so Ard and I were able to convince the Snow Dragons that it was not one of us."

"Why would a Changed One attack the Snow Dragons?" wondered Azure. "He probably had family in the town they were attacking. This is one thing that we never considered. We suspected that some of the Changed Ones would not help us in our war with the humans, but we never thought that they would fight against us," said Gek quietly.

"That is troubling. So, what did the Council decide?" "We realized that there are probably more Changed Ones on the west side of the river, since their magic-users are not actively seeking out those with the spark, so we will concentrate our attacks on the humans on this side of the river where there are hopefully fewer Changed Ones. Also, the agreement that all Fire and Stone Dragons must stay west of the river is canceled. We will need them in our fight." "What did they say about this ridiculous truce we have with the human navy?" asked Azure.

Gek smiled, "Ard pointed out that our treaty just says that we will not attack their *ships or port facilities*; it does not restrict us from attacking the humans farther inland." Azure smiled, "That is an excellent point! I had not considered that." "Hopefully, the humans have not either. Ard also suggested that the Dragon Clans begin cooperating and attacking together, rather than each Clan on its own. This is a new and radical idea, and the Clan Chiefs all said that they would have to discuss it with their Clans. We will decide at the next Council meeting."

"That could be effective, but it is not the Dragon way," said Azure. "I know, but it could be a big advantage for us. I also raised the possibility of letting the humans know about our Changed Ones and our ability to speak and do magic," said Gek. "Are you crazy! Our ability to speak and do magic has been a closely guarded secret for centuries!" "I know," said Gek, "but the human magic-users already know about it. I think that they have not told their non-magic-users for fear of starting a panic and civil unrest. I agree it is a big decision, but it could really work in our favor."

"I guess we will have to wait and see what the Council decides," said Azure. "In the meantime, what are we going to do about Anna and Richard?" "I guess we keep an eye on them until they learn to speak and Richard can perform enough magic to defend himself from his sister." "And what do we do if he does not have the spark?" asked Azure worriedly.

277

King Donald

Chapter Fourteen:

ALL IS NOT AS IT SEEMS

Edward and Kathy landed just east of Baize, on the outskirts of the city. Quickly changing into human form and putting on their robes, they proceeded into the city on foot. It took most of the morning to reach the palace, and the summer sun had them dripping with sweat by the time they arrived. They made their way to the throne room, where the King was listening to a report from Minister William about all of the new construction projects in the kingdom, made possible by Edward's Sand and Adhesive spell combination.

As they entered, the King said, "Speak their names, and they appear! Mage Kathy! Wizard Edward! I never expected you back so soon! Come in, come in. Page, summon Wizard James at once. Minister William, is there anything else you wish to report?" "No, Sire, but I would like to ask Wizard Edward a question about his construction technique." "Of course," said the King.

"Wizard Edward, we've been using the Sand and Adhesive spells that you employed to repair our watering stations, but our magicians are not having the same success as you had. Is there a secret to the process?" Edward smiled and asked, "Minister, as a child, did you ever make sand castles on the beach?" "Of course," replied the Minister, confused. "And were you able to make your walls and towers with dry sand?" The Minister thought for a moment, then said, "No, the sand needed to be moist; dry sand can't be molded." "Exactly," said Edward. "The sand I used around the watering holes was already damp, so I didn't need to conjure any water to mix with the sand. If you're trying to make walls out of sand, you need to add a little water –not too much, or the Adhesive won't stick. Just make it moist." "Of course…" said Minister Williams, "thank you for the clarification, Wizard Edward."

As Minister Williams departed, considerably happier than when he arrived, Wizard James entered the throne room. "Kathy! Wizard Edward! How in the world did you get here so quickly?" Edward looked at Kathy and they both said in unison. "We flew." The King sat up straighter on his throne and said, "Flew?" "Just so, Your Majesty," said Kathy. "We transformed ourselves into dragons and flew here from our construction site near Springfield as soon as we received your message."

Wizard James realized that his mouth was hanging open and shut it quickly. "How does one transform into a dragon?" he asked.

"It's a long story, and we should probably start at the beginning," said Edward. He then explained about Donovan's surprising arrival, the news that he had passed his Sorcerer's Test and could change into a dragon, and finally, about his impending marriage. They then related how they asked Donovan to transform into a Great Dragon and scout out the water channels that led to the Great Salt Flats from the Caperian and Grey Mountains. This led to the story of Donovan fighting off the Snow Dragons that were attacking Snowton, his injury, and his return to the Academy for his wedding. He also told them about the attack by the Stone Dragon during the wedding reception and the casualties.

"We would have come sooner, Your Majesty, but as soon as we returned to the construction site, there was a tremendous thunderstorm that lasted three days. Your Messenger Hawk barely survived the journey."

When Edward was finished, the King said, "You certainly have an amazing family, Sir Wizard. The next time you see your son, please convey my personal thanks for his timely rescue of my citizens. Before we get to the 'change into a dragon' explanation, how is the construction project going?" "We are making good progress, Sire," said Kathy. "The apprentices are all working hard, and we hope to have the initial trench completed within the month." "You're joking," said

James. "Not at all," replied Edward. "You see, it's only thirty feet down to bedrock along the outer edge of the Salt Flats, so it's taking less than half the time I anticipated to dig the trench. I'm sure the distance to bedrock will increase as we begin excavating the middle of the reservoir, but since we won't be building any walls, the work should proceed on schedule."

"Did the big storm you mentioned cave in your walls?" asked James. Edward smiled, "No. While he was touring the site, my son suggested that we use the Heat spell to melt the sand into glass along the inside edge of the trench. This kept the sand and substrate in place so the rain did not cause the walls to collapse. There's about fifteen feet of water in the trench right now, which is actually a good thing, since it means that the bottom of the trench is firmly adhered to the bedrock below. The water in the trench should evaporate out in a few weeks."

"Have there been any dragon attacks?" asked the King. "No, but we did have to eliminate one Changed One among the apprentice magicians, and a merchant from Springfield attempted to sneak into Mage Kathy's tent one afternoon and poison her water pitcher," said Edward. "Why would a Springfield merchant try to kill you?" the King asked Kathy. "He was a Fire Dragon Changed One, Sire. He claimed that I killed his daughter, Char," replied Kathy.

"Who is Char?" asked James. "Char was Admiral Vandall's secretary, Charolette," said Kathy. "She tried to push me out of my bedroom window, and I killed her and vanished her body. I suspected that she was acting on orders from Wizard Louis, but I had no proof." "Why didn't you report this?" asked the King. "Sire, this was weeks before Wizard Edward exposed Louis as a dragon Changed One. I had no proof that Louis was behind the attack on me or the subsequent instances of finding poison in my meals or a sand viper under my bed."

The King shook his head sadly, "I'm sorry, Mage Kathy. I had no idea." Silence hung over the room for a time, and then James said, "So, how do you change yourself into a dragon?"

Home repair was *not* Donovan's thing. As expected, the first thing Rachel wanted changed about their new home was the shower. The water tank was too small and required them to refill it with water more often than Rachel liked. They had become accustomed to the showers at the Wizards Academy that automatically refilled when the water level in them dropped below a certain amount. The cabin's shower had no such refilling system. The first thing Donovan did was to Enlarge the size of the water tank. Unfortunately, when he filled the larger tank with water, the weight of the water was too heavy for the brackets holding the tank to the wall, and the tank came crashing down, splashing water and hurling ceramic shards everywhere.

For Donovan's next attempt, he created a copper water tank, which was big enough to hold enough water, and he Adhered and bolted it to the shower wall. After a few trials, he found that the copper conducted heat much better than the ceramic tank, and the water came out scalding hot. To refill the water tank, Donovan constructed (magically) a large water tank on the roof of the cabin, remembering to reinforce the rafters to account for the weight of the tank. Besides drawing water from the nearby river, the roof-top storage tank also had the ability to capture rainwater. Donovan was very proud of his shower system until his first shower, when steaming hot water with twigs, seaweed and river algae came pouring down on him. This required a series of screens and filters designed to keep river flotsam (and small fish) out of the shower water.

Tired and hungry, Donovan sat down to a bowl of cold *and* burned beef stew. Rachel was *not* a good cook. Since she had entered the Wizards Academy at age twelve, she had never learned to cook from her parents. At least they had some fresh bread they had bought at the market on their way home. Donovan made a mental note to suggest to Wizard Noland that a cooking class be added to the Wizards Academy curriculum.

When they arrived at the Officer's mess the next morning, Donovan spoke to Major Gerald, "Sir, do you think it would be alright if either Rachel or I helped out in the kitchen for a few days? You see, neither of us ever learned to cook. Rachel entered the Academy when she was twelve, and *I* certainly never learned. I think we would both agree that our first meal together last night was *awful*." The Major laughed, "I would have thought the Academy would have taught you about cooking." "We can both brew *Serums*, but that's not food." The Major thought for a moment, then said, "I never met a cook that didn't want more help. They'll probably be pleased to show you their skills."

"What are we going to be working on today, sir?" Donovan asked. "In garrison, our training schedule is pretty much the same every week: on Firstday, we focus on individual combat skills in the morning and crossbow training in the afternoon; on Twoday we conduct maneuvers at the squad level, pitting one squad against another; on Midweek we practice Company level exercises; Foursday we focus on equipment maintenance, and on Endday we have an equipment inspection, then release the men for the rest of the day. Other than showing me that you have not lost your

Concealment cloaks and that your mount's shoes are in good order, you two will be released early on Enddays."

After breakfast, Donovan and Rachel headed out with their respective companies. When they reached the training area, Captain Fletcher, the commander of 2nd Company, said, "OK, men, as usual, 1st squad will go against the 1st squad from 1st Company, our 2nd squad against their 2nd squad. Third squad, you know what to do. This morning, the 1st squad from 1st Company will defend that tree line over there," he said, pointing at the tree line about half a mile away. "Sorcerer Donovan will accompany our 1st squad, while Sorceress Rachel will go with 1st Company's 2nd squad; the rest of you know the drill. Move out."

As the 1st squad gathered around Sergeant Brown, the squad leader, Donovan, asked, "So, how does this work?" The squad leader grinned. "We usually just put on our new Concealment cloaks and try to sneak up on the other squad. Sometimes, it works, and sometimes, they're able to detect our approach. Anyone we can touch without being detected is 'dead,' if they find us, we're 'dead.'" "I see," said Donovan thoughtfully, "and they're in that tree line?" "They're supposed to be, but that doesn't mean that they can't move and take a position forward of the trees or deeper in the woods," said Sergeant Brown.

"How long does this exercise last?" asked Donovan. "Usually until lunch," replied the Sergeant. "Why?" "Well, I have a sneaky idea, if you want to try it." "Tell me," said the Sergeant, grinning. "Well, how about if we just sit here for the next couple of glasses. That will make them think that maybe we're trying to sneak around behind them. They'll start jumping at shadows and random noises in the forest. I can actually Sense where they are from here. When we're ready, we can walk across the field and surprise them," said Donovan.

"That won't work," said Sergeant Brown, "in the past, they've always seen our footsteps in the tall grass as we approach." Donovan thought for a second, then said, "They won't if I conjure a brisk wind across the grass as we approach." The Sergeant smiled, "I like it. I don't like losing this game to Sergeant Jackson, the 1st squad leader in 1st Company."

The men in the squad sat down in a circle and introduced themselves to Donovan while they waited. As they sat and discussed life in the Royal Expeditionary Force, Donovan noticed that the soldier's armor 'clinked' as they moved around. "Sergeant Brown, would it be OK if I put a Silence spell on everyone's armor? That would keep them from giving themselves away as they get close to the other squad." "Is it that loud?" asked the confused squad leader. "Not really, but if the other side has a magician who is using a Hearing Enhancement spell, it's loud enough to detect." "Please proceed then." Donovan went around to each soldier and cast a Silence and Stamina spell on their armor. When he was done, he sat down, took a drink from his water bottle and rested for a moment. The amazed soldiers began jumping around, shocked that there was no noise from their armor plates as they rattled against each other.

"This is fantastic!" exclaimed Sergeant Brown. "Now we're invisible *and* silent!" "Yes," said Donovan, "but there are limits to the silence." "What does that mean?" "It means that the armor will not make any noise when it strikes something, but whatever strikes the armor *will* make a noise." "I don't understand," said the Sergeant. "Let me demonstrate," said Donovan. "Corporal Dinning, please stand up and hand me your sword." The Corporal looked confused but stood and handed over his short sword. Donovan took a gentle swing at the armor covering the Corporal's shoulder, and the sword made a soft ringing sound. Donovan handed the Corporal back his weapon.

"You see? The armor did *not* make a sound; what you heard was the sound that the sword made when it struck the armor." The assembled soldiers murmured their understanding. "So, if you're sneaking up on someone, and you step on a twig and it snaps, that will make a noise. Similarly, if an acorn falls from a tree and hits your armor, the acorn will make a sound. You understand?" The soldiers all nodded their understanding about the limits of the Silence spell.

"Now, I can Sense that the opposing squad is moving back, deeper into the woods. They probably think we're trying to sneak up on them from behind. Let's go surprise them, shall we?"

The squad rose and, with Donovan in the lead, proceeded single-file across the field. Donovan conjured a brisk wind across the field, covering their approach. As they entered the wood line, Donovan and the squad leader directed the men of 1st squad to each member of the 'enemy' squad. When they were all in position, Sergeant Brown yelled, "NOW!" Eight swords tapped eight soldiers from behind, making them jump. One soldier actually screamed in surprise.

Sergeant Jackson from 1st Company complained, "No fair. Next time we get the Sorcerer." "Agreed," said Donovan. "I'll also put the Silence spell on all your men's armor, just to make it fair." The soldiers headed back to the garrison for lunch, each discussing the morning's exercise.

"How did it go?" asked Major Gerald as Donovan entered the Officer's Mess. "It was actually unfair, one squad having a magician while the other did not," replied Donovan. "We sat and waited for about two glasses; by that time, the 1st Company squad was jumping at every noise in the forest. I put a Silence spell on my squad's armor, so they were able to sneak up on them and surprise them completely. I also used a Wind spell to hide our footsteps through the tall grass. I promised to put a Silence spell on 1st Company's armor this afternoon, just to make it fair."

"I can see that having magical support is going to be a huge combat multiplier," said Major Gerald. "Where's Rachel?" asked Donovan. "She came back over a glass ago. She's back in the kitchen helping the cooks. The squad she was with was also able to sneak up on their opponents and win the game. You two are making quite an impression on our soldiers." "I guess I should go back and help Rachel, or I'll never hear the end of it," said Donovan. "Just don't forget to eat something," said the Major.

Donovan went back into the kitchen and found Rachel watching Corporal Fry cook mutton steaks. "The key is to brown the meat on both sides without cooking all of the moisture out of it," explained the cook. "Oh, hello, sir." Donovan approached and said, "Sorry I'm late. What can I do to help?" Rachel frowned at him, "Well, lunch is almost done. Why don't you help clean up the dishes?" "There's no need for that…" said Corporal Fry. "Oh no! If I cooked, he gets to clean. There's the sink," she said, pointing. Donovan shrugged and walked over to the stack of dishes and cooking utensils that were soaking in the warm, soapy water. Donovan thought for a minute, then drained the water as the cooks and kitchen helpers looked on, wondering just what their new Sorcerer was up to.

Once the water had drained, Donovan picked up the first baking sheet, murmured a Remove spell, and proceeded to clean the dishes at lightning speed, much to the surprise of the kitchen staff. Donovan was done before the last of the cooking implements were finished being used, and he was dry as a bone. Rachel said, "Cheater." Donovan merely shrugged and headed into the dining area with her to get their meal.

After lunch, Donovan accompanied 1st Company's 1st squad to the training area. The exercise was the same as the morning drill; 2nd Company occupied the tree line, and 1st Company was tasked to sneak up and attack them. After applying the Silence spell to each soldier's armor and explaining the limits of the spell, Donovan asked, "So, Sergeant Jackson, how would you like to proceed?"

"Well, I can tell you, we were all inside our heads waiting for 2nd Company this morning. I was convinced that you were trying to circle around and get behind us. The waiting was stressful." Donovan grinned, "I'll bet that Sergeant Brown will expect us to try the same thing on his squad. Maybe we should head over immediately while their guard is down."

Sergeant Jackson considered the idea, then said, "I like it. Can you tell where they are right now?" Donovan thought for a moment, using his Sensing ability, and then he said, "They're in the grass, about a hundred yards in front of the tree line. I guess they don't want to get spooked by all the noises in the forest." "So how do we get close without them seeing us approach through the tall grass?" asked Sergeant Jackson. Donovan said, "When we walked across the field this morning, I cast a brisk breeze across the grass to mask our footsteps. What if I cast the breeze across the east side of the field to get them looking that way, then we approach from the west side?" "I like it. Let's go."

The men donned their Concealment cloaks and moved off to the west side of the meadow. Donovan concentrated and cast a Wind spell on the east side of the field. As expected, the soldiers from 2nd Company saw the grass moving and arrayed themselves to repel an assault from the east, and the 1st Company soldiers were able to sneak up and surprise them. After the day's exercises, it was obvious that having a magician on your side was a decisive advantage.

Donovan entered the kitchen ahead of Rachel and went to the preparation area to see what he could do to help. "What's for dinner?" he asked. "We're making a stew out of the leftover mutton," said Corporal Fry. "What can I do to help?" asked Donovan. The cook looked around and said, "Well, you could wash and chop some vegetables." Donovan moved to the sink and began washing the carrots, peas, onions and potatoes.

"Did I miss anything important this afternoon?" Donovan asked. "Not really. Sorceress Rachel and I mainly talked about the importance of avoiding cross-contamination," said the cook. "Cross-contamination? What's that?" The cook explained that, when working with raw meat, you had to avoid transferring germs from the raw meat to the cooked meat, either with your hands or the utensils you were using. He also stressed the need for washing your hands frequently and keeping the cooking and preparation surfaces clean. "Food poisoning fells more soldiers than enemy swords," the cook explained. "That's one reason that you only get tea to drink in the field. The boiling of the water kills the germs and makes the water safe to drink. We also make sure that we carefully clean the cook pots after each meal."

After the warning, Donovan carefully washed the vegetables before chopping them and adding them to the pot. The stew was in the pot and over the fire before Rachel came in. "How did it go?" asked Donovan. "About the same as this morning. It's really not fair to the squad without magical support," replied Rachel. "We do Company against Company tomorrow, so the forces will be more evenly matched," said Donovan.

"You two ready to learn how to make bread?" asked the baker. "Absolutely," the two magicians replied.

The dinner was passable but not the best meal either of them had ever eaten. "It's the mutton," explained Corporal Fry. "Beef makes a better stew, but we use what we have. Will we see you two tomorrow?" "Probably not for lunch," replied Donovan. "We're doing Company-level drills tomorrow." The cook nodded his understanding and headed back to the kitchen.

The next day, after breakfast, Major Gerald and the Expeditionary Force rode a little way out of the city to a small, round hill surrounded by woods. Major Gerald reigned up and addressed his troops, "This morning, I want 1st Company to defend this hill and 2nd Company to attack it. Defenders, you have two glasses to prepare your positions. Use every weapon at your disposal, but try not to injure each other."

As 2nd Company moved down into the trees, Donovan asked Captain Fletcher, "How does this usually work?" The Captain replied, "Well, *without* magical support, the defenders normally dig shallow trenches and earthworks to hide behind, then mow down the attacking force with their crossbows. I'm not sure the attacking force has ever won this game." "Well, Sorceress Rachel will undoubtedly use the Dig spell to make the trenches and use Sensing and Hearing enhancements to detect our approach." "So, you're saying we can't win," said Captain Fletcher. Donovan thought. "Not at all, sir. Tell me how the defenders can use crossbows without injuring the attackers; even the training bolts my father constructed would seriously injure someone at close range."

"The crossbowmen don't load the bolts; they just draw the bows and fire them empty. If you're targeted by a crossbowman, you're considered dead." Donovan smiled, "Then I have an idea."

After two glasses of time, the soldiers of the 2nd Company began climbing the hill quietly. The Senior Specialists, Lance and Dirk, were each off, looking for one another. The 2nd squad had left their bows behind in favor of their short swords. When they were just inside crossbow range, Donovan conjured a Seeming of the Company, charging up the hill towards the dug-in 1st Company. When they heard the twang of the crossbows being fired, Donovan dropped the Seeming, and the real soldiers quickly closed the distance before the confused crossbowmen could reload.

Second Company rolled over the trenches and surrounded Rachel, Captain Smith, and Major Gerald. "HOLD!" shouted the Major. The winded soldiers from 2nd Company stopped in their tracks. "Victory to 2nd Company! That was a fine bit of trickery, Sorcerer Donovan! First Company expended all of their crossbow bolts shooting at a Seeming, and you overran them while they were reloading. Take a break for lunch, and in two and a half glasses, it's 1st Company's turn to attack." Rachel walked down the hill with 1st Company, shaking her finger at Donovan.

While they ate their trail rations, Donovan asked Captain Fletcher how he usually defended this hill. The commander replied that the hill was normally defended just like what 1st Company had done, trenches or embankments, maybe some forward scout positions, but, given an equal number of attackers and defenders, equally armed, the defenders usually won. "Well, Sorceress Rachel is probably going to try something you've never seen before, like sneaking up close and casting a Sleep spell on all the soldiers," said Donovan.

"So, what do you recommend?" "I'll track Rachel," said Donovan. "Wherever she is, that's most likely where 1st Company will be. Once we determine which side of the hill they're coming up, you can move your troops to intercept them. I'll try to counter-act her Sleep spell."

After about a glass, Donovan Sensed Rachel moving around to the east side of the hill. He advised Captain Fletcher to position his troops accordingly. Once the defenders were in place, Donovan conjured a rain storm to make climbing the hill more difficult for the approaching 1st Company and potentially make it easier to detect the soldiers under their Concealment cloaks.

Just as Rachel was coming into Tether spell range, Donovan realized that he'd been tricked. "BEHIND US!" he shouted. But it was too late, as soldiers from the 1st Company came spilling over the hilltop from the west side, behind the waiting 2nd Company. Donovan quickly conjured a Seeming of a swooping dragon and sent it hurtling towards the charging soldiers, but they were not fooled. "HOLD!" shouted a soaking wet Major Gerald. "Victory to 1st Company!"

Donovan canceled the Water spell, and the downpour stopped. He reached out and helped his soaking-wet wife the rest of the way up the hill. "I knew you would track me," she said. "You were right, but I'll do better next time," replied Donovan. As the soldiers of the Royal Expeditionary Force headed down the hill to where their mounts were waiting, the soldiers conversed among themselves about how tricky their new Sorcerers were.

Chapter Fifteen:

SILVER AND GOLD

"That should do it," said Wizard Noland tiredly. The Wizards Academy faculty, with the help of Wizard Cassandra, the Franconian Court Wizard, had just finished replicating the 10,000 gold coins that Jasmine, the former Minister of Internal Security, had stolen or simply destroyed with a Remove spell, in order to undermine the finances of the Kingdom. The theft had been discovered by Leonard, the Franconian Minister of Finance, during a routine audit of the Treasury. Minister Leonard had reported the shortage to Wizard Noland immediately, and the Headmaster had agreed to begin an immediate search for the missing currency. It had taken almost a week to replicate all of the missing coinage, with the Academy instructors and the Court Wizard working several hours each night to replace all the pilfered gold.

The good news was that the King had not returned from his visit to Southport, where he was overseeing the final touches on his new 'Winter Palace,' and so had not become aware of the missing gold.

"The rest of you head back to the Academy," said Noland, "I'll go and inform Minister Leonard that we found the missing gold and that it's all back where it should be. Thank you for your tireless efforts." "Michael," said Wizard Daniel, the History and Enhancements instructor, "How do we know that this hasn't happened in other towns and cities throughout the Kingdom?" Wizard Noland considered this disturbing thought, "That is a troubling question," he replied. "You may be right, if Jasmine had other co-conspirators in other cities and towns. We should probably conduct a quiet audit of all of the Treasuries in the Kingdom."

"How on earth are we going to do that?" asked Wizard Dylan, the Forces instructor. "We can't just all leave our duties at the Academy, and only a magician will be able to replicate any currency that's found to be missing." "I'll give it some thought," said Noland. "Right now, I need to go speak with the Minister of Finance. Give this problem some thought tonight, and we'll discuss it in my cottage tomorrow after Mentor testing."

The Wizards departed the Treasury vault, which Noland secured with the key. After some consideration, Noland used a Change spell to create a new key and lock mechanism, just in case someone had obtained an unauthorized key to the vault. After re-keying the lock, he went upstairs and proceeded to the Finance Minister's office. As expected, the lamp was still burning, even though it was well past midnight. Wizard Noland knocked softly.

"Yes? Come in," said the weary voice of Leonard, the Finance Minister. Noland entered with a beaming smile, "Minister, I just wanted to inform you that we found the missing gold!" Leonard practically leaped from his desk to embrace the Wizard. "Thank you, thank you, thank you!" he exclaimed. "That's the best news I've ever heard! Where did you find it?" Noland answered, "It was hidden in a secret room in Jasmine's apartment. I suspected as much. After all, 10,000 golds take up quite a bit of space and are much too heavy to move around easily. She probably took a little at a time, over several years."

"But you recovered it all?" asked the relieved Minister. "We recovered a little over 10,000 gold coins, Minister. I don't know if that's what we *should* have found. Not knowing what the accounts say, I can only tell you what we *actually* found." "Of course, of course," said Leonard, "You would have no idea of what should be in the Treasury. I should have thought of that." "It's also likely that Jasmine spent some of what she stole, so the final tally may come up short of what you expect."

The Finance Minister considered this possibility. "You're correct, of course, Jasmine undoubtedly spent some of her ill-gotten gains, but if you recovered 10,000 golds, then there's not too much missing." "You understand that we didn't actually *count* all of the recovered gold; we just seized whatever we found and returned it to the Treasury vault. There may be more or a little less than 10,000 golds, but I judge the amount is close to what you determined was missing." "Of course," said Leonard. "Thank you so much! You have saved my job and probably my head and rescued the Kingdom from financial ruin. I'll have my staff conduct a full inventory in the morning."

"I took the liberty of re-keying the lock to the Treasury vault," said Noland, handing over the new key. "Just in case, Jasmine had an accomplice helping her remove funds from the vault. This is the only key that will open the door now. Is one key enough, or would you like me to replicate a few more?" asked Noland. The Finance Minister considered the question and replied, "You know, one key might be best for now. If I need additional keys made, I assume that Wizard Cassandra can assist me?" Noland nodded, "Wizard Cassandra is more than capable of replicating a simple vault key."

"That's good to know. Thank you again," said Leonard, yawning. "I suggest you get some sleep, Minister. I know it's been a stressful few days since you discovered the theft." "You can say that again," replied

Leonard, "I was just calculating how much we were going to have to raise taxes in order to compensate for the missing gold, and I assure you, the citizens and merchants of Franconia would not have been pleased."

"Good night then, Minister," said Noland as he eased his way out of the door. "Good night, good night," replied Leonard. Noland left the palace and returned to the Wizards Academy, wondering if Daniel could be correct and if other local Treasuries had been plundered by dragon Changed Ones.

Sorceress Anne landed back on the HMS VALOR. This time, before changing back into her human form, she asked the sailors to kindly turn their backs. The crew grudgingly complied, and Anne quickly transformed and dressed. "Thank you, gentlemen. As you were," she said. Mage Andrew came over and said, "Is it Anne or Celeste? You two really need to start dressing differently, or maybe one of you could wear her hair shorter, so we could tell the difference."

"Hello, Mage Andrew," said Anne, "It's me, Anne." "Welcome back. How was Grotton?" "The Admiral was very glad to receive the message about the Stone Dragons, and we selected a large abandoned warehouse near the Navy Headquarters building, where Dragon Messengers can land and transform before delivering their messages." "Won't someone see?" asked Andrew. "Not if we cast a Concealment shield over ourselves before we land. We should also probably wear our Concealment cloaks as we walk from the warehouse to the Admiralty."

"Dragon Messengers?" asked Andrew. "Yes, that's what Admiral Cross wants to call us," said Anne. "*US?*" "Yes. Celeste and I have been appointed by Wizard Noland as the official Dragon Messengers to the Royal Navy." Andrew let that news set in for a moment, then asked, "Are you sure that's what you want? The crew has grown very fond of you."

"I know, Andrew. But the fact of the matter is that whenever I'm on deck, *they stare at me* like I'm a circus attraction. They don't say anything, and they're always respectful, but can you imagine being leered at every minute? That's why I spend almost all of my off-duty time in my cabin instead of up on deck." Andrew said, "I could ask them…" "What? Not to stare? You know that would be an unenforceable order. Besides, once another ship arrives, I'll be reassigned there. No, I think this is for the best. This way, my sister and I can still help the Navy and the crown." "I suppose you're right," said Andrew. "So, what brings you back to the HMS VALOR?"

"I need to let Commodore Matthews know about my new assignment and give him new orders from the Admiral," said Anne. "I think he's below, checking on the food stores. Let's go find him."

The two magicians headed below decks and found the Commodore inspecting a barrel of apples. "These still look all right," the Commodore said, "but let's serve them in the next few days before they start to go bad." "Aye, Aye, sir," said the Galley Steward. The Commodore looked up and, seeing the two magicians approaching, said, "Anne! Welcome back. What's the news from the Admiral?" Andrew looked mystified. "How did you know it was Anne?" he asked. "Because Celeste is on her way to Kingston with the draft Peace Treaty," replied the Commodore.

Anne smiled at the Commodore's insightfulness. "Here is a message from Admiral Cross," she said, handing over the message pouch. "Let's go up to my cabin," said the Commodore. They climbed the steep staircase to the next deck up and headed aft to the Commodore's cabin. Once inside, the Commodore sat in his Captain's chair and opened the message pouch. He read the message quickly. "So, Official Dragon Messenger to the Royal Navy, eh? Well, I knew that someone would be assigned that duty, and it had to be a magician who'd seen a dragon. I don't suppose there are many to choose from."

"No, Commodore. Other than my sister and me, there are only the instructors at the Wizards Academy, Mage Andrew, and two Sorcerers with the Royal Expeditionary Force, and none of them are available for this duty." "So, what about your sister?" "She is also a Dragon Messenger, Sir. I believe that she'll be assigned to deliver messages to the 2nd Fleet, while I serve in the 1st Fleet." The Commodore nodded, "I guess I can understand that. A single Dragon Messenger would be run ragged flying between both Fleets. So, where are you bound for next?"

"I have a message for Vice Admiral Jordan, informing him of my new assignment and delivering the Concealment cloaks to the magicians in his squadron." "We'll miss you, Sorceress. I admit, I had my doubts about a woman serving in the Royal Navy, but you did yourself proud. Let's head up on deck and get you on your way." The Commodore gave a subtle nod to Andrew, who headed forward to find the Bos'n.

As Anne stood on the aft deck and prepared to transform, Andrew erected a Seeming to conceal her from the crew as she disrobed. Once in dragon-form, the Bos'n raised his pipe and blew a three-note signal. "DRAGON MESSENGER, DEPARTING!" shouted the Commodore. All of the sailors on deck saluted Sorceress Anne as she flew off to the south and the HMS SENTRY.

As the locksmith finished installing the lock on the cabin door, Donovan paced around the living room. "What's wrong?" asked Rachel. "I'm worried about the training we've been doing this week," Donovan replied. "Is this because I beat you on Midweek afternoon?" "No. You were very clever and I thought I knew what you were going to do, and I was wrong. That's not it at all," said Donovan.

"All done, sir," said the locksmith. "Here are your keys." Donovan thanked the locksmith and paid him three silvers for installing the lock on their front door, a task that was beyond his homemaking ability. After the locksmith departed, Donovan looked at Rachel and continued, "I don't think we're doing the *right* kind of training. I realize it's what the Royal Expeditionary Force has always done, and it's worked out in the past because the Expeditionary Force was facing conventional forces or brigands. But soon, we'll be fighting *dragons*, and these squad-on-squad training exercises will not help us fight them. Even the individual skills training is questionable. Only the axmen are getting any training at attacking a dragon. I think we need more crossbow training and not just the kind we're doing."

"What do you mean?" asked Rachel. "When we were headed towards Farmdale, my father built a wooden target that he strung between some trees. He used a Wind spell to blow it back and forth and had the crossbowmen try to hit it. Only I succeeded. The rest of the force was unable to hit a moving target, and we lost most of their crossbow bolts. The bowmen decided that the crossbows were useless for engaging flying targets. That's why most of the crossbows were still in the wagons when we attacked the dragon," said Donovan.

"So, you're saying that we need to start shooting at flying targets," said Rachel. "Well, at least *dragon-shaped targets,*" said Donovan, "but yes. We need to adjust our training regime. We need to practice for the *next* war, not the last one." "So, what will you recommend to Major Gerald?" "More crossbow practice, maybe at flying Seemings of dragons. But, unless we figure out a way to recover the bolts, we're going to run out of them in about two days."

"What if we practiced inside the Wizards Academy?" asked Rachel. "The shield should keep the crossbow bolts from flying away." "That's an interesting idea," said Donovan, "but I'm not sure how we could use one of the training areas without disrupting lessons." Rachel considered the problem, and then inspiration struck, "What if we made a training area on the *outside* of the shield, near the boundary. Then we could fire crossbows at Seemings without losing any of the bolts!"

"That's brilliant!" said Donovan. "That is, as long as a crossbow bolt can't penetrate the shield. We'd have to do some tests and get Wizard Noland's permission. Any idea what's on the outside of the shield?" "Well, the south side has the portal to the marina, the north side faces the city, and the west side is along the river. We would have to use the east side, and I have to admit, even after ten years at the Academy, I never stopped to consider what was on the other side of the shield."

"We'll talk to Major Gerald in the morning and then Wizard Noland if the Major approves. It's a good thing that tomorrow is Firstday. I doubt that we'll miss anything by skipping sparring practice."

The next morning at breakfast, Donovan and Rachel explained their ideas to Major Gerald. "Yer probably right," he admitted. "Our current training schedule hasn't changed in years, except the crossbow training. I've been thinking about how to construct flying targets, but you remember what a disaster that was, Donovan." "I know," said Donovan, "but that was when we weren't sure it *was* a dragon. Now we know. I'll bet that the soldiers will be much more enthusiastic and focused now." "Huh, you're probably right about that. What would we use for a target? That wood thing with a streamer wasn't a very good likeness."

"Well, Rachel or I could cast a Seeming of a dragon. If they hit it, it would vanish in a flash of light," said Donovan. "That's a great idea! I wonder why your father didn't think of that," said the Major. "It's because he'd never seen a dragon before," said Donovan. "You can't cast a Seeming of something you've never seen." "Riiiight," said Major Gerald.

"I suppose, in a pinch, I could transform into a dragon and act as a target. You'd have to use the dummy bolts, though," said Donovan. "I don't think so," said Rachel. "We don't know how much damage even a training bolt would do to you." "That reminds me, Sir, I need to go back to the Wizards Academy sometime and ask Wizard Noland if there are any Great or Fire Dragon Changed Ones at the Academy. I need to figure out how to breathe fire when I'm in dragon-form. Besides screaming when I get scratched in the face."

"Why don't you two go back there today? You can find out about what's on the east side of the Academy. I admit, I have no idea. Meanwhile, I'll start thinking about a new training regime. One geared towards evading and killing dragons," said Major Gerald.

As Rachel and Donovan rode through town, they observed several teams of carpenters busily affixing what looked like Stone Dragon scales to the roofs of the palace buildings. "I wonder what in the world they're doing?" asked Rachel. "Let's ask," said Donovan. They rode into the palace courtyard and asked the carpenter's foreman what they were doing. "Civic improvements," was the somewhat terse reply from the supervisor.

"Are those dragon scales?" asked Rachel. "I'm not really sure what they are, Miss," said the Foreman, with a much more respectful tone towards the attractive young lady. "We got a wagon load of 'em delivered with orders to have 'em installed on every roof in the palace before the King returns next week. I'll tell you this much, I've never seen the like of 'em. They're hard as steel but a bit lighter; inflexible too. Why, we can't even drill a hole through 'em to make installation easier!" "How are you attaching them?" asked Donovan.

"The only way we can! Tar!" said the foreman. "We spread out tar on the roof and then stick 'em down. Overlapping, of course, so the rain washes down 'em. They're so heavy, we're having to reinforce the rafters to hold the extra weight." "Can I see one?" asked Rachel. The foreman walked over to a nearby wagon and brought back a Stone Dragon scale for her examination. "Definitely a Stone Dragon scale," murmured Donovan.

"Are they all the same size?" asked Rachel. "Unfortunately," said the worker. "I sure wish we had some that were about half as wide, for the edges, you know." "We might be able to help with that," said Donovan. "How?" asked the foreman, suspiciously. "Well, we're both Sorcerers," said Rachel, "we could use a simple Reduce spell and shrink some of these down in no time."

The foreman removed his cap respectfully, "I'm sorry. I didn't know. I would really appreciate your help." Donovan and Rachel moved to the wagon, and Rachel asked, "How many would you like Reduced?" The foreman thought for a minute, then said, "If you just made those on that pallet there smaller, say half the size, width-wise, that would be a tremendous help."

"We can certainly do that," said Donovan, "but you need to unstack them and lay them flat for us." The supervisor grabbed a couple of workers, and in short order, the pallet of Stone Dragon scales was laid out on the ground in a single layer. "I'll take the left half; you take the right?" asked Donovan. Rachel nodded, and both magicians said *"REDUCTO,"* while pinching their right thumb and index fingers together. The scales instantly shrank to half their width.

The foreman looked on in wonder. "Fantastic!" he said. "This will make our job so much easier! Thank you both!" "Our pleasure," said Rachel. "Now we really have to be off. Good luck!" The foreman waved happily as Rachel and Donovan continued on towards the Wizards Academy. "I wonder why someone wants Stone Dragon scales on the roof of the palace," said Rachel. "It's certainly not very stylish."

"I'll bet it's really good insulation, though," said Donovan, "and it will surely protect against hail damage." Rachel shrugged.

They rode up to the hitching post in front of the grey, nondescript building that was the entrance to the Wizards Academy. "I hope we can get them to open the door for us," said Rachel. "You know they usually only open on Midweek mornings. "I'll bet if I knock hard enough, maybe with a Blast spell, I can get their attention," said Donovan. Before he reached the door, it opened, and Wizard Faith said, "Please don't Blast my door. I have to live here, you know."

Wizard Faith

Chapter Sixteen:
BELLS AND WHISTLES

"What's on the east side of the Academy boundary?" asked Wizard Noland. "I honestly have no idea, Why?" Donovan and Rachel were seated in the Headmaster's parlor, having tea. "Sir, Major Gerald wants the Royal Expeditionary Force to do some crossbow training against flying targets. We just can't think of a way to do it without losing too many bolts."

"Dragon-shaped flying targets, I assume?" asked Wizard Noland with a smile. Donovan shrugged. "I know we can't practice in here," said Donovan, "it would disrupt the lessons, but we thought if we used the outside of the barrier…" "I see," said Noland, "well, the only way to find out will be to walk around from the marina, I suppose." "Will the barrier stop a crossbow bolt?" asked Rachel.

"That's a good question," said Noland. "Personally, I've never fired one at it. I think it *should* hold. I mean, students have tried burning through it, Blasting through it and digging under it without success. I suppose we should go find out, though." They walked across the courtyard to the Academy Armory, where Donovan's crossbow was still stored. "My crossbow! I'd forgotten all about it," said Donovan. "Yes, I was going to send it to you, but since you're here, you can take it with you when you leave," said Noland.

Armed with his crossbow and a couple of iron bolts, they proceeded past the stables into the Forces Training area. They continued on until they came to the boundary of the Wizards Academy, delineated by a smooth, curving line in the sand. When they got within one hundred feet of the barrier, Wizard Noland said, "I think this is close enough. We don't want to get hit by shrapnel if the bolt shatters. Donovan, you may proceed."

Donovan put on the belt with the hook, which was required to draw the stiff steel bow, placed his foot in the stirrup, and flexed his legs and back, drawing the crossbow. The bowstring was held back by a metal post, which was lowered by pulling the lever under the stock. Donovan carefully loaded an iron bolt into the groove on the top of the stock and placed the back end of the bolt next to the taut bowstring. Donovan took aim, and Wizard Noland said, "You break my barrier, and you bought it." Donovan fired.

The barrier rang like an enormous bell, and the crossbow bolt bent in half and fell to the ground, but the shield held. A few minutes later, Wizard Faith, Wizard Dylan and Wizard Daniel came running to find out what had happened. "Let's *never* do that again," said Wizard Noland, shaking his head, his ears still ringing. "What happened?" asked Wizard Faith. "We were trying to see if the barrier could be used as a backstop for crossbow practice for the Royal Expeditionary Force. The answer is 'absolutely not.' Everyone inside would go deaf."

"Well then, I guess there's no point in walking around to the other side to see what's there," said Rachel. "What? Over there?" asked Wizard Dylan, "That's a swamp." "And just how would you know that?" asked Wizard Noland. Wizard Dylan blushed, "You see, when I was a Level Three, my girlfriend and I went exploring one Endday afternoon. We left the portal at the boat dock and decided to see what was on this side of the barrier. It's a pretty deep, nasty bog, full of biting insects and snakes. We couldn't get out of there fast enough."

"Well, that settles that! Donovan, Rachel, I guess the Royal Expeditionary Force will have to find someplace else to practice shooting crossbow bolts at flying targets." "Have you considered the old amphitheater?" asked Wizard Faith. "The what?" asked Donovan. "The amphitheater, out on the east edge of the city? It shut down years ago, after the Kingston Opera House was built. It's got a big half-dome made out of plaster and mortar, but if you used the wooden training bolts, it should work just fine." "I knew we'd come to the right place," said Rachel.

As they walked back into the courtyard, there was a commotion of students leaving the student dormitories. "What's going on?" asked Wizard Noland. "Did you hear that bell? Well, all of the students thought it was the dinner bell and headed off to the dining rooms until the cooks shooed them out. Dinner won't be ready for another hour yet." Donovan laughed.

Donovan, Rachel, Wizard Faith and Wizard Noland walked back to the gatehouse. Before they left, Donovan said, "Sir, one more thing, I need to talk to a Fire, Stone, or Great Dragon Changed One to learn how to breathe fire while I'm in dragon form. Who can I ask?" They entered the gatehouse and sat down in Wizard Faith's parlor. "I've already made inquiries," said Wizard Noland. "Before the Stone Dragon attack, the Changed Ones here at the Academy were very reluctant to explain the process. After the carnage during your reception, they all came by to explain it to me."

"Well, at least *something* good came out of it," grumbled Donovan. Wizard Noland continued, "As I understand it, there are 'lumps' inside a dragon's mouth, both on the top and bottom. These 'lumps' are, in fact, sacs of *inferno,* a gelatinous substance that the dragon ignites. Apparently, you push on the inferno sac with your tongue, which squirts the inferno out towards the target, then, as the inferno leaves your mouth, you ignite it by dragging your tongue across your teeth, which creates sparks." "That sounds complicated," said Donovan.

"Yes, and it gets worse. It seems that each sac squirts inferno in a slightly different direction. According to the Changed Ones, it takes a long time to learn how to hit what you're aiming at and light the inferno. It's not uncommon for young dragons to spit unlit inferno, then emit sparks from their mouths too late to ignite it," said Noland. Donovan groaned, "How am I going to practice that?" Wizard Noland said, "I suppose we could use the Forces Training area in the evenings after supper. We'd have to make the area 'Off Limits' to students practicing their Tracer skills, playing hide-and-seek, or Blind-Man's-Bluff."

"How much inferno does a dragon have?" asked Rachel. "It seems to depend on what type of dragon," replied Wizard Noland. "Fire Dragons have the most, followed by Great, then Stone Dragons. That's undoubtedly why the Stone Dragons that attacked Weaton stopped breathing fire after a time. They ran out of inferno." "Do we know how long it takes for the inferno to regenerate?" asked Donovan. "One day, according to the Changed Ones."

"Well, this has certainly been an interesting day," said Rachel. "By the way, do you know why carpenters are sticking Stone Dragon scales to the roofs of the palace?" Noland smiled, "To make them fireproof. We couldn't really think of any other useful purpose for them, but as a hard, fireproof material, that is easily replicated, it must be good for something," said Noland. "Can we have one?" asked Donovan. "Between the two of us, we might be able to think of something."

Donovan and Rachel returned to their cottage, each carrying a Stone Dragon scale, with Donovan's crossbow and iron bolts.

Sorceress Celeste was sitting alone in her guest chambers when a young Page knocked on her door. "Come in, please," she said. "Sorceress, the King asked me to extend an invitation for you to dine with him this evening, if you are not too weary from your travels." "I would be honored," said Celeste. "Where and what time?" "The King usually dines at six, and if it's acceptable, I'll come back and escort you to His Majesty," said the Page. "That will be fine," said Celeste. "I hope what I'm wearing is appropriate. You see, I have no other garments with me."

"I'm sure what you have on will be fine," said the young man. "I will return in a few hours to escort you. Meanwhile, there is a washroom behind that door," he said, pointing, "if you wish to refresh yourself before dinner." The Page left, closing the door quietly. *Dinner with the King,* thought Celeste. She had certainly come far since being dismissed from the Grotton Regional Mage's Office.

After a short nap, Celeste rose and availed herself of the washroom, then used a spell to clean her dress and shoes. She was waiting patiently when the Page returned to escort her to dinner.

The same guard was outside the door to the dining room. As Celeste approached, he said, "I apologize for earlier, Sorceress. It's just that *everyone* wants an audience with the King lately, and he did ask not to be disturbed." "I understand completely. Please think nothing more of it," said Celeste graciously. The Page left quickly as the guard opened the door and announced, "Sorceress Celeste, Your Majesty!"

Celeste entered the room and discovered that this was not the large formal dining room that she had expected but a much smaller, more private eating area, and the King was alone. Astonishingly, the King rose from his chair as Celeste entered. "Sorceress Celeste, it's so kind of you to join me this evening," said the

King. "It is my honor, Your Majesty," replied Celeste. "Please, call me Henry when we're alone. Believe it or not, hearing 'Your Highness' or 'Your Majesty' all day long gets somewhat tiring."

The King actually held the chair out for her as she sat down at the table. Once they were both seated, a servant appeared on cue and brought two flutes of white wine. "This is one of my favorites," said Henry, "and I can only get it here in Southport. Apparently, it does not travel well, either by ship or by wagon." Celeste sipped the wine carefully. It would *not* do to become inebriated when dining with the King.

"So, tell me about yourself, Sorceress," said the King. "Celeste, Please, Your—Henry," replied Celeste. "Well, I grew up in Grotton with my parents and my identical twin sister, Anne." "Identical twins? Does she also have the spark?" asked the King, interrupting. "Yes," said Celeste, "we entered the Wizards Academy together when we were only eleven winters old. Anne was recently assigned to the HMS COMFORT as the only woman in the Royal Navy."

"The COMFORT?" asked Henry, "Didn't I see a report that she was lost during a Sea Dragon attack?" "Yes, sire," said Celeste, slipping. "But Anne survived the attack and made it to the southernmost of the Coral Islands." "Wasn't that the one we set fire to?" "Yes. But she really didn't have any other choice. Anne barely made it to the shore before she passed out from the exertion of the battle and the struggle to reach the island." "But she survived?" "Yes. She was ultimately befriended by a Sea Dragon and her Great Dragon mate, who spared her life because they thought she was me."

"Why would these dragons want to spare your life?" asked the King curiously. Celeste related the story of how Gek had been captured while he was in human form by Mage Charles, the Grotton Regional Mage, and she was assigned to transport the boy to the Wizards Academy. "Neither of us realized that 'Jed' was actually a Great Dragon Changed One," said Celeste. She went on to explain how Azure had attacked the coach and left both her and Jed badly injured in the wreckage of the coach.

"How terrible!" said Henry. "Yes, well, when I crawled out of the coach the Sea Dragon, her name is Azure, was distraught because she didn't know how to help her mate. Jed was badly wounded with a shattered shoulder, broken ribs and internal injuries. He also had a head wound and would likely have died. So, hoping that they would be friendly Changed Ones, like those remaining at the Wizards Academy, I offered to heal him. I gave him some of the Healing Serum I had with me and cast a Healing spell." "Did he survive?" "Yes, but then the dragons began discussing whether they needed to kill me, in order to keep their secret."

"They obviously didn't." "No, instead, they named me a dragon-friend and promised to spare me. That is undoubtedly why they didn't kill Anne when Gek found her on that beach." "Truly amazing. And it was these two dragons that proposed the Peace Treaty you brought to me earlier today?" "Yes. Gek and Azure landed on the HMS VALOR to negotiate the truce, but it was really because of what my sister did after they captured her on that beach."

"And what was that?" "Well, during the fight with the 1st Squadron, fifteen of the Sea Dragons were killed, and 37 more were grievously wounded. Gek and Azure convinced Anne to heal those she could." "Why would she agree to that?" asked the King, growing angry. "Because she made each dragon she healed submit to a Binding spell, never to harm a human. Anne was able to heal 35 of the injured Sea Dragons, but there were two that she could not save," said Celeste.

"I see," said Henry, "so Commodore Matthews killed 17 Sea Dragons and 35 more are bound never to attack humans. That's quite an accomplishment! Tell me, Celeste, what happens if they break the Binding spell?" "They die. Instantly. That may be why the Sea Dragons have sued for peace. I believe that their numbers have been reduced considerably, and unlike the other dragon species, Sea Dragons have an abundance of prey in the sea and do not suffer from hunger as the other dragons do."

Celeste suddenly realized that during the course of her story, she had finished her wine, and also eaten all of her dinner. The King rose from the table and said, "Celeste, this has been the most enjoyable dinner I've had in years. I hope to see more of you while I consider the Peace Treaty. The Page outside will escort you back to your room. I wish you a pleasant evening." The King took and kissed the back of her hand, then departed through one of the other doors.

Celeste's head was buzzing, and it was *not* from the wine. She walked out the door and back to her room, thinking of Henry.

After Anne departed for the HMS SENTRY, Commodore Matthews said, "Andrew, come with me. There was more in the Admirals' order than simply assigning Sorceress Anne and her sister as Dragon Messengers." They went back to the Commodore's cabin, and he said, "Our new orders are to return to Sundock, refit and resupply, then head north to relieve

2nd Squadron in patrolling the seas between Frostberg and Sundock. We'll need more foodstuffs because it's a much longer patrol route and winter garb for the sailors, since the weather is much colder around Frostberg."

"We may also have to deal with Snow Dragons, going that far north, Sir. And we don't have a Treaty or even a truce with them." "Correct," said the Commodore. "You might also start thinking about how those Seabows are going to operate in the cold. You may need to work out some way to 'winterize' them." "I just hope that, with us in a different patrol area, the dragons can find us in two months to finalize the Peace Treaty."

"I'll be sure to mention that fact to the Admiral. Maybe we'll be back around here by then. Meanwhile, let's get this Squadron turned around and headed back to port."

"So, you're saying that all I need to do to Change into a dragon is picture one in my mind, then perform the Change spell?" asked Wizard James. "That's correct. Just remember to think of a dragon who can speak, or you won't be able to cast the spell to Change back into a human," said Edward. "Right now, you will only be able to Change into a Stone Dragon," said Kathy, "because that's the only type of dragon you've seen. You also have to remove your human clothes before you transform, or they'll be torn to shreds when you change into a dragon."

"Remind me of a Stone Dragon's strengths and weaknesses," said James. "On the plus side, Stone Dragons have the hardest scales and are difficult to kill. However, Stone Dragons cannot swim, they do not fly very fast (because they're so heavy), and they apparently have a limited amount of fire breath," said Edward. "And you both have done this?" asked a somewhat skeptical Wizard James. "Three times, actually. Once to travel to the Franconian Wizards Academy for my son's wedding, once to return to the construction site, and once more to travel here," confirmed Edward.

They were standing in the center courtyard of the Baizian Palace. Everyone had been cleared out, and palace guards stood in all of the windows and doorways to prevent onlookers. James disrobed and took a deep breath, then clapped his hands, saying, *"MORPHIOUS."* Instantly, a large Stone Dragon stood in the courtyard. King Donald came forward reluctantly, "James?" he asked. The dragon shook his head and replied, "Yes, Your Majesty, it is me. What an unusual experience!"

"How do you feel?" asked the King. "Hungry," said James. The dragon walked around the courtyard and then spread his wings. He flapped briefly, rising about five feet off the ground, before setting back down. "This is *weird,*" said James. Then he reared up on his hind legs and clapped his dragon hands together, transforming back into human form. He dressed quickly.

The King clapped enthusiastically. "Well done! Let's go back inside and talk about what use we can make of this wonderous new capability." The three magicians and the King retired to his private study and sat around the small conference table. "So, what else should I know about being a dragon?" James asked Kathy and Edward. "For one thing, when you're flying, you have to flap your wings constantly, or you begin to fall. Dragons are not like birds that can ride the air currents and glide," said Edward.

"The higher you fly, the colder it gets, and the harder it is to breathe," said Kathy, "and clouds are ephemeral, like fog in the sky." "We know from experience that crossbows and magician's Blast spells are generally ineffective against Stone Dragons but can kill all other types of dragons. We also have not learned the secret to how dragons breathe fire. When my son, Donovan, was attacked by the Snow Dragon, he says that he screamed and fire came out, but screaming has not worked for us.

There must be some trick to it that we have not discovered yet," said Edward.

"Lastly, while Stone Dragon scales are impervious to fire, I suspect they could be killed by *inhaling* fire, like the method of igniting flour that we used to kill the last two Fire Dragons outside of Springfield," concluded Edward.

"So, what can we do with this newfound knowledge?" asked the King. "Well, we can certainly send messages quickly across long distances," said Edward. "It's unlikely that we could infiltrate a dragon clan, as the dragons have done to us. Being family units, I fear that we would quickly be discovered. If Snow Dragons attack, we have seen that Great, Fire or Stone Dragons could defeat them or drive them off. I really wonder how the dragons have reacted to my son's attack on the Snow Dragons that were assaulting Snowton. The Snow Dragon clan cannot be very happy."

"So, we have a secret weapon, but we don't know how to use it fully," said the King. "And we must keep this knowledge from the dragons at all costs. If they discover that we can change into dragons, we lose our advantage." "I believe that is correct, sire," said Edward. "I will continue to make inquiries and perform experiments to try and determine how to affect the fire breath. I understand that Snow Dragons breathe ice, not fire and that the Sea Dragons spit high-pressure jets of water. Unfortunately, I have never seen a Fire, Snow or Sea Dragon, so I am unable to Change into one."

"Very well," said the King, "We will continue to explore this new knowledge and keep it very close-hold for now. Wizard Edward, it might interest you to know that King Henry and I have agreed to the restoration of normal relations between our kingdoms. The borders are re-opened, and the former Franconian Ambassador is now in residence. We have also opened negotiations to acquire a supply of those marvelous Concealment cloaks you mentioned, although, I admit, ten golds seems a heavy price for a single cloak."

Edward whistled, "That does indeed seem a high price, Your Majesty. Perhaps it's just a high starting point for negotiations." "Let's hope so," said the King. "Oh, my. The thought just occurred to me that, with the Franconian Ambassador in residence, I have no suitable guest quarters in the palace for you, Wizard Edward."

"That's all right, Your Majesty. I will take care of Wizard Edward," said Kathy. Kathy and Edward left the King's private study together, and Wizard James began to whistle *Strangers in the Night*.

Chapter Seventeen:
TARGET PRACTICE

enry was in love. There was simply no other explanation. The young Sorceress fascinated him. She was beautiful, shy, and kind, and Henry made excuses to see her repeatedly since her arrival in Southport, from asking her to help him pick out the drapes for the throne room, to crafting the specific wording of the Peace Treaty with the Sea Dragons, Henry seemed to want Celeste's advice on *everything*. They had dined together every evening, foregoing the normal dinners with Ministers and functionaries. Celeste had initially tried to insist that she might be needed to deliver messages for the Navy, but the King implored her to stay, saying that, whenever he finished with the precise wording of the Peace Treaty, she could deliver it to the Admiral immediately.

Celeste realized that there might be other important messages that the Navy needed delivered, but one does not refuse the King's command, and she really didn't want to. Celeste was attracted to Henry, and was frankly enjoying all of the attention. The court Ministers had begun to fawn over her, buying her expensive clothes and asking her for assistance with matters that they hoped the King would decide in their favor. Celeste was becoming a very important person, someone who had the King's ear. It was a new experience for her.

After dinner one evening, as the King and Celeste strolled around the impressive palace gardens, Henry kissed her, then wanted more, but Celeste rebuked him, saying that she didn't want to become a dalliance, to be used and then discarded. Henry assured her that his affection was genuine and that he was not looking for that sort of relationship. So, they began courting (officially). Celeste was at the King's side for every meeting, event and meal (except breakfast). When Celeste reminded Henry of her duties as the Dragon Messenger to the Royal Navy, the King changed her assignment to "Dragon Messenger to the King," *and that was that.* A Messenger Hawk was dispatched to Wizard Noland, informing him of this change and directing him to appoint another Sorcerer to serve as the Dragon Messenger for the 2nd Fleet.

"Henry, you really have to finish modifying that Treaty and get it back to the Admiralty," said Celeste. It had been a month, and the Treaty still wasn't ready. Henry and his Ministers continued to pick at it, adding clauses about fishing rights, what constituted a "port facility," and on and on. What had started out as a simple, two-page document now took up ten pages of parchment with no end in sight. "I know, beloved, but this must be exact! For example, what constitutes a

'Navy ship'? What we really want is for them not to attack *any* Franconian ships, right down to the smallest craft with a couple of fishermen in it. Additionally, the Treaty says that no one can go ashore on the Coral Islands; but what if some unfortunate sailor is swept overboard in a storm and is *washed ashore? Is he doomed? Or is there grace?* These are important issues."

"I know they are dearest, but we don't have forever. The dragons expect to sign this in just over a month from now, and someone has to take it to the Admiral in Grotton, then to a ship near the Coral Islands." "I know, but I should also consult with my advisors and Ministers in Kingston. I'm sure they'll have ideas also. I guess we need to schedule our departure and return to Kingston so we can get this treaty approved and on its way."

While she knew it was inevitable, Celeste was in no hurry to return to the capitol. She knew that the sycophants there would multiply several times over as every petty administrator would woo her in order to get her to influence the King on their behalf. *Well, there really was no avoiding it,* she thought. *We might as well get it over with.* "When should we leave?" she asked. "If we sail tomorrow, we can be there in a week. The flow of the river is against us, you know," said Henry. "Not if I use a Wind spell," Celeste reminded him, "I can have us there in four days."

"Very well. Bruno!" the King shouted for the guard outside the door. Bruno opened the door immediately and stepped inside, "Yes, Your Grace?" "Tell my Ministers that we depart at sunset tomorrow! It's time for me to get back. Arrange for Sorceress Celeste's things to be secured on board and find her an appropriate cabin, not too far from mine." "At once, Sire," said Bruno, hurriedly closing the door and summoning messengers to announce the King's imminent departure.

"Celeste, my dear, once we return to Kingston, our relationship will quickly become common knowledge. Before the rumormongering goes too far, I would like to announce our engagement at the Winter Ball two months hence. You need not give me an answer right now, but sooner is better than later."

"What a dump!" said Donovan. "Well, at least we won't get into a bidding war with anyone else trying to buy this place." The Kingston Royal Amphitheater had certainly seen better days. The stage's floorboards were cracked, broken, weathered, and generally unstable. There were nail heads sticking up everywhere, and the boards creaked and groaned with every step he took.

Donovan, Rachel and Major Gerald had come to the outskirts of Kingston to examine the old amphitheater to see if it could be used for crossbow practice. Major Gerald was having doubts. Seating for this outdoor venue was semicircular tiers of compacted dirt with stone risers. The dirt was overgrown with weeds and knee-high grass, and the stones were cracked, moss-covered and collapsing in some places. The tall, half-dome backdrop, which was designed to help carry the actor's voices or the music, depending on the performance, was still standing, but just barely. The formerly smooth interior was cracked and pitted, with several wooden slats separated and hanging out from the otherwise uniform surface of the dome.

"I suppose we could use Enlarge and Adhere spells to repair the stage and do something to reinforce the backstop and smooth the surface," said Donovan. "I mean, it doesn't have to be perfect. It just has to stop training crossbow bolts." "Right," said Major Gerald. "You two stay here and see what you can do with it; we'll try it out tomorrow morning."

The Major rode back to the compound to supervise the day's training, hoping that his new magicians could repair the old structure and that it would help train the members of the Expeditionary Force to shoot at flying targets. At least the old amphitheater was on the outskirts of the city, and it was unlikely that any of the

Kingston residents would see what was happening there. It would not do to alarm the populace.

When the two companies of the Royal Expeditionary Force reigned up before the Kingston Royal Amphitheater the next morning, the transformation was startling. The stage was smooth and gleamed like it was new, and the dome was newly painted a sky-blue color, with whisps of clouds depicted in the background. The grass tiers were newly cut and weed-free. The entire facility looked like it was anticipating a performance by the Royal Ballet Company.

"This is incredible!" exclaimed Major Gerald. "I thought you said this place was a disaster," said Specialist Dirk. "It was," replied the Major. "I can't believe the change, and in only a day!" "We're glad you approve, sir," said Donovan as he and Rachel emerged from behind the dome. "Rachel and I have been working on it all night."

"It's fantastic," repeated the Major, "but why did you paint the background like the sky?" Rachel smiled, "Because that's what it'll really look like if you're trying to shoot a flying dragon." "Of course," said Gerald. "Well, we might as well get started. How do you recommend we proceed?" "We've given it some thought, and we think that it would be best if one squad at a time took turns shooting at a Seeming of a flying dragon. If a bolt hits the Seeming, it will vanish. Donovan can produce Seemings of Great, Stone and Snow Dragons. I can only make Great and Stone Dragon Seemings. Neither of us has ever seen a Fire or a Sea Dragon."

"You've been working all night. Are you sure you're up to this?" asked the Major. Donovan grinned, "Seemings are easy, Major. Cutting that much grass was hard. We're ready whenever you want to begin. I would suggest that one of us cast the dragon Seeming, while the other casts a Seeming of a forest around us to avoid prying eyes." "I admit that I was a little worried about that. Let me get the men organized, and we can begin."

In short order, the 1st Company's 1st Squad was positioned on the stage with their crossbows, looking very apprehensive. "Relax, men," said Donovan. "The dragon will look real, but it's just an illusion. Concentrate on leading the target, and try not to shoot over the top of the dome. *I'm* not going back there to find your lost crossbow bolts." The men smiled in understanding.

"Ready?" Suddenly, a large, golden dragon flew over the top of the dome and directly at the line of soldiers. The men fired wildly, shocked despite the warning from Donovan. None of them hit the target.

"THAT WAS PATHETIC!" yelled Major Gerald. "THAT THING FLEW RIGHT AT YOU, AND YOU ALL MISSED. IF THIS HAD BEEN A REAL DRAGON, YOU'D ALL BE DEAD! GO TO THE BACK OF THE LINE. NEXT SQUAD!"

Second squad took position on the stage and loaded their crossbows; this time, Donovan brought the Seeming from behind them, flying over their heads and through the dome in front of them. Again, eight shots, eight misses. As the day wore on, Donovan continued to vary the flight path of the dragon Seemings, their speed, and eventually, the type of dragon that was the target. Despite the range being less than 100 yards from the soldiers to the backstop, there were very few hits. The backstop was riddled with crossbow bolts, but at least they hadn't actually lost many.

As they rode back to the garrison for dinner, Major Gerald expressed his disappointment with the day's training. "Don't be so hard on the men, Major," said Rachel. "I was watching, and Donovan was making it very difficult to anticipate the direction and speed of the target. Maybe we need to start slower tomorrow." "But we killed seven fire dragons with those darn crossbows!" said Major Gerald. "Yes. But as I understand it, they were all stationary, and you crept up very close behind them." "I guess that's true," conceded the Major. "I just expected to do a lot better today."

"I'll conjure the dragons tomorrow, and they'll move slower and in a consistent pattern," said Rachel. "We'll increase the level of difficulty as the men's proficiency increases." "That might be for the best," said Major Gerald. "I don't want the men to get discouraged, but I don't want them thinking that this is going to be as easy as shooting fish in a barrel either."

Donovan and Rachel again helped out in the kitchen, preparing the evening meal. Tonight, the entrée was some sort of fish. "You use less heat to cook fish," Corporal Fry explained. "You see, the meat is not as robust as beef or pork. Too much heat and you burn the fish, and *nobody* likes burned fish for dinner." As the weeks went by, the couple's cooking skills had improved dramatically, to the point that they were fairly confident in their skills.

"I think this will be our last night in the kitchen," said Rachel. "Thank you all so much for the instruction. We really appreciate it." The cooking staff smiled and said that they were welcome back anytime before returning to their duties.

As Rachel and Donovan rode home that evening, they heard more construction work going on around the palace. Reigning up, Donovan asked the same foreman what they were working on this time, since it appeared that all of the roofs had Stone-dragon-scale shingles.

"We're installin' these darn Guardbows on the watchtowers and the ramparts on the outer walls. Wizard Noland had about a dozen of 'em delivered and said we need to get 'em installed before the King gets back this week."

"The King is coming back this week?" asked Rachel. "That's what Wizard Noland said, and I guess he'd know. Anyway, these things aren't hard to install; the hard part is hoisting them up over the battlements." Donovan looked at Rachel, and she nodded. "If you want, we could move them wherever you want without your having to set up and reposition the hoist each time."

"How would you do that?" asked the foreman suspiciously. "We could shrink them down, take them to wherever you want them, then enlarge them back to actual size," explained Rachel. "Really?" asked the surprised supervisor. "Easily," confirmed Donovan. The foreman agreed, and within the hour, twelve Guardbows (the new name for stationary Seabows) were positioned on the palace battlements, waiting for the construction workers to affix the rotating pedestals to the stone floors.

"You two have been a great help to us lately," said the construction foreman, "If there's anything we can do to repay you, just say the word." "Now that you mention it," said Donovan, receiving a scowl from Rachel, "we just bought a cabin out by the river, And I'm not sure how sound the roof is. If someone could take a look, we'd sure appreciate it. If you have the time." The foreman beamed, "I'll see to it as soon as we get these Guardbows installed! Goodnight!"

"You shouldn't have done that," said Rachel. "Why not? We've helped those carpenters save dozens of man-hours over the last few weeks. First, with the dragon scales and now with the Guardbows. It would have taken them days to move those heavy weapons up to the battlements, and you know it. Plus, they were under a time crunch, having to get them installed before the King returns." "I still don't like asking for favors in return for magical assistance. It doesn't seem right." "I didn't ask him to *rebuild* the cabin, just check the roof. It probably just needs a couple of new shingles and maybe some tar. It's no big deal." Rachel 'Humphed.'

The next day, Rachel conjured much slower dragon Seemings, which always appeared from the right side of the dome and moved from right to left at a constant speed and height. The soldiers were much more successful at hitting the targets and left the amphitheater that evening feeling much more confident. As Donovan and Rachel rode past the palace, they noticed that each watchtower and battlement wall had Guardbows and that there were soldiers manning the positions and practicing drawing the massive weapons with the crank system.

"I wonder what the King is going to think of all these new upgrades," said Donovan. "You know the King," smiled Rachel, "He'll probably want the Guardbows gold plated." Donovan laughed.

As they rode up to their cabin, they were shocked by the transformation. The cabin roof had been replaced with new rafters and Stone Dragon scale shingles, the shower system had been reconstructed by someone who actually knew what he was doing, and the somewhat dilapidated stable (which was next on Donovan's 'To-do list'), was completely rebuilt and looked amazing. Both Stam and Rachel's horse, Ginger, seemed to really appreciate the new accommodations. As Donovan closed the new stable door, Rachel scowled.

"What?" "You know what! They went overboard and did way too much for the help we provided. You better scrape up some gold and find that foreman tomorrow! This is just too much!" Realizing that this was not an argument that he was going to win, Donovan merely nodded and headed inside. There was a note on the mantlepiece.

Sorceress Rachel,

Please accept these small upgrades as our thanks for your magical assistance on our recent projects for the King. Without your help, it's unlikely that we would have been able to complete our work in time. In case you are wondering, every merchant in Kingston is now clamoring for the new fireproof roof shingles, and all of the construction firms in Kingston are in the process of hiring more workers to meet the demand. If you ever need anything else, please don't hesitate to ask.

Bob Thatcher

Kingston Roofing
and Construction

"See?" said Donovan, "we not only made him happy; we've made all the construction companies in Kingston happy, and news of these new shingles will probably spread throughout the Kingdom." "I suppose," admitted Rachel, grudgingly.

As the days went by, the soldiers of the Royal Expeditionary Force gradually improved their skills at hitting the Seemings of dragons, although Donovan pointed out that hitting a dragon in the tail was not going to kill it but only make it mad. Donovan suggested that he could transform into a Stone Dragon, which they knew was generally impervious to crossbow bolts and act as a more realistic target, but Rachel and Major Gerald absolutely forbid it. "You might get hit in the eye, and that might kill or blind a Stone Dragon, even with a training bolt," said Rachel. "Your scars are bad enough; I don't want you needing an eye patch too!" Donovan dropped the idea.

On Endday as they wandered through the city on their way to Rachel's father's shop, they stopped to watch the King's celebratory return parade. He rode through the city in his elaborately decorated Royal Coach, waving at the (seemingly) enthusiastic citizens, welcoming him back. As the coach passed, Donovan asked, "Was that Sorceress Celeste in the coach with the King?"

The trench was done. It was ten feet wide, about thirty feet deep, depending on the depth of bedrock, fifty miles long and twenty-five miles high on each side. The twenty-foot-high walls sat atop the outer edge of the trench, making it a fifty(ish) foot-deep trench. The walls were adhered to the sides of the trench, which were adhered to the bedrock below. All of the seams had been tested, and even after several more rainstorms, the walls and the trench held without collapsing.

Now for the hard part. As Wizard Edward faced the throng of tired but proud apprentice magicians, he explained how they were going to excavate the middle of the reservoir. "Ladies and Gentlemen, you have all done excellent work, and we are ahead of schedule on this project! We are going to have a brief pause in our efforts as we move our campsite to the area inside of the trench. We are going to put it in the exact center of the Salt Flats. Once re-established, we'll be traveling back to the southern trench and Removing the glass, sand, salt and dirt from the surface all the way down to bedrock. We'll make a linear hole, working backward, excavating from south to north."

"Cooks, prepare a box lunch for everyone, then take down the kitchens and load the equipment into the wagons. Magicians, pack all your belongings and load them into the wagons. Engineers, I want you all to take down the tents and latrines and get them loaded. We need to get moving as soon as the wagons are loaded. Once the magicians have loaded their belongings into the wagons, Mage Kathy, Mage Elianna, and I will begin teaching them the Remove spell. Surveyors, once you have completed surveying the northern boundary of the reservoir, you are released to return to Baize. Let's get moving."

Students rushed to their tents and quickly packed their meager possessions into backpacks and duffle bags. Cooks quickly began preparing 150 box lunches with cheese sandwiches, fruit and crackers. Engineers put the horses in their harnesses and waited patiently for the magicians to clear their things out of the tents. Once a tent was empty, it was immediately taken down and loaded into a wagon.

As the students finished stowing their gear in the wagons, they gathered around the three senior magicians. Once all of the apprentice magicians were assembled, Edward led them off to the large landfill that had been dug to contain all of the trash generated by the campsite over the past three and a half months. As they stood on the edge of the rubbish pit, Edward explained the Remove spell.

"Ladies and gentlemen, today, those of you who do not already know the Remove spell will learn it and the dangers it presents to careless magicians. First the incantation is *"DELERE,"* say it with me please." *"DELERE,"* repeated the students. "Again, please," said Edward. *"DELERE,"* said the students. "Very good. Now, the gesture is flicking your right wrist toward the object that you wish to remove. Like so," said Edward, demonstrating the gesture. He had all of the students practice the gesture several times as he,

Mage Kathy and Mage Elianna moved among them and corrected any mistakes.

"Now," said Edward, "I need to tell you about how dangerous this spell is for careless magicians. If there is *anything* between your right hand and the object you are attempting to Remove, that object will vanish. Objects vanished by this spell cannot be recovered. EVER. Do you understand?" The students looked at each other, confused.

"Let me explain," said Edward, "let's say that you are removing dirt from the reservoir, and a distracted fellow magician accidentally walks in front of you while you are casting the spell. What do you think will happen?" No response. "The distracted magician vanishes and cannot be resurrected. They are gone forever." There were gasps from the crowd. "At the Franconian Wizards Academy, we had a senior student accidentally position his left hand between his right hand and the object he was trying to Remove. What do you think happened?"

A student in the front raised his hand. "Yes, Ethan?" "He removed his own hand?" "Exactly right!" said Edward. "He removed his own hand, and, as you know, many spells require both hands or just the left hand. The student was unable to continue his magical education," said Edward somberly. "What happened to him?" asked a girl in the back of the crowd. "He is currently a cook's helper at the Academy," replied Edward. The students quieted, considering the dangers of the Remove spell.

"Now, I want you to form a line, single-file, and approach the rubbish pit. Concentrate on removing as much of the trash and refuse as you can, then perform the spell. Once you're done, move to the back of the line. As soon as the tents and other gear are loaded in the wagons, we need to be on our way to our next campsite," said Edward.

The students walked up to the edge of the pit and, one by one practiced the Remove spell. Most of them held their left hand behind their back as they performed the spell, which Edward decided was probably a good safety precaution. As expected, some of the students were able to Remove much more rubbish than others, and all felt the energy drain much more significantly than that caused when performing the Dig, Wind, Shield, or Adhesive spells.

"Before you try again, you need to drink some water," Edward cautioned. "As you can see, the energy drain from this spell is much more than for the other spells that you've been using so far." Despite there being a large amount of rubbish, the pit was empty before each student came around for their third attempt at conjuring the Remove spell.

"Very good, everyone!" said Edward. "Now, when we get to the trench, you will have to stand back a ways when casting your Remove spell. Otherwise, you might remove the sand and soil underneath your feet and fall into the trench. It's a thirty-foot drop in most places, and that's a long way to fall. I *really* don't want to have to Heal any of you. Understood? Good. It looks like the wagons are all loaded, but before we go, everyone, please gather around and use Wind spells to fill in this hole."

The apprentice magicians quickly blew the ever-present sand into the now-empty trash pit, then climbed aboard the wagon with their personal belongings on it. The convoy of wagons headed out for the new campsite in the middle of the Great Salt Flats.

The HMS VALOR and the rest of 1st squadron arrived in Sundock near sunset. After receiving their pay, the crews disembarked for two days of shore leave, which was all the Commodore could give them because he had orders to depart for the sea around Frostberg soon. As the crews left the ships, shore facility personnel began offloading empty barrels that had been full of fresh water, food, and other supplies. The

Commodore and Andrew headed to the supply warehouse to requisition winter gear for the sailors of 1st squadron.

"So, Andrew, now that you have a couple of days off, what are your plans?" asked the Commodore. "I really haven't given it much thought," said Andrew. "I'll probably just find an Inn that looks reasonably clean and take it easy for a couple of days in a bed that doesn't rock and bob. There's also probably a couple of good places to eat around here. Do you have any suggestions?" The Commodore smiled, "I'd recommend the Royal Arms for the Inn and the Salty Dog for the food. Steer clear of the Mermaid Tavern, it's a little rough, and the food's not particularly good." "Then how do they stay in business?" asked Andrew. "While the food is not *particularly good*, it's still better than Navy rations or what's served on most commercial ships. The food doesn't have to be the best, just better than what the sailors are used to getting."

Andrew grinned, "I understand, sir. Thanks for the recommendations. Is there any place I should avoid in Sundock?" The Commodore considered the question, then said, "I'd steer clear of the west side of the docks after sundown. Lots of sailors end up getting robbed when they wander down there, usually drunk." "What about the city Enforcers?" asked Andrew. "They mainly patrol the center of town or the Navy piers. There aren't many of them, only about three or four; Sundock is a town, not a city. There's only one Mage in town currently, so that limits the patrol area." "I understand," said Andrew.

The Commodore and Andrew parted ways, and Andrew headed for the Royal Arms Inn. He arrived just as the clerk was getting ready to leave for the evening. "I need a room, please," said Andrew. The clerk looked Andrew up and down, "You off one of them ships that just ported?" "That's right," said Andrew. The clerk scowled, "Then check with your shipmates, and you'll find out what I told them—our rooms cost two silvers a night. You'd be better off at the Warf Inn, down by the docks; it's generally all Navy sailors can afford."

Andrew drew himself up and said, "That may be, but I'm the Battle Mage for 1st squadron, and I think I can afford four silvers for two nights." "Forgive me, sir," said the clerk, "I mistook you for one of the crew. Most sailors prefer to spend their coins on wine, women and song, if you know what I mean. Here at the Royal Arms Inn, we cater to a more *genteel* clientele, if you know what I mean." "I do," said Andrew, smiling. The clerk opened the door quickly and moved behind the reception desk. "You said two nights?" "Yes," replied Andrew. "That's all the time we'll be in port." "I understand," said the clerk. "Most Navy ships only stay a couple of days, a week at most. It must be a hard life."

"It's not for everyone," said Andrew, handing over four silvers.

The clerk produced a key from the desk drawer and handed it to Andrew. "Room five, sir, just along that hallway. We serve a light breakfast from six until eight. It comes with the room, at no extra charge. We only have two other guests at present, an arms merchant and his daughter from Fairview. They're in town on business. You'll probably meet them at breakfast tomorrow."

Field Marshall Guzman

Chapter Eighteen:

ON THE ROAD AGAIN

The King immediately noticed the changes to the palace. He stormed into the throne room and found Wizard Noland there waiting for him. "What is that on the roof?" he demanded, "and what are those things on the battlements and watchtowers?" "Your roof has been covered with Stone Dragon scales to make it fire-proof and impervious to arrows, stones hurled by catapults, or any other projectiles, sire," said Wizard Noland. "After our fight with the Stone Dragon at the Academy, we discovered that its' scales are so incredibly hard that even a magician's Blast spell cannot penetrate them. Unfortunately, while we can Replicate them, we have not found very many uses for them yet other than roof shingles. The weapons on the ramparts are called Guardbows. They are an adaptation of the Seabows that are currently being installed on all Royal Navy ships. The Guardbows are cumbersome and slow to operate, but the projectiles they fire can penetrate most dragon's scales, causing critical injuries."

"What about Stone Dragon scales?" asked the King. "We have not tested the Guardbows against Stone Dragon scales yet, Sire, but even if they do not penetrate, they will certainly cause shock damage to even the fiercest Stone Dragon," replied Noland. The King smiled.

"It seems as if you've accomplished a great deal while I was away," said the King. "With conflict with the dragons imminent, I thought it best not to dawdle, Your Majesty. Hello, Sorceress Celeste; it's good to see you again." "Wizard Noland, it's good to be back in Kingston. Were you able to find a replacement for me as a Dragon Messenger for the Royal Navy?" asked Celeste.

"Level Three Phillip will be taking his Sorcerer's Test next week. Since he grew up in Southport, I think that he's an excellent candidate for that duty," said Wizard Noland smoothly. "Excellent!" said the King. "What else has been happening?" Noland looked at the soldier guarding the door and nodded; Minister Leonard entered hesitantly. "Your Majesty," said Wizard Noland, "in your absence, Minister Leonard brought a very serious matter to my attention. It appears that former Minister of Internal Security, Jasmine, removed several thousand golds from your Treasury, prior to our discovering her treachery."

"WHAT?" raged the King. "How could such a large theft go unnoticed! Minister Leonard?" "Sire—" began the Finance Minister, before Wizard Noland cut him off, "Jasmine removed the gold and replaced it with a Seeming, sire. It's not Minister Leonard's fault. Fortunately, when he reported the theft to me, I and the faculty from the Wizards Academy immediately searched Minister Jasmine's house and found almost all of the missing golds hidden in a secret room she had constructed to hide her ill-gotten golds."

"How much did I lose?" asked the King, considerably calmer. "It appears that only about sixty golds are unaccounted for, Sire," said Minister Leonard. "Undoubtedly, Minister Jasmine spent the missing coin, but we were most fortunate that Wizard Noland was able to recover most of the ten thousand missing golds." "*Ten thousand golds*?" asked the King. "Yes, Sire. It would have been a devastating loss to the kingdom if the Wizards had not been able to recover them," said Leonard.

Celeste looked at Wizard Noland and raised an eyebrow. Wizard Noland gave an almost imperceptible shake of his head, and Celeste nodded her understanding. The King said, "Wizard Noland, you have my sincere thanks. You and your associates have saved the kingdom from financial ruin." "I appreciate the compliment, Your Highness, but I have another concern."

"What is that?" asked the King. "I am concerned that Minister Jasmine may have had additional accomplices in other cities and towns in the realm. The Treasury in Kingston is by far the largest in the kingdom, but Fairview, Southport, Grotton and Three Forks all have substantial deposits in their vaults. I fear that their vaults may also contain less than we believe." The King looked worried, "What can we do?" "Sire, I have an idea. While you were in Southport, Major Gerald asked me to assign some organic magical support to the Royal Expeditionary Force. With Wizard Edward still in Baize and Sorcerer Curtis now assigned as the Kingston Regional Mage, the force was bereft of magical support. Sorcerer Donovan, the young man who saved Marshall Guzman's life at the Royal Ball, recently passed his Sorcerer's Test, so I assigned him and his wife, Sorceress Rachel, to the Expeditionary Force.

"Very well. So?" asked the King. "Sire, if the Royal Expeditionary Force were to conduct a sweeping tour of all of the major cities and towns in Franconia, they could accomplish two things: First, they could conduct a discrete audit of the city's Treasuries and check for any shortages; and second, they could make sure there are no dragon Changed Ones posing as Regional Mages or members of their staff," said Noland.

The King considered the idea carefully, then said, "I like the idea, but won't that take a long time?" "Yes,

Sire. Several months, at least. Even traveling by ship with magicians to increase the wind in the ship's sails, it will still take time to get to each town and city, conduct the audit and inspect the Regional Mage's Offices. I estimate perhaps five months, maybe longer, but I think it's worth the time. Plus, the Royal Expeditionary Force will be a reassuring presence to the citizens of Franconia," said Wizard Noland.

"I like it," said the King. "I'll give Major Gerald his new orders tomorrow and send them out by the end of the week." "Very good, sire," said Noland, "If I may, I need to have a word in private with Sorceress Celeste." The King gave his grudging approval, and Celeste and Noland left the throne room together. Once in the hallway, Wizard Noland cast a Silence spell around them and asked, "Celeste, is your relationship with the King of your own free will? I would not see you coerced in any way, even by a King."

Celeste smiled, "I am not being coerced, sir. Our relationship is absolutely consensual, but thank you so much for asking." The relief on Noland's face was evident. "Jasmine vanished the golds, didn't she?" Celeste asked. Noland nodded grimly, "Yes, and it took all of the Academy staff a week to replicate that much coin. Celeste, even though you may be the next Queen of Franconia, you *must* keep it a secret that we can replicate coins. Otherwise, any monarch could demand that we spend all of our time replicating golds, which would ruin the economy of the Kingdom!"

"I understand, Wizard Noland. I would never divulge that to Henry," said Celeste. Noland smiled, "In that case, would you mind if I cast a Secrecy spell on you to ensure it?" Celeste considered the request and reluctantly agreed. Once the spell was cast, Wizard Noland returned to the Academy, much more confident and happier about Celeste's attraction to the King. Having a magician close to the King added a level of protection and would make him more supportive of the magicians in Franconia.

Andrew entered the Royal Arm's small dining area a little past seven in the morning and found the other two guests enjoying a simple breakfast of porridge, fruit and toast. "Good morning, sir," said Andrew, "How are you today?" "I'm fine, sir, thank you for asking. My name is James, and this is my daughter, Maria." Andrew shook hands with both James and his daughter. "I'm Mage Andrew. What brings you to Sundock?" he asked.

"Well, I manufacture and sell arms to the crown," said James. "My production facility and main office is in Fairview, but I brought my daughter on a little vacation to the coast while I conducted some business. You see, the steel produced in Smithville is far superior to the steel I've been getting from my supplier in Colton. I really came out this way to see if I could find a way to economically import steel from so far away."

"Hmm," said Andrew, "While Sundock is the closest port to Smithville, it's a rough road over the Black Mountains. It might be easier and cheaper to ship the steel to Eastport, then transport it by ship to Fairview. Still, that's a long way…" "I know," said James. "The problem with Eastport is the taxes. They're even worse than those imposed in Fairview! It may be impossible. The profit margin on my weapons is pretty good, but not enough to pay for the shipping costs and the Eastport city export taxes."

"What are you making that takes so much steel? Armor?" asked Andrew. James looked around the dining area, then said quietly, "Crossbows." "Indeed?" asked Andrew, "Then you know Wizard Edward?" James frowned, "I knew a Battle Mage named Edward Francis. He was a good friend, but I heard that he was killed by a dragon," he whispered. Andrew smiled, "No. Edward survived the attack by the dragon," he replied quietly. "He was just in a healing coma, as is common with magicians who expend too much power during a battle."

"Are you sure?" asked Maria. "Positive. You see, Edward is my uncle. After he unmasked a traitor in the palace in Kingston, he passed his Wizard's Test. I think he's somewhere in Baize now, working on a project for King Donald." "That's wonderful!" exclaimed James. "Wait, Edward, is your uncle? Does that mean you know Donovan?" asked Maria.

"Of course! Sorcerer Donovan is my cousin," said Andrew. *"Sorcerer Donovan?"* asked James. "That seems impossible, why, he's only been at the Wizards Academy for a few years!" "Yes. Donovan graduated from the Academy faster than anyone ever has before. After Donovan passed his Sorcerer's Test, Wizard Noland assigned him and his wife, Sorceress Rachel, to the Royal Expeditionary Force," said Andrew.

"HIS WIFE?" asked Maria. "Yes, he married Sorceress Rachel a couple of weeks after he passed his Sorcerer's Test," said Andrew. "I see," said Maria, somewhat despondently. "You know him?" asked Andrew. "We dated when we lived in Kingston. I really liked him," said Maria, wiping a tear from her eye. "I'm sorry," said Andrew, taking her hand, "I had no idea."

"So, Mage Andrew, what brings you to Sundock?" asked James, changing the subject. "I'm the Battle Mage for 1st Squadron, assigned to the HMS VALOR. We ported last night and have a couple of days shore leave before we head north to relieve 2nd Squadron in the seas around Frostberg." "So, you know about the crossbows?" asked James. Andrew smiled, "Yes, indeed. In fact, I made a modification to them that might be of interest to you." "Really? What did you do to them?" asked James. "I enlarged them to about four times their original size, then put them on rotating pedestals and bolted them to the decks of our ships. I call them Seabows."

"Fascinating!" exclaimed James. "Do you think I could see one?" "I don't see why not," said Andrew. "After we eat, we can head down to the docks, and I'll take you aboard. I'm sure that Commodore Matthews won't mind." They quickly finished their meal and headed down towards the port; Andrew was wearing his Concealment cloak (inside out, of course). As they walked over the rough, cobblestone streets, Maria stumbled. Andrew caught her before she fell and gave her his arm for the rest of the walk to the ship. He wasn't exactly sure if the stumble was intentional or not, but he found that he liked Maria's touch very much.

When they reached the HMS Valor, Andrew took Maria's hand and guided her up the steep gangplank. James followed them up. When they reached the deck, the Bos'n blew three notes on his pipe, "BATTLE MAGE ON DECK!" he shouted. "As you were, men," said Andrew. "Is the Commodore aboard?" Andrew asked the Bos'n. "No, sir. He's still in town, trying to convince the Naval Quartermaster to issue us some winter gear. It seems we need some sort of written authorization." "If he can't get it sorted out, let me know, and I'll try to convince the Quartermaster," said Andrew with a wink. The Bos'n smiled.

As they headed towards the starboard Seabow, the Bos'n said, "Ahem, sir. A word, please?" Andrew let go of Maria's hand and walked off a few paces with the Bos'n. "Sir, we don't allow civilians on board Royal Navy ships." Andrew smiled and said loudly, "This is Master James, the inventor of the crossbow, and his daughter, Maria. I was just going to show them the new Seabow and get his expert opinion on how we might improve it. I'm not giving them a tour." "Yes, sir, sorry, sir. Please proceed," said the Bos'n.

"Sorry about that," Andrew said to James as they walked over to the Seabow. James looked it over carefully. "Does it work?" he asked. "Remarkably well," replied Andrew. "As you can see, the stouter bow requires a lot more power to draw. That's why I added the crank mechanism. Even so, it takes two men to operate the crank." "Or one magician," said a nearby crewman. Andrew blushed, "Well, yes, using a Strength Enhancement, I can draw the Seabow with the crank."

"Hmm," said James, "you know, maybe you need some sort of mechanical advantage, like a couple of pulleys. That would make it easy enough for one man to draw," said James. "How would that work?" asked Andrew. "We could split the steel into two pieces on each side, then put a pulley on each end and re-rig the drawstring. It would take some trial-and-error to get it right, though. You said that you sail in two days?" asked James. "That's the schedule, but I could ask the Commodore for a brief delay, not long though," replied Andrew.

"What's this then?" asked Commodore Matthews as he stomped onto the deck. "Andrew! Are you giving tours to civilians?" "Sir," said Andrew hastily, "Might I introduce Master James, the inventor of the crossbow, and his daughter, Maria. James was just telling me how we could modify the Seabow so that it could be drawn by one person." "Is that so?" asked the Commodore, softening his bellicose tone. "How is that now?"

"Sir, I mean, Commodore, I was just telling Mage Andrew that if we split the steel bow and put a pulley on each end of the bow, we could gain some mechanical advantage and make the Seabow easier to draw. It might also make it more accurate and powerful." The Commodore looked interested. "How long to make the modification?" he asked. James thought, then said, "It shouldn't take more than a day or two. The Blacksmith in town has all of the parts I'd need. Probably cost about four silvers for the materials, then there's my labor. Call it seven silvers?"

"What do you think, Andrew? Is it worth the delay and the cost?" asked the Commodore. "Sir, if we can make a Seabow that can be drawn by a single crewman, then we *could* put six or eight on every ship without adding too many additional crewmen. Think how much that could save the entire Navy!" "You're right," said Commodore Mathews. "So, James, what do you need from us?"

James said, "I need four silvers for the parts, the use of a magician, and someone to watch my daughter while I work. I don't want to leave her all on her own in a strange town for two days." "I think I can help with that," said Andrew quickly, "and Sorcerer Jason from the VICEROY can assist James." The Commodore laughed at Andrew's rapid volunteering to spend time with the Arms merchant's attractive daughter but said, "I guess it's settled then. Let me get you the silvers out of the strongroom." The Commodore went below and returned quickly with the silvers. "I'll inform the Bos'n that you're to be given access to the weather deck. Now hurry off and get what you need. We really do need to get to Frostberg soon."

Andrew, James and Maria headed back down the gangplank and into town to procure the necessary supplies. Once off the ship, James said, "Why don't you two run along and explore the town? I can handle the Blacksmith. I'll see you both back at the Inn for breakfast. Don't wait up, I may be very late. Maria, tell the Innkeeper that we'll be staying at least two more days. I'll pay him when I get back to the Inn."

Maria and Andrew headed into town, hand in hand. Andrew felt like the luckiest Mage in the world.

Major Gerald, along with Captain Fletcher, Captain Smith, Donovan and Rachel, entered the King's private study and found Finance Minister Leonard, Wizard Noland, Marshall Guzman, and Sorceress Celeste already seated around the conference table. They all rose as the King entered and took his seat next to Celeste. "Major, I have a new assignment for the Royal Expeditionary Force, and I'm afraid that it is one that will take you several months to complete."

"The Royal Expeditionary Force stands ready for any task you command, Sire," said Major Gerald. "Good. You are, of course, aware of Minister Jasmine's treachery," said the King. Gerald nodded. "What you don't know is that before she was uncovered, she stole almost ten thousand golds from the Royal Treasury here in Kingston." "Ten thousand golds!" exclaimed Major Gerald. "Indeed," said the King. "Fortunately, Wizard Noland and the other magicians at the Wizards Academy managed to find almost all of the golds that Jasmine had removed and hidden in her home. Only sixty golds were actually lost."

"My concern is that Jasmine may have had additional accomplices in other cities and towns in Franconia. I want you to embark on a nationwide tour of all of the cities and towns in the realm. You are to conduct a discrete audit of their Treasuries to determine if there is any *unreported* shortage, and if such a shortage is discovered, determine who was behind the theft and deal with them accordingly. I *do not* want news of this widespread audit becoming common knowledge. Also, you will obviously make a thorough search to try and locate any missing coins. Lastly, I want your Sorcerers to visit the Regional Mage's Offices and ensure that all of these dragon Changed Ones have been identified and dealt with. I would like you to brief me on your plan and depart within a week."

"At your command, Sire. I will need some kind of document, signed either by you or Minister Leonard, which will allow me to audit the Treasuries. This is not a function normally carried out by the Royal

Expeditionary Force, and we'll likely encounter some resistance from the men and women tasked with securing and accounting for your assets," said Major Gerald. "A very good point, Major," said the King. "Leonard, please draft such an order immediately. We will both sign it and Major— I will brook no interference with your mission. I would expect anyone culpable of stealing from the Royal Treasuries to be most insistent that you are not authorized to conduct such an audit. Deal with any such person as you deem appropriate."

"I'll consult with a judge to determine the appropriate punishments for various levels of theft prior to our departure, Sire," said Major Gerald. "Why is that necessary?" asked the King. "Sire, I doubt that we will find *every* Treasury's accounts completely accurate. However, the theft of, say, three golds, should certainly be punished less severely than someone who stole a hundred." The King considered Major Gerald's words for a moment. Celeste whispered something in his ear, and he said, "You are right, of course, Major, and a simple accounting error must be dealt with much less harshly than deliberate theft. Consult with one of the Superior Court judges before you depart. You are dismissed."

As they filed out of the King's private study, Donovan and Rachel approached Wizard Noland,

"Jasmine vanished the golds, didn't she, sir?" asked Rachel quietly. Wizard Noland cast a Silence spell over the three of them and nodded grimly. "Yes, and it took all of the Academy instructors and Court Wizard Cassandra a week to replace that much gold. You two will have to do the same if you find any significant shortages. If you need time to accomplish the Replication, you may have to inform Major Gerald and cast a Secrecy spell on him. Our ability to Replicate golds *must not* become known. Do you understand?" They both nodded. "Now, I expect at least one of the magicians in the Regional Mage's Offices is a dragon Changed One, and it is unlikely that he or she will submit to a Binding spell, so be prepared for that and act quickly and mercilessly if the situation warrants."

"Sir, before we depart, I really need to practice breathing fire, and so does Rachel," said Donovan. "I anticipated that," said Noland. "I have placed the Forces Training Area 'off limits' to Academy students for the next week. All Forces training will either be conducted on water or in the Seemings Training Area. I want you to practice near the burned patch next to the shield. That way, your efforts may go unnoticed." Donovan and Rachel nodded. "Anything else, sir?" asked Donovan. Noland thought for a moment, then said, "Yes. While we will try to keep this unannounced audit and inspection quiet, news of it will undoubtedly get out eventually. Once that happens, you may find accountants and magicians missing from their posts. Watch your backs."

When they got to what Edward thought was the middle of the Great Salt Flats, there was a problem. The sand and salt were too deep to pitch a tent in, and the sand/salt mixture billowed into the air with every footstep, making breathing difficult. Edward planted a stake in the middle of where he wanted the campsite and assembled the apprentice magicians. "We can't pitch the tents and get the kitchens and latrines set up until we get rid of this sand. I know that we could blow it away with Wind spells, but that would just make more work for later, and the billowing cloud of sand and salt would get worse. So, we're going to begin Removing the sand now. Start right here, and teams one through four, make a line facing South and start Removing the sand. Stop when you get to dirt and rocks. Teams five through eight, face east and do the same. Teams nine through twelve, face north, and teams thirteen through sixteen face west. I'll tell you when we've cleared enough space. Wagon drivers! Reposition to the north. I'll bring you back in once we've cleared enough space for you.

Kitchens first, then the latrines, then the wagons with the tents and personal gear. Move."

As soon as the wagons were clear, the apprentice magicians began Removing the sand and salt mixture, remembering to keep their left hands behind their backs. Initially, there was almost no progress being made; as soon as the sand was removed, more sand poured back into the empty space. Eventually, however, the young magicians got below the sand and reached the substrate of soil and rock. Looking at the layers, it seemed as if the sand was about five feet deep. "Well, it could have been worse," said Edward, "and this should be the area where the sand is deepest. It should only get easier from here. I just hope it doesn't rain anytime soon."

"What will we do when it rains?" asked Kathy. "I suppose we'll have to melt the sand on the north and west sides of the camp to keep from having any salt-infused sand pour into the campsite. We better go help the apprentices; clearing this area is going to take the rest of the day and most of the night."

Edward was correct. It took a hundred magicians all afternoon and all night to clear an area big enough for their campsite. The final touches, a ramp entering from the north for the supply wagons and one going south for their egress to the dig site, were completed shortly after the sun rose the next day. Fortunately, the engineers erected the kitchens, latrines and most of the tents before the entire area was cleared of sand and salt, and it took less than a glass to pitch the remaining tents and move the personal gear inside.

"That was a job well done, everyone!" said Edward. "We'll take a break for the rest of the day and start digging tomorrow at noon with first shift. The cooks will have some hot soup and tea ready shortly, but if you just want to get some sleep, I understand. First shift, be ready to depart here a glass before noon tomorrow."

As the apprentices began sorting themselves out and finding their tents, Edward walked over to Kathy and Elianna. "Kathy, you and I need to ride out now and mark the trail to where we'll start excavating. I don't want to get turned around and lost on our way there tomorrow. Elianna, you stay here and provide magical support. I don't expect trouble right away, but I have a feeling that sooner or later, the dragons are going to pay us a visit, even if it's just out of curiosity."

Edward walked over to the line of wagons, took a length of rope out of the back of one, and tied it to a wooden pallet he placed on the ground behind the lead wagon. He informed the wagon driver that he and Kathy were going to use the wagon and pallet to mark the trail to the dig site. Then he hopped up onto the driver's bench and called for Kathy, who quickly walked over and climbed up onto the bench beside him. Edward drove the wagon out of the camp, dragging the wooden pallet behind. Once he left the campsite area, the pallet made a smooth, shallow depression in the sand behind the wagon. "Do you know where you're going?" asked Kathy. "Of course," replied Edward. "I'm heading for the southeast corner of the trench. As long as I keep the sun on my left shoulder, we should be fine. We don't have to hit it exactly, just close enough to find our way there tomorrow."

"Why the pallet?" Kathy asked. "I'm afraid that the tracks left by the wagon wheels might be covered by the wind. The pallet is making a wider trail, and we'll come back the same way, so it should be even deeper when we're done." Despite the heat and the glaring sun, Kathy snuggled up next to Edward on the wagon bench and put her arm around him. "Do you think this is going to work?" she asked. Edward smiled, "I was actually very happy when we discovered that the sand was only five feet deep in the middle of the Flats. That should be the deepest section. I was afraid it would be ten or twelve feet deep. It's going to get shallower and shallower as we move towards the edges. Right now, it's the weather that concerns me."

"Why?" asked Kathy. "We're moving into autumn, and winter will not be far behind. As the temperatures drop, the apprentices will be more miserable. Working in the cold for eight hours, with no break from the wind, can really sap your strength, and at night, the temperature is going to get much colder. We may have to consider limiting ourselves to daytime digging only." "What will that do to our schedule?" asked Kathy. "Well," said Edward, "We're almost a month ahead of schedule right now, and the sand is much shallower than I expected. It will all depend on how deep it is to bedrock as we excavate towards the middle."

It was a little before noon when they reached the trench. They were not exactly at the corner but were within 300 yards of their intended destination. "Let's see just how hard this is going to be," said Edward as he climbed down off the wagon. He gave Kathy a helping hand down, then gave the horse some water. As they moved over the glassy area that bordered the trench, the thin sheet of glass cracked and spider-webbed underfoot. When they reached the edge of the trench, they backed up about fifty yards and began using Remove spells to excavate the glass-covered soil down to bedrock. It was easy, but it was going to take a while to remove all the soil.

"This is going to work," said Kathy, "but it's going to take a while." "You're right," said Edward, with a sigh. "I wish there was an easier way." They sat in thought for a while. "What if we excavated from *inside* the trench?" suggested Kathy. Edward shook his head,

"No, I thought of that, but that's thirty feet down. If the trench walls collapse or we have a sudden rainstorm, the diggers would be trapped in the trench."

Eventually, they just decided that the simplest way was probably the best way. It was just going to take some time and patience. At least it was still only about thirty feet down to bedrock.

As the afternoon wore on, Edward and Kathy continued Removing soil and actually accomplished quite a lot. As the sun set and the air grew colder, Edward and Kathy retreated to the wagon. Kathy saw that Edward had brought along blankets, pillows and a light dinner meal. "Did you have this all planned?" she asked playfully. Edward shrugged, "I thought it unlikely that we'd be able to make it all the way here, do anything productive, and get back to camp before nightfall. I'm also not planning to try and find my way back to the campsite in the dark. I guess you're just stuck with me."

"That sounds like a fine idea," said Kathy, snuggling under his arm. They lay in the wagon bed, using each other for warmth as the sky darkened and a million stars brightened the night sky. As they lay there, looking at the stars, a fast-moving shape blacked out the stars as it passed overhead. "Was that a cloud?" asked Kathy. "No," said Edward. "That was a dragon."

Chapter Nineteen:
DRAGON FIRE

Mage Andrew had a wonderful time in Sundock with Maria while her father worked tirelessly on modifying the Seabow. They spent two glorious days together exploring the city and sampling the various cuisines that the local taverns had to offer, before James returned to the Inn on the second afternoon and declared that he was finished. The three of them returned to the HMS VALOR, boarded quickly and examined the new and improved Seabow. Andrew was stunned. It hardly looked like a Seabow. The split bow metal arms each had a lopsided pulley attached at the ends, and the draw string was a complicated configuration of crossed strings and connections.

"Does it work?" asked Andrew. "Try cranking the handle," said James. Andrew steeled himself and grabbed the crank handle. To his amazement, it turned smoothly and easily, drawing the bowstring back and locking it into position. This was certainly a major improvement. *But how were they going to retrofit all of the Seabows in the fleet?* He wondered. It was at this moment that the Commodore appeared. "So, all finished?" he asked.

"Yes, sir, and it works incredibly well! One man can easily draw the bowstring now," exclaimed Andrew. "Excellent! Can you replicate it?" asked Commodore Matthews. Andrew's face fell as he examined the complicated pulley arrangement, the crisscrossing bowstrings and the way it attached to the crank system. "No, sir," he finally admitted. "This weapon is much more complicated than the ones I enlarged and replicated. This one has too many moving parts. It would take me more time than we have to figure out how to replicate this."

"So, where does that leave us?" asked the Commodore. "Well, I suppose that James could make up a modification package for all the Seabows and install them whenever we get back into port," said Andrew. "He could also modify all of 2nd Squadron's Seabows when they come in, then 3rd Squadron's later. I suppose we'd need permission from the Admiral to pay for all that." "You got that right. Let's see, we have eighteen Seabows in 1st Squadron, because we put six on each of our three ships, the other two squadrons have four ships with four Seabows on each ship, that's thirty-two, plus eighteen equals fifty Seabows in 1st Fleet. At seven silvers each, that comes to…" "Thirty-five golds, Sir," finished Andrew.

"Figure the same for 2nd Fleet, and that's a seventy-gold order. Are you interested, Master James?" James chewed his lower lip, "Sir, I'm certainly *interested* in such an order, but I can't stay here in Sundock for months at a time, waiting for an answer from the Admiral, then waiting on ships to arrive in port. The Inn alone would cost me nine golds a month, plus food! Besides, I have a business to run in Fairview, and hundreds of crossbows to make and deliver to the Royal Guard."

The Commodore immediately saw how difficult this would be for James and his daughter. Then inspiration struck Andrew, and he whispered something to the Commodore. "Do you think that would do it?" asked the Commodore. Andrew said, "We can only try." Commodore Matthews smiled and said, "OK, James, here's my offer. You and your daughter stay in Sundock for a couple months. The Navy will pay for your room and board, and pay thirty-five golds for modifications to all of the Seabows in 1st Fleet; and, as a sweetener, I'll get you a letter from the King, exempting you from all Eastport taxes on the export of steel used to make weapons for the crown."

James thought for a second, then extended his hand, "Done. I will need a deposit in order to purchase the materials, though." "Will twenty golds be enough?" asked the Commodore. "Certainly," replied James. The Commodore went below to retrieve the coins from the ship's strongbox. After he returned and handed over the golds to James, he said, "Andrew, I need you to go to the Inn and give the owner this voucher. It states that the Royal Navy will be paying James's bill. Try to negotiate a monthly rate that's less than nine golds. Be back here at dawn. We sail with the tide."

"Were you able to get the winter gear from the Quartermaster?" asked Andrew. "Yes, but I had to come back here and get the order from the Admiral, directing us to Frostberg. I got parkas, boots and mittens for the crews of all three ships. They'll be delivered later today," said the Commodore. "I need to send a Messenger Hawk to the Admiral to get authorization for the purchase I just made, and get that letter from the King. The letter is not a big deal, I understand that several merchants who make things for the crown have letters, exempting them from local taxes," he whispered to Andrew.

Andrew, James and Maria disembarked from the HMS VALOR and headed back into town. James told Andrew and Maria to head back to the Inn and secure the extended stay, while he went to the Blacksmith. "I want to pay for these materials as soon as possible," he explained, "I don't like carrying this much coin around."

Andrew and Maria made the short trip back to the Inn, and Andrew asked to speak to the owner. A short, chubby, elderly man came out from the back office. "You asked to see me, sir?" he asked. "Are you the owner?" "Yes, I am. Thomas Hilton, at your service. How can I help you?" "You have a guest here, an arms merchant named James, and his daughter Maria. James has just been contracted to do some work for the Royal Navy, which will require him to remain in Sundock for at least two months, maybe longer. The bill will be paid by the Royal Navy," said Andrew, handing over the letter from Commodore Matthews.

"Naturally, since this is work for the crown, and he will be here for an extended period, we need to negotiate a monthly rate for their stay," said Andrew. The owner of the Inn thought for a moment, then said, "You know, I might have a better solution for us both. You see, my mother passed away recently, so her cottage is currently vacant. I would be more than willing to rent it to James for... five golds a month?" the Innkeeper said hopefully. "Four golds," countered Andrew. The Innkeeper shook his head, "That's too low. How about we split the difference, say four golds and five?" Andrew frowned at the counteroffer, sensing that there was more leeway to be found. "Four and a half, if they still get a complimentary breakfast here every morning." "Done!" said the relieved owner. "Let me get you the keys!"

The owner of the Inn retrieved the keys to the vacant cottage and led Andrew and Maria out the door and down the street. Surprisingly, the cottage was just across the lane from the Blacksmith shop. "Here we are," said the Innkeeper, "um, I do need the first month's rent in advance, you understand." Andrew glowered at the Innkeeper for not mentioning this earlier, but he said, "Let's look at the cottage first, then we'll see about payment in advance."

"Of course, of course. Right this way." The cottage was cozy, with two bedrooms, a living room with a fireplace, and a well-stocked kitchen. "This might do," said Andrew, "but I see the Blacksmith shop across the road, how noisy does it get in here? I'd hate to have their sleep interrupted by the clanging of hammers on hot steel." The Innkeeper's face fell as he feared the loss of the agreement. "It can get rather loud from time to time," he admitted. "How about we knock off the five silvers from the monthly rent and they just pay four golds a month?"

"I think they could live with that, as long as you have two keys to the door. James and Maria will both need one," said Andrew smiling, "and I'll need to retrieve the golds from my room at the Inn," said Andrew. The Innkeeper handed the keys to Maria. Andrew and Maria walked back to the Inn to retrieve James and Maria's things from their room. Andrew went into his room and

Replicated four golds from his single gold coin. When he came down to the front desk, Maria was already there with two packs, stuffed with clothes. Andrew paid the Innkeeper the four golds. "By the way, I'm sorry for your loss," said Andrew. The Innkeeper waved him off, "Mother passed six months ago, but thank you for your condolences."

Andrew helped Maria transport their personal belongings back to the cottage. As soon as the door to the cottage closed behind them, Maria turned and gave Andrew a kiss. "Thank you so much for helping us. The Inn was OK, but this is much nicer. You're a shrewd negotiator." Andrew paused as he recovered from Maria's kiss, then said, "My pleasure. We should probably go across the street and inform your father, so he doesn't go all the way back to the Inn looking for you."

They locked the door and headed into the Blacksmith shop, where they found James and the shop owner having tea while they concluded their agreement. James expressed surprise at their appearance. "I expected you two to be off exploring the town together. I know that Andrew is leaving tomorrow," said James. "We just came by to let you know that we have the cottage across the street for the next two months, and free breakfast at the Inn if we want it," said Maria. "That cottage over there?" asked James, pointing. "Yes. Here is your key," said Andrew, handing over the second key. "I hope you didn't pay more than five golds a month for it," said the Blacksmith.

"The Royal Navy paid four golds a month," said Andrew. The Blacksmith whistled, "Then you got a better deal than the last renters." Andrew smiled.

Maria and Andrew spent the rest of the day wandering through town, enjoying each other's company. After dinner, Andrew walked her back to the cottage and kissed her goodnight. "I have to be back on the ship before dawn," said Andrew, "but I hope to see you again when we return in about a month." "I'll wait for you," said Maria. "Please be careful, and come back to me."

The next morning, the HMS VALOR sailed from Sundock, headed for the seas east of Frostberg. The prevailing wind out of the west allowed the ships to trim their sails to a beam reach configuration, and reach their destination in just over a week, without Mage Andrew or the Sorcerers on the other ships in the squadron needing to spend their strength by conjuring Wind spells. The weather grew colder the farther north they traveled, and eventually, there were floating blocks of ice in the water to contend with.

The ship's magicians had to position themselves on the forecastles in order to see these small icebergs and either Blast them apart, or order the ships to change course to avoid the floating hazards. When they reached the port town of Frostberg that evening, they found the four ships of the 2nd Squadron tied to the piers, loading supplies for the journey back to Sundock. "Commodore Lang, how is it out there?" asked Commodore Matthews. Commodore Lang, the thin, blonde-haired commander of the 2nd Squadron, said, "It's cold, bleak and barren out there. That's how it is. My crew's half frozen to death, and my ships are all bashed up from the ice floes out there. It's bad enough during the day, but at night, you can hardly see the blasted things! My magicians are all exhausted from Blasting icebergs, or trying to blow them aside with Wind spells!"

"Any problems with dragons?" asked Mage Andrew. "None at all," replied Commodore Lang. "I doubt that they'd even come this far north. The water's freezing, and the fishing is terrible, they tell me." "Then how do the people of Frostberg make a living?" asked Andrew. "They fish for crabs," replied Commodore Lang. "Their ships head out and drop crab pots or traps attached to buoys, then come back in a few days and drag them back up off the sea floor. It's cold, dangerous work, but apparently very profitable."

"Well, now that we're here, you can head back to Sundock whenever you're ready. By the way, the Arms Merchant, James, who invented the crossbow, is in

Sundock. He's come up with a modification to our Seabows that allows them to be drawn by a single sailor. It'll probably take a couple of weeks for him to modify all the Seabows in your squadron, but he's already been paid for the job. Make sure you look him up. I understand that he's staying in the cottage across the street from the Sundock Blacksmith shop. Also, the Sea Dragons seem to be abiding by the truce so far, and we haven't had any attacks, but I guess that could change at any time," said Commodore Matthews. "We're ready to depart anytime, so we'll plan to head out at dawn. A word of caution about the Seabows, you need to keep them warm. It's so cold out there that we had two of the metal arms snap when we tried to draw them. Too cold, I guess. I hope to be out of these ice-infested waters before sunset tomorrow," said Commodore Lang.

The two commanders parted, and Commodore Matthews and Andrew headed for the nearest Inn, the Ice House. They entered to find a roaring fire in the fireplace and a warm and inviting bar area. "What'll ya have?" asked the heavyset barmaid. "A couple of ales, and two rooms for tonight," said Commodore Matthews. "The ales are two coppers each, and the rooms are a silver for a room on the first floor, two silvers for the second-floor rooms, and three silvers for a room on the third floor." "Why are the rooms on the higher floors more expensive?" asked Andrew.

"Because heat rises," said the barmaid. "Rooms on the third floor are much warmer than those on the second, and the second-floor rooms are warmer than those on the ground floor."

"These old bones are too used to the warm southern seas," said Commodore Matthews, handing over three silvers and two coppers. "I'll take a room on the third floor." "Second floor," said Andrew, as he gave the barmaid two silvers and two coppers. "Be right back with the ales and the keys," said the barmaid. She headed back into the kitchen and returned quickly with two ales and the keys to the rooms.

Gek awoke to someone slapping his leg. He looked around and found Richard next to him. "How did you get out of your bed?" he asked sleepily. Richard giggled and scooted quickly across the floor into the living room. Gek shook his head. "Great. Now we will never get any sleep," he groused. He got up and headed into the living room after Richard. "Just where do you think you are going, young man?" Gek asked, scooping Richard up in his arms. Richard laughed and squirmed. "DADA!" he said.

"What did you say?" asked a stunned Gek. "DADA! DADA!" said Richard. From the corner of the room, Bruce looked on, shaking his head in amazement. "These dragon Changed Ones sure mature fast," he said. "At this rate, he'll be walking soon." "How do you suppose he got out of his bed?" asked Gek. "He probably just sat up and pulled himself over the side. I guess it's time for that crib I told you about. Let's go out to the shed and get it."

Gek and Bruce headed out to the dilapidated shed outside the hut, where Bruce had constructed a crib out of a shallow shipping crate and four sections of picket fencing that had washed up on the shore sometime over the past five years. The fence sections were held together with baling wire and nailed to the crate. "This should hold him for a while," said Bruce, grinning.

Gek set Richard down on the sand and helped Bruce carry the makeshift crib into the back room that Gek, Azure, Anna and Richard had been using as a bedroom. As they entered, Azure stirred from sleep. "What is that?" she asked. "It is Richard's new bed," said Gek. "He has learned to crawl and escape from his crate. Bruce says this thing will contain him for a while." "Where is Richard now?" asked Azure.

Gek bolted outside to find Richard crawling towards the surf. "HEY! GET BACK HERE!" roared Gek.

Richard giggled and crawled faster. Gek raced across the sand, picking Richard up before he plunged into the water. Gek sat down at the edge of the shoreline, holding Richard in his lap as the waves grew closer and closer as the tide came in. After a few minutes, a wave washed over their legs and Richard squealed with delight.

After a few minutes in the surf, Gek picked Richard up and headed back to the hut. He set him down on the floor in the living room and sat down in one of the driftwood chairs. Gek dozed off for a moment, and when he opened his eyes, Richard was eating a plum from the kitchen table, the juice running down his chin. Gek watched, fascinated. "Well, your mother will be relieved," he said, "it looks like you are eating solid food, but why are you eating *that*?"

Bruce entered the hut and spied Richard and his plum. "I thought dragons only ate fish or meat?" he asked. "We do," said Gek. "I do not understand it. Even Changed Ones do not eat fruits or vegetables." "Maybe it's because he's *not* a Changed One. Maybe, he's more of a human. I mean, Changed Ones are born dragons, right? Then they learn how to change into humans. Richard was born a human." "I do not know," replied Gek. "That is a question for Beau or the other Changed Ones in Grotton, but I am reluctant to go back there. The Regional Mage would recognize me for sure."

Richard finished his plum and was gnawing on the pit when Bruce said, "No, Richard, you don't eat that part." Bruce gently pried the plum pit from Richard's hand and threw it into the fireplace. Richard reached for another plum and began again. Bruce just shook his head. "Like I said, I've never seen a baby grow so fast." Once Richard was finished with his plum, Gek picked him up and immediately said, "What is that stench?"

Bruce laughed, "I warned you what was coming once he started eating solid foods. It goes right through 'em. Take him outside and get that messy diaper off him. Wash him off in the surf and clean the diaper. Your life just got a lot messier and smellier. *And I don't change messy diapers!*"

Gek held Richard at arm's length and dunked him, diaper and all, into the seawater. He gently removed the soiled diaper and threw it up onto the beach. Once he finished cleaning Richard's bottom, he placed him on the sand and picked up the diaper, plunging it into the surf as quickly as he could. Once the diaper was relatively clean, Gek took it out of the water, then chased down Richard, who was now crawling towards the tree line. Gek tossed the soaking wet diaper towards the hut and picked up Richard, who was now covered with sand.

After washing Richard in the surf again, Gek took him inside, where he woke Azure and informed her of the new developments. "Wait, are you telling me that Richard can crawl, eat solid food, mess his diaper and *talk*? All in one day?" "Yes," said Gek. "Although I am not sure why he was eating fruit. Richard, can you say 'MAMA'?" Richard looked at Azure, "DADA!" he cried. "No," said Azure, "MAMA." "DADA! DADA!" screamed Richard.

"What an idiot," said Annalise.

A shower of sparks erupted from Donovan's mouth, then a glob of unlit inferno hit the shield that encircled the Wizards Academy. "Again!" said a frustrated Donovan. "How in the world do dragons ever figure this out?" he raged. He'd been at it all morning, and mastering dragon's breath was not as easy as it looked. He had figured out how to expel the inferno from the sacs, but not quite forcefully enough to hit anything at a distance, and making sparks by running his tongue along his teeth was too easy; but using the sparks to ignite the inferno was proving to be exceedingly difficult.

Rachel was out with the Royal Expeditionary Force, helping them practice shooting crossbow bolts at Seemings of flying dragons, while Donovan spent the morning trying to learn how to breathe fire. They were going to change places after lunch. Donovan hoped his wife was having more success this morning than he was. "Excuse me, sir," said a voice behind him. Donovan turned to find Vida, a Level Three student, standing behind him. "Yes, Vida, what is it?" asked Donovan crossly. "Well, Wizard Noland thought I might be able to help you. Me, being a Fire Dragon Changed One and all."

Donovan softened his tone and said, "Actually, that is a great idea. I am having great difficulty shooting inferno and igniting it." "That is a common problem for young Dragons, sir. It is not easy to master, yet, once you know how to do it, it is like second nature. So, here is how I learned: first, you need to practice expelling the inferno and hitting your target. You know that each sac of inferno shoots out at a different angle, right?" Donovan nodded. "So, you have to turn and sometimes twist your head to hit what you are aiming at. My mother made me practice shooting inferno for *weeks* before she let me try igniting it," said Vida.

"I do not have *weeks*," said an exasperated Donovan. "I have *this week* to learn. Then I have to leave with the Royal Expeditionary Force! Is there a faster way you can teach me?" Vida considered the problem, then said, "Well, if you concentrate on using just one sac, say the one on the upper right side of your mouth, you might learn faster. Here is what you do: Push down on the sac with the right side of your tongue, and drag just the tip of your tongue across your teeth. It really does not take many sparks to ignite the inferno; it is really quite flammable."

"OK, I will try it," said Donovan. "Just realize that you will run out of inferno after about three tries," said Vida, "Great Dragon sacs do not hold as much inferno as Fire Dragon sacs. If you run out, you will have to wait until tomorrow before the sacs refill." Donovan concentrated, then tried again. This time, a stream of inferno spewed from his mouth, followed by sparks.

"Oooh! That was so close!" said Vida. "Try again, and just be a hair quicker with the sparks." Donovan worked his jaw back and forth and tried again. This time, a blast of fire erupted from his mouth, and flaming inferno coated the inside of the Academy shield. "You got it!" exclaimed Vida. "But now that sac is empty," said Donovan. "You can try the same thing with the top left sac," said Vida. "It is basically the same thing, only push on the sac with the other side of your tongue. The sacs on the bottom of your mouth are harder to control, and the one on the roof of your mouth is the most difficult, because your tongue is in the way, so you have to push the sac, and quickly lower your tongue and hit your bottom teeth as you do. It is actually quite complicated."

Donovan tried using the upper left sac of inferno, but was unable to hit the target. "That is why you have to turn your head slightly," said Vida. "You are really spitting fire out of the side of your mouth." "I will practice some more tomorrow," said Donovan as he transformed back into human form. "Will you be here to help Rachel this afternoon?" asked Donovan. Vida shook her head. "No, I have History and Martial Arts practice this afternoon. I believe that Level Three James is going to come help Rachel during Fourth period. He is already very good with a staff." "I will let Rachel know to expect him. Thank you for your help," said Donovan.

Donovan met Rachel in the officers' mess for lunch. "How did it go this morning?" he asked. "They're getting better. I think they are a little more motivated now that we're headed back out soon. How was your fire-breathing practice?" "It's complicated. I only managed one good blast before I ran out of inferno. Fortunately, Wizard Noland sent Level Three Vida, who is a Fire Dragon Changed One, to help me. I think Level Three James is going to come help you during fourth period." "I admit, I'm a little nervous about Changing into a dragon for the first time," said Rachel.

"Believe me, I understand," said Donovan. "Would you like me to come with you?" "Yes. At least for my first time," admitted Rachel. Donovan rose and went over to where Major Gerald was having his lunch. "Sir, would it be alright if I accompanied Rachel to the Wizards Academy for the first glass after lunch? She's a little anxious about Changing into a dragon for the first time."

"No problem whatsoever," replied Major Gerald. "Besides, we need some more practice riding under concealment. Why don't you stay with her the whole afternoon? Did you have any luck breathing fire this morning?" "I accomplished it once before I ran out of inferno. I'm sure I'll get the hang of it before we leave on Firstday," replied Donovan. Major Gerald nodded. "We need to discuss our route through Franconia soon. This is going to take us a while, and we need to decide the fastest and most efficient route. You two meet me here after dinner, and we'll plan it out in my office. I'll invite the company commanders and the Specialists as well. I need to brief the King on our plan on Midweek."

"You got that, Dirk?" asked Donovan. Specialist Dirk lowered the hood of his Concealment cloak. "Yes, Specialist Lance and I will be here. Do you want Corporal Knox here too?" "No. The seven of us should be more than adequate," said Major Gerald.

Donovan went back to the table where Rachel was just finishing her lunch. "Major Gerald said I could spend the afternoon with you. The rest of the Force is going to take a break from crossbow training and concentrate on riding while Concealed. We have a meeting with the other officers after dinner tonight in Major Gerald's office to plan out the route we will take through the Kingdom." Rachel nodded. "I'm afraid I won't be much help. I've never really been anywhere outside of Kingston."

They arrived at the Wizards Academy and were greeted by Wizard Faith. "More dragon training?" she asked. Rachel nodded worriedly. "Worried about making the Change?" asked Faith. Rachel nodded. "It's as easy as pie. If Celeste can do it, anybody can." "Is it true that she's dating the King?" asked Rachel. Wizard Faith nodded, "Yes. I certainly never expected that. We'll just have to see where *that* goes. Well, good luck."

Donovan and Rachel walked over to the Forces Training Area, to the section where the grass was scorched and blackened. Donovan said, "Let me Change into a dragon first, so you will have a clear picture in your mind of what one looks like. He stepped back, disrobed, and said *"MORPHIOUS,"* while clapping his hands together. Instantly, a large gold dragon stood in his place. "Just picture a dragon like me that can talk," he said encouragingly. "You can do this."

Rachel smiled at hearing the very words she told Donovan before he made the Change for the first time during his Sorcerer's Test. She steeled herself, took off her clothes, looked at Donovan, smiled at his staring eyes, and said, *"MORPHIOUS,"* and clapped her hands. Instantly, she transformed into a golden dragon. "Congratulations!" said Donovan. "Now, feel around inside your mouth, there are several lumps on the sides, top and bottom of your mouth. Those are inferno sacs. You need to practice pushing on them, one at a time, with your tongue to force the inferno out. You spit the inferno at your target, but since the sacs are in different places inside your mouth, the inferno comes out in different directions, depending on which sac you press. You light the inferno by dragging your tongue along your teeth, which makes sparks."

"That sounds complicated," said Rachel. Donovan laughed, "It is *very* complicated! Vida said that it takes weeks for young dragons to learn how to spit and ignite inferno accurately." "But we do not have *weeks*!" said Rachel. "That is exactly what I told Vida," said Donovan with a smile. "You should practice making sparks first."

Rachel moved her tongue across her dragon teeth, and a shower of sparks erupted. "Very good," said Donovan (as if he were an expert), "but you need to use just the tip of your tongue; otherwise, the rest of it gets in the way of the inferno." Rachel tried again several times, making a less prodigious number of sparks. "Vida says not to worry about how many sparks we make, it only takes a few because of how flammable the inferno is," confided Donovan. "Are you ready to try spitting inferno?"

"I guess so," said Rachel. She concentrated and opened her mouth, spitting inferno at the shield ten feet away. The inferno landed short, in the blackened grass. "Try again, but push harder on the sac," said Donovan. It took multiple tries, but Rachel eventually managed to hit the shield. "Now try igniting it. Right after you spit, while the inferno is just leaving your mouth, make sparks with your tongue." Rachel opened her mouth, and a blast of fire erupted, striking the shield and rebounding. "Beginner's luck," grumbled Donovan. Several more successful trials, and it was obvious that Rachel had figured out how it worked. Donovan looked sulky.

"Do not pout! It is unbecoming of a Great Dragon," teased Rachel. "It certainly is," said James, as he walked up behind them, "and I should know." Donovan and Rachel turned to greet James, a Great Dragon Changed

One. "So, Rachel, it seems like you have figured out the trick of spitting and igniting inferno. Well done! Now, I have to tell you that just being able to breathe fire is only the beginning. You have to learn how to hit your target while stationary, running and flying, and your target may also be moving, so it is much more complicated than either of you realize. Unfortunately, you are not going to be able to fly around the Academy, spitting flaming inferno at targets, so that is something you will have to practice elsewhere."

Donovan and Rachel were silent. They both realized that James was right; mastering this skill was going to take a lot more practice, which they had no time for. "However," continued James, "you do not need to become experts, since any need for fire breath from either of you is likely going to involve close combat, not long-range engagements. As you have heard, Donovan, Dragons are not fireproof. It is even possible for one Dragon to ignite the inferno in another Dragon's mouth, if the Dragon in question opens his or her mouth too wide; and while we breathe fire, we cannot *breathe* fire, if you take my meaning. If you *inhale* smoke or flames, you will die. Keep that in mind."

With that final word of advice, James headed off to the Martial Arts training area. Donovan Changed back into human form, got dressed, and told Rachel, "Now, just picture yourself as you were, rear up on your hind legs and conjure the Change spell." Rachel conjured the spell, but something went wrong, and she was left standing naked, with bright golden hair. Donovan grinned. "What?" asked Rachel, as she quickly put her clothes back on. "Your hair is gold," said Donovan. "You mean light brown with gold highlights," said Rachel. "No. I mean gold, like a gold dragon. You're going to be quite the topic of conversation at dinner tonight." Rachel looked scandalized.

Just as Donovan predicted, all of the soldiers stared at Rachel's golden hair during dinner. Rachel was extremely embarrassed, but couldn't think of a spell to turn her hair back to her natural color. Donovan suggested that after dinner, she change back into a dragon, then back into human form again; this time, concentrating on her hair color. She ate quickly, then retreated outside, behind the dining hall (Donovan reminded her about taking off her clothes before Changing into a dragon). When she returned, her hair had returned to normal.

After dinner, the officers and Specialists assembled in the Major's office. He laid out a map of Franconia and said, "OK, the King wants us to visit all of the main towns and cities in the Kingdom, take an inventory of their Treasuries, and the Sorcerers will check the Regional Mage's Offices for any dragon Changed Ones. Our job will be to support them and protect their backs.

That means you, Specialists Dirk and Lance. Now, we need to map out the most expeditious and efficient route.

The assembled men looked over the map, thinking about how to get from place to place without backtracking. Finally, Captain Smith said, "It looks like two loops to me, sir: Southport to Westport, to Weaton, then Prarrieville, Colton, Riverton, Fairview, Farmdale, Hayford, Three Forks, Frostberg, Sundock, Eastport, Grotton, then home. We miss the towns of Haven and Smithville, but they're small, and I doubt that either of them have significant Treasuries."

"Hmm, the King might go for that, but I'm not sure he'll accept missing those two towns," said Major Gerald. "What if Rachel and I Changed into dragons and visited them while the Force rested in Hayford? I mean, it looks like a short flight, and it would only take about a day in each town. Of course, that would leave you without any organic magical support." "Any other comments?" asked Major Gerald. "I don't like them going alone," said Dirk. "Haven and Smithville may be small towns, but there could be rogue magicians or dragon Changed Ones in one or both of them."

"Dirk's right," said Major Gerald, "Any other ideas?" Donovan grinned, "Dirk, have you ever wanted to ride on a dragon?"

Chapter Twenty:
SURPRISE, SURPRISE!

"Just what do you mean by that, young lady?" asked Azure, somewhat shocked by Anna's pronouncement. "Just what I said. That thing," she said, pointing at her brother, "is an idiot!" Gek's mouth fell open. "And just when did you learn to talk?" he asked. "This morning, I guess," said Annalise smugly. "I have understood you for some time now, but I guess that I just learned how to talk. So, can I *please* have some fish to eat? I am starving, and the crabs I have been eating are not very filling." "Come with me, and I will find you some fish to eat," said Gek finally.

They walked into the kitchen and found Bruce repairing a fishing net. "Bruce, this is Annalise," said Gek. "I know her name. What's the matter with you? Did the sun get to you?" asked Bruce. "It is nice to meet you, Bruce," said Anna. "Thank you for being kind to me." Bruce dropped the net on the floor. "SHE SPOKE! I thought you said that she was only six months old!" cried Bruce. "I am. I guess Dragons just learn to talk sooner than…. What are you again?" asked Anna.

"I'm a human," said Bruce, "like your brother, and your father at the moment," stammered Bruce. "Human. Hmm. OK, I guess you know what you are. Can you change into a Dragon?" Bruce laughed, "No. There are no humans that I know of who can change into dragons. But, there are some dragons, like your parents, who can change into humans." Annalise thought for a moment, then said, "I guess that makes sense, but why is my brother a human?"

"That is a long story that we will discuss later. I thought you were hungry," said Gek. Anna nodded, and Gek retrieved some leftover fish from breakfast. "Here you go." Anna devoured the fish quickly and said, "Is there any more?" Gek sighed. "There are plenty of fish in the sea, but wait for your mother to go with you." "Why?" asked Anna. "Because some fish are big enough to eat *you*, instead of the other way around," said Azure, as she carefully entered the room.

"A fish could eat me?" asked Annalise. "Some could. At least until you get bigger. So, let us go out and see what we can find for lunch." Azure and Anna left the hut and proceeded down the beach before diving into the water. "That was a surprise," said Bruce. "You are telling me," confirmed Gek. "Here, I was impressed with how fast Richard is growing. I had no idea how quickly Dragons matured."

"How old were you when you started talking?" asked Bruce. "I have no idea," confessed Gek. "We did not exactly keep track of the time in the Snow Fields.

One day, I could just talk. It took almost a year before I learned how to fly, and longer still before I could breathe fire." "Well, at least now you can make sure that Anna understands not to hurt her brother," said Bruce. "She may understand, but keeping her from doing it is a whole other matter," said Gek.

After catching and eating their fill of seabass, Azure and Anna walked along the beach. Anna asked, "Mother, why are you and daddy different?" "What do you mean?" Azure asked. "You are the color of the water, and daddy is the color of… I do not know what color he is!" Azure laughed. "That is because I am a Sea Dragon, while your father is a Great Dragon. His scales are gold, while mine are blue." "Are there other differences, besides color?" "Of course, Sea Dragons spit water," said Azure, spraying Anna with a low-pressure jet of water. Anna giggled, "Stop it! You mean daddy does not spit water?"

"No, Great Dragons breathe fire." Fire?" "Yes, fire. Sea Dragons are much better swimmers than Great Dragons. You see how my tail is flat, and I have webbing between my fingers? That helps me swim better." "But you cannot breathe fire?" "No. I cannot." Annalise thought for a minute, then asked, "What am I?" "You are a Great Sea Dragon," said Azure. You will learn how to spit water *and* breathe fire." "When will I be able to breathe fire?" Anna asked excitedly. "Not for a while yet, dear. Your body needs to grow some more." "Why?" "Imagine if all baby Dragons could breathe fire without any training! They could set their homes on fire, or the forest."

"Who is Bruce?" Anna asked. "Bruce is our friend. We met him a little over a year ago. He was helping us find other Sea Dragons." "Why? Are they lost?" "Not *lost*, exactly. It is just that our islands, the place where you were hatched, got too crowded, and so, some of the Sea Dragons moved here, and we lost track of them."

"Why do you and daddy look like Bruce sometimes?" "We have learned how to change into humans. It makes it easier for us to search human towns for other Sea Dragons," said Azure, predicting where this conversation was going. "Why do you call that small human my brother?" "Because you are *both* my children," said Azure. "I gave birth to Richard while I was in human form, and you while I was a Dragon."

"I do not like him," said Anna. "Maybe not today, but someday you will," said Azure.

Edward and Kathy rose early the next morning, watered and fed the horse, then headed back to the campsite. "I hope that dragon was just passing by last night," said Kathy. "It was moving fast and headed due west, towards the Grey Mountains, and it was flying pretty low. If it stayed on that same course, it might not have seen our campsite. Although, with all of the campfires, it's probably not hard to spot from the air at night," said Edward.

"What do you think they'll do?" asked Kathy. "I have no idea. First, why would the dragons care if we dig a big hole in the ground? If it fills with water, as I hope, that's probably a good thing for them. Additionally, I suspect that they'll hesitate to attack a camp with over a hundred magicians in it." "You think that they can detect the spark?" asked Kathy. "It's possible, but even if they can't, they'll surely notice that we're using magic to dig this hole so fast."

They arrived back at the campsite around mid-morning and found the camp bustling with activity. Edward asked Kathy to find Mage Elianna and round up the apprentices for a quick meeting. Once everyone was assembled, Edward said, "So, we are about a two-hour ride from the trench. I've decided to make a change to our schedule. From now on, we'll only work during the day. We're going to line up in a row and Remove the glass, sand and soil all the way down to bedrock, then move west and do it again."

"We'll depart an hour before sunrise each day and leave the dig site at sunset. The camp will be empty except for some of the wagon drivers and the cooks, who'll stay here at the campsite; the rest of us, stay together. Load up!"

The apprentice magicians all piled into five wagons, and they headed out. The apprentice magicians seemed to be happy that there would be no more night shifts. As they rode, Edward gathered Mage Kathy and Elianna together. He told Mage Elianna about the dragon they'd seen during the night. "Once we get back tonight, I want to minimize the number of campfires we have going and keep them very small. I'm sure the campsite can be seen for miles from the air, especially at night. We all need to be on the lookout. I don't want to be surprised by a dragon attack. I'm not sure how the apprentices would react."

"Should we start teaching them the Blast spell?" asked Elianna. "Maybe," said Edward. "I don't want to overload them or cause them anxiety. As long as they know how to conjure Shields, they should be safe. Just remember, if we're attacked by a Stone Dragon, the best way to kill it is by enclosing it in a shield and suffocating it."

"How would you know that?" asked Mage Elianna. "That's how I had to kill the Stone Dragon that attacked us at the palace in Baize," replied Edward casually. "Blast, Sleep and Paralyze spells were ineffective, although a strong Wind spell kept him on the ground. Stone Dragons are not strong fliers." Elianna looked at Kathy, who nodded. "How many kinds of dragons are there?" Elianna asked. "Five," said Edward, "Fire, Stone, Snow, Sea and Great Dragons. But only the Fire and Stone Dragons should be living on this side of the Amber River. Of course, the Snow Dragons live in the Snow Fields, so they are in Baize too."

When they got to the glassy area in front of the trench, Edward had all of the student magicians form one long line, with about ten yards between each apprentice. The line was a little over half a mile long. "REMOVE," commanded Edward. His voice wouldn't carry to the end of the line, but as the students saw the magician next to them cast the spell, they followed suit. In short order (less than a minute), the first half-mile of sand, salt and dirt had been vanished all the way down to bedrock. Students loaded back into the wagons and moved down the trench line. They cleared the entire length of the southern trench on the first day.

"So, how are we doing?" Kathy asked Edward. "It was OK for the first day, but we need to move faster if we hope to be finished by the time the King arrives. At least the travel distance will get shorter each day as we work our way north. In the meantime, I need you to go into Springfield and check on the accounts. The next allotment of 250 golds should have arrived by now, and we're going to need it to procure some winter gear for the workers."

"You're right. I'll leave in the morning. Is there anything else I should do?" asked Kathy. "Yes," said Edward. "Warn Wizard Timothy and Captain Douglas of the Baizian forces about the dragon."

The Royal Expeditionary Force departed on Firstday morning on the FS LUMBERJACK, headed for Southport. The merchant ship was transporting cut lumber to Westport with a stop in Southport. The ship was not ideal for transporting three wagons and fifty-three soldiers with mounts, but it would do. The ship would remain in Southport for three days; after that, the Royal Expeditionary Force would have to find other transportation to Westport.

"Once we get to Southport, I'll take some of the men and head for the Treasury. You two go and check out the Regional Mage's Office. Dirk, you go with the Sorcerers. We'll do the same thing in every place we visit. The Captains and I can count the golds, while you two make sure there are no Changed Ones in the local Mage's office," said Major Gerald.

"If we want to be thorough, we'll need to check the magicians in the 4th Regiment also," said Donovan. "That means the Battle Mage and the four Sorcerers in the Regiment. I hope no one is out on maneuvers, or we'll have to track them down." Major Gerald scratched his beard and said, "Yer right. I don't think the King thought of that. What will you do if you find a Changed One?"

"We'll have to Tether their arms, so they can't change into a dragon. Then ask if they will submit to the standard Binding spell. If they won't, we'll have to kill them." "And just how are you going to find all of the magicians and get them to come to you?" asked Gerald. "Easy," said Donovan, "we brought them their Concealment cloaks. Our wagon is full of them. Which reminds me, we're going to need guards for the wagon. We certainly don't want anyone making off with an armload of Concealment cloaks." Major Gerald grunted, "We certainly don't."

Four uneventful days later, the FS LUMBERJACK ported in Southport. The ship's captain, Captain Wood, said to Major Gerald, "We sail in three days. That's on Midweek morning. Don't be late, or we sail without you." Major Gerald nodded his understanding and continued offloading his command. "Once everything is off the ship, we'll head to the 4th Regiment garrison, they should have enough room for all the men and mounts. I want a twenty-four-hour guard on the magician's wagon. There's valuable cargo in there. After we get settled, the magicians will go meet with the Regiment's magicians, while the company commanders and I will go inspect the City Treasury, I believe it's in the King's new winter palace."

When the Expeditionary Force arrived at the garrison that housed the 4th Franconian Regiment, a guard at the entrance challenged them, "Who are you, and what's your business here?" he asked. "Major Gerald with the Royal Expeditionary Force, on an inspection tour ordered by the King. Open up!" The portcullis was immediately raised, and the Expeditionary Force entered. Major Myers, the Regimental Commander, was summoned and appeared quickly.

"Gerald! What brings the Royal Expeditionary Force to Southport?" asked Major Myers. "The King sent us out on some damned inspection tour of every garrison in Franconia," grumbled Major Gerald. "He wants us to inspect all of the Treasuries in the Kingdom and check on the Regional Mage's Offices, just to be sure everything's in order. If you ask me, he just wanted something for us to do." Major Myers laughed, "Well, you know the King."

"I do indeed," said Major Gerald. "We also have some fantastic new gear for all of the magicians in your command," he said quietly. "If you could assemble them all, my new Sorcerers will hand out the new kit." "So, you finally have some organic magical support? It's about time! What's this new gear?" "Let's get inside and I'll tell you all about it," said Gerald.

Once the Majors were in the Regimental Commander's office, Major Gerald explained about the new Concealment cloaks that were being issued to all of the magicians in the Kingdom. "That'll be a real help!" said Major Myers. "Let me summon my magicians."

The 4th Regiment's Battle Mage, Jeffery, and three of the four Sorcerers assigned to the Battalions arrived shortly. Sorcerer White, from 3rd Battalion, was missing. "Someone go find Sorcerer White," ordered the commander, "and get him in here. I don't care what he's doing!" An orderly rushed to obey the commander. Donovan took the other four magicians out to the wagon and began issuing them their Concealment cloaks. He conjured a Smell Enhancement on the way and checked each magician carefully before issuing them their cloaks.

"These Concealment cloaks cost a gold each to replace, so don't lose them," said Rachel. "I recommend folding them inside out whenever you're not wearing them; otherwise, if you put them down somewhere, you may never find them again." As the last of the cloaks was issued (and signed for), Sorcerer White came running up.

"I am sorry! I was inspecting the armory. What is this new equipment we are receiving?" he asked. Sorcerer White smelled like a lizard wearing perfume. Donovan immediately Tethered his arms. "What is the meaning of this outrage!" shouted Sorcerer White. "Say 'can't,'" said Donovan. Sorcerer White struggled against his bonds, but remained mute. "I thought so. What are you, a Snow Dragon?"

"What are you talking about? I am not a dragon!" "I think you are, and unless you can convince me by using a contraction, *RIGHT NOW*, I'm going to kill you. Your other option is to submit to a Binding spell never to Change back into a dragon and never to harm a human," said Donovan. The Regimental Battle Mage was stunned. "You're saying that Sorcerer White is a *dragon*?" "Yes," said Rachel, "use a Smell Enhancement and you'll see that he smells like a reptile."

The other four magicians all conjured Smell Enhancements and agreed that something was wrong. "So, what's it going to be, Binding spell or death?" asked Donovan. Sorcerer White slumped, then said, "Binding spell." "Promise never to Change back into a dragon, and never harm a human," said Rachel. "I promise never to change back into a Dragon, and never harm a human," said Sorcerer White, as Rachel drew her finger along the ground and said *"PROMISA."* A shower of sparks descended and engulfed Sorcerer White. Donovan released the Tether spell. "Please escort Sorcerer White to his quarters. He'll need to be reassigned to the Regional Mage's Office," said Donovan.

"Why is that?" asked Mage Jeffery. "What good is a Battalion Sorcerer who can't harm another human? He'll only be useful for detecting rogue magicians now." "What about his cloak?" asked Jeffery. "I don't think so," replied Donovan. "While he can't harm another human, he could certainly 'lose' or give away his cloak to an enemy without violating the Binding spell. We'd better go see the Regimental commander."

As they entered Major Myers' office, he stood and asked, "What's wrong?" "Sir," began Donovan, "Sorcerer White was a Snow Dragon Changed One. Sorceress Rachel has placed him under a Binding spell never to change back into a dragon, and to never harm a human. He needs to be transferred to the Regional Mage's Office. He's no good to you now." Major Myers sat down in shock.

"Let me get this straight, you're saying that Sorcerer White, from 3rd Battalion, is a dragon, disguised as a human?" "Exactly right, sir. At the Wizards Academy, we discovered that dragons can perform magic, including the Change spell, and that some of them have taken human form and are living amongst us," said Donovan. "To what end?" asked the commander. "Well, sir, some of them just had miserable lives as dragons; constantly hungry, afraid of their own kin, endlessly hunting for food. Life as a human was preferable for dragons like White." "And the others?"

"The other dragon 'Changed Ones,' which is their word for dragons living in human form, are spies, intent on doing us harm. Those Changed Ones have to be killed," said Donovan. "Is that why the Royal Expeditionary Force is visiting every town and city in Franconia? To find these Changed Ones?" asked the commander. "That's one reason. The other is to distribute the Concealment cloaks to all of the magicians in Franconia. It would be too disruptive to make them all travel to Kingston to pick up their cloaks," said Rachel.

"What about this audit of all the Treasuries?" asked Major Myers. Donovan shifted his feet. Finally, he said, "Dragon Changed Ones are not only impersonating magicians, but also some of the key people in the realm. The King is concerned that some of his gold may have been misappropriated by dragon Changed Ones. We are checking to allay his fears." "I see," said Major Myers. "You have a daunting task ahead of you. I wish you well. Before you go, can you tell me how to identify a Changed One?" Donovan explained about Changed Ones not using contractions, and how they smelled different than humans. The Major promised to keep a sharp lookout for any other Changed Ones in Southport.

There were no Changed Ones in the Regional Mage's Office, and all was as it should be in the Treasury. One down and fifteen to go. The Royal Expeditionary Force boarded the FS LUMBERJACK on Midweek morning and headed for Westport.

Chapter Twenty-One:

SNOW, COAL AND GOLD

Andrew and the HMS VICTORY were preparing to cast off when he saw them, seven Snow Dragons, flying low through the fog towards Frostberg. "DRAGONS!" shouted Andrew. "MAN THE SEABOWS! BATTLE STATIONS! LOAD CROSSBOWS!" Sailors rushed to their posts, winding the cranks to draw the Seabows, gathering crossbow bolts and preparing for the assault.

But the ships were not the target of the attack. The dragons flashed over the docks and headed for the town, breathing ice. A few sailors got off wildly inaccurate shots from their crossbows, and one or two of the Seabows fired, trying to bring down the Snow Dragons. Everybody missed the smaller Snow Dragons. "CEASE FIRE!" shouted Commodore Mathews, "Those bolts are going to land in the town and could hit someone!" "What can we do?" asked Andrew. "We need to form up and march into town, where we have a better shot with our crossbows," said the Commodore. "Unless you have a better idea."

Andrew thought for a moment, then said, "I have an idea, but it's risky." "What? Quickly, man!" "I could Change into a dragon and try to drive them off." "Do you really think a Sea Dragon can fight off a pack of Snow Dragons?" "No, I would need to Change into either a Great Dragon or a Stone Dragon," said Andrew. "Well, between my sailors and Sorcerers, and the Frostberg Sorcerer, the air is going to be filled with crossbow bolts and Blast spells, won't those hurt a Great Dragon?" "You're right, sir, a Stone Dragon it is."

Andrew ran for the aft deck and yelled, "MAKE ROOM! CLEAR THE DECK!" Once the deck was clear, he threw off his Concealment cloak and immediately changed into a Stone Dragon. As soon as his head was clear, he launched himself into the air and raced towards the town.

Commodore Matthews and the other ship Captains assembled their men and quick marched them into the Frostberg town square, searching the air for targets. The Snow Dragons began their assault at the east end of the town, freezing the roads, houses and any exposed people they could find. They were working their way into the center of the town when Andrew attacked. He managed to kill two of the Snow Dragons before the others raced off and circled around, screaming at him for attacking his cousins.

Andrew quickly discovered that a Stone Dragon flew much too slowly to keep up with the smaller and faster Snow Dragons, and without fire breath, he could only hurt them at close range. Their ice breath didn't hurt him, but he couldn't seem to turn fast enough to catch the elusive Snow Dragons. Suddenly, he was struck on the right side by a magician's Blast spell, as the Frostberg Sorcerer entered the fight. Andrew quickly flew out of range of the Sorcerer, realizing that, while the Blast spell had not penetrated his scales, he would be bruised tomorrow (if he survived the attack).

The sailors from 1st Squadron entered the town square and began firing at the Snow Dragons with their crossbows. Several bolts missed the Snow Dragons and struck Andrew instead, but none penetrated his scales. Between the Sorcerer, the sailors and the Stone Dragon, the Snow Dragons were not causing very much damage to the town or its people, but they continued their attack, determined to punish the humans in the town.

One of the Snow Dragons broke off from the others, trying to slip around to the west side of the town while the sailors and the magicians were busy fighting the other four on the north and east sides of the town. Andrew spied the lone Snow Dragon and descended, flying just below the level of the roofs of the town. While he was slower, he came around and collided with the faster Snow Dragon head-on. Andrew snapped and clawed, severing the Snow Dragon's head before it even knew that Andrew was there. The decapitated Snow

Dragon fell on a small fruit cart that was parked in the street where its owner had abandoned it.

Andrew repeated the tactic, staying low and circling around to the north. There were only four Snow Dragons left at this point, but they were now focusing their attacks on the exposed sailors, who were trying (rather unsuccessfully) to find cover on the deserted streets of the town. The Snow Dragons slowed their speed to concentrate their ice breath on the crouching sailors. That was a mistake. Andrew smashed into the pack of Snow Dragons, clawing, biting, and thrashing his tail. One Snow Dragon fell, critically injured, and, as another turned to engage Andrew, took a crossbow bolt through the back, which went clear through and struck Andrew. The last two Snow Dragons quickly fled north. The attack was over.

Andrew landed back on the HMS VALOR and waited for assistance. He was pierced by at least ten crossbow bolts, and he needed them removed before he transformed back into human form. He had no idea what would happen if he changed back into a human with crossbow bolts in him, but he didn't think it would be good.

Eventually, Commodore Matthews and several of the sailors reboarded the ship and found Andrew on the aft deck. "Why haven't you changed back into a human?" asked Commodore Matthews. "There are people in the town who are injured and need healing." Andrew nodded, then explained, "I have about ten crossbow bolts in me that need to be removed before I transform, or I might be seriously injured or killed. It might also be a good idea to bring a Sorcerer here to heal my injuries. I took a Blast spell from the Frostberg Sorcerer during the fight."

The Commodore sent the First Mate with orders to find the first Sorcerer he ran into and bring him to the ship. The First Mate ran off and returned quickly with the Sorcerer from the VICEROY. After the crew removed the eleven crossbow bolts stuck in Andrew's scales, he immediately transformed back into human form. The crossbows left small, harmless but painful pinpricks in Andrew's skin, but the damage from the Blast spell was more serious. Andrew had two cracked ribs and would be bruised for the next few days.

A quick dose of Healing Serum repaired the broken ribs, and Andrew headed below to find some new clothes. He'd been in such a hurry to confront the Snow Dragons that he had not taken the time to disrobe, and the remnants of his clothes were scattered about the aft deck. Only his Concealment cloak was still intact. Andrew headed into Frostberg (gingerly) to see if he could be of any assistance.

The town had come through the attack fairly well. There were casualties, of course, but there were many fewer than if Andrew had not intervened. After healing several of the townsfolk, Andrew met Sorcerer Stewart, the Frostberg Regional Sorcerer. "Sorry about the Blast spell," said Stewart, "I had no idea that a magician could turn into a dragon. It's a good thing that one of your sailors grabbed me and told me who you were, or I might have kept firing." "It's really hard to kill a Stone Dragon with a Blast spell. As far as I know, it's only been done once before, at point-blank range, and the Sorcerer did not survive the power drain." Stewart gulped, "Then how do we kill Stone Dragons?" "You have to encase them in a shield and suffocate them, which I'm kind of glad you didn't know." Stewart smiled his understanding.

"Is there anything I can do to help now?" asked Andrew. "No. The other Sorcerers and I have already thawed out the frozen buildings and tended to the frostbite injuries. You don't look so good. I think you should go back to the ship and rest." "You're probably right," replied Andrew. "I am kind of..." Andrew began, before he lost consciousness and fell into the street.

"The next Dragon Council is coming up soon. Do you want to attend?" asked Gek. "I do," said Azure, "but what will we do with the children?" "Well, we talked about leaving Anna with your mother, and maybe Ard and Cobalt can watch Richard on Perfo." "That will not work," said Azure. "They are both on the Dragon Council. Have you forgotten?" Gek considered the problem. "Richard cannot get into the underwater cavern system on Acropo, and I do not want the Dragon Council to know about him."

"Why not?" asked Azure. "At the last Council meeting, the Dragons were so angry about the Great Dragon Changed One's attack on our Snow Dragon cousins, they were ready to kill all of the Changed Ones they could find. I am not sure how they would react to a human born to Dragon parents," said Gek. "Could we leave him here with Bruce? It would only be for a couple of days. Now that Richard is eating solid foods, he does not need Dragon milk," said Azure.

"That may be the least bad of our choices. The only other option is for me to stay here with him while you go to the council meeting," said Gek. "I guess we should ask Bruce," said Azure. "Ask me what?" asked Bruce as he entered the hut, dragging a large piece of driftwood. "If you would consider watching Richard for us for a few days while we attend the Dragon Council.

Anna would stay with her grandmother on the Coral Islands."

Bruce considered the proposal for a while, then said, "I guess it would be all right, as long as it's only for a couple of days." "Thank you," said Azure, "I'll leave in the morning to take Annalise to Acropo and be back in four days. Then Gek and I will need to leave in order to make it to the Council meeting on time." "OK," said Bruce.

The next morning, Azure told Anna that they were going back to Acropo, where her Grandmother was, so that she and Gek could travel to the Dragon Council meeting, and that it would only be for a few days. Anna was eager to see her grandmother again and tell her that she could talk, and was happy to get away from her human 'brother' for a few days (or forever). As evening fell, Azure changed into human form and said goodbye to Richard, then, after transforming back into a dragon, she and Anna headed down to the beach. Gek watched them go from the hut, with Azure carrying her daughter in her talons. *I hope Anna learns to fly soon,* he thought, *before she is too big to carry.*

Azure and Anna stopped for the day in the old coal mine in the mountains just east of Smithville. As they entered the mine, Azure said, "Your father and I have spent a few nights in here. This abandoned mine is a good place to hide during the day, and is about halfway to the islands. If we leave at nightfall, we should be home by morning. Anna yawned and said, "It smells funny in here." "I know," said Azure, "but you will not notice it while you sleep. Good night."

Azure and Annalise slept fitfully. The mine was cold, and Anna kept wanting to go exploring. Knowing that there were vertical shafts and confusing side tunnels, Azure tried to keep her inquisitive daughter by her side, but it proved impossible. When Azure woke around noon, Annalise was nowhere in sight. Azure growled and headed down the mine shaft, looking for Anna. It took nearly an hour of searching and backtracking to find the side tunnel that Anna had headed down. As Azure walked down the mine shaft, her heart stopped as she heard human voices coming from the tunnel up ahead.

"I told you, the entrance is back this way," said the first voice. "It is not! We came past that old ore cart on our way down to the clubhouse! We need to go *that way!*" said a second voice. "Wait, *what's that?*" asked the first voice. "It looks like a dragon," said the second voice, "only *smaller*, like it's a baby." Azure panicked. She had to protect Anna! Rushing forward, she spied two human children, about ten or eleven winters old. Thinking quickly, Azure said, *"INCOGITA, "* and made the required gesture. Both children fell immediately, sound asleep.

"Anna, get out here this instant!" shouted Azure. Anna walked slowly forward, her head bowed. "Do you know the danger you have just placed us both in? We have to get out of here. Now." "I am sorry, I was just bored and wanted to have a look around. I did not expect to find humans in the mine. Are they dead?" "No. Just asleep. Now, we need to get out of here and never come back," said Azure. "But why?" asked Anna.

"Because these humans will tell others that dragons live in this mine! The humans will come searching for us, and I cannot put them all to sleep!" "Why not?" asked Annalise. "Because the Sleep spell does not work on human magic-users! If either of those two boys had the spark of magic, my spell would not have worked. Hurry now, before their parents come searching for them!"

As the two dragons reached the entrance to the mine, Azure was relieved to see that the day was overcast, with low cloud cover. She grabbed Anna and leapt into the air, climbing as quickly as she could, hoping to get above the clouds before she was spotted. She failed.

The Treasury in Westport had all of the golds that it should have had, and the Regional Mage's Office was free of Changed Ones. After visiting the 10th Battalion and ensuring that their Sorcerer was human, the Royal Expeditionary Force boarded a merchant cargo ship, headed for Colton, with a stop in Weaton. The town of Weaton was still a mess, with many burned-out buildings and a shocked and somewhat paranoid population. The Treasury had fewer coins than expected, but that was understandable, as the town council spent freely in an attempt to rebuild the city quickly.

The Regional Mage, Alfred, was human, and doing his best to help rebuild the city. Sorcerer Justin, the Sorcerer from 15th Company, who had killed the Stone Dragon during the attack on the city, and died as a result, had yet to be replaced, so there was only one magician in Weaton. While they wished they could have stayed longer to help the city, the burden of supporting the Royal Expeditionary Force would have been too much for the city coffers, so Major Gerald ordered the Force to move on after only a day in Weaton.

The Expeditionary Force rode on to Prarrieville, eschewing river transport, and proceeding by the road. After weeks at sea, both the men and horses were glad to be back on solid ground for a while. The weather was turning colder as autumn faded into winter, and

Donovan found that campaigning in winter was much less enjoyable than the spring and summer months. The stiff wind out of the north moved across the open grassland and made everyone feel colder.

The soldiers were glad when they finally reached the garrison in Prarrieville, both for the shelter from the weather and the break from the monotony of the road. Prarrieville only had two Sorcerers in residence, Sorceress Megan, The Regional Sorcerer, and Sorcerer Bernard, the magical support for the 11th Battalion. Both Megan and Bernard were human, but the Prarrieville Treasury was almost empty.

"I just don't understand it!" said Luke, the city Treasurer, "the chests looked full, and my assistant, Miss Blaze, assured me that she counted every coin each month!" "The coins were Seemings," explained Rachel, "illusions, made to look like currency. Where is Miss Blaze?" "Well, it's a little past her time, but she should be here any minute," said Luke.

"Perhaps we should go and check on her," suggested Donovan. "Where does she live?" "I have no idea," confessed the Treasurer, "it never occurred to me to ask." "How long has she been employed here?" asked Rachel. "Almost twenty years!" said Luke. "And she always did the inventories?" asked Donovan. "Of course! She was the Assistant Treasurer when I was hired several years ago. I never suspected her of any wrongdoing."

Donovan motioned for Rachel and Major Gerald to join him in the hallway, then he cast a Silence spell over them. "When my father and I lived in Prarrieville, he was investigating the theft of weapons from the Garrison armory. Now we discover that the Treasury has been looted. I suspect that Miss Blaze is a Changed One. We need to find her and see if we can locate the missing coins." Releasing the Silence spell, Major Gerald told Luke to determine *exactly* how much was supposed to be in the Prarrieville Treasury, and to find someone who knew where the Assistant Treasurer lived.

To everyone's relief, Miss Blaze arrived a glass later, claiming to have been visiting a sick relative. Rachel brewed her a comforting cup of tea, laced with a healthy dose of Truth Serum. "So, Miss Blaze, do you live near the garrison?" Rachel asked. "Oh, no, I live on the edge of town, near the Blacksmith shop. It is a bit of a walk each day, but the house was less expensive because of its location. Most people do not want to live near a smithy, it is noisy and the smell of hot iron and burning coal is offensive to some people," said Miss Blaze.

"I imagine it smells wonderful to a dragon," said Rachel casually. "Yes. It smells like home…" said Miss Blaze before she realized her mistake. Donovan seized her in a Tether spell, pinning her arms to her side, the teacup falling to the floor. "So, what did you do with the coin you stole from the Treasury over the years?" asked Rachel. "Some of it I sent to Wizard Victor, and some is hidden under the floorboards in my bedroom," said Miss Blaze, compelled by the Truth Serum.

"Who was responsible for the theft of the weapons from the Prarrieville armory?" asked Donovan. "The previous Company commander, Lieutenant Gravel, sold the weapons to a traveling peddler who visited about once a month. Unfortunately, the Lieutenant suffered a heart attack some years ago, and that lucrative enterprise dried up," Miss Blaze confessed.

Donovan's face hardened as he asked, "Who killed Mage Edward's wife?" Miss Blaze struggled against the Truth Serum, but eventually said, "I did." Donovan stepped back, shocked at the news, he struggled to regain his composure, then asked, "How many more Changed Ones are there in Prarrieville?" "There are three more Fire Dragon Changed Ones in the city," Miss Blaze said softly. "Who are they?" asked Rachel. Miss Blaze was silent for a long time, but Rachel persisted, "I asked you, who are they?" "The Blacksmith and his two assistants."

"I think we've heard enough," said Donovan. *"THERMO REDUCTUS,"* he said, placing his right hand on his chest, fingers closed. Miss Blaze screamed as she froze to death.

Sorcerer Christopher trudged up the rocky slope towards the old abandoned mine, hurrying after Mrs. Hammond, who had come to him earlier in the day, begging him to help her locate her two sons, who had apparently gone off to explore the old mine. With no other more pressing matters, the Sorcerer reluctantly agreed to help. The old mine was *creepy*. It had been abandoned almost two decades ago after the coal seam played out. The entrance had been boarded up to keep curious people out, but vagrants and children continuously removed the boards to gain entrance, and the town had eventually given up replacing them.

Christopher hoped that the children had not gone in there. As he remembered, it was dark, dusty and dangerous. There were open vertical air shafts that someone could fall into, and it was easy to get lost in the maze of twisting side tunnels. He *thought* there were six levels to the mine, each one deeper and more dangerous than the preceding level. He hoped the children had stayed on the upper level, *if they were in there at all,* he thought.

They were within a hundred yards of the mine adit, when Christopher spotted movement. He started to call out to the boys, then stopped. He grabbed Mrs. Hammond and pulled her down next to the tall bush beside him. As they watched in stunned silence, a large blue dragon, carrying what looked like a baby dragon emerged from the mine and took off into the air. Sorcerer Christopher immediately cast a Sight Enhancement, to make sure he was not hallucinating, but it was true. It was another dragon, this one very similar to the one who had recently ravaged the town before fleeing east.

Once the dragons vanished into the low altitude clouds, Mrs. Hammond rushed up the slope, screaming for her children, "Josh! Jeremy! Where are you?" Christopher raced to catch up with her, then quickly cast a Silence spell around her. He grabbed her by the shoulders and turned her to face him. "SHUT UP, WOMAN! There may be more dragons in the mine!" said Christopher. "But my babies!" screamed Mrs. Hammond. "I know," said the Sorcerer, "but we will not do them any good by rushing in when we don't know what might be waiting for us inside. Listen to me! I need you to go back to town and get Sorceress Karen, from the 15th Company. Ask her to bring Lieutenant Harris and the rest of the company up here. Tell them what we saw, and ask them to bring their crossbows."

It was quickly apparent that Mrs. Hammond was *not* going to listen to reason, so Christopher had to cast a Compulsion spell on her to get her to obey him. As she raced back down the hill, the Sorcerer considered what to do next. It was very possible that both children had been killed by the dragons, and that all they would find inside were their bodies, and maybe more dragons. He was *not* going in there alone.

Less than a glass later, Lieutenant Harris, Sorceress Karen, a squad of eight men with crossbows, and an aging civilian came trudging up the hill to the mine. None of them looked happy. "So, Sorcerer Christopher, what's this I hear about a dragon?" asked the Lieutenant. Christopher explained the situation and asked what happened to Mrs. Hammond. "I spelled her to sleep," said Sorceress Karen. "She was hysterical and would not have been an asset on this mission," Christopher grunted his agreement with Karen's assessment.

"So, how do you want to proceed, sir" asked Karen. "Mr. Black, here," said the Lieutenant, pointing at the civilian, "is familiar with the mine. That's why we brought him along. Mr. Black?" The old miner mumbled under his breath about being pressed into service hunting dragons, but eventually said, "The mine has two main shafts, this one here," he said, pointing, "and another one about half a mile to the east. If'n the kids went in, they most likely used this adit." "Adit?" asked Karen. "It's the word for an entrance to a mine," said Mr. Black. "If one of you magicians comes with me, I'll lead the way."

"Do we take torches?" asked Christopher. "Only if you want to see anything beyond about a hundred yards in," replied the ancient miner. "Otherwise, it'll be pitch black in there and we won't find nothin.'" The commander unpacked a bundle of torches he had brought along and Sorceress Karen lit them with the Fire spell. Christopher erected a shield in front of himself and the old miner. "Let's go," he said.

The party crept into the mine cautiously, jumping at every shadow (which were many) and sound. When they came to a fork in the tunnel the miner stopped. "They could have gone either way here. Do we want to split up?" "No," said Lieutenant Harris. "We stay together, no matter what." Sorcerer Christopher examined the ground, then said, "Go right." The group took the right-hand shaft and kept going. "Why did you choose this tunnel?" whispered the miner. "Because the dragon tracks came out this way," whispered the Sorcerer. "Terrific," replied the miner.

Another two hundred yards, and they spotted the bodies of the two children lying on the floor. Christopher rushed forward and examined them. "They're alive, just sleeping. I wonder what happened. This is an odd place for a nap." He sprinkled some water on the children and shook them awake. "Where are we?" asked Josh, the older boy. "You're in the old mine, Josh. What are you doing here?" asked Christopher. "Me 'n Jeremy was going to start a club. I found an open cavern down that way," he said, pointing. "We was on our way out when we seen what looked like a baby dragon, only it was gold and blue. We was talkin' about it when I heard someone say "INCOGITA," next thing I knew, you was splashin' water on us."

"Pick up the boys. We need to get out of here immediately," said Christopher. Two of the soldiers slung their crossbows and picked up the boys, and the adults jogged quickly out of the mine. Once clear of the shaft, Sorcerer Christopher knelt before the two boys, placed his right index finger in front of his lips, and said, *"CONFIDO,"* "Take the boys to their mother. Say nothing about this to anyone. Karen, Lieutenant Harris, a word."

The old miner and the squad of soldiers headed back down the hill towards the town. Sorcerer Christopher looked at Karen and the Lieutenant and said, "We have a problem." "I know," said the Lieutenant. "Dragons are using the abandoned mine as a home." "It's worse than that," said Christopher, "the dragons can do magic."

Rachel recoiled in shock at what Donovan had done. "Why did you do that?" she asked. "You heard her. She admitted to killing my mother," replied Donovan. "Yes, but why did you freeze her to death instead of using the Death spell?" "Because that's how she killed my mother," said Donovan, coldly. "Sorcerer Donovan, I need a word," said Major Gerald. The Major led Donovan out into the hallway, then said, "I understand why you killed Miss. Blaze, but you were hasty. She might have told us much more before you summarily killed her," said the Major.

"She already told us about the Blacksmiths!" said Donovan. "Yes, but she might have known about other Changed Ones in other towns and cities. Your rash action may have deprived us of valuable information. You acted in anger, and without authorization. I am fining you one week's pay for your actions. Do not let it happen again." Major Gerald re-entered the room to find that Rachel had already removed the dragon Changed One's body. "You need to have a talk with your husband. His actions today were unacceptable," said the Major sternly.

Just then, Luke came running down the hallway and said, "There are two hundred and forty golds and fifty silvers missing from the inventory!" Major Gerald nodded and said, "Well, we know where some of the stolen money is. We'll go retrieve it and let you know what your actual losses are. In the future, I recommend that *two* people inventory the Treasury each month."

Major Gerald, Donovan, Rachel and the two Senior Specialists left the Treasury building and headed towards the west end of Prarrieville to confront the Blacksmiths. "How do you want to handle this?" asked Rachel. Major Gerald considered the problem. Finally, he said, "Since we know that all three of them are Changed Ones, I want Dirk and Lance to enter first and use their blow guns to put at least one of them to sleep. You and Donovan will each Tether one, and we will question them carefully. Understood?" Donovan nodded, but did not speak, still fuming at his rebuke from the Major.

They reined up a block from the smithy and dismounted, approaching on foot. The two Specialists went in first, followed a few seconds later by Donovan and Rachel. But the smithy was empty, the fires, cold, and the adjoining house was vacant. "It looks like they fled," said Specialist Lance. "These forges have not been lit today," said Donovan. "They must have been tipped off somehow and left Miss Blaze to take the fall." "Possibly," said Major Gerald. "It took us a week to get here from Weaton. I suppose a Messenger Hawk or some other messenger may have beaten us here and warned the Changed Ones. This bodes ill for the rest of our mission. In the future, we'll need to secure the message centers." "If they're Changed Ones, they don't need Messenger Hawks," said Donovan quietly. "They can just transform into dragons and fly to the next town."

"How do we stop them?" asked the Major. Rachel and Donovan considered the problem for a few minutes. Donovan snapped his fingers, "I think Rachel and I need to fly to Colton and inspect the magicians there before the Royal Expeditionary Force arrives. If we can get a head of the information flow, we can stop the advanced warning." "That's assuming that the three Fire Dragons flew to Colton, and not to Fairview, Riverton, or back across the Amber River," said Dirk.

"We'll discuss this later," said Major Gerald, "right now we need to go see if we can find some missing gold." They walked to the house next to the Blacksmith shop, noting that it seemed rather *elaborate* for someone on an Assistant Treasurer's salary. They proceeded to the master bedroom and began examining the floorboards. Lance and Dirk immediately discovered the hidden panel and were about to open it when Rachel said, "HOLD UP!" The two Specialists looked at her questioningly. "I think there's something in there. A boobytrap," she said. "Stand back." The two Specialists retreated a few steps, then Rachel vanished the floor board with a Remove spell. A sand viper lunged from the exposed cavity in the floor. *"TERMINA,"* murmured Donovan quietly, while making a slashing motion with his right hand. The viper died instantly.

The two Specialists gulped and stammered their thanks to the magicians. "I hate snakes," said Dirk. "There's only two golds in here," said Major Gerald. "Is that all there is?" "Hopefully not," replied Rachel. "We asked Miss Blaze where the gold was that she stole. She couldn't lie, but this may only be part of it. We need to search the house. The rest of the gold may still be here." "Less what she sent to Wizard Victor," said Donovan. They began a thorough search of the house, and found the gold, not secreted in any one place, but scattered around, in dresser drawers, behind picture frames, under carpets, even in the smokehouse. When they were finished, they had recovered almost two hundred gold coins.

"I think that's about all we're gonna' find," said Major Gerald. "Let's get this back to the Treasury and inform Luke that he only needs to report about forty-five golds missing to the King. It could have been worse."

Back at the garrison that evening, Donovan sat alone outside, thinking about the day's events. Specialist Lance walked up (uncloaked) and sat down next to him. "Silver for your thoughts," he said. "I'm not sure they're worth that much today," replied Donovan sadly. "Still thinking about the Changed One that killed your mother?" asked Lance. "I guess," said Donovan. "I was just so angry. I thought I showed great restraint by letting it answer two more questions, when I wanted to kill it the second it confessed to killing my mother."

"I understand," said Lance, "I felt the same way when that merchant cheated my father all those years ago. He didn't kill him, but my family was faced with financial ruin by an unscrupulous villain." Donovan considered the Specialist's words. I'm surprised you didn't kill him." "Oh, I thought about it, but his death would not have helped my family." "I suppose not," said Donovan. "Anger is not a bad thing," counseled Lance, "it can help overcome fear, or cause you to act decisively, but you have to learn to control your anger, or it can cause you to hurt those around you." Lance patted Donovan on the shoulder and walked off towards the mess hall.

Rachel came out of their room and sat beside him. She put her arm around his shoulders. "Do you think I was wrong to kill that Changed One?" Donovan asked. "Not wrong, my love, *hasty*, perhaps. That Changed One was unlikely to submit to a Binding spell; but Major Gerald was not wrong in saying that she might have told us more. After all, she had been working against us for over twenty years." "I didn't consider that. I guess I owe Major Gerald an apology," said Donovan. "By the way, he fined me one week's pay," Rachel laughed, "As if money has ever been a problem for you. I think we can survive without the five silvers. Just don't make a habit of it." Rachel gave him a peck on the cheek and went back inside.

Donovan rose and walked over to the office that Major Gerald was using. He knocked timidly. "Come in!" called Major Gerald from behind his desk. Donovan entered and said, "I just came by to apologize for my actions today, sir. It won't happen again." "Sit down, Donovan. Do you know why your father is such a valuable asset to the military?" Donovan was somewhat taken aback by the question. He thought for a moment, then said, "Because he's a powerful magician?"

Major Gerald shook his head, "No. Because he *anticipates* problems. Think about our trip to Farmdale. Edward anticipated the attack on the Force outside

Fairview and the attempt to delay us in the city. He constructed a target that looked like a dragon and had the bowmen practice firing at it. He immediately understood the utility of the crossbow, even when some of us thought it was useless. On our way to Springfield, he saw the Fire Dragon that was following us, *because he was looking for it.* Without him, we would have marched into an ambush that would likely have wiped out the entire Expeditionary Force. Wizard Edward plans ahead and considers the consequences of his actions carefully before acting. You did not do that today, and we could have used whatever additional information that Changed One knew."

Donovan lowered his head. "I know. I acted in anger at hearing that she killed my mother. I did not consider what else she might have known," "You know that you are the youngest Franconian Sorcerer ever, right? Wizard Noland cautioned me that you might act impulsively at times, but that your instincts were usually right. So, putting today's events behind us, what do you think we should do next?" asked the Major.

Donovan sat in thought for a moment, then rose and walked over to the map of Franconia that Major Gerald had put up on the wall. Major Gerald rose and walked over next to him. "The largest Treasuries in the Kingdom are in Kingston, Southport, Fairview, Three Forks and Grotton," said Donovan. "Agreed," said

Major Gerald, "So?" "So that's where the most damage can be done," said Donovan. "The Treasuries of Colton, Riverton, Farmdale and Hayford combined won't match the amount of gold in the Fairview Treasury!"

"Are you suggesting that we should divert to Fairview from here?" "I don't know, sir. Something in my gut says that everything is not as it should be in Colton, but even if a Changed One emptied the Colton Treasury, how much could be lost? Two hundred golds? Three?" Major Gerald nodded, following Donovan's logic. "But what about distributing the Concealment cloaks and looking for Changed Ones? We still have to do that."

Donovan thought and reached a difficult conclusion. "Sir, I think you need to split the Force. Send one Company to Colton and the other to Fairview. We can meet up again in Riverton, then continue on to Farmdale together." "Which Company goes where?" asked Major Gerald. "I would send 2nd Company to Colton, but I can't tell you why," said Donovan. "Perhaps because you want to follow your instincts. Very well. We'll leave at dawn."

"Where will you be, sir?" "I'm going with 1st Company to Fairview. If we expect to inspect the Fairview Treasury, it may take someone of a higher rank than a Captain to get them to open the vault."

Chapter Twenty-Two:
WAR AND PEACE

Azure landed on Acropo. She was tired. The rapid daytime flight from Smithville without a good day's sleep had taxed her. Carrying Anna had been no picnic either. As they stood on the overlook above the entrance to the Sea Dragon colony, Azure wondered if Anna jumping off the cliff was such a good idea. "What are we waiting for, mommy?" Anna asked. Azure said, "Normally, I jump off from here and my momentum carries me down almost to the mouth of our cavern. I am not sure it is wise for you to jump from so high above the water."

"I have done it before," said Annalise. "When?" asked Azure. "That time you and daddy left me here," Anna replied. Grandma pushed me the first time." Azure was somewhat shocked by this news, but Aqua always was a stern parent. "OK, then, JUMP!" Both Azure and Annalise jumped from the cliff and landed in the water with a splash. They both swam down to the underwater entrance to the Sea Dragon's system of caverns and emerged in the grotto. They climbed out of the water and padded down to the chamber currently occupied by Aqua, Azure's mother.

The old, blue-green dragon was asleep. "Grandma! Grandma!" shrieked Anna. Aqua opened one eye and said, "Hello, Annalise. What brings you by today?" "I came to show you that I learned how to talk!" said Anna proudly. Aqua snorted, "You are six months old! I should hope you could talk! Have you started hunting for your own prey yet?"

Anna was disappointed that her grandmother was not more impressed with her ability to speak. "No. I can catch and eat fish, but mommy is always with me. She says that there are fish in the sea that are big enough to eat me." Aqua rose and said, "I suppose that is true, but if you are careful and stay in the shallows, you should be fine." Azure yawned, "Is there someplace I can sleep for a while? I have been flying almost non-stop for two days, and I have to get back to Gek so we can leave for the Dragon Council."

"So, you just came by for the free dragon-sitting, eh?" asked Aqua. "That and to let you know that Annalise can talk, swim and eat solid food," said Azure. "I thought that was significant." "So, how long do you plan to leave her here?" "It is two days back to Grotton, then two days to the Dragon Council meeting, one day for the meeting, then four days to get back here. Call it nine or ten days." "*Fine,*" said Aqua. "Have you two given any thought as to when you might move back to the islands?"

Azure hesitated, then said, "Richard is crawling and eating soft food now. He should be walking soon. Once that happens, we can start making plans to move to Cobalt's cave on Perfo. How do you think the rest of the Clan will react to our raising a human child?" "Not well. There is a reason the other Sea Dragon Changed Ones moved to the mainland," said Aqua. "That does not leave us with many options," said Azure.

"This is a problem of your own making," said Aqua. "You two will have to find a solution. Enjoy the Dragon Council. We will see you in two weeks. Come, Anna, let us go for a swim while mommy rests." Anna and Aqua headed off to the grotto and the open sea.

The next evening, Azure said goodbye to Anna, promising to return soon. The parting was much less difficult than the previous time when Anna had held on to Azure's leg, crying. This time, Anna just said, "Please return soon." Azure flew through the night, letting the wind wipe her tears away.

Rather than returning to the mine outside of Smithville, Azure landed on the east side of the swamp. The weather was turning colder, and that made the swamp slightly less miserable. There were no fish in the swamp—at least none that Azure would consider eating, and the wading birds looked bony and meatless. Eventually, Azure found a family of turtles that served as a snack, but she decided that this was *not* a place to hide out for very long. A dragon could starve to death in here, unless she decided to try alligator again. So, she found a dry spot and fell asleep for the day. As night fell, she completed her journey to Bruce's hut near Southport.

As Azure entered the hut, Richard came toddling over, "MAMA, MAMA," he cried. Azure said, "Well, that did not take long." "No," said Bruce from his chair. "The little guy started walking the day after you left. He's spent the last two days wandering around looking for you." Gek heard Azure's voice and came out of the back room, rubbing sleep from his eyes. "Welcome back!" he said. "How was Acropo? Did you see Cobalt and Ard?" "No. Cobalt was away, spreading news of the Treaty to the Sea Dragons in the north, and Ard has apparently already left for the Dragon Council meeting. Sky says that he is ailing again. Aqua is watching Anna, but she does not seem happy about it. She wants to know when we are moving back to the islands."

"Hummph," said Gek, "That is a good question. I suppose once Richard can walk a little better, we could move into Cobalt's cave on Perfo, but I am not sure how the other Sea Dragons will react." "My thoughts exactly. What did Aqua think?" "She said that there was a reason the Sea Dragon Changed Ones moved to the mainland." "Well," said Gek, "that is not very helpful."

That evening, as they prepared to depart for the Dragon Council, Richard was *not* cooperating. He would not sleep. He would not stay in his crib, and Gek was having no luck in distracting him. Finally, Azure decided that they should use the Sleep spell to get Richard to settle down. In human form, she walked over and said, *"INCOGITA,"* while performing the gesture. Nothing happened. *"INCOGITA,"* she said again. Still nothing. "Well, I guess that means that he has the spark," said Gek happily.

"INCOGITA," *"INCOGITA,"* said Richard exuberantly, waving his hands from side to side. Bruce slumped in his chair, fast asleep. "OH NO!" said Azure. *"INCOGITA,"* *"INCOGITA,"* repeated Richard, like a child with a shiny new toy. "What are we going to do now?" asked Azure. Gek considered the situation, then said, "I guess you are going to the Dragon Council alone."

Andrew awoke when something hit the side of the ship. He was in his bunk, and his head hurt. *How did I get here?* He wondered. *I was in Frostberg.* He got out of bed and put on his boots. As he headed for the door, he remembered where he was and grabbed his parka. As he walked on deck, the First Mate called out, "BATTLE MAGE ON DECK!" Andrew waved the crew back to their duties, too weary and disoriented to give his standard "As you were" command. He walked over to the First Mate. "What's going on? What did we hit?"

"It's all these damned icebergs, sir. We can't seem to avoid them. They're everywhere! And these rough seas aren't helping." Andrew nodded his understanding and moved forward on the deck. He noted that the ship's sails were mostly reefed, with only a bare minimum of sail exposed to keep the ship moving slowly forward. As Andrew reached the forecastle, another sizable iceberg slammed into the hull, throwing him to the deck. He got up and walked carefully to the rail. In the tossing waves, he saw them, large blocks of ice, bobbing in the sea unpredictably, slamming into the hull as the ship tried to navigate a steady course.

Andrew started Blasting every ice floe in sight, but there were just too many, and most of their mass was underwater, so the Blast spell was generally ineffective. He tried using the Remove spell, which was a bit more effective, but took twice as much power. He was getting lightheaded. Then suddenly, they were out of the ice field. The waters were calm and ice-free. It happened so suddenly that Andrew could scarcely believe it. One minute, they were surrounded by perilous icebergs; the next, they were in flat seas with no ice in sight. The

Commodore came forward and clapped Andrew on the back. "Well done! I never thought we'd get through that patch!"

"Where are the other ships?" asked Andrew. "Right in our wake, of course," said Commodore Matthews. "That's the only way to get through the ice pack, single-file." "You sound like you've been here before," said Andrew. "Aye," replied the Commodore, "I spent several years as a First Mate on the HMS IMPECCABLE, which patrolled these seas. That's why I asked for a command in the 2nd Fleet, so I'd never have to face this cold again."

"Captain! We're taking on some water!" called the Bos'n. "I'm on it," said Andrew. He hurried below and found several small cracks in the hull where water was seeping through. A few Enlargement and Adhesive spells, and the water stopped coming in. The pump crews cheered his efforts. "Sorry, I can't just vanish the water with a Remove spell, men, but the last magician that tried that ended up removing the keel of his vessel," said Andrew. The bilge pump crew laughed as they continued moving the pump levers back-and-forth, back-and-forth.

"No worries, sir, we'll have her pumped out in no time, now that there's no more water comin' in." Andrew went back on deck. The sun was shining brightly, and the temperature rose noticeably. He walked over to the Commodore and asked, "Did I miss anything important?" The Commodore laughed, "No. I guess you just overdid it. The local Sorcerer told us that you'd be fine, just might be out for a couple of days. We couldn't wait, so we cast off and hoped for the best. That's the first time I've seen you weaken."

"I should have drunk some water after I changed back into a human," confessed Andrew. "But I was in such a hurry to get into town, I forgot. As soon as I was dressed, I just rushed into Frostberg to help. I didn't realize how taxing being a Stone Dragon was." "How so?" asked the Commodore. "Well, for one thing, as soon as you transform, you're hungry. Then, to fly, you have to flap your wings every damn second, and Stone Dragons are much heavier than Sea or Great Dragons, so flying is harder. Trying to catch up with those Snow Dragons was no easy task either. They're much smaller and faster."

"Well, just don't ever do that again. That's an order," said the Commodore. "Aye, aye, sir," replied Andrew. "So, what's our patrol route?" asked Andrew. "We sail around this area for about a week, then head back through the ice pack, and back to Frostberg. Then back to Sundock, maybe signing a Peace Treaty with the Sea Dragons along the way.

Just then, an enormous beast broke out of the water off the port bow. It towered over the HMS VALOR, before splashing down and submerging. "What kind of sea monster was that?" asked Andrew. "That was a whale, son. And he's just playing. No need to worry about him."

Donovan kissed Rachel goodbye. "I'll see you in a couple of weeks," he said. "Watch your back." "You do the same," said Rachel. "I'd advise checking out the local Blacksmith shops in Fairview. It might be the preferred place for Fire Dragon Changed Ones," said Donovan. Major Gerald came up and asked, "Any final thoughts, Sorcerer Donovan?" "Well, sir, I think it may be time to try riding Concealed. The weather is cooler, so the horses won't overheat, and it might prevent our movements from being noticed."

Major Gerald grinned, "Now that's thinking ahead. Good idea. But what about the wagons?" "A couple of wagons on the road isn't really cause for concern. A company of the Royal Expeditionary Force is," said Donovan.

Major Gerald moved off, giving orders to his company commanders to put on the horse Concealment blankets and get the men into their cloaks until further notice. Donovan took out his horse blanket and put it on Stam. "Easy, boy, I know this is different, but you'll get used to it. Besides, I'm riding in the wagon. The horse nickered as if it understood. Once the 2nd Company was mounted and ready, they headed out the gate and on the road to Colton.

Donovan looked back to wave 'goodbye' to Rachel, but 1st Company was already out the gate and moving at a quick trot. "She'll be fine," said Specialist Lance. "I know," said Donovan, "but it's still hard. I don't think we've been apart more than a week since we started dating." "Buck up," said Captain Fletcher, riding up. "Almost every man in the Royal Expeditionary Force has a wife or sweetheart somewhere, and *our* wives don't get to accompany us on missions." Donovan laughed, "I guess that's true."

"The commander said that you said you had a 'bad feeling' about Colton. Can you tell me why?" asked the Captain. "Not really, sir. And that bothers me. I know that Colton is along the border with Baize, but that shouldn't matter. Maybe it's because it's the city closest to where the Dragon Council meets." "Really?" asked Captain Fletcher. "Where does this Dragon Council meet?" "In an abandoned rock quarry about two miles north of Colton. I have no idea when, or how often they meet, but it sure might be nice to listen in on one of those meetings."

"Put that thought out of your mind," said Captain Fletcher sternly. "That is *not* our mission. We are going to inventory the Treasury, and check for Changed Ones in the 9th Battalion, and the Regional Mage's Office. Nothing more. Do you have any idea how big the Regional Mage's Office is?" "As I recall from the Academy, Colton has one Mage, Arnold, and a single Sorceress, Janice," said Donovan. "I don't know who the Sorcerer is with the 9th Battalion. There have been a lot of reassignments lately."

They rode quickly, stopping after dark each day, and, at Donovan's recommendation, lit no campfires at night. The soldiers grumbled, but then soldiers always grumble about something. As they reached the outskirts of Colton, Captain Fletcher pulled Donovan aside and asked for an opinion about how to approach the situation. "How about if Specialist Lance and I go into town under Concealment and check out the Sorcerer in the 9th Battalion first, then the Regional Mage's Office. If that's all clear, we bring the rest of the Company in to check the Treasury." "OK, but I want Healer Bone to go with you."

As they rode toward Colton, Donovan began to get a very bad feeling. Finally, he reined up and said,

"Something's wrong. Let's get off the road and I'll conjure a Seeing spell to find out what's ahead." They left the road and stopped in a strand of trees. Donovan dismounted and pulled his map and truncheon out of his saddlebags. After spreading the map on the ground and casting a Seeing spell, Donovan, Lance and the Healer were shocked to find the companies of the 9th Battalion were arrayed in an "L-shaped" ambush a few hundred yards ahead.

Donovan held the spell, searching for any magicians. He found a Mage with the Commander, and two sorcerers in the tree line along the road. Donovan released the spell before becoming weak. "Why would 9th Battalion be setting an ambush for the Royal Expeditionary Force?" asked Healer Bone. "I suspect the Mage has cast a Compulsion spell on the 9th Battalion Commander, and will blame him for any 'mistake' that occurs," said Donovan.

"So, what do we do?" "I'd say we should circle around on the open side and get behind the Mage and the Commander. I'll put a Silence spell around them, then Paralyze the Mage. You two try to talk some sense into the Commander." "Can you hold two spells at once?" asked Specialist Lance. "I thought it took a Mage to do that." Donovan grinned, "The only spell I will be *holding* is Silence, which takes minimal power. I will *cast* the Paralysis spell. Once cast, it takes *no* power." "You're the magician," said Lance. "What do I do?" "You have your blow gun ready for any rear sentry we come across," said Donovan. "I'm not making that mistake again."

They tethered their mounts out of sight of the road and put the feedbags on to keep them quiet, then crept around behind the 9th Battalion, who were anything but quiet: "How long are we going to stay out here?" "I'm cold!" "What's for dinner?" "Who're we expectin' anyway?" Donovan shook his head as they worked their way around. These men were not trained very well, which meant that they were probably not *led* very well either.

Suddenly, Lance put his arm in front of Donovan, bringing him to a halt. Up ahead in the tall grass was a rear sentry. He wasn't very well trained either. He kept moving around, fidgeting. Then he actually stood up to look around. Lance crept forward silently and shot him with a blow dart from *very* close range. The sentry fell, more quietly than he had been. Lance quickly bound and gagged him, just in case, and the three Expeditionary Force soldiers continued on.

Finding no more sentries, they moved in stealthily. The Mage and the 9th Battalion Commander were talking. "You're sure they're coming?" asked the Commander. "I'm sure," said Mage Arnold. "They should be here within the hour. You remember the orders?" The Captain nodded grimly, "No survivors." Donovan tapped Lance on the shoulder and murmured, *"SILENTIUM,"* while putting his left index finger to his lips. He followed up immediately with *"LIGARE,"* while making a fist with his left hand. Mage Arnold froze in mid-sentence. Specialist Lance and healer Bone opened their Concealment cloaks and asked, "Can we help you, Captain?"

The Captain turned and shouted to his men, but the Silence spell kept his command from being heard. Donovan walked forward and said, *"CODA NECESSITAS."* The Captain shook himself like a wet dog and said, "What's happening?" "You were placed under a Compulsion spell by Mage Arnold here, and ordered your Battalion to ambush the Royal Expeditionary Force, Captain," said Donovan. "What? That's Impossible! We would never attack Franconian troops!" said the Captain.

"Then what are you doing here, Captain?" asked Specialist Lance. The Captain looked around and saw his men in dug-in positions across the road. He could also detect the two companies in the tree line along the right side of the road. He looked very confused. "Who is your Battalion Sorcerer, Captain?" asked Donovan. "Why, Sorcerer Scott. He's new. Just assigned from the Wizards Academy," said the Captain. "I'm going to release the Silence spell," said Donovan. "Please send for Sorcerer Scott." Donovan released the Silence spell, and the Captain had his orderly go and fetch Sorcerer Scott.

As Scott approached, he said, "Donovan! It's good to see you! I see that you made Sorcerer in record time! What are you doing way out here?" "Hello, Scott. I've been assigned to the Royal Expeditionary Force. Can you tell me why the Battalion is set up in an ambush formation?" Scott looked confused and said, "Captain Bond told us that a large band of brigands was approaching from Prarrieville and that we were going to surprise them and wipe them out. He said the King would be most pleased."

"Is Janice the other Sorceress from the Regional Mage's Office?" asked Donovan. "Yes, she's right behind me. Janice, say 'Hello' to my friend, Sorcerer Donovan." Sorceress Janice came forward and extended her hand, then suddenly raised it and started to bring it down in a slashing motion. *"DELERE,"* said Donovan quickly, with a rapid backhand flip of his right hand. Sorceress Janice's right hand was removed cleanly, and her incantation of *"TERMINA"* was not conjured. Janice looked shocked and immediately clapped her hands together, saying, *"MORPHIOUS,"* but, again, without a right hand, nothing happened. "Lance, please put her to sleep," said Donovan. A quick puff of the blow gun and Sorceress Janice fell in a heap.

"Captain, please recall your troops to the barracks. Healer Bone, would you please ride back and tell the rest of the Company that it's safe to proceed, and Lance, would you please bring up our horses?" ordered Donovan. "Yes, sir," said Lance and Healer Bone respectfully. "Captain, we'll need a wagon to transport Mage Arnold and Sorceress Janice in. Don't mind the Mage, he's paralyzed and will be stiff as a board until I release him. The Sorceress should sleep for several hours. Both need to be held for questioning."

In short order, the 9th Battalion was back in garrison, and the Mage and Sorceress were in the city jail. Once Captain Fletcher and the rest of 1st Company arrived, Donovan explained what happened and told the Captain, "I need to remove both of Mage Arnold's hands so he cannot conjure any spells. Then I will remove the Paralysis spell so we can question him. I've already removed Sorceress Janice's right hand, I just need to remove the left also." "Is that really necessary?" asked Captain Fletcher. "With just her left hand, Sorceress Janice could heat your blood to boiling; conjure a gust of wind and push you off a cliff; put you to sleep; paralyze you, or compel you to do her bidding," said Donovan. The Captain gulped and told Donovan to proceed.

Once both hands were removed from both of the Changed Ones, Donovan brought them a pitcher of cold water, laced with Truth Serum. Janice drank eagerly, not anticipating the Serum. "So, Janice, what species of dragon are you?" asked Donovan. "I am a Snow Dragon," said Janice. "And what is Mage Arnold, here?" "He is a Fire Dragon, of course. What else could he be?" "Stone?, Great?, Sea?" asked Donovan. "Stone Dragons are too stupid, Sea Dragons are too passive, and I am not sure there are any Great Dragons left," said Janice smugly.

"JANICE, SHUT UP!" raged Mage Arnold. Donovan cast a Silence spell on Mage Arnold and continued the questioning: How many Changed Ones were there in Colton? *Seven.* Who were they? Did Janice know of any Changed Ones in other towns in Franconia? *Only Victor.* Had they stolen coins from the Colton treasury? *Of course, they had.* Janice was a wealth of information, and incredibly, the more she talked, the thirstier she got, and the more Truth Serum-laced water she drank. The interrogation lasted for hours, until, finally, there was nothing more to learn from Janice.

Donovan turned to the Mage and removed the Silence spell. "So, Fire Dragon, as you heard, I learned quite a lot from Janice here. More than enough, really. There is only one thing I want from you: The location of the Fire Dragon colony," said Donovan. "Never!" replied Arnold. "We'll see. Thirst can be a powerful motivator. I'll check back in with you in the morning."

As Donovan left the Jail, he was exhausted. Captain Fletcher, who had been listening in on the interrogation, asked, "What should we do with Janice?" Donovan shook his head sadly, "Even without hands, that Changed One could still betray us. Tomorrow, I will give her some water laced with Death Serum. It is really the most merciful thing we can do."

As expected, the Colton Treasury was almost empty. There were over five hundred golds missing, but with the information gleaned from Janice, all but fifty golds were recovered. Janice died peacefully after drinking water laced with Death Serum, and Arnold lasted four days and died without giving up the location of the Fire Dragon colony. The seven Changed Ones in Colton were hunted down. Three accepted Binding spells, three had to be killed, and one escaped. After Mage Arnold's passing, the 1st Company headed toward Riverton, after Donovan sent a Message Hawk to Wizard Noland, informing him that both magicians in the Colton Regional Mage's Office had been Changed Ones, and that the city needed new magicians assigned.

The project was moving along ahead of schedule. The apprentice magicians were really getting the hang of the Remove spell, and great swaths of soil were being removed every day. The weather had turned colder, as expected, but Mage Kathy had managed to procure enough winter clothing so that everyone was prepared for the cold weather. As the digging moved closer to the campsite, and the travel time decreased, Edward, Kathy, and Elianna began spending more and more time each evening teaching the students the Blast and shield spells, and testing the students to improve the strength of their individual shields. Several of the older students were almost ready for the Sorcerer's test, except for the Serums portion.

"So, Kathy, Elianna, how can we provide instruction on making Serums to the more advanced students?" asked Edward. "The students from Middleberg already know how to make Healing Serum," said Elianna. "That's good," said Edward, "But we need to teach them how to make Truth, Sleep, Stamina, Love and Death Serums before we can give them the Sorcerer's Test. At least that's how we do it in Franconia."

"It's the same here," said Kathy. "I suppose we could take some of them into Springfield for Serums classes," said Elianna. "I'm not sure," said Edward. "If we do that, then we take our best apprentices off the construction line. How many students are we talking about?" "I think there are about ten apprentices who are about ready. What if we took two of them into town each day? If they worked on Serums all day, once a week, they might be ready by the time we're finished with this project." "I like it," said Edward, "but it's a two-and-a-half glass trip to Springfield, each way."

"They could sleep in the wagon, each way," suggested Elianna. "We have plenty of wagon drivers; besides, the drivers can sleep while the students practice making Serums." "That will work," said Edward. "So, who's going to teach the Serums class?" "I think I have the most experience teaching classes," said Elianna. Edward looked at Kathy, who shrugged. "OK. That's settled. Mage Elianna will move back to Springfield tomorrow and set up a Serums classroom in one of the garrison offices. We'll need Serum supplies, and I suspect they won't be cheap. At least they're not in Franconia."

"I think you'll find that most of the ingredients for Serums are considerably cheaper here in Baize," said Elianna. "That's good to know, because we can't spend too much of King Donald's gold on Serum supplies.

We're supposed to be using it on the reservoir. Kathy, why don't you go into town with Elianna tomorrow and check with our vendors? If my calculations are correct, we're going to have to move our campsite again in the next two weeks."

"I'm still worried about the dragons," said Kathy. "So am I," said Edward. "I've seen them flying overhead towards the Grey Mountains several times. The Fire Dragon colony must be in there somewhere. I thought I saw two dragons flying east last night, but they were too big to be Fire Dragons, I think they were Stone." "Why would Stone Dragons be flying east? I thought they were restricted to this side of the Amber River."

"If I ever catch one, I will so inform him or her," said Edward with a smile. "*I* certainly didn't give them permission to cross the river." Kathy and Elianna laughed.

Azure landed in the rock quarry just as the full moon was rising. Ard was already there, and he did not look happy. "What is wrong?" asked Azure. "It is those damn Snow Dragons again! They claim that they attacked the human city of Frostberg and were set upon by a Stone

Dragon Changed One. The Stone Dragon Clan Chief insists that none of his clan live in Frostberg because it is too cold that far north. The Snow Dragons insist that a Changed One can live anywhere."

"ENOUGH!" shouted Cobalt. "This argument is getting us nowhere! It seems that, for the second time, the Snow Dragon Clan has attacked the humans and been confronted by a Changed One. We discussed this at our last meeting! Our only hope of avoiding this is to attempt combined-Clan attacks. That way, if a Changed One intervenes, we can deal with them accordingly."

"So, where can we strike?" asked Jasper, the Stone Dragon Clan Chief. "There are several possibilities," said Rose, the Fire Dragon. "The first is the human town of Colton. It is close enough to the Snow Fields for the Snow Dragons, and I know of eight Fire Dragon Changed Ones in the town who will support us." The Dragons murmured their agreement. "Alas! That is no longer true," said Fern, as she landed in the quarry. "I have just received a report from the lone surviving Fire Dragon Changed One in Colton. Somehow, the humans discovered all of our kin in the city and either killed or co-opted them. I would not choose to attack the town of Colton."

"How were they discovered?" asked Ard. "It seems that the King has a force sweeping the Kingdom, searching for Changed Ones. They have started in the west, and are moving east, slowly, but methodically." "Then we must strike in the east before they have a chance to discover our allies," said Jasper. "What about Three Forks?" asked Azure, speaking for the first time. "You are not a member of this Council," said Rose. "Why are you even here?" "My mate, the Great Dragon, Gek, is a member of this Council. I am here in his stead."

"And where is Gek?" "He is tending our child. He attended the last Council meeting, so I came this time," said Azure. The dragons began to argue amongst themselves as to whether a mate of a member of the Council had the right to attend or not. "ENOUGH!" shouted Ard. "I care not whether Azure is permitted here or not. The question is: Does her suggestion have merit? Who can tell us about this city of Three Forks?"

Bliz, the Snow Dragon Clan Chief, responded, "It is a major human city at the junction of the Ivory, Sapphire and Emerald Rivers. It is within the reach of the Snow Dragon Clan. There is also another abandoned rock quarry, much like this one, just north of the town." "The Sea Dragons can reach this town and attack it also," said Cobalt. "How is that possible? Did you not sign a ridiculous Peace Treaty with the humans?" sneered Jasper.

"The Treaty is not signed yet, but when it is, we will promise not to attack the Franconian ships or port facilities, and the city of Three Forks is neither." The Dragons murmured their approval of this cunning deception. "When will this Treaty be signed?" asked Fern. "Before the next full moon," said Cobalt. "Then we strike at the second full moon from tonight," said Jasper. "I will send two Stone Dragons for this attack." "I will send two also," said Rose. "The Sea Dragon Clan will send two as well," said Cobalt. "If the other Clans, in fact, send two, I will dedicate two Snow Dragons to this attack," said Bliz. The dragons looked to Ard. "The Great Dragon Clan will support this attack as well."

"What are the humans doing in the desert west of Springfield?" asked Jasper. "I noticed a large camp as I traveled here." "It appears as if they are digging a large hole in the ground," said Rose. "To what end?" asked Ard. "We have no idea. They have been working on it for several moons. It is an enormous hole, with walls around the sides," said Rose. "Have you attacked the camp?" asked Cobalt. "No. There are dozens of human magic-users there. It would be suicide," replied Fern.

"Perhaps we should just begin harassing them," suggested Azure. "How so?" "Well, as Gek suggested, as Dragons pass over the camp, they could drop stones on it, like rain. There would be minimal risk. Drop the stones at night, or while Concealed." "I like this idea," said Rose. Fern and I will drop rocks on our way back to the Fire Dragon Colony." "As will we," said Jasper.

"There is one more matter to discuss," said Ard. "At the last Council meeting, we considered the possibility that there may be other Dragons in the far west of Baize, but we did not select someone to go in search of them." "I have three perfect candidates for this mission," said Rose. "They are Fire Dragon Changed Ones who abandoned one of my Clan in the human town of Prarrieville. Sear, Fry, and Broil will make this journey. If they find no Dragons and perish in the attempt, it will serve them right!"

"Henry, you've got to finalize this Peace Treaty! The Sea Dragons expect to sign it this month," said Celeste. "I know, my darling, but the Minister of Commerce is insisting on some assurances about crabbing rights in the North Sea. It is a crucial industry for Frostberg!" said King Henry. "I'm sure," said an exasperated Celeste. "Yesterday it was the eel fishing grounds around Grotton, and the day before, something about reparations to the town of Smithville for damage caused by a Sea Dragon! As if Sea Dragons have money!"

"I quashed the reparations demand, beloved. I agree, that one was ridiculous, but we have an opportunity here. Admiral Cross thinks that we have dealt a decisive blow to the Sea Dragons. We need to take advantage of it." "I understand, I just don't want to squander this opportunity for peace over fishing rights."

The King took her hand and kissed it. "You're right. I'll make it known that all amendments must be finalized by this Endday. After that, it will be too late. Celeste softened, "That should be plenty of time, dear. Have you heard anything from the Royal Expeditionary Force yet?" "Only sporadic reports, it appears that the Southport Treasury was untouched, but that some few golds were missing from Prarrieville and Colton. Nothing of consequence, mind you. They have also uncovered fourteen of these infernal dragon Changed Ones! It was very wise of you to suggest having them search for them in addition to auditing the Treasuries. It seems that Sorcerer Donovan and his wife are able magicians," said Henry.

"I believe that Sorcerer Donovan completed the course of instruction at the Wizards Academy faster than anyone in history," said Celeste as she rose and came over to sit on Henry's lap. "What a remarkable family," murmured Henry, as he leaned in for a kiss.

Chapter Twenty-Three:
ROCKS AND DUST

The rocks came out of nowhere. Four large stones fell from a clear blue sky and slammed down in the middle of the campsite. One hit an empty tent, another a women's latrine, and the other two fell harmlessly on the ground. Fortunately, all of the students were at the dig site when it happened. The cooks, guards and wagon drivers screamed and searched for cover under the wagons. As quickly as the rocks began to fall, the deluge ended, leaving the men confused and worried.

When the magicians returned that evening, the cooks and servants told Wizard Edward what had happened. "And you didn't see anything?" Edward asked. "Nothing, Sir Wizard. There wasn't a cloud in the sky! If it were a dragon, we would've seen it." "Hmm, not if it was concealed. This is new. We'll have to start leaving a couple of magicians here during the day to watch for this. We'll also need to be more vigilant during the night. If that tent had been occupied, someone might've been killed," said Kathy.

"Why are the dragons attacking now?" asked Mage Elianna. "This wasn't an attack," said Edward. "If it had been an attack, there would have been several dragons, and they would have flamed the camp, not just dropped some rocks on it. I think this is just harassment, designed to hurt morale and cause a little damage, without any risk. We need to be on our guard and make them pay the next time they try it, or the harassment will continue," mused Edward.

"I think it's time we moved the campsite for the last time," Edward said, "and we leave a small contingent here to keep the campfires lit at night. That may confuse the dragons, or at least entice them to drop stones on the wrong target. We'll break camp in the morning and move north. We'll have to spend some time clearing the sand and salt away from the new campsite, but it shouldn't take as long as last time, because the sand won't be as deep. I'll go tell the cooks and drivers. You two tell the students and have them pack their things tonight. We leave after breakfast tomorrow."

Mage Elianna left to inform the apprentice magicians, while Edward and Kathy told the cooks and wagon drivers. They seemed to be relieved that they were leaving this place, where rocks rained down from the sky without warning. Edward didn't have the heart to tell them that it was likely to be a short reprieve, and that the dragons would undoubtedly find the new campsite in short order.

As the adults made preparations to depart in the morning, Edward paced around the camp. He was concerned. The danger was greatest at night, while the students were sleeping, and the guards were focused on threats from the ground. Kathy found him and asked, "Edward, what's wrong?" "I'm concerned about the safety of the camp at night. I think we need to douse the fires, at least for tonight. The problem is, it's getting colder, and the guards will be miserable. I may just cancel the watch tonight. We haven't had any threats while we've been out here," said Edward.

"What about the kitchens? We can't just shut them down," said Kathy. "I'll have them make up some cold sandwiches for breakfast tomorrow, and we can magically heat the water for tea and porridge, a glass before dawn," said Edward. "You really are worried, aren't you?" "Yes. This new tactic will spread terror, and I'm not sure the students are mentally prepared for it. Besides, I need them focused on finishing the reservoir, not worrying about falling rocks."

Edward and Kathy moved around the campsite, telling the guards that there would be no need to stand watch tonight, then extinguishing the campfires. The cooks were happy to be able to get a full night's sleep. They shut down the cooking fires and began putting their equipment in the wagons. Once all of the fires were out, the camp was dark. Except for the light of the moon, which made it possible to navigate around the camp without running into tents or wagons.

Edward climbed up on one of the wagons and scanned the sky for threats. With no cloud cover and a nearly full moon, Edward could see for miles, especially with a Sight Enhancement. He focused his attention to the west, where he assumed the Fire Dragon colony was. The night was quiet. Edward could hear the conversations of the students, the snoring of the adults, and the work of the cooks as they packed their equipment into the wagons for an early departure in the morning.

Kathy walked over to the wagon and asked, "Are you going to stand watch all night? We have a busy day tomorrow." "I know," said Edward. "I just have a bad feeling about this. I think one of us needs to stand watch tonight, just in case." "I'll let Elianna know. What are you thinking? Three glass shifts? Now until midnight, midnight until three, three until dawn?" "That sounds about right," said Edward. "I'll take the middle shift." "Oh no, you won't," said Kathy forcefully. "You always take the hardest shift, where you get the least sleep. You take the last shift. Elianna and I will toss a coin to see who gets the middle shift. Now get into the tent!" "Yes, ma'am," said Edward submissively.

When Kathy did not come to bed immediately, Edward surmised that Elianna had lost the coin toss and would be standing watch from midnight until three. Edward rolled over and fell into a fitful sleep. He roused briefly when Kathy came to bed just after midnight, but quickly fell back to sleep.

Screams erupted from the camp about a glass after midnight. Edward and Kathy rushed outside, just as a hundred-pound stone smashed into their tent. Edward blocked out the shrieks of the students and scanned the skies. He detected a slight distortion in the air and fired a Blast spell at it. The Blast spell was not as effective as it could have been because of the extreme range, but Edward saw a Fire Dragon cartwheel across the sky, right itself, and continue flying west.

"STUDENTS ERECT PERSONAL SHIELDS! ADULTS TAKE COVER BENEATH THE WAGONS!" Edward shouted. Stones continued to fall. Dozens of stones. Most were deflected by shields, but several wagons were hit, and four latrines were destroyed. As quickly as the attack began, it was over. Edward could just make out a dozen dragon shapes, flying west as they dropped their Concealment shields. "I'll be right back," Edward told Kathy as he quickly disrobed and transformed into a Great Dragon.

Edward launched himself into the air and took off after the fleeing Fire Dragons. He was not intending to do battle, just determine where they were going. As he flew on through the night, following the dragon pack, Edward cast a Concealment shield around himself and struggled with the energy drain. *Wherever they're going, I hope it's close,* he thought.

The Fire Dragons descended into a narrow valley between two steep mountains and entered a partially concealed cave. *Got you!* Thought Edward, as he banked away, heading back towards the campsite. Once he was well away from the Fire Dragon colony, he dropped his Concealment shield and increased his speed back to the camp. He landed outside the camp and rushed in. The sun was just cresting the horizon as he surveyed the damage. Several tents were damaged, and Kathy had organized a triage system for treating the injured. "Where's Elianna? She should be helping you!" said Edward. Kathy's eyes brimmed with tears, "She's in that tent, and she's in a bad way. The Healing Serum has kept her alive, but she still has severe injuries."

Edward rushed into the tent and found Elianna on a cot, feverish and delirious. "No, No. No!" she shouted, "Go away! Leave us alone!" Edward asked Stephen what her condition was. "She took a hit to the torso from a large stone. She had several broken ribs and internal injuries. She has been given Healing Serum, and it repaired her ribs, but she is fading," said Stephen as tears rolled down his face. "Where were you?" Stephen asked accusatively.

Edward brushed off the hurtful comment by Stephen and focused on the problem. He told Stephen to go into his tent and bring him a vial of Healing Serum from the chest under his bed. "I told you, she's already had Healing Serum!" Stephen shouted. "Not one of *my* Healing Serums," replied Edward angrily. "Now do as you're told, and hurry!" Stephen rushed out of the tent. Edward placed a cool cloth on Elianna's brow and whispered, "It's going to be all right. I won't let you die." Stephen hurried back in, bringing the entire chest of Serums. Edward opened the lid and scanned the contents, looking for one vial in particular. He pulled it out and uncorked it.

Raising Elianna up, he said, "Drink it all. I know it tastes bad." Elianna drank the Serum, and her breathing eased. Edward handed the empty vial back to Stephen and said, "It may not be enough. Stand back." Edward placed both hands over Elianna's chest and said, *"SALVARE. "* Elianna's back arched, then she fell back onto the cot. Edward fell to the floor of the tent, unconscious.

Andrew hated the ice pack. It was dangerous and unpredictable. Their week-long patrol of the northern ocean was over, and it was time to get back to Frostberg, then the Coral Islands for the Treaty signing. Andrew only hoped that the King's bureaucrats had not delayed the final draft of the Peace Treaty too long with their petty arguments and self-interests. Sailing south was actually a little easier for the small fleet of three ships, with a light tailwind to keep them moving.

"How much further, Commodore?" Andrew asked. "Oh, I'd say about five leagues yet." "Terrific," muttered Andrew as he Removed another small iceberg from the ship's path. The Commodore laughed, "Relax, Andrew. Our ships sail through here all of the time, and we almost never lose any!" "That's not very comforting, sir," said Andrew. The sea ahead was dotted with ice floes, and Andrew was growing tired of Blasting and Removing them. *What about a shield?* He wondered. Deciding that it was worth a try, Andrew cast a protective shield around the bow of the ship.

Bracing for the next impact, and unsure of what was going to happen, Andrew was pleasantly surprised when the shield shoved the floating ice aside with no impact to the ship. The HMS VALOR pushed through the ice field, like a knife through butter. After a few minutes, the Commodore came forward and asked, "What are you doing? I haven't felt a bump for the last half-glass." "I cast a protective shield around our bow, sir," said Andrew. "It seems to be pushing the ice out of the way before it has a chance to hit the ship. It may be making it harder on the trailing ships, though. We should tell their Sorcerers to do the same thing."

The Commodore had the Signalman transmit the message. It was a complex series of flags and motions, but eventually, the VICEROY and the VICTORY got the message and shields sprang up in front of their ships. The squadron carved a straight line through the ice pack, emerging unscathed. As the last of the ice floes receded behind them, Andrew released the shield and sat down, taking a drink from his water bottle.

"That was brilliant!" said the Commodore. "I can't believe that none of the other Navy Sorcerers ever tried that shield thing. This will make patrolling the Northern Ocean much easier and safer. Well done!" "Thank you, sir," said Andrew. "I figure the shield cost us maybe three knots in speed, but I suppose we could have put on more sail to compensate. That might not work, though; more speed would create more water resistance against the shield." "That's no matter. We made it through the ice pack in record time with no damage. The crews manning the bilge pumps are very happy."

The fleet docked in Frostberg that afternoon, and the happy crew headed into town with several hours of additional shore leave. While Andrew was glad to be back on solid ground, he'd much rather be with Maria in Sundock. "How long will we stay here, sir?" Andrew asked the Commodore. "Two days," replied Commodore Matthews. "We sail at noon on Midweek. Are you going to stay in the Ice House Inn again?" "Probably," replied Andrew, "but I'll most likely take a room on the ground floor this time. Somehow, it doesn't seem so cold here now."

When Andrew arrived at the Inn, the barmaid greeted him exuberantly, "You're the Mage that killed all those Snow Dragons, aren't you?" Andrew admitted that he was the one. "I heard that you were injured," said the proprietor. "Not injured, really, just fatigued. It happens when magicians expend too much power conjuring spells and forget to eat and drink to keep up their strength. I was fine after a couple of days."

"Well, I'm glad to know it. You have a room on the third floor and it's on the house! How long will you be in town?" Andrew said that the ship would be leaving in two days. The owner seemed both relieved, that she wouldn't be out too many nights' rent, and worried that the town's protection would be leaving so soon. Sensing her unease, Andrew said, "I doubt that there'll be any trouble with the Snow Dragons any time soon."

Azure landed back on Acropo nine days after she left. As she entered the underwater cavern, she hoped to find Annalise waiting for her, but neither she nor Aqua was anywhere to be found in the colony. Azure returned to the island and sunned herself on the warm, white sand for a while, enjoying the peace and quiet. Suddenly, Anna landed next to her with a 'thump.'

"Mommy, mommy! Did you see me? I can fly!" said Anna excitedly.

The Peace Treaty was finalized. All 37 pages of it. It was just before midnight on Endday when the final Royal seals and ribbons were attached, and King Henry XI signed the "Formal, Permanent, *Everlasting* Agreement of Non-Aggression between the Franconian Royal Navy and the Sea Dragons of the Coral Islands." Once the ink was dry and three certified copies were made (one for the Navy, one for the Dragons, and one for the Wizards Academy) the treaty was placed into an oversized message pouch and given to Sorceress Celeste for delivery to Naval Headquarters in Grotton, where the Admiral of the Fleets would affix his signature, before Celeste would take the Treaty to the HMS VALOR, which was patrolling the sea near the Coral Islands.

"Deliver the Treaty and return to me quickly, my love," said King Henry. "The Winter Ball is in a few short weeks, and I would not have you miss it." "I promise to return in time," said Celeste. She hurried to the courtyard, ducked behind a privacy screen erected for just such an occasion, where she disrobed and transformed into a Sea Dragon, destroying the privacy screen in the process. Celeste lifted off and headed southeast, following the road to Grotton.

She arrived in Grotton before dawn, landing in the newly renovated, roofless Navy Supply warehouse. After landing, she Changed back into human form and secured a jumpsuit from the closet in the corner of the warehouse, then took her Concealment cloak out of the message pouch and put it on. She slipped out of the warehouse and walked to the Naval Headquarters building in the cold morning light.

Upon her arrival, the night guard escorted her to a prepared sleeping chamber, promising to wake her once the Admiral arrived. Celeste took off her cloak and used it as a blanket as she settled on the plush, full-sized bed. She fell asleep quickly. At a little past nine, the receptionist knocked on the door discreetly, "Sorceress? The Admiral will see you whenever you're ready." Celeste rubbed the sleep out of her eyes and splashed some water on her face from the basin in the corner. Re-donning her cloak, she opened the door and headed to the Admiral's office.

She stopped outside the door and knocked (she was not the Queen—yet). The door opened immediately, and the Admiral escorted her to a chair. "Welcome back, Sorceress Celeste! Were the arrangements satisfactory?" "Perfectly satisfactory, Admiral, thank you. I have the Peace Treaty for your signature," said Celeste. "Wonderful!" said the Admiral. "I was beginning to worry. Let me just take a quick look before I sign it, and you can be on your way this evening. Oh my!" said Admiral Cross, looking at the sheaf of paper Celeste handed him. "All this?" "I'm afraid so, Admiral. Every minister and wealthy merchant wanted something added to what I thought was a fairly simple agreement."

The Admiral leafed through the pages, reading out loud to himself, "fishing rights, definition of what constitutes a 'port facility,' which personnel are considered 'sailors,' inclusion of merchant ships and fishing vessels, personal watercraft, provision for the rescue of castaways, definition of the word 'attack,' only pure-bred Sea Dragons included, arbitration procedures, procedures for termination, parties subject to the Binding spell, this is quite a contract!"

"Yes," said Celeste. "Henry's solicitors wanted there to be no misunderstandings or loopholes." "Sorceress, this is going to take me a while to read. Would you like to wait in the sleeping chamber while I digest all this?" "That's really not necessary, Admiral. Since the King has already signed the Treaty, this is a courtesy only. One of these copies is for you, and you may read it at your leisure, but the King was insistent that there be no alterations whatsoever. Just sign the Treaty, please, so I can be on my way. I have a long journey ahead of me."

It took a moment for the Admiral to grasp what Celeste was saying. His opinion no longer mattered. This was the Treaty the King wanted, and there was to be no further discussion. The Admiral angrily took his quill from the inkwell and signed his name on all three copies of the Treaty, then handed two copies back to Celeste.

"Thank you Admiral. I do understand the awkwardness of the situation. Trust that I will try to keep the best interests of the Royal Navy foremost in my mind in the future." Realizing that he was probably speaking to the future Queen of Franconia (news travels fast), the Admiral put on his best diplomatic smile and said, "Always a pleasure to see you, Sorceress Celeste." Celeste closed the message pouch and headed back to the sleeping chamber, "Admiral, could you please arrange for someone to awaken me at dusk?" "Of course," said the Admiral through clenched teeth.

The 1st Company of the Royal Expeditionary Force rode into Riverton and proceeded at once to the 7th Battalion's garrison. After ensuring that Sorcerer Gil was not a Changed One, Captain Fletcher and his squad leaders proceeded to the city Treasury while Donovan headed to the Riverton Regional Mage's Office. Riverton had one Mage, David, and one Sorceress, Teresa. Donovan was relieved to discover that they were both human. After issuing them their Concealment cloaks, Donovan went back to the garrison headquarters.

"Has there been any news from 2nd Company?" he asked Captain Fletcher. "No, but the Fairview Treasury's much larger than any we've looked at before. It's probably the second-largest in the Kingdom, after Kingston. They also have a full Regiment and a Regional Mage's Office that's one of the biggest. Don't worry, traveling by water, they'll be here soon.

The evening of the second day, the FS LORTON pulled in to the Riverton pier and the 2nd Company of the Royal Expeditionary Force disembarked. Donovan was waiting on the pier for them. "How'd it go?" he asked. "There was one Changed One in the Regiment, but the Regional Mage's Office was clean. The idiot Treasurer didn't want to let us audit his accounts, so that took some time, *and a Sleep spell*," said Rachel. "I don't know what all the fuss was about, because everything was perfectly in order." "Some accountants are just like that," said Donovan.

"So, how was Colton?" Donovan explained about the intended ambush, and how the entire Regional Mage's Office was manned by Changed Ones. He described his interrogation of Janice and how they recovered most of the pilfered gold. "You're telling me that you snuck up on a Mage, and then cast two spells simultaneously?" asked Rachel. Donovan sighed, "I didn't *hold* two spells at once; I held the Silence spell, then *cast* the Paralysis spell. It's not the same as holding two spells at once. I've told you this before." Rachel just shook her head.

"Anyway, Riverton is clear. No Changed Ones, and all of the gold that should be in the Treasury, *is* in the Treasury," said Donovan. "How far is it to Farmdale?" asked Rachel. "Probably about two weeks, if we don't get rain or snow," said Donovan. Rachel shuddered at the thought.

As they settled in for the evening, Specialist Lance knocked on Donovan and Rachel's door. "Yes, Lance what is it?" asked Donovan. "The Major would like a word with Sorcerer Donovan," said Lance. Donovan grumbled as he put his boots back on, then he walked across the compound to the office Major Gerald was using. He knocked on the door firmly. "Come on in, Donovan," said Major Gerald. Donovan entered and the Major motioned him to a chair. "Captain Fletcher has told me how you anticipated the ambush, then circled around behind them, took out the rear sentry, paralyzed the Mage, and convinced the Battalion Commander of the error of his ways," said Gerald smiling.

"Specialist Lance tranquilized the sentry, and the Commander was under a Compulsion spell by the Mage, all I did was remove it," said Donovan modestly. "Yes, but you *thought ahead*," said Gerald. "How did you know the Company was riding into an ambush?" "It was just a feeling, sir. Like I told you before, my gut told me that there was something wrong in Colton. My Seeing spell showed us the ambush." Gerald smiled, "You ever have a 'gut feeling' like that again, you be sure to tell me. I'm awarding you one week's pay for saving 1st Company. My men are good, but I don't think a single Company could best a Franconian Battalion waiting in ambush. Well done!" Donovan smiled.

"You have any gut feelings about Farmdale or Hayford?" "No, sir. Just bad memories. I *am* a little concerned about Three Forks though, but again, I can't tell you why." "Hmm, well, that city is still weeks away. Maybe you'll figure out something as we get closer." "When are we leaving, Sir?" Major Gerald grinned, "I think there's a storm moving in tonight. We'll stay here until it blows over. I'm not going to go out riding in a storm just to prove we can. Go get some…sleep."

Azure and Anna landed outside Bruce's hut just after sunset, and Anna rushed inside. "Daddy, Daddy! I can fly! Wanna watch?" Gek raised his head from the table and smiled, "Sure baby, just let me talk to mommy for a minute and I will be right out. Annalise bounded outside, headed towards the surf. "Stay in the shallows,

Anna!" yelled Azure. Gek came out of the hut, looking bedraggled. "You look terrible!" said Azure, "What happened?" "I have not had more than a few hours sleep since you left. Richard is driving me crazy!" said Gek. "What is he doing?" asked Azure.

"He keeps putting Bruce to sleep!" said Gek. "Bruce is so frustrated, he is talking about evicting us, because every time Richard sees him he yells *"INCOGITA,"* and Bruce falls asleep. Richard thinks it is a funny game, but Bruce is no longer amused. We have to find a way to put a stop to it, or find another place to live," said Gek. "Where is Richard now?" "In his new bed. He broke out of the crib the day after you left," said Gek.

"Daddy! Daddy! Watch" screamed Anna as she leapt into the air, flapping madly. "When did Annalise learn how to fly?" asked Gek. "My mother taught her while I was at the Dragon Council. Can you believe it?, she flew up above the water and just dropped her!" "Well, Ard told me that Great Dragon parents dropped their children above the forests to teach them how to fly. He said that those who failed to learn, died." "How did your mother teach you how to fly?" asked Azure. "She never did. She was killed before she got the chance. Ard taught me how to fly."

"How did he do that?" "He blew fire at my feet and screamed at me until I flapped hard enough to get off the ground and across the river in our path," said Gek, smiling at the memory. "How did Ard get across the river? I know he cannot swim."

"I waded across," said a gravelly voice. "The river was only a couple of feet deep at that spot." "Ard!" cried Gek. "It is good to see you!" "I am glad to see you too, Gek. I have been searching for you for three days now. I would not have found you except that I saw my great-granddaughter flying around as I walked down the beach."

"Annalise! Grandpa is here!" yelled Gek. Annalise came bounding down the beach, half-running, half-flying. "Grandpa! Did you see me fly?" asked Anna. "I did indeed, and you are very advanced for one so young. You will be a Great Dragon!" said Ard. "No, I am a Great Sea Dragon," said Anna. Ard smiled. "That is a good thing to be."

"Where is Richard?" asked Ard. "He is in the hut sleeping," said Gek. "I would like to see him before I go," said Ard in a gasping breath. "Go? But you just got here! Where would you go?" asked Gek, fearing the answer. "I am dying, Gek. Cobalt healed me, and my scales are shiny and my talons are strong, just as they were in my youth. But I am still 320 years old, and I think that must be the life span of a Great Dragon. While I can be healed again and again, extending my life, it is only a short-term solution. I am ancient *inside*, and no amount of healing can change that. I have no injuries, and no diseases. They have all been healed, and I feel no pain, but my age cannot be healed."

"Grandfather," wept Gek. "It is all right Gek. I have lived a good life and seen my offspring grow. I wanted to come and see my great-grandchildren one last time before the end." "Azure, go get Richard," said Gek. Azure raced inside the hut and returned with Richard. "Richard, this is your grandpa, Ard," said Gek. "Hello, Ard." "Hello, Rich*ard*," said the ancient Great Dragon.

"I need you to be a good boy and listen to your parents, OK?" asked Ard. Richard nodded, sensing some oncoming sadness. "Annalise," said Ard, "go play with your brother, and *be nice*," said Ard, "I need a final word with your parents." Astonishingly, Anna and Richard headed down to the surf together, as Ard walked into the tall sedge grass on the slope above Bruce's hut.

"Gek, Azure, I am at the end. I just came to see the children one last time, and give you a final piece of advice that was given to me by my father during the last war: ***If we can win the war, but only with unacceptable consequences, then we must consider an imperfect peace.*** This was true two hundred years ago, and it is still true today. Do not forget my words…" Ard closed his eyes and exhaled. He did not inhale again.

Chapter Twenty-Four:
REJECTED!

Edward woke slowly. He'd been here before. This was not the first time he'd expended too much power on a spell, so he recognized the effects: the pounding headache, the sore muscles, the disorientation, and the dry mouth. He sat up gently and looked around. He was in his tent, but the sounds he expected to hear were absent. He could hear the rustling of his tent flaps as they swayed in the breeze, so he knew his hearing was fine, but he did not detect the noise of apprentice magicians moving about the camp or the cooks scrubbing pots and pans.

He rose gently, and put on his clothes and boots. As he exited his tent, the blinding sun was a stark reminder of where he was: The Great Salt Flats. But, this was *not* the campsite he was familiar with, the tents were more spread out, there were fewer firepits, and the kitchens and latrines were not where they once were. Edward staggered out of the tent and immediately ran into Frank, his ever-present privacy-keeper. "Frank, where in Baize are we?" asked Edward.

Frank rose quickly and replied, "Sir Wizard! Mage Kathy said she didn't expect you to wake for another couple of days yet! We're in the new campsite, just north of the line that the surveyors laid out as the top of the reservoir." "Where is everyone?" asked Edward. "Why, they're all at the dig site, sir. Mage Kathy said to keep working," replied Frank. "How long have I been asleep?" "Three days, sir. Are you sure you should be up and about?"

Edward nodded and said, "Yes, Frank. Lying in bed will only delay my recovery. How is Mage Elianna?" "She's fine, sir. She's in Springfield, setting up some sort of Serums lab, I think. She should be back later today." "Last question, What day is it?" Frank smiled and said, "It's Midweek, sir, about ten in the morning." "How many people were injured during the dragon attack?" asked Edward. "Mage Elianna suffered the only serious injury, the other injuries were from broken tent poles, or splinters from the wagons being hit. There were no deaths." Relieved by the news, Edward nodded his thanks and walked over to the nearest kitchen.

"Wizard Edward! It's good to see you up and about!" said the head cook. "Thank you, Bill. Do you have anything that I can snack on? I need something to eat and some tea if you have any." "Right away, sir! Why don't you have a seat over there," said the cook, pointing to a nearby table. "I'll bring it right over." Edward nodded his thanks and walked over to the table. He sat down heavily, his legs a little shaky. The cook brought over some fried eggs and ham, with fried potatoes, bread with jam, and a pot of tea. Edward thanked him and began devouring the food, knowing that eating was the fastest way to regain his strength after expending too much power and passing out.

"I've got to stop doing that," he thought aloud. After finishing his food and returning the plates to the kitchen staff, he walked around, surveying the new campsite. The campsite was larger than before, with wagons, tents and kitchens more spread out. *Probably a good idea if dragons start dropping rocks on us again,* he thought. Edward moved around the camp, talking to the guards and wagon drivers. Apparently, they had moved here the morning after the attack, cleared the sand and salt and set up the campsite quickly, then got back to work. *That's good,* Edward thought, *keeping them busy will take their minds off the attack.*

Shortly after midday, Edward spotted a lone rider headed for the camp. Using a Sight Enhancement, he determined that it was Mage Elianna, returning from Springfield. Edward mounted his horse and rode out to meet her. "Edward! We didn't expect you up for a few days yet," said Elianna. "I have over-extended myself so often that I recover quickly," replied Edward. "How do you feel?" "Still a little sore on the right side, but I'm alive, thanks to you. Stephen told me all about how you healed me. Tell me though, how are *your* Healing Serums better than the ones we prepared in

Middleberg?" Edward smiled, "Not necessarily *better*, but more specific to the injury. The serums you prepared were sort of general Healing Serums. Mine are more tailored, some for burns, some for broken bones, others for internal injuries. I even have one for excessive bleeding. Plus, mine were made more recently. You realize that Serums begin losing their effectiveness as they age, right?"

Elianna shook her head, "No. I was taught that Serum lasted about six months if stored-" "In a cool, dark place," finished Edward. "I was taught that too. However, I've learned from experience that a three-month-old Serum is a little less effective than one prepared a week ago." "How do you 'tailor' your Healing Serums?" "Well, for broken bones, I add a half-measure more bone marrow, for burns, a half-measure more agave, internal injury Serums need a full measure more of Yarrow root, and I add an eighth measure of Arsenic to my Bleeding Serum."

"But Arsenic is poison!" exclaimed Elianna. "Yes, but in small doses, it constricts the blood vessels, and slows bleeding," said Edward. "How in the world did you learn all this?" Edward sighed, "Being a Battle Mage, I've seen more than my fair share of injuries, so when I had the time, I experimented." "On people?" asked Elianna. "No, mostly on horses that were injured, or, in rare cases, on injured soldiers that didn't respond to traditional Healing Serums."

"Well, I'm glad yours worked on me. Thank You," said Elianna. "You're welcome. How did you get hit by the stone anyway?" Elianna blushed, "I was in the latrine and never saw it coming. It was just bad luck I guess." "Hummph, I'm not so sure about that. The tent Kathy and I share was also hit with a large stone just after we left it. It's a strange coincidence that all of the senior magicians seemed to have been targeted during the attack," mused Edward.

"You think the dragons can sense where we are?" asked Elianna. "I'm not sure, I just find it curious that all of us were either hit, or nearly hit, by falling stones dropped by magical dragons."

"So, the next full moon is in a couple of days," said Gek. "Who from the Sea Dragons is going to the ship to sign the Peace Treaty?" "I guess Cobalt and I will have to go. Will you be all right with the children for a few days?" asked Azure. "I suppose," said Gek. "Now that Richard has stopped constantly putting Bruce to sleep. Even Richard and Anna seem to be getting along better."

"Just make sure that she does not try to take him for a swim," said Azure. Both children had taken Ard's death hard. They had both searched the shore and the surrounding area for him, thinking it was a game of hide-and-seek. Ard's body had surprisingly turned to dust almost immediately after his death. All that remained was a gold shimmer to the sand on his final resting place.

"I'll leave tonight, then," said Azure. "Hopefully the human King did not demand anything unreasonable." "As long as they think their ships are safe, and the treaty does not restrict us from attacking the humans at Three Forks, we should be fine. I am not sure I like the idea of you being under another Binding spell though," said Gek. Even with Ard's passing, Gek and Azure were unsure whether his Binding spell on them, not to eat humans, and to spare the magic-users Andrew and Donovan, was still in effect, or whether it ended with his death. Neither one was eager to test the Binding spell to find out.

Azure departed at sunset, stopping for the day in a clump of trees on the north side of the Black Mountains. She didn't dare go back to the mine near Smithville after her encounter with the two human children. She slept wonderfully, not having to deal with her children's restlessness. The next night, she completed the journey to Acropo and the Sea Dragon Clan.

She found Cobalt, pacing the largest cavern anxiously. "Azure! At last! I was beginning to think you were not going to make it in time. Where are Gek, Ard, and the children?" "Gek is on the mainland with the children. Ard passed away. He came to Southport to see the children one last time, then just stopped breathing. It was awful, yet peaceful at the same time."

"I knew he was ailing. I tried healing him several times. Each time he revived a little, but then grew worse again. The time between healings grew shorter and shorter. I guess that healing cannot cure old age," said Cobalt. "That is what he told us before the end. He said that he had no pain, but no strength either."

"Anyway, there are three Navy ships, I think one of them is the VALOR, sailing around the islands. I think they are waiting for us to arrive to sign the Peace Treaty. Are you prepared?" asked Cobalt. "I will need to borrow that white dress again, and you need some presentable human clothes if we are going to a Treaty signing ceremony," said Azure. "Already prepared," said Cobalt. "Then we should leave just after dawn," yawned Azure.

The next day was overcast, with a light rain, but Cobalt and Azure left the colony and proceeded to the HMS VALOR. Azure circled the ship, holding the white dress in her talons. Sorceress Celeste waved from the aft deck that it was safe for them to land. Cobalt landed first, and after Celeste conjured a Seeming of a curtain across the deck, Changed into human form and donned a fancy night-blue velvet outfit. Azure landed next, transformed and put on the white dress she had been carrying. Once transformed into human form and clothed, the two dragons came forward. "Hello, Anne, it is good to see you again," said Cobalt. Celeste giggled and said, "I'm sorry to tell you, but my twin sister Anne is not here. I'm Celeste. Hello Azure, it's good to see you again. Where is Gek?"

Azure ignored Celeste's question and said, "Hello Celeste, this is Cobalt, Chief of the Sea Dragon Clan and Gek's father." "Greetings, Cobalt. It is nice to make your acquaintance," said Celeste. Cobalt looked Celeste over carefully, trying to find some way to tell her apart from her sister Anne, but finding none. Finaly, he asked, "How do you know Gek?" "I saved his life once," said Celeste.

"AHEM," said Commodore Matthews, "If we're ready, we should proceed with the business at hand. It looks like rain, and unlike you, *I* am not waterproof." Surprisingly, Cobalt laughed. "I like this human. He does not dither. Very well. Let us see the Treaty your King has signed and get this agreement finalized."

Celeste opened the message pouch and brought out the two copies of the Peace Treaty. Cobalt looked at the multipage document and said, "You are joking." "Not at all," said Celeste hurriedly, "King Henry wanted every detail of the agreement documented, so there could be no misunderstandings later." Cobalt drew himself up to his full height and said, "No." "What do you mean 'No'?" asked Commodore Matthews. "I mean that our agreement was that we would not attack your ships or port facilities, and you would not attack us. You would cede control of the Coral Islands to us and we would allow up to five ships to shelter in the cove on Acropo during a storm. What is all this?" he asked, waving the lengthy document.

"Well, it defines other aspects of the Treaty," explained Celeste, "like fishing rights, and protection of merchant ships, and..." "ENOUGH!" said Cobalt angrily. "This was not our agreement! I will not sign it!" "But the King..." said Celeste. "Celeste," said Azure, "you are mistaken if you believe that Dragons can read human writing. Just because we can speak, does not mean that we can read. It is just not something taught to Dragons."

Celeste's countenance fell, "I could read it to you..." "No," replied Cobalt. "After the last betrayal by the humans, I would not trust the words of any human, reading such a lengthy document. Besides, after we leave here, if we forgot anything in the Treaty, we could die from the Binding spell, *over a few fish*." "Our agreement was simple, but you have enlarged and complicated it. We will not sign. I see now that you have just used this delay to construct more of those weapons," said Cobalt, pointing to the new Seabows.

"That was not our intent," said Celeste, desperately. "Perhaps not, but it is the *result*," said Cobalt. "We will not sign this trash. Moreover, the temporary truce between us will end at sundown today. I recommend you depart these waters immediately. Celeste, you have been named a Dragon-friend, and we will try not to injure you when we attack, but if you remain on this ship, I can make no promises."

Cobalt and Azure stomped back to the aft deck, and caring nothing for the human clothes they were wearing, transformed and dove off the ship, taking no chances of the humans firing on them as they flew away. The tattered remains of their clothes were as shredded as the Peace Treaty.

As the Royal Expeditionary Force rode into Farmdale, they were treated like heroes. The people lined the streets, waving flowers, and showering the soldiers with praise. Mayor Norville rushed out of his office to greet Major Gerald. "Captain Gerald! Welcome back! What brings you to Farmdale this time? "Actually, I've been promoted to Major, and it's good to see the town doing so well, Mayor. "Yes, most of the citizens returned after you so heroically disposed of that dragon. The town is thriving again, and most of the damaged farms have been repaired."

"That's good to hear. Is there someplace I can quarter the men for a day or two? We won't be here long," asked Gerald. "Of course! How about that barn you stayed in last time? I know it's not much, but it's out of the weather. It's mostly empty right now, since the crops have been sent to Hayford for transport to Kingston." "The barn will be more than adequate," said Major Gerald.

"Company commanders! Move your companies into the barn we stayed in the last time we were here. Tend to your mounts, while the magicians and I arrange for provisions." The companies headed down the street to the large barn at the north end of the town. As they groomed and fed their mounts, Major Gerald, Donovan and Rachel met with the Mayor.

"I know you're curious as to what brings us way out here," said Gerald. "The King dispatched the Royal Expeditionary Force on a tour of Franconia. We're visiting every city and town in the kingdom." "That seems like a long journey," said Mayor Norville. "Yes, it is, but we're also auditing all of the Treasuries in the towns and cities we visit, and inspecting the Regional Mage's Offices."

"Farmdale doesn't have a Mage, only a single Sorcerer, Sorcerer Winthrop," said the Mayor. "I know," said Donovan, "I just need to talk to him for a few minutes, and issue him some new gear that all of the magicians in Franconia are receiving." "Easily done," said Norville, "Billy, go fetch Sorcerer Winthrop. He's probably in his office." Billy, a lad of about thirteen raced out the door to find the town's magician. "Why are you auditing all of the Treasuries?" asked the Mayor.

"Well, Mayor, it's like this, we've discovered that these dragons can do magic and change themselves into people. Some of them have gotten jobs with the Treasuries in various towns and cities, and quietly stolen quite a bit of coin over the years. The King wants to put a stop to that, and determine just how much is missing. I'm sure you can understand," said Major Gerald. "Dragons masquerading as humans? You can't be serious!" exclaimed the Mayor.

"I'm afraid so," said Donovan. "You remember Wizard Victor?" Norville snorted, "You mean that idiot who claimed that dragons were mythical?" "Yes. It turns out that *he* was a dragon. That's why he didn't want anyone coming out here to investigate your report." Mayor Norville shook his head in amazement. "It's almost impossible to believe." Just then, Billy knocked on the office door, "Sir, Sorcerer Winthrop is here." "Do not say anything before we can examine Winthrop," whispered Rachel. The Mayor nodded his understanding, now a little worried.

"Come!" he said, his voice a little higher pitched than normal. Sorcerer Winthrop entered. "You asked to see me, Mayor?" Sorcerer Winthrop was tall, about six foot seven, with red hair. Donovan and Rachel's suspicions were immediately aroused. "Yes, Sorcerer Winthrop, this is Major Gerald, the commander of the Royal Expeditionary Force, Sorcerer Donovan, and Sorceress Rachel. They'll be staying in town for a couple of days, so I wanted you to meet them."

"I'm pleased to meet you," said Winthrop, extending his hand. Donovan smiled and relaxed. He shook the offered hand and told the Mayor, "It's OK, he's not a dragon." "What? Of course I'm not a dragon! If I was a dragon I'd have wings!" said Sorcerer Winthrop. "You also wouldn't use contractions," said Rachel, shaking his hand. "I don't understand," said Winthrop.

Donovan explained the situation with the dragons to the Farmdale Sorcerer. "Let me get this straight, you're saying that dragons can do magic, and have mastered the Change spell?" "Unfortunately," said Rachel. "I can't believe it!" said Winthrop. "Do you remember Wizard Stuart from the Wizards Academy?" asked Donovan. "Of course, he was the gatekeeper," said Sorcerer Winthrop. "He was also a dragon Changed One. He'd been at the Academy for *decades*, and we never suspected a thing."

"So, how do you unmask one of these 'Changed Ones'?" asked Winthrop. "First, dragons don't use contractions, and second, they smell different than humans." "They smell different? How so?" "They have a reptilian scent," said Rachel, "but they've learned to mask it with cologne or perfume." Sorcerer Winthrop sat quietly for a minute, then said, "So, what should I do?" "Well," said Donovan, dragons also have the spark, so while you're on the lookout for rogue magicians, use a Smell Enhancement spell, and listen to their speech carefully. Many of the Changed Ones we have encountered were willing to submit to a Binding spell, never to transform back into a dragon, and never to hurt a human. Those we Bind, we let go back to whatever job they were doing."

"And those that won't agree to a Binding spell?" asked Winthrop. "Kill them immediately," said

Donovan, "before they can escape or transform. I can tell you from experience, it's not easy to kill a dragon."

Before they left the Mayor's office, Donovan and Rachel told Winthrop and Norville about the different types of dragons and the best way to kill a Stone Dragon. Donovan escorted Winthrop out to his wagon, where he issued him his Concealment cloak. Winthrop got the standard warning about the replacement cost and to turn it inside out when he wasn't wearing it.

"If you walk us over to the Treasury, Mayor, we can be out of your hair tomorrow," said Major Gerald. Norville smiled and said, "No walking required, Major. The town Treasury, such as it is, is right down the hall." The Farmdale Treasury consisted of a mere 69 golds and a few silvers. "When everyone fled from the dragon, there was no one to pay the taxes. We lost almost a year's worth of crops because there was no one here to harvest them. We'll be better next year."

Major Gerald and the two magicians walked over to the barn and found that the grateful townsfolk were stuffing the Expeditionary Force soldiers with more food than they could possibly eat. "Don't get too comfortable, men," said Gerald. "We leave Farmdale tomorrow morning." Both the soldiers and the townsfolk groaned. "Well, I guess we can leave *after* breakfast tomorrow."

Celeste landed back at the Naval Supplies warehouse in Grotton. She needed to inform the Admiral that the Treaty had been rejected by the dragons, and that even the temporary truce was off. She felt dejected, and was very remorseful at how she had treated the Admiral on her last visit. She transformed and changed into the standard-issue jumpsuit, then put on her Concealment cloak and headed for the Naval Headquarters building. She arrived just after dawn, having timed her arrival better this time.

When she entered the building the receptionist was already at her desk, "Good morning, Sorceress Celeste. Did everything go well?" "No," said Celeste sadly. "In fact, things couldn't have gone worse. I need to see the Admiral when he has a minute." "Of course," said the receptionist, "he's in a meeting with his staff right now, would you like to wait?" "Actually, my news is probably something they should all hear."

They walked down the hallway until they came to the conference room. The receptionist knocked softly then stuck her head in, "Excuse me Admiral, but Sorceress Celeste has returned, and it seems she has some rather bad news." "Show her in at once," said

Admiral Cross. Celeste entered with her head down. "Sorceress, what's wrong?" asked Wizard Lake, the Chief of Naval Wizardry. "The Sea Dragons rejected the Treaty. They accused us of adding other items that they had not agreed to, and stalling for time while we built more Seabows. Cobalt, the Sea Dragon Clan Chief, said that our temporary truce is over, and that their war with us will resume immediately."

The Admiral sighed, "I was afraid this would happen. What, specifically, did they object to in the Treaty?" *"Everything,"* said Celeste. "They said that they had proposed a simple agreement: They would not attack us and we would not attack them. We cede the Coral Islands to them, and they will not attack our port facilities, and we were allowed to shelter up to five ships in the cove on the northern island. Apparently, dragons can't read, so the lengthy document prepared by the King's Ministers was incomprehensible to them."

"Dragons can't read," said the Admiral, "we should have thought of that." "I offered to read the Treaty to them, but they said that they would not trust *any* human to read such a lengthy document to them; and that they would not be able to remember all of the clauses and stipulations in the Treaty. They said that if they agreed to a Binding spell, to abide by the Treaty, they could be killed for eating some fish from the wrong part of the ocean."

"So, where does that leave us?" asked the Admiral. "Commodore Matthews is sailing for Sundock. Apparently, there is an arms merchant there who created a modification to the Seabows that allows them to be drawn by a single crewman. The Commodore paid thirty-five golds for enough modification kits to outfit all of the ships in 1st Fleet. I believe 2nd Squadron already has the new Compound Seabows. It seems that they are too complicated for a magician to replicate. Once 1st Squadron has the modifications, I believe they were going to contact 3rd Squadron to put into Sundock for the upgrade."

"That sounds like a wise decision," said the Admiral. "Well, gentlemen, we need to put the Royal Navy back on a war footing; inform all of your subordinates of this new development and restart the convoy escort operations. As soon as 1st Fleet has the new Seabow modifications, I want one squadron at a time to rotate back to the Low Sea. I'll send along another thirty-five golds for the modifications for 2nd Fleet. Dismissed."

The Admiral's staff hurried out of the conference room, preparing to send out new orders to the Fleets. The Messenger Hawks were going to be busy today. Once the staff was gone, Celeste, Wizard Lake and Admiral Cross were left alone in the conference room. "I'm sorry, Admiral. I tried to talk Henry into keeping the Treaty short, but he has so many people in his ear, and the temptation to get the best conditions was too great. It never occurred to me that dragons can't read."

"Don't be too hard on yourself, Sorceress, none of us realized that dragons can't read. Do you think they will be open to trying again, with a simple treaty, like the one they initially proposed?" "I'm not sure, sir. Cobalt basically told me that they were going to resume their attacks immediately, and that, despite my being a dragon-friend, he could not guarantee my safety if I remained on the HMS VALOR."

Azure landed back on the beach near Bruce's hut. She was shocked to hear Annalise and Richard laughing and playing in the surf as Gek watched on. "Well, those two sure seem to be getting along," said Azure. "Yes, ever since Richard saved Anna from the cougar, they have been getting along swimmingly," said Gek. "Wait, *what cougar?*" Azure asked.

"Anna was playing in the tall grass at the top of the hill, probably still looking for Ard, when a cougar started stalking her through the grass. Richard saw the big cat, and when it pounced on Annalise, he put it to sleep. I had no idea that the Sleep spell would work on animals," said Gek. "After that, I guess Annalise decided that her brother was not such an idiot after all," said Gek. "How did the Treaty signing go?"

"It was a disaster. That idiot king wrote up a Treaty that was dozens of pages long, then expected us to agree to something we could not read! Celeste offered to read the Treaty to us, but Cobalt said he would not trust a human to do that, and that we would not be able to remember everything the humans had added to the Treaty." "What sort of things did they add?" asked Gek curiously. "Something about *fishing rights*," said Azure. "As if we would ever agree to a restriction on where we could hunt for prey! It was insulting!"

"So, what did Cobalt do?" asked Gek. "He said that he would not sign the Treaty, and that our temporary truce with the humans would end at sundown. I guess we are back at war," said Azure. "He told Celeste that he could not vouch for her safety if she remained on board one of the ships around our islands." "How was Celeste supposed to get off the ship?" asked Gek.

"I do not know, she was on the VALOR, so we would not have attacked it anyway, because of Andrew being there, but the humans do not know that. Anyway, the ships left immediately, heading back to their port in Sundock," said Azure.

"Maybe it is time to strike Sundock again," said Gek. "Maybe, but the Dragon Council has decided to attack the city of Three Forks in two cycles of the moon. Each Clan will send two Dragons and we will attack together," said Azure. "Without Ard, I may be the only Great Dragon able to participate," said Gek. "Maybe Ig or his mate will help," offered Azure.

"What else did the Dragon Council decide?" asked Gek. "The Snow Dragon Clan Chief reported that his Clan attacked the human town of Frostberg, but were driven off by a Stone Dragon Changed One. This is becoming a real concern. Also, seven Fire Dragon Changed Ones in the town of Colton were discovered and either killed or driven off by human magic-users. The Fire Dragons are going to start dropping rocks on the humans in the salt flats of Baize, and they are sending three of their Clan to the far west to determine if there are other Dragons living there."

"Now that sounds like a plan," said Gek happily.

Edward was sleeping when Kathy and the apprentice magicians returned that evening. "Wake up, sleepyhead," said Kathy playfully. Edward opened his eyes and said, "It's good to see you." Kathy kissed him and said, "Don't you *ever* do that again, you hear me?" "Would you rather I let your friend Elianna die?" Kathy thought for a second, then said, "I take it back, but why did you change into a dragon and fly off?"

I was following the Fire Dragons back to their colony. Now that I know where it is, we can drop some rocks on *them*!" "I don't know, just the three of us would be no match for a colony of Fire Dragons," said Kathy. "Who said anything about just the three of us?" asked Edward. "Once we get this reservoir dug, and the ten most advanced students pass their Sorcerer's Tests, we could attack with twelve or thirteen!"

"That sounds pretty ambitious, let's finish one impossible task at a time, shall we?" asked Kathy. "So, how is the construction coming?" "Actually, it's moving much faster than I anticipated. The sand is only a couple feet deep here, and the bedrock has risen to only about twenty feet," replied Kathy. "That's fantastic! I had a feeling that the sand would be shallower up here," said Edward. "Why?" asked Kathy.

"Because it's been flowing south and east for decades! I should have realized it would be much less up here. I didn't anticipate the bedrock being this shallow though. How much time do you think it will be before we're finished?" asked Edward. "At this rate? Less than a month," said Kathy. "Then we need to move on to the next step," said Edward. "Which is?" "Which is digging out and reinforcing those channels from the mountains that Donovan discovered. Once we have the hole dug, we will need a way for the water to get *in.*"

Chapter Twenty-Five:
DRAGON RIDERS

The HMS VALOR pulled up to the pier in Sundock. It had been a quick trip from the area around the Coral Islands, with the Sorcerers conjuring Wind spells to hasten the trip. Second Squadron was still in Sundock, and the dock was crowded with seven Navy ships in port at once. Commodore Matthews walked quickly over to the HMS SEAHAWK to find Commodore Lang, the commander of 2nd Squadron, and give him the bad news about the Peace Treaty.

The SEAHAWK, as the command ship for the squadron, had been fitted with the new Compound Seabows first, and the crew was marveling at the ease with which they could now be drawn. "How's it going?" asked Commodore Matthews. "Modifications are done on the SEAHAWK, and the ABLE is almost complete," said Commodore Lang, "another week, and we should be finished with the re-fit. How did the Treaty signing go?" "It didn't," growled Commodore Matthews. "The King and his blasted Ministers added so much extra crap to the document that the dragons wouldn't agree to it. And frankly, I didn't blame them."

"What else did the King add?" "It was stuff about fishing rights, what constitutes a ship, what about castaways, what is the definition of a 'port facility.' On and on," said Commodore Matthews. "So, why wouldn't they sign it?" "Because dragons can't read! The dragon Clan Chief said that they offered a simple agreement, 'you don't attack us, and we won't attack you,' and what the King sent back was a 37-page Treaty that was incomprehensible to them. I wouldn't have signed it either."

"Fishing rights?" "Yes. Probably some damned Minister's idea. Anyway, the Treaty's off, and so is the temporary truce. The dragons gave us until sundown two days ago before they said they'd start attacking again." "I'm so frustrated!" "Then I guess we should speed up the modifications to the Seabows," said Commodore Lang. "You got that right. Where's James?" "He's on the ABLE, installing the modifications."

"I better get over there and see if I can get him to speed things up. I imagine that we're going to go back to convoy escort duty again. Do you know when the next merchant ships are planning to head out?" "Not off the top of my head, but I'll go ask the Harbor Master, and inform him of the renewed threat. I'll leave it to him to notify the traders." Commodore Lang headed to the

Harbor Master's office, while Commodore Matthews walked down the dock to where the ABLE was moored.

As he came aboard, Commodore Matthews heard James swearing, "No! You idiot! That line goes *across* to here! How many times do I have to tell you?" The Commodore smiled, James was a man after his own heart. "James! How goes it?" he asked. James wiped grease off his hands and extended his hand, "Commodore Matthews! It's good to see you again, but I didn't expect you for another two weeks." "The Treaty with the dragons fell through and we're back at war with the Sea Dragons. I brought 1st Squadron back to get the new modifications as soon as possible."

"That's unfortunate," said James, "I was hoping we'd have more time." "Me too. What can the Royal Navy do to help speed this effort up?" James thought for a moment, then said, "Well, I have most of the parts made. If you could have some men transport the parts from the Blacksmith shop to the ships, that would be helpful. If your ship's Carpenters could lend a hand, that might speed up the installation. Inserting the new split arms is easy, routing the longer bowstring through the pulleys correctly is complicated. If the bowstring is installed wrong, the Compound Seabow won't work at all."

"I'll get some men to the Blacksmith shop right away, and have all three of the ship's Carpenters report to you here within the glass. Would magicians help?" James shook his head, "Not really. There's nothing magical about these things." "How long will it take with the extra help?" asked the Commodore. "I'll be finished with 2nd Squadron in three days. Figure another three days for 1st Squadron, since you only have three ships. Call it a little over a week," said James. "I just hope we have a week," said the Commodore.

Mage Andrew was waiting for the Commodore when he returned to the VALOR. "How long on the modifications, sir" he asked. "At least a week. James has only finished the SEAHAWK so far. He's working on the Frigate HMS ABLE right now. He says if we send some men to the Blacksmith shop to pick up the modification kits and take them to the ships, it will speed things up. He also requested the ship's Carpenters to help with the modifications. He said that he doesn't need any magical support."

Andrew smiled and said, "I'll be happy to guide some men to the Blacksmith shop and help load the new gear. We'll probably need a wagon to transport it." "I never knew a Blacksmith that didn't have a heavy-duty wagon," said the Commodore. "Once you get the modification kits loaded, take the rest of the week off." Andrew smiled, "Thank you, sir. I'll check in each day just to make sure you don't need anything." "Life is short, Andrew. Don't let it pass you by."

Andrew hurried off, grabbing ten idle sailors to come with him to the Blacksmith shop to load the modification kits for the new Compound Seabows. The men grumbled (slightly) but followed Andrew across the town to the Blacksmith shop. The Blacksmith was actually eager to get the twenty-nine kits out of his smithy, since they were taking up space, and he still had sixteen more kits to make up for 3rd Squadron. "We're going to need them sooner than expected," said Andrew. "The Royal Navy will pay any *reasonable* charge for the expedited work." The Blacksmith smiled and nodded, always glad to make a few extra coins. As the Commodore predicted, the Blacksmith had a large wagon, reinforced to hold the weight of the steel bar stock, which he eagerly lent to the Navy (for only a silver). Andrew paid the silver and helped load the kits. Once loaded, he instructed the sailors to take the kits to each ship, and place one modification kit next to each Seabow on all the ships in both fleets, telling them that the SEAHAWK had already been fitted with the new weapons.

Once the sailors were on their way back to the port, Andrew walked to the cottage across the street and knocked on the door. Maria answered. She was wearing an apron and her hands were covered with flour. She looked beautiful. "Andrew! I didn't expect you back so soon! Come in, come in!" Andrew entered the cottage and the aroma of baking bread wafted through the air. "That smells wonderful," he said. "You'll have to excuse me, I have rolls in the oven. Come on in to the kitchen and keep me company," said Maria.

Andrew followed her into the kitchen. "So, how is the cottage working out?" he asked. "It's almost like home," said Maria. "Except, it's a little quieter. At home, my father works late into the night sometimes, and our house is attached to the smithy. At least here, the Blacksmith shop is across the street, and Mr. Smith, the Blacksmith, doesn't usually work too late." "That may change for the next week," said Andrew. "Why?" Andrew explained about the dragon's rejection of the Peace Treaty, and the end of the temporary truce.

"That's why we're back so soon," Andrew explained. "We need the new modifications as soon as possible." "Oh, that's too bad," said Maria. "I was so hoping that the Treaty would put an end to the hostilities." "Maybe at sea," replied Andrew, "but the Sea Dragons were very clear that they didn't speak for the other dragon clans." "Let's talk about something else," said Maria. "Where are you from?"

"I grew up in Southport. My father worked unloading cargo from the merchant ships and my mother was a seamstress," said Andrew. "When did you know that you had the spark?" "I suspected it when I was about twelve, but my father never believed it. He kept insisting that I should get a job, gutting fish on the docks, like all the other boys my age. So, I ran away from home and went to the Wizards Academy," said Andrew. "How did you get to Kingston?" asked Maria.

"I got a temporary job on a merchant ship that was headed that way. Once I arrived, the Wizards Academy admitted me right away. I spent eight years there as a student, then two years as a Mentor, before Wizard Noland assigned me to the Royal Navy." "And they let you be a Mentor for your cousin?" asked Maria. "I didn't know that Donovan was my cousin when he arrived. At the time, I just thought that he was a very talented, older student. I didn't know we were cousins until Wizard Edward told us when he returned. But enough about me, were you born in Fairview?"

"No. We lived in Kingston until I was eighteen, then my father moved his business to Fairview, thinking that there would be less competition. There are a *lot* of arms merchants in Kingston."

Andrew and Maria lost track of time as they talked, and suddenly the smell of burned bread wafted from the oven. "My rolls!" exclaimed Maria. She rushed over and opened the oven door, burning her hand on the hot handle. She yelped, then grabbed a hot pad to remove the charred dinner rolls. "Oh, no!" said Maria, moving to the water pump to put some cool water on her hand. "Let me see," said Andrew, He took Maria's slightly burned hand in his left hand and said, *"ALEVIO,"* while holding his right hand over the reddening skin, palm down, his fingers closed. The burn faded immediately. "That feels wonderful! Thank you!" "Anytime," said Andrew. "But what about my dinner rolls? Is there anything you can do for them?" asked Maria.

Andrew thought for a while, searching for an appropriate spell, then he smiled and walked over to the baking sheet of blackened dinner rolls, clapped his hands together and said *"MORPHIOUS."* The burned rolls instantly turned into a bouquet of roses. "How are we going to eat that?" asked Maria. "I can't *unburn* bread," said Andrew, "so I guess I'll just have to take you out for dinner tonight."

The Royal Expeditionary Force departed Farmdale after a hearty breakfast the next morning, headed toward Hayford. This journey from Farmdale to Hayford was much more pleasant than the last one for Donovan, since the last time he made this trip, he was escorting what he believed to be his father's coffin, and a severed dragon's head. As they traveled down the road, Major Gerald approached, "Donovan, do you notice anything different?" Donovan paused to consider the Major's question, then he answered, "The animals have returned to the forest. The last time I traveled down this road, there were no sounds, not even birds."

"Senior Specialist Lance said the same thing. That might be a good sign, that there aren't any dragons about," said the Major. "At least not any in dragon-form," confirmed Donovan. Major Gerald smiled and rode off to the front of the column of soldiers, and Donovan asked Rachel to take the reins of the horse pulling their wagon. After Rachel had control of the horse, Donovan jumped down and unhitched his horse, Stam, from the back of the wagon, mounted, and rode off, looking for Sergeant Kindred.

Donovan reined up beside Sergeant Kindred, the Archer from 2nd Company's 3rd Squad, and asked, "How does it feel to be going home again?" "Hello, sir. I admit it's strange. I haven't been back since our last visit, and as you may recall, our parting wasn't exactly joyful." Sergeant Kindred's parents had not approved of his joining the Royal Guard, and had been disappointed when he returned home, and immediately asked to borrow one of the family's small fishing boats to depart for Kingston the next day.

"Maybe we can stay a little while longer this time," offered Donovan. "Plus, now you're a Sergeant, they should be proud of you." "Maybe, but there's still the fact that I didn't take over the family's fishing business. I hope they found someone to help them, or I'm going to hear more complaints when I get home." "Would you like me to talk to them?" asked Donovan. "To what end?" "I don't know, maybe a mild Compulsion spell; that's the only *'Get off your son's back-type'* spell I know." Sergeant Kindred laughed.

"Thanks for the offer, but I'll just have to deal with it," said Sergeant Kindred. "OK, just let me know if you change your mind. Is 12th Company still stationed in Hayford?" asked Donovan. "As far as I know. At least, that's the Company I joined when I enlisted." "That's just an independent Company, right? No magical support?" "Correct. The only magicians in town are the Regional Mage, Dean, and Sorcerer Nathan. They've both been there for years." "That's good to know. Thanks," said Donovan.

Donovan rode back to the wagon, re-hitched Stam to the hitching ring on the back, and climbed up onto the bench with Rachel. "What was all that about?" she asked. "I was talking to Sergeant Kindred, the archer in 3rd Squad. He was born and raised in Hayford. I just wanted his take on the magicians in the town. There's only the Regional Mage's Office, and Mage Dean and

Sorcerer Nathan have been there for years. I don't expect any problems in Hayford."

"Where do you expect problems?" asked Rachel. "Three Forks, although I can't say why. I just have a bad feeling about that place," replied Donovan, wiping his brow with his left hand. "The last time you had a 'bad feeling' about a town, your company was almost ambushed on the road," observed Rachel. "I remember," said Donovan. "I'll do a Seeing spell before we head up there to check for anything like that."

The Royal Expeditionary Force entered Hayford a week after departing Farmdale. As expected, neither of the magicians in the Regional Mage's Office were Changed Ones, but the Treasury was a little light. "It's not our fault," said Tom, the Hayford Mayor, "Farmdale sent us fewer crops to export to Kingston this year. The tax revenue we were expecting didn't materialize!" "Hmm," said Major Gerald, with a tone of skepticism in his voice, "the King might buy that excuse this year, but I'll recommend that he look at your accounts more closely next year." The Mayor gulped.

As they left the Mayor's office, Major Gerald asked Rachel, "What do you think?" "I think the Mayor has been skimming some of the tax revenue off the top. Not much, but enough that we noticed it. How short was the Treasury?" "Six golds, eight silvers. Like you said, not much, but a year's wages for a fisherman," said the Major. "I think it's a good thing we caught this early, before it got out of control," said Donovan. "Agreed," said Major Gerald. "Where do you two think we should go from here?"

Donovan diplomatically let Rachel offer the opinion that they had discussed the night before. "I think that Donovan and I should transform and head to Haven and Smithville separately. They're both a day's flight away, and fairly small towns. Haven only has one Regional Sorcerer, and Smithville has one Regional Sorcerer and the 14th Company with one Sorcerer," said Rachel. "Any preference as to who goes where?" asked Major Gerald. Donovan shrugged.

"OK, Sorceress Rachel, you and Specialist Dirk head to Haven; Donovan, you and Lance go to Smithville. I'll expect you both back here in three days. Please leave tonight." Donovan and Rachel both nodded their understanding and went to find the Specialists. As he walked through the 12th Company garrison compound, Donovan spied Sergeant Kindred. Walking up, he asked, "Did you see your family? How did it go?" "Yes, I saw them. They were actually impressed that I made Sergeant so fast. My father has found a capable young man to help with the business, so he wasn't quite as grumpy this time."

"I think the Expeditionary Force will be staying in town for a few more days, so you could probably take a couple of days leave to visit more and help around the house, if you wanted to," said Donovan. Sergeant Kindred smiled at the idea. "I thought we had to get to Three Forks, why are we delaying here?" asked the Sergeant. "Rachel and I are going into Haven and Smithville tonight with Dirk and Lance. We should be back in three days," answered Donovan. "Do you know anything about either town?"

"Smithville is a mining town; mostly steel, but some coal too. I've only been there once. The miners are kind of a rough crowd, and the whole town smells like smoke and ash. The 14th Company is stationed there. Haven is a small town on the Emerald River. It's really just an intermediate stop for goods going from Three Forks to Sundock, there's no military unit there," said Sergeant Kindred. "Thanks," said Donovan. "Did you get all that, Lance?" asked Donovan, looking over his shoulder at the empty air. Senior Specialist Lance lowered the hood of his Concealment cloak, and said, "Got it, boss. When do you want to leave?"

"We'll leave at sundown, that should get us there before morning. As long as you aren't too heavy and don't fall off."

Donovan gave Rachel a quick kiss as they prepared to depart. "See you in three days," he said. They were on the outskirts of Hayford, in a clearing in the trees. Donovan cast a Seeming around Rachel as she disrobed and transformed into a Great Dragon. Then he packed her clothes into her backpack and gave it to Specialist Dirk to carry. Dirk climbed up on Rachel's back gingerly, unsure of where to put his feet. "You need to move up higher on my neck," said Rachel, "otherwise, I'll knock you off with my wings." "Wonderful," murmured Dirk.

Donovan disrobed and similarly put his clothes in his pack, handing it to Lance. He transformed instantly and Lance climbed aboard. "Ready?" Donovan asked. Both Specialists nodded, somewhat uneasily, and the two dragons took flight, Rachel heading east, while Donovan and Lance took a more southeasterly course.

Celeste landed in the area of the palace that King Henry had designated for Dragon Messengers. There was a privacy screen already in place, so Celeste changed back into human form and got dressed. She was dreading telling the King the news about the dragons rejecting the Treaty. She walked through the palace, and headed towards the King's chambers. As expected, she found a guard outside the door, but he let her in immediately.

While it was still before dawn, Henry was already awake and working on some papers on his desk. "Celeste, my love! Welcome back! I've missed you! How did it go?" asked Henry. Celeste gave Henry a passionate kiss, then said, "Not well, I'm afraid. The Sea Dragons refused to sign the Treaty. Apparently, dragons can't read. They refused to sign anything so lengthy that they could not understand. I offered to read the Treaty to them, but they said that they would never be able to remember all the words, and that a Binding spell would put them at too much risk if they agreed to it. They also said they weren't going to agree to any restrictions on where they could gather prey."

The King sat down and sighed. "I'm sorry, dear. I tried, I really did," said Celeste. "It's not your fault," said Henry. "I warned those darn Ministers that they were expecting too much, but they insisted. So, where does that leave us?" "The dragons were pretty angry. They accused us of stalling for time while we built more Seabows. They even canceled the temporary truce we had, and gave us until sundown to leave their waters before they attacked again. Commodore Matthews took 1st Squadron back to Sundock to get the Seabows modified as quickly as possible."

"What modification is that?" asked Henry. "That arms merchant, James, you know, the man who invented the crossbow, has come up with a modification to the Seabows that enables them to be drawn by just one man, instead of two. He added a pulley system to the bow, and calls them Compound Seabows. They work really well, so Commodore Matthews paid him seven silvers for each modification kit, thirty-five golds in all, including installation, for every ship in 1st Fleet." "I guess that sounds reasonable," said the King. "I really hope that the Royal Expeditionary Force doesn't find that we are missing a lot of gold from our Treasuries."

"You must be tired. Why don't you retire for a while? I still have some work to do, working on the arrangements for the Winter Ball next week. The invitations are all out, but I need to increase security. I can't afford another assassination attempt at this Ball," said the King. "I understand completely, dear. Maybe you should invite some of the Wizards from the Academy for extra security," said Celeste. "An excellent idea! I'll prepare some additional invitations today, and you could deliver them this afternoon. I know it's short notice…" "I'm sure they'll be honored to attend. But they might not have time to purchase formal attire." Henry smiled, and said, "Wizard's robes will be formal enough."

While the apprentice magicians finished digging the last few acres of the reservoir, Edward and Kathy transformed into dragons and scouted the ravines and wadis that Donovan had located, leading down from the Caperian Mountains in the north, and the Grey Mountains to the west. When they found what they were looking for, they began Removing the (thankfully) small amounts of sand from the channels, and adhering the side walls where they looked weak. There had been several rainstorms in the past few weeks, and the reservoir was slowly beginning to fill.

"We need to decide what to do about the northern edge of the reservoir," said Edward. "What do you mean?" asked Kathy. "Well, we've constructed channels for the runoff and snow melt from the mountains to get into the reservoir, but do we need walls on the north end?" "I'm not sure," said Kathy. "What do you think?" "My initial idea is to create a beach area along the north edge, like a swimming pool, with the shallow end in the north, and the deep end in the south. I mean, as far as we know, all of the water is going to flow south and east," said Edward.

"How do we control how much water is in the reservoir?" asked Kathy. "First, for the water coming in from the east, we need to construct underground culverts with gates, which will allow water to flow into the reservoir, but not out. Once we determine how much water we're talking about, we can devise some overflow channels and holding ponds. That is, if this lake ever fills up. Only time will tell how much water will accumulate and not evaporate off," said Edward.

"It would be a shame if the lake never filled," said Kathy. "Maybe," said Edward, "but the goal was to keep the salt from getting into the Amber River, and I think we've accomplished that admirably." "So, what do you think we have left to do?" asked Kathy. "We need to finish digging out the spoils, gradually digging shallower and shallower until we reach the level we want at the north end. I figure that will take another week. Then, we need to construct the culverts and water intake channels. Lastly, we should create some sort of recreation area along the beach at the north end. Then we send for the King. Call it a month, tops."

Rachel landed in the forest outside of Haven a few hours before dawn. It had been a relatively short flight, even with Dirk clinging to her back. "Turn around, please," said Rachel, "and hand me my backpack." "Oh, right," said Dirk. Once transformed and clothed, the Sorceress and the Specialist headed into town.

Haven was a small village, barely a town. There were less than sixty buildings, including the ones along the modest piers along the Emerald River. Clearly, few of the ships from Three Forks actually stopped in the town. Rachel and Dirk were immediately noticed by the few townsfolk, there being so few visitors to the village. "Good morning. Can I help you?" asked an elderly gentleman. "We're looking for the Mayor and the town Sorcerer," replied Dirk. "Can you direct us?"

The old man smiled and said, "The Mayor's house is just down the street, on the right side. It's the red brick building next to the General Store, which the Mayor owns." "The Mayor operates the General Store?" asked Rachel. "That's not unusual in a small town," murmured Dirk. They thanked the man and wandered down the street. It was still early morning, and the General Store wasn't open yet, so they walked next door and knocked on the door of the red brick building.

A woman, presumably the Mayor's wife, answered the door, "Yes, can I help you?" "We're looking for the Mayor," said Rachel cheerfully. "You got her, Mayor Silvia Moss, at your service. How can I help you?" "I'm

Sorceress Rachel, and this is Specialist Dirk," said Rachel. "We're from the Royal Expeditionary Force. King Henry ordered the Expeditionary Force to visit all of the towns and cities in Franconia to meet the Regional magicians and audit the Treasuries. I hope that won't be too much of an inconvenience."

"The Royal Expeditionary Force is coming to Haven?" asked the Mayor. "But, we don't have room for that many visitors! Why, Mary's Boarding house only has four rooms, and the tavern doesn't have near enough tables or food to feed a company of soldiers," said the worried Mayor. "We anticipated this," said Dirk, "the Expeditionary Force isn't coming here, just us. The rest of the Force is in Hayford. We just came down to do a quick check of things, and then we'll be on our way."

"Oh, that's much better. I don't mean to seem inhospitable, but we're a small town…" "I understand completely," said Rachel. "Where might we find the town magician?" "Sorceress Cindy? Why, she should be in the Exchequer Building, just around the corner. It's not open yet, I'm afraid. Cindy is the town Treasurer, you see. We don't have much in the way of local government here in Haven," said Silvia. "Is there someplace we could wait, and maybe get something to eat?" asked Rachel. "Well, Martha's Café should be open by now. You could get some tea and muffins for breakfast while you wait," said the Mayor helpfully.

"That would be lovely," replied Rachel. "Where is the Café?" "It's right across the street, dear. The building with the green door." Rachel and Dirk expressed their thanks and headed across the street. Martha's Café was a small eatery with only three tables and a small counter area with two stools. The tea was marginal, but the blueberry muffins were excellent.

As they left the Café, Dirk and Rachel ran into the Mayor. "There you are! I found Sorceress Cindy and told her you were looking for her. Poor thing got all nervous and rushed right over to the Exchequer to make sure everything was in order for you. I'll walk over with you and introduce you." As they entered the Haven Exchequer building, it was obvious that all was *not* in order. There were papers strewn about the floor, and the safe was open. "Cindy!" called the Mayor. "Where are you?"

Dirk immediately donned his Concealment cloak and made a rapid search of the small treasury building. There was no one in the building, and the back door was ajar. "There's no one here," said Dirk as he reentered the room that housed the safe. "Where could she have gone?" wondered the Mayor, "I just spoke to her a few minutes ago."

"I suspect that Cindy has fled with the town's funds," said Rachel. "We've seen this before. That's one reason the King wanted this audit. Mayor, do you have any idea how much is missing?" The Mayor blanched and stammered, "No, not *exactly,* but it should be here in the ledger," she said, pointing at the scattered papers on the floor. "Dirk, why don't you see if you can locate Sorceress Cindy?" said Rachel. "I'll stay here and try to help the Mayor reconstruct the town's accounting ledger, though I suspect that Cindy took the last few pages with her."

As Dirk headed outside, Rachel followed him and whispered, "I'm sure that Cindy is long gone. Just see if anyone saw a dragon flying away this morning." As expected, the last few pages of Haven's treasury records were nowhere to be found. Rachel asked how much coin the Mayor thought was in the Exchequer. "It should have been about forty golds! How could Cindy do this to us? I thought she was my friend!" the Mayor sobbed. "The town may never recover from this loss! I know it might not seem like much to you, but it's all we had!" Rachel nodded sympathetically and said, "Where did Cindy live? Maybe she stashed some of the coins in her residence."

The Mayor guided Rachel to a small log cabin along the river. "That's Cindy's place. There's no smoke from the chimney, so I doubt that anyone's home." Rachel nodded, Sensing that the cabin was, indeed, empty. "Why don't you go back and clean up the Exchequer? I'll make a quick search and come let you know what I find." The Mayor nodded despondently and headed back into town.

Rachel entered the cabin cautiously, searching for any hidden traps, but it was obvious that when Cindy left that morning, she wasn't expecting trouble in the form of a visiting Sorceress. Rachel made a quick search of the cabin, but found nothing of value. The bedsheets, however, reeked of lizard. Feeling sorrow for the Mayor and the town, Rachel quickly Replicated forty golds and put them in an empty canvas bag she found under Cindy's bed. It had "Haven Exchequer" written on the side.

She found Dirk waiting in the Exchequer when she returned, and he reported that no one had seen anything out of the ordinary that morning. Rachel told him that she had recovered forty golds from Cindy's cabin. Dirk raised an eyebrow suspiciously, but didn't say anything. They found the Mayor in the General Store, dusting cabinets and muttering to herself. "Good news, Silvia!" said Rachel, "I found about forty golds in Cindy's cabin. They were in her closet, under some dirty clothes. I guess she didn't have time to retrieve them before she fled."

The Mayor looked somewhat relieved. "Well, that's a mercy. I just can't believe that Cindy would do such a thing! Did you find her?" "No," said Dirk. "I suspect she fled downriver in a small boat. We'll search for her when we visit Sundock later. What did she look like?" The Mayor described Cindy as a short, plump middle-aged woman with red hair. "She shouldn't be hard to notice," said Dirk. "Maybe she'll turn up." "In the future, Silvia, I recommend that you always have two people inventory the town's funds. Like I said, this isn't the first city in Franconia where we've found something like this."

Dirk and Rachel ate lunch in Martha's Café, then said their farewells to Martha and Silvia, before walking north along the road back to Hayford. They found a vacant fishing shack along the river and decided to use it to get a few hours of sleep before returning to Hayford at sundown. When they arrived in Hayford the next morning, they found Major Gerald pacing his office worriedly. "What's wrong?" asked Rachel. "Donovan and Lance aren't back yet, and Mage Dean just got a Messenger Hawk from Sorcerer Christopher, the Regional Sorcerer in Smithville, stating that there are dragons living in the mines above the town. He is asking for help."

Donovan landed in the hills outside of Smithville just as dawn was breaking. It was a longer flight to Smithville than to Haven. He Changed into human form, and he and Lance headed toward the town. They hadn't gotten very far before a contingent of soldiers from the 14th Company, carrying crossbows, along with Sorcerer Christopher, approached them. "Did you see it?" asked Christopher. "See what?" asked Donovan. "The dragon! I think it landed just over that ridge!" "What color was it?" asked Donovan. "Gold," said Sorcerer Christopher.

Realizing that he'd been seen, Donovan took the excited Sorcerer aside and quickly explained that it was him and Lance that they had seen. Which quickly devolved into an explanation about dragons and how they could do magic, and what Donovan and Lance were doing in Smithville. "You're telling me that you can change into a dragon?" asked Christopher. "Yes," said Donovan, "but keep that to yourself. We don't want the dragons learning about our ability, and we certainly don't want to scare the populace."

"Well, it's too late for the people of Smithville, I can tell you that," said Sorcerer Christopher. "Why do you say that?" asked Lance. "For one thing, a blue, water-spitting dragon ravaged Smithville about six months ago, and lots of people saw it. Then, just recently, two boys wandered into the old coal mine where they claim they found a baby dragon. When they tried to approach it, they fell dead asleep. Right there on the floor of the mine. Their mother dragged me up here to look for them, and just before we got to the entrance, a big blue dragon, carrying a baby dragon, flew out of the mine, heading east."

"You're sure it was a dragon?" asked Donovan. "I used a Sight Enhancement, so yes, I'm sure it was a dragon." "Have you explored the mine?" asked Donovan. "Do I look stupid to you?" asked Christopher angrily. "I'm the only magician in this town! I sent out all of the Messenger Hawks we had, asking for assistance. We've been staking out the entrance, waiting to see if any more dragons come out, or if any go in."

"Did you send a Messenger Hawk to Hayford?" asked Donovan. "Hayford, Haven, Sundock, and Kingston," replied Sorcerer Christopher. "We only had four hawks." "Well, I guess we should go check out this mine, then," said Donovan. "Just the two of you?" asked an exasperated Christopher. "No. You are coming with us," said Donovan.

They crept into the mine, the two Sorcerers conjuring Silence spells, and Lance cloaked and invisible. Donovan carried a torch and led the way. "If I find a Sea Dragon, don't be shocked if I Change into a Great Dragon," Donovan said to Christopher. "Why would you do that?" "Because Great Dragons breathe *fire*, not water," said Donovan. "Right," said Christopher, apprehensively.

They reached the spot where the two boys had been found, but there was no sign of dragons. Donovan scanned the floor of the mine carefully, then pointed, "That way," he said. They began creeping up the mine shaft on the left. "Why are we going this way?" whispered Christopher. "Because that's where the dragon tracks came from," whispered Lance, pointing at the faded, but still detectible dragon tracks. As they crept along the mine shaft, Donovan signed to Lance, *This may be the dumbest thing I have ever done.* Lance smiled and signed back, *No, you once said that you didn't have the Spark. That was dumber than this.* Donovan smiled.

They followed the larger dragon tracks to the main entrance. "The dragons entered here," said Donovan. "It looks like the baby dragon wandered off, probably exploring, and the older dragon went after it. That's when they ran into the children. The older dragon spelled them to sleep, grabbed the baby, and flew off."

"Why didn't they just kill the two boys?" wondered Christopher. "Consider yourself lucky they didn't. I don't think there are any more dragons in the mine right now, but they've clearly used it for shelter before, and may again someday, so keep an eye out."

Once they were out of the mine, Donovan released his Silence spell and the two Sorcerers, five soldiers and one Specialist headed into Smithville. A check of the town's Treasury revealed that all was in order, but it took longer than expected to conduct the inventory because the Treasurer had atrocious handwriting, and there were more coins in the Smithville treasury than in either Hayford or Farmdale. It was almost midnight by the time Lance and Donovan finished counting coins. "We'll have to stay another day," said Donovan. "Otherwise, we'll end up flying during daylight, and I don't want to alarm the people of Hayford." Lance yawned sleepily and said that he had no objections. They found an empty office in the Treasury building and caught a few hours of sleep. The next day, they offered to go back out to the mine and try to board up the entrances more securely, at least good enough that children couldn't break in.

As they finished boarding up the second entrance, a gold dragon came swooping out of the sky towards them. Sorcerer Christopher raised a shield and shouted a warning to the soldiers, who hastily attempted to draw and load their crossbows, their hands shaking with fear. "HOLD YOUR FIRE," yelled Donovan. "THAT'S JUST MY WIFE."

Chapter Twenty-Six:

THREE FORKS

They were finished. The Great Salt Lake was complete. It had taken almost ten months, but they had finished ahead of schedule and under the 1,000-gold budget allocated by King Donald of Baize. Edward had instructed Wizard Timothy in Springfield to send a Messenger Hawk to the King about two weeks ago, so he should be there anytime (depending on his Royal Calendar).

The reservoir was slowly filling with water. There had been additional rainfall, and a good bit of runoff from the Grey Mountains. Mercifully, there had been no more dragon attacks in the last month. The water intake channels were complete, and a slow trickle of water was continuously streaming in. The water was not overly salty, more brackish, but certainly not fresh drinking water. It would have to be desalinated for that.

The recreation area along the north end of the lake was already being used by the people of Springfield, who suddenly had more disposable income as a result of the incredible engineering project that had taken place over the last year. All of the advanced apprentices were working hard on their Serums mastery in hopes of taking their Sorcerer's Test before departing. Edward wanted everyone to remain on site until the King arrived, as he hoped that some kind words from the King would be encouraging to the apprentice magicians who had worked so hard for so long.

Edward, Mage Kathy, and Mage Elianna took turns Changing into dragons each evening and flying along the road to Baize, watching for the King's approach. They finally spotted his entourage approaching and decided to meet him along the road, just south of the reservoir. Clothes were mended and cleaned, shoes were shined, hair was cut, and everything was made ready for a visit from the King. Similarly, the people of Springfield were hoping that the King would visit the city.

As the King's party rode up the road, Wizard Timothy, Wizard Edward, Mage Kathy, Mage Elianna, and Captain Douglas, the commander of the 1st Baizian Infantry Battalion were drawn up on the road to greet him.

"Wizard Edward! Mage Kathy!" said the King, "You have surprised us yet again. I expected it to take several more months and hundreds more golds to complete this monumental project, and here, after barely ten months you are complete." "It is entirely due to the hard work and dedication of the apprentice magicians of Baize, Your Majesty," said Edward modestly. "Without their dedication, we would have accomplished nothing." "Of course," said the King graciously. "Let's go see this masterpiece of engineering!"

Edward and the others guided the King's party around the reservoir. The view from atop the southern berm was spectacular, you couldn't see the entire reservoir. It was just too big. There was less than ten feet of water in the basin, but the potential was immediately obvious. "How long do you think it will take to fill the reservoir?" asked Minister William, the Baizian Public Works Minister. "That's hard to say," said Edward, "it depends on the rainfall and snowfall in the mountains. It may be several years before the lake fully fills. There is also the amount of evaporation to consider. That will slow the water level increase." "True, true," said the Minister. "This is a great achievement, Wizard Edward."

"I'm glad I was able to be of assistance. If you'll all follow me, I'll take you to the recreation area," said Edward. "Recreation area?" asked Wizard James, the Court Wizard of Baize. "Yes, you see, there are no walls on the north end of the lake, since all the water flows south and east, so we created a beach and recreation area. You'll see," said Edward. When they reached the north end of the lake, they saw what Edward meant. There were elevated life guard chairs dispersed every hundred yards down the beach, picnic tables, concession stands, even a few small craft rental vendors were in evidence. The King was stunned. "This looks like our facilities at Seaside!" he exclaimed.

"So I've been told by Mage Kathy. While I've never been to Seaside, I can imagine a restful place on a lake to relax. This might help revitalize Springfield as a resort destination, and generate additional income for the Kingdom. It should certainly generate some tax income, while encouraging small businesses." "Remarkable," was all King Donald could say.

The King stood in thought for a long while, taking in all that Edward and his workers had accomplished. Finally, he said, "Wizard Edward, you have gone above and beyond what I expected. I am awarding one gold to everyone who worked on this project. Mage Kathy, I offered to release you from your service to the kingdom of Baize if this project succeeded. I am more than pleased, and hereby grant your release from any obligation to the crown. I hope you will both return to visit from time to time, and I wish you happiness in your life together."

"Thank you, Your Majesty," said Edward and Kathy together. "When will you return to Franconia?" asked James. "Once we get all of the apprentice magicians and engineers on their way home, and administer the

Sorcerer's Test to the ten advanced students we've been working with, we should be ready to depart. I had planned to begin the Sorcerer's Testing tomorrow if you'd like to observe it," said Edward.

James shook his head, smiling. "No need, Edward, you've done more than enough. I'll handle the testing tomorrow. Bid everyone your goodbyes and feel free to depart as soon as you're ready." Edward was surprised by the rush to see Kathy and himself off, but nodded and said, "There's one other matter that I need to make you aware of: A month ago, our campsite was attacked by dragons, who were hiding under Concealment shields. They dropped several large stones on us, injuring several students and damaging some of the wagons. It seems as if, myself, Mage Kathy, and Mage Elianna were specifically targeted. The dragons have not returned, and I followed them as they flew back to the Fire Dragon colony. It's in a narrow glen on the east side of the Grey Mountains."

"We'll keep that in mind. Thank you for the warning, and the information," said James. "Now, I need to get the King to the relative safety of Springfield before night falls. Goodbye Edward, Kathy. Thank you for all you've done."

Just like that, Wizard James, Minister William, the King, and his entourage, rode off toward Springfield.

Edward was shocked by the abrupt departure and dismissal. "Well, that was sudden," he said to Kathy, Timothy, and Elianna. Timothy said, "The King and his staff are embarrassed that it took a foreign Wizard to accomplish something they've been unable to do for decades. It seems they want you two gone, so that they can begin spreading the word of their wonderful achievement."

"Please assemble the apprentices and everyone else in the camp, so we can say farewell. Kathy and I will leave at sunset," said Edward quietly. Later that afternoon, Edward addressed the apprentice magicians, praising them for their hard work and dedication. He relayed the King's promise of a one gold reward for each of them for all their hard work, and he bid them farewell. As he and Kathy packed up their belongings, Edward took Timothy aside and said, "Not that I doubt the King's word, but there should be over 150 golds left in the project funds in the Springfield Treasury. Please ensure that everyone gets what they were promised before you send them home. Keep the rest for Springfield." Timothy nodded and said, "What about you and Kathy? Surely you deserve some reward for this miracle."

Edward looked at Kathy lovingly and said, "I'm leaving with the greatest treasure in the Kingdom."

James was just finishing the last of the Seabow modifications on the HMS VICEROY, the last ship in 1st Squadron to receive the upgrade. It was early morning, and he was tired. He'd been working late into the night, sleeping on board the ships, in order to get them prepared for the next attack. He walked away from the newly modified Compound Seabow to get a cup of water, when a large stone slammed into the ship next to the Compound Seabow.

He looked up, frantically, trying to imagine where such a large stone could have come from, when another hit the HMS VICTORY. The few sailors on board scrambled to man the Seabows, looking for a target, but finding none. Stones and rocks continued to rain down on the Navy ships of the 1st Squadron. All except the HMS VALOR, which was unscathed. Then stones began falling on the moored merchant ships, breaking through the decks, crushing merchant sailors who were defenseless against this attack.

James regained his senses and ran to the Compound Seabow he had just finished modifying. He drew the drawstring and loaded a bolt, scanning the skies carefully. He detected what he thought was a slight distortion in the air and fired. A fatally injured Sea Dragon appeared, its Concealment shield vanishing as it died. The dragon fell into the water beside the VALOR. James reloaded the Seabow, just as three large stones smashed into him, killing him instantly.

Out of stones, the Sea Dragons flew off, feeling *very* pleased with themselves.

Andrew and Maria were having breakfast at the Inn when the alert came in. Dragons were attacking the port! Andrew told Maria to go home, and he would see her later, then rushed quickly to the ship. By the time he arrived, the attack was over. Eight ships were damaged, four new Compound Seabows were destroyed, and James was dead. Commodore Matthews surveyed his damaged ships. "I want the decks repaired and the Seabows Replicated in the old style. We need to get out of this port. We're sitting ducks here. The dragons could return anytime."

"I need to see Maria, and tell her about her father," said Andrew sadly. "This will break her heart." "I'm sorry son. Death is never easy. Go now, we can handle the repairs. Just return quickly. We need to get to sea. Meanwhile, I've got to send a Messenger Hawk to the Admiral. Do we know how they did this?" "From what I heard, the dragons cast Concealment shields around themselves, then dropped heavy stones and rocks on the ships. Most of the crew was ashore, including the magicians. We could have cast shields to deflect the rocks, but we weren't here."

"It's not your fault, Andrew. Surprises happen in war. No one can anticipate everything. Go see Maria. I want to sail with the evening tide."

Andrew hurried across town, wondering how he was going to break the news to Maria. When he arrived at the cottage, she was waiting. "What happened ? Is everyone all right?" she asked frantically. Andrew took a deep breath, and said, "The dragons attacked the ships that were tied to the dock. They cast Concealment shields around themselves and dropped heavy stones from high in the sky. With most of the sailors on shore leave, there were very few crewmen aboard to try and fight them off. None of the magicians were on board."

"My father was on the VICEROY," said Maria, "Is he alright?" Andrew shook his head sadly and said, "No, sweetheart, he's not alright. Your father was killed." Maria broke down in tears, inconsolable. All Andrew could do was hold her as she wept. Eventually, the tears stopped, and the fear set in.

"What am I going to do now?" she asked. "How am I going to support myself? How will I even get back to Fairview? What am I going to do?" she asked tearfully. Andrew wept with her, then an idea occurred to him. It was crazy, but not too crazy. "Maria, I love you. Marry me," said Andrew.

"What?" "I said, 'Will you marry me?'" repeated Andrew. Maria shook her head, confused, "Andrew, I think I love you, but how can I marry you the day of my father's death?" Andrew thought, "I can get Commodore Matthews to marry us," he said. "I'll buy this house instead of rent it. Then we'll make our way home to Fairview as soon as I'm reassigned from the VALOR." "What am I supposed to do in this town, alone?" Maria asked.

"Did your father teach you how to assemble the modified Seabows," asked Andrew, dreading the answer. Maria's face hardened, "Yes. I know how to assemble them." Andrew sighed, "Well, you could work on putting the new modifications on the 3rd Squadron's ships when they arrive. I'll insist that a magician remain on board to protect you while you make the modifications." "Agreed. Anything I can do to help kill dragons."

That evening, after meeting with Mr. Hilton and purchasing the cabin for twenty golds, Maria and Andrew stood on the deck of the HMS VALOR as Commodore Horatio Matthews pronounced them 'man and wife.'

"In recognition of this auspicious occasion, I have postponed our departure until *tomorrow* evening," said Commodore Matthews.

The Royal Ball was the same as all Royal Balls. Lots of receiving lines, expensively bad food, pretty women dancing with fat old men who were not their dates, and frustrated young men standing around the food and drink tables, wishing it was over. The difference this time was the incredible amount of security. Soldiers guarded every entrance, anxious food testers sampled every dish, wine tasters were getting drunk on 'just one sip' at a time, and Wizards prowled around the dance floor, using Smell Enhancement spells to check for anything that smelled *reptilian*.

In a strange order, the King had demanded that absolutely no perfume or cologne was to be worn by *anybody* except himself and Sorceress Celeste. That meant everyone smelled like sweat, or alcohol. Midway through the evening, the King had stopped the music and announced his engagement to Sorceress Celeste Mace, of Grotton. There was thunderous applause, then the music resumed.

There were many Ministers and functionaries who just *had* to go and offer their congratulations to the King and Celeste. As the ball went on, the Royal Announcer shouted, "Wizard Edward Francis, and Mage Kathy Francis." *That announcement* certainly got some people's attention. Wizard Noland was the first to approach Edward and Kathy.

"Edward! Welcome back! So, have you finished?" Edward took Michael's hand and said "All finished, my friend. As soon as we showed the new reservoir to King Donald, he release Kathy from any responsibilities in Baize, and hustled us out of the country." "I'm not surprised," said Wizard Noland, "and 'Kathy Francis'?" "Yes," said Kathy, blushing. "We had Wizard Timothy marry us just before we left Baize." "Congratulations!" said Noland. The other Wizards from the Wizards Academy gathered around to congratulate Edward and Kathy, then suddenly, the King was there.

"Wizard Edward! Welcome home. I trust your project in Baize is complete?" "Yes, Your Highness. The Great Salt Flats are no more. Instead, there is a Great Salt Lake in their place, and we never need worry about salt entering the Amber River, and causing economic or ecological harm to either of our Kingdoms." "Splendid, Splendid," said the King, "When did you arrive back in Franconia?" "We landed just a few minutes ago, sire, but I understand congratulations are in order," said Edward smoothly. "Thank you. I hope we can be married in the spring, and I *certainly* hope to have a less *exciting* reception than your son's."

Edward laughed, "I would sincerely hope so as well, Your Majesty. Your Highness, may I introduce my wife, Mage Kathy, formerly the Assistant Court Wizard of Baize." "Mage Kathy, it is a great honor to meet you," said the King graciously. "Wizard Edward, have you given any thought to your next assignment?" "Not really, Your Highness, did you have something in mind?" "Yes," said the King. "The Chief of Military Wizardry post has been vacant for many years now. I can think of no one better suited to the post than you." Before Edward could utter a word, Wizard Noland said, "An excellent choice, Sire. I shall note it in the Wizards Academy files this evening." "Excellent! Well, now that that's settled, you must excuse me, we're leaving for our, excuse me, my, Winter Palace in Southport in the morning," said the King.

The King and Celeste left the ballroom, leaving Edward in stunned silence. "The Chief of Military Wizardry? Do I get an Assistant?" he asked. Noland grinned, "As the Chief of Military Wizardry, you get anything you want."

Donovan, Rachel and Lance arrived back in Hayford close to dawn the day after Rachel arrived in Smithville. They had searched the town of Smithville for any Changed Ones, but it was difficult with the odor from all of the forges and smithies. Major Gerald was very happy when they arrived back safely. "What took you so long?" he asked. Specialist Lance answered, "The Smithville Treasurer's handwriting looked like chicken scratches, and the coins were covered with soot and ash. It was hard to tell a silver from a gold!"

"It might also be because we had to search a played-out coal mine for dragons," said Donovan. "There were dragons in the mines?" asked Major Gerald. "They'd used at least one of them for shelter recently. I don't think they were *living* in the mine, there would have been more signs, but it may be a place where they hide during the day, before flying off to somewhere else at night."

"All right," said the Major. "Next stop, Three Forks. What do we know about it?" "Three Forks sits on the junction of the Sapphire, Ivory, and Emerald Rivers," said Captain Fletcher. "It is the biggest city in northern Franconia, with a population of about 15,000 people.

It's primarily a trading hub, making most of its money from the shipping of furs, timber, gold, and other commodities to Kingston and Southport. The 6th Regiment is stationed there. The Regional Mage is Mage Roark, and he has three Sorcerers working for him."

"How could you possibly know all that?" asked Major Gerald. "I was born and raised in Three Forks, sir," replied Captain Fletcher. "Donovan, do you still have a 'bad feeling' about Three Forks?" asked Major Gerald. "Yes, sir, but again, I'm not sure why. I've never been there, and I understand that Mage Roark is a competent Mage who can also perform the Seeing spell."

"All the same, let's get out that map and take a look." Donovan retrieved his map and truncheon from his wagon. He spread the map out on the ground and held the truncheon over it. "What exactly am I looking for, sir?" "Troops waiting in ambush, dragons, that sort of thing," replied Major Gerald.

Donovan concentrated, the 6th Regiment appeared to be in garrison in the city, except for one Battalion that was a little ways to the east, there were two Mages and seven Sorcerers in the city, as there should be. Everything seemed to be in order. Then Donovan remembered the recent Snow Dragon attacks, so he cast his gaze north of the city, towards the Snow Fields. He found a rock quarry a few miles north of the town, then dragon symbols began appearing on the map, two red, two white, two black, two blue, and one gold dragon, all in the quarry. That could not be a coincidence.

Donovan felt himself becoming lightheaded, and Rachel grabbed his hand holding the truncheon. "Enough!" she said, "We can't have you passing out now!" Donovan released the spell and quickly took a drink from his water bottle. "Nine dragons," he gasped, "two from each clan except the Great Dragons. That can't be good."

"Maybe it's a meeting of the Dragon Council," said Major Gerald. "No," said Donovan. "They meet in the quarry north of Colston, by the Amber River. I think these dragons are going to attack Three Forks! We have to warn them."

"It's three days by clipper ship, even with a tail wind," said Major Gerald. "I don't think we *have* three days," said Donovan. "If the dragons are already assembled, they may attack at dawn tomorrow!" "What do you suggest?" "I think Rachel and I need to transform and head to Three Forks *now*. We warn the forces and the magicians; eleven magicians against nine dragons is an even fight. Plus, there's a Regiment of soldiers with crossbows!"

Major Gerald thought it over. Every minute brought the city of Three Forks and its 15,000 citizens closer to disaster. Finally, he said, "Go! Warn the Regiment and the Regional Mage. Make sure they know how to kill Stone Dragons."

Donovan and Rachel quickly disrobed, not waiting for Seemings or screens to cover their nakedness. They stuffed their clothes in their packs, then quickly transformed into Great Dragons and flew northeast as fast as their wings could carry them.

They landed just outside the city and quickly Changed and dressed. Then they ran for the garrison. They arrived out of breath and panting. "Halt!" said the guard at the gate. "I'm Sorcerer Donovan, and this is Sorceress Rachel. We're from the Royal Expeditionary Force, and we have an urgent message for the Regimental Commander!" said Donovan. "Is that so?" sneered the guard, "You'll have to do better than that! I happen to know that the Royal Expeditionary Force doesn't have any magical support!"

"We don't have time for this," said Donovan, *"INCOGITA."* The guard fell down, asleep, but the gate was still locked. *"DELERE,"* muttered Rachel, flicking the back of her right hand at the gate lock. The lock dissolved. Donovan and Rachel rushed in, looking for the likely location of the commander's office. "Hold it right there," said a voice as a strong Tether spell enveloped both Donovan and Rachel. It was the Battle Mage.

"Sir," said Donovan, desperately, "You've got to believe us, we're from the Royal Expeditionary Force, with an urgent message for the 6th Regimental Commander, this city is about to be attacked by nine dragons!" "Really? Nine of them? I don't suppose you brought any proof with you?" asked the Battle Mage. "If you release me, I can conjure a Seeing spell and show them to you on my map!" said Donovan. The Battle Mage scoffed, "A Seeing spell! There are only a few magicians in all of Franconia who can conjure that spell."

"Yes, I know," said Donovan, becoming angry, "My father, Wizard Edward Francis, Mage Curtis Martin, Mage Roark, and myself! Now will you let me go! This is urgent, I tell you!" Battle Mage Gregory hesitated, he was surprised at how this young magician knew the names of everyone in Franconia who could cast a Seeing spell, although he had heard that Mage Edward was dead. "You may have heard those names anywhere! Convince me that you're telling the truth!"

"Give me a dose of Truth Serum if you don't believe me!" shouted Donovan. "Just get on with it, we don't have any time to lose!" Still unsure what to make of these two young magicians, Battle Mage Gregory pulled out a bottle of Truth Serum from his robe and held it to Donovan's lips. He was surprised when Donovan drank eagerly.

He waited a moment, then said, "Well?'

Donovan said calmly and clearly, "There is a force of nine dragons in the rock quarry a few miles north of here. I located them with a Seeing spell earlier today in the town of Hayford, where the Royal Expeditionary Force is currently boarding a ship to get to Three Forks as fast as possible to render assistance. I am Sorcerer Donovan Francis, assigned to the 2nd Company, Royal Expeditionary Force, and this is my wife, Sorceress Rachel. Rachel is assigned to the 1st Company, Royal Expeditionary Force. Please summon all of your magicians. We have little time."

The Battle Mage immediately released the Tether spells. "My sincere apologies, Sorcerer Donovan. Come with me, and I'll take you to the commander."

Major Franklin, the 6th Regimental Commander, whistled as he viewed the Seeing spell conjured by Mage Roark. "It appears that you're correct, Sorcerer Donovan, there are indeed nine dragons in the quarry. But why are they different colors?" "Two are Fire Dragons, Two are Stone Dragons, two are Snow

Dragons, two are Sea Dragons, and the gold one is a Great Dragon, sir," said Donovan.

"How do we fight them?" asked the commander. "Sir, all of the dragons except the Stone Dragons can be killed with crossbows. The scales on Stone Dragons are too hard. A magician has to encase them in a shield and suffocate them." "A shield?" scoffed one of the Sorcerers from the Regional Mage's Office. "Of course," said Mage Gregory, "the dragon uses up his air, breathing fire, plus he can't hurt anyone with his fire breath while he is in a shield. Won't that work for the others as well?"

"It might," said Donovan, but the Snow Dragons are smaller and exceedingly fast. The Stone Dragons are very slow and ponderous; the other breeds are quicker. It might be hard to get a shield around a fast-moving target." "So, how do we kill the Snow Dragons?" asked Mage Roark. "The last time I faced them, I Changed into a Great Dragon and killed them with my talons." The assembled magicians started, "*You* changed into a dragon?" "Yes, it's something that they've been teaching at the Wizards Academy for the last few months, it's how Rachel and I got here so fast from Hayford to warn you."

"Remarkable," said Mage Gregory. "So, when do you think the dragons will attack?" "They've been attacking at dawn," said Donovan, just as the booming peal of the city's alarm bell rang. "Although, I could be wrong," said Donovan, belatedly.

The soldiers and magicians ran for the battlements. The commanders yelled at their soldiers to get their crossbows from the armory. Meanwhile, the dragons rampaged over the town, setting buildings on fire, smashing them with their talons and tails, or freezing them. The Sea Dragons were spraying water, which the Snow Dragons quickly froze into ice. This combination of dragons was proving to be very destructive.

"Blast spells!" shouted Mage Gregory. Eight of the nine magicians began firing Blast spells at the dragons, who were really too far away to be affected by the spells. The other magician, a Sorcerer from the 6th Regiment, fled. "I'm going after the Snow and Sea Dragons," yelled Donovan. "Don't shoot me!" Donovan Changed into a Great Dragon and flew off into the fray, with Rachel, in Great Dragon form, right behind him.

The two Sea Dragons were too focused on spraying water for the Snow Dragons to freeze, and didn't notice Donovan and Rachel closing behind them. They both fell, headless, a moment later. When the water stopped, the Snow Dragons turned to see what had happened. One took a crossbow bolt through the head, and the other dove low, ducked under a bridge, and fled back to the snow fields. That left two Fire Dragons, two Stone Dragons and the Great Dragon.

The Fire Dragons were so intent on setting fire to everything they could see that they had not been paying attention to what was happening behind them. Donovan slammed into the back of one of them and grabbed the Fire Dragon's back and wings, shredding the wings to pieces with the talons on his hind legs, then Donovan carried the screaming dragon high into the air, before dropping him to the ground. His wings shredded and useless, the fire dragon screamed all the way to the ground.

Rachel was trying to flame the other Fire Dragon, but was not having much luck. The dragon's scales seemed to be resistant to the burning inferno. Remembering what the dragon Changed One, James, had told them back at the Wizards Academy, Donovan circled around and waited for the Fire Dragon to open its mouth. When he did, Donovan quickly spat inferno down the Fire Dragon's throat and ignited it. The Fire Dragon died in agony.

That left the two Stone Dragons and the Great Dragon. The fight had gone on so long that the Stone Dragons were out of inferno. However, stubborn as ever, they refused to withdraw. Side by side, they strolled down the main street of Three Forks, smashing buildings and biting the numerous vendor carts that lined the street. "You get the one on the left," Donovan said to Rachel. She nodded in agreement.

Donovan and Rachel landed side by side in the street and quickly Changed back into human form. They simultaneously cast protective shields around both Stone Dragons and held on tight. Soldiers ran up and asked how they could help, and Donovan said, "Keep an eye out for a gold dragon! He's still out there somewhere!"

By this time, the two Stone Dragons were beginning to feel the effects of the shields and were starting to become concerned. They blew what little inferno they had left, they clawed the shields, they struck with their tails, but nothing worked. Without Blast spells and rocks hitting the outside of his shield, Donovan was able to hold his shield around the Stone Dragon until it died. Then suddenly, the building next to Rachel collapsed towards them. It was the Great Dragon!

Donovan released his shield on the dead Stone Dragon and cast a shield around Rachel and himself, protecting them from the falling bricks and stout wooden beams that engulfed and buried both of them under tons of brick, stone, and timber. One of the Sorcerers from the Regional Mage's office wasn't quick enough and was crushed by the falling debris. While effective at distracting the magicians, the heavy falling stones also finished the remaining Stone Dragon.

Gek paused and realized that this battle was over; as he turned for the safety of the Snow Fields, Mage Gregory fired a blast spell, which missed his torso, but sheared off two fingers on his left hand. Gek cursed; he had become complacent and was now injured. He flew back to the rock quarry, wondering how many dragons had survived the first-ever combined dragon assault.

As he landed in the rock quarry, yellow dragon blood dripped from his left claw, where he was missing two talons. Only one Snow Dragon returned. *What a disaster!* Just then, a young Fire Dragon landed in the quarry. This was not one of the dragons that had begun the attack with Gek and the others. "Who are you?" asked Gek, wearily. "I am Cinder, a Fire Dragon Changed One. I am called Cliff by the humans. I was disguised as a Sorcerer in the 6th Regiment in Three Forks. I fled when the attack began because I have vital news for the Dragon Council. How did the attack go?"

"We were attacked by two Changed Ones who transformed into Great Dragons and killed the Snow, Sea and Fire Dragons," said Gek. "No," said Cinder, "They were not Changed Ones. The human magic-users have learned how to transform into Dragons." "Are you sure of this?" asked Gek. "Positive. I was present when Sorcerer Donovan and his wife, Sorceress Rachel, explained how to make the change to the Regional Mage and the 6ᵗʰ Regiment's Battle Mage."

"Sorcerer Donovan? Battle Mage Edward's son? I thought he was still at the Wizards Academy!" said Gek. "No. He arrived in Three Forks just before the attack. Is that a problem?" asked Cinder. "Potentially a very great one, especially if he is married to another magician. Do you know if he was killed or injured in the battle?" asked Gek. "I have no idea. I fled here as soon as I was out of sight and could Change without being seen," replied Cinder. Were you compromised?" asked Gek. "I do not believe so," said Cinder. "Then I need you to return to your post as a Changed One, Pretend to have been injured in the attack. That will allay suspicion. If you can determine whether Sorcerer Donovan was killed or injured in the attack, that would be helpful information. You have done well, but we need you inside the enemy's counsels," said Gek. "I will inform the Dragon Council of your heroism. Before you go, can you heal my injury?" asked Gek, holding out his damaged foreleg. Cinder looked at the leg, then reared up on his hind legs, reciting the incantation, *"MORPHIUS."* Once back in human form, Cinder examined the injury and said, *"ALEVIO,"* while holding his right hand over the wound, palm down, fingers closed. Gek's claw stopped bleeding, but he was left with two short stumps where the middle and index talons used to be.

"Your missing fingers may prevent you from being able to cast some of the spells that use the left hand," said Cinder. "The Sleep spell, for instance." "No matter," said Gek, "I have rarely found a use for that one anyway. Now, return quickly. You will be contacted later."

Cinder returned to his Dragon-form and flew back towards the burning city, intent on resuming his place as Cliff, Sorcerer in the 6th Franconian Regiment.

Gek waited in the abandoned rock quarry until nightfall, then flew south, following the Sapphire River. Two nights later, he landed outside Bruce's hut. He reared up on his hind legs and clapped his hands together, saying, *"MORPHIOUS."* Nothing happened.

THE END OF BOOK IV

Watch for Book V, The Peace of Minds

Coming soon.

Chapter One:

A TON OF BRICKS

Donovan frowned as the flames slowly covered his shield. He and his wife, Sorceress Rachel, were trapped under tons of bricks and timbers. The Great Dragon had collapsed the building next to them while they were busy suffocating the two Stone Dragons with protective shields. The Stone Dragon that Donovan had encased had died first, and Donovan had seen the building coming down on top of them just in time to erect a shield around both of them. The problem was, they were now trapped underneath tons of rubble, and the dragon had apparently spewed burning inferno on top of the debris, just for good measure.

"Donovan?" "Yes, my love?" "Where are we?" asked Rachel, regaining consciousness. "Well, it seems that we're trapped under several tons of bricks and timber. That Great Dragon pushed over the building we were standing next to and collapsed it on top of us. I barely managed to get a shield around us in time," said Donovan tiredly. "OK, but why is there fire outside the shield?" asked Rachel. "Either the dragon flamed the debris as he left, or the structure caught fire as it fell. I'm not sure which."

"Are you going to do something about it?" "I was planning to. Do you want me to put the fire out?" asked Donovan. "Yes, please." *"AQUARITOUS,"* said Donovan, cupping his right hand and turning it over. Several hundred gallons of water rained down on the debris over their heads, completely extinguishing the fire, but leaving them in total darkness.

"Well, that's not optimal," observed Rachel. "Are you injured?" asked Donovan. "I hit my head, but I'm alright, other than being trapped under a ton of bricks," replied Rachel. They lay in silence for a moment. "Are you planning to get us out of here?" asked Rachel. "I'm working on it. I'm just not sure which spell to use. Any suggestions?" "Wind, maybe," suggested Rachel. "Can you try a strong wind spell?" asked Donovan. Rachel nodded and said, *"GUSTO,"* with a backhand wave of her left hand. Nothing happened.

"How about Blast?" asked Rachel. "I'm not sure that will work," said Donovan, "have you ever fired a Blast spell *through* a shield before?" "No." "Neither have I. I keep thinking back to my first shields class as a Level One; you know, when you throw rocks at each other." "What about it?" "Well, Level One Kelly kept angling her shield, sending the rocks I threw back at me, so I tried erecting a shield, then throwing the rock. The rock bounced off the inside of my shield and hit me in the leg. I don't fancy trying that with a Blast spell," said Donovan.

"Hmm," said Rachel, "there's always the chance that the Blast spell would shatter the shield. I kind of like that shield right where it is right now." "There's another problem, even if I could fire a Blast spell outside the shield, I might hit one of the rescuers who, I assume, are trying to dig us out as we speak. That wouldn't be very appreciative," said Donovan. "No, it wouldn't. OK, not the Blast spell. What else have we got?" asked Rachel. "Well, the Remove spell might work, assuming it doesn't just remove my shield, but then we have the same problem about rescue personnel."

"Can you conjure a Hearing Enhancement to determine if there's anyone digging through the rubble around us?" asked Donovan. "Why can't you do it?" "You always ask me how I can hold two spells at once, and I always tell you that I don't. I hold one spell, then *cast* the other. Right now, I'm *holding* this shield. If you want me to try *holding* a Hearing Enhancement, I'll try, but it might not last very long," explained Donovan. Rachel grinned and said, *"AUDIO,"* while putting her left hand behind her left ear, palm forward. She listened for several long minutes. "I hear someone," said Rachel, "maybe quite a few people, digging, but I can't tell how close they are. It could be that we're under several feet of bricks."

"So, I guess we can't use the Remove spell. It would probably vanish the shield, anyway," said Donovan. *It was maddening! They taught me 38 spells at the Wizards Academy, and now that I need one to save our lives, I can't think of a useful one,* thought Donovan. "I don't mean to be a nagging wife," said Rachel, "but we're going to run short of air if we don't think of something soon."

Suddenly, Donovan smiled, "You're a genius!" He craned his neck and gave Rachel a kiss on the cheek, then lay flat on his back and said, *"REDUCTO,"* while pinching his right thumb and forefinger together. The layer of bricks and timber next to the shield shrank to red brick dust and sawdust. Three more attempts, and it seemed like the shield was only covered with dust. "Try that Wind spell again." This time, the dust was blown high into the air, and sunlight streamed down through the shield.

"OK, I'm going to release the shield. We need to stand up and get out of here before the bricks on the sides cave in. Ready? *CODA!"* Donovan's shield vanished, and the two magicians stood quickly. The bricks on Rachel's side began to collapse into the hole, and several bricks struck her on the left ankle. Donovan grabbed her, conjured a Strength Enhancement, and jumped clear of the debris field.

Donovan and Rachel landed, somewhat unsteadily and looked around. They were surprised to find themselves standing next to Mage Gregory, the 6th Regiment's Battle Mage. Gregory recoiled in shock at Donovan and Rachel's sudden emergence from the rock pile. "Thank goodness! Everyone in the city has been digging through the rubble looking for you two! We thought you were goners! How did you survive?"

"I put a shield over Rachel and myself just as the building started coming down. The problem was the fire and all the bricks," said Donovan. "Yes, we figured that at least one of you was alive when it started raining without a cloud in the sky." "The problem with putting out the fire, was that it left us in complete darkness," said Rachel. "Hmm," said Mage Roark, as he walked up. "What spell did you use to get out from under all that, Dig?" "No," said Donovan, "I didn't think Dig would work through my shield."

"Blast? Remove?" asked Mage Gregory curiously. "Same problem," said Rachel, "Can you fire a Blast spell through a shield? We were afraid that it would crack the shield and let the bricks fall on us. Remove might have just vanished the shield. Besides, even if it worked, we didn't want to risk hitting someone on top of the rubble." The two Mages stood there, stumped. Finally, Mage Gregory said, "Off the top of my head, I can't think of another spell that would have freed you from that pile. How did you do it?"

"Reduce," said Donovan with a smile. "Reduce?" "Yes, Donovan shrunk the bricks outside the shield to dust-size, then I blew the dust away with a Wind spell." "That's brilliant!" said the two Mages. "Yes, it was. Now, can someone heal my ankle, please? Some of the bricks toppled in from the side as we made our way out of the hole." Donovan knelt down, put his left hand on Rachel's ankle, palm down, fingers closed, and said *"SANA,"* before collapsing on the road.

www.ingramcontent.com/pod-product-compliance
Lightning Source LLC
Chambersburg PA
CBHW051129300726
48978CB00011B/200